# A BAD, BAD THING

# A BAD, BAD THING

## Elena Forbes

This first world edition published 2018
in Great Britain and the USA by
SEVERN HOUSE PUBLISHERS LTD of
Eardley House, 4 Uxbridge Street, London W8 7SY
Trade paperback edition first published
in Great Britain and the USA 2018 by
SEVERN HOUSE PUBLISHERS LTD

British Library Cataloguing in Publication Data
*A CIP catalogue record for this title is available from the British Library.*

ISBN-13: 978-0-7278-8832-7 (cased)
ISBN-13: 978-1-84751-947-4 (trade paper)
ISBN-13: 978-1-4483-0157-7 (e-book)

*All Severn House titles are printed on acid-free paper.*

Severn House Publishers support the Forest Stewardship Council™ [FSC™],
the leading international forest certification organisation.
All our titles that are printed on FSC certified paper carry the FSC logo.

Typeset by Palimpsest Book Production Ltd.,
Falkirk, Stirlingshire, Scotland.
Printed and bound in Great Britain by
TJ International, Padstow, Cornwall.

# ACKNOWLEDGMENTS

This is a work of fiction, of course. But a number of people have helped me in the research and writing process and it would have been a much duller experience without them. Particular thanks are due to my wonderful agent Sarah Lutyens and to Francesca Davies and Juliet Mahony at Lutyens & Rubinstein; to Tracy Alexander and David Niccol, both always so incredibly generous with their time, as well as delightful company along the way; to Peter Jensen for all his help, as well as his hospitality at Newmarket and Lincoln – both hugely enjoyable occasions (I can see why people easily become hooked!); also to John Ferguson for martinis and his invaluable insight into the racing world; George and Candida Baker for welcoming me to their yard at Manton; and to my neighbour Chris Goulding. On the editorial front I am grateful to both Lisanne Radice and Susan Opie for their input, as well as to my husband George and mother Jeanne, my chief readers.

*For Jeanne Scott-Forbes*

# ONE

'You sure about this?' Jason asked, shielding his eyes from the sodium glare of the streetlamp as he peered up at the dark façade of the house in Park Grove, Wood Green. It was as quiet as a churchyard, no movement or glimmer of light anywhere in the dark, empty windows above, or behind the tightly drawn curtains on the ground floor and basement. They were late. Maybe Liam Betts had already gone.

'It'll be all right,' Eve said softly. 'Trust me. You said the info was good. He's probably hiding out around the back.'

He could just make out the contours of her lovely face in the half-light. Whenever he looked at her, he felt weak. He wished suddenly he had never told her about Liam Betts, or at least not waited until the very last minute. But he'd been dithering, some little voice in his head telling him it wasn't a good idea. Even now, it didn't feel right. He'd give anything to be back at her flat, in bed with her, instead of hanging around in a dank, muddy garden in North London on a wild goose chase. But he knew she wouldn't let go of it that easily. She'd been wanting to find Liam Betts for weeks. It was all she seemed to care about.

He sighed and gave her a mock salute. 'Yes, ma'am.'

She rewarded him with one of her rare smiles and kissed him lightly on the lips. The touch was electric. He reached for her, but she pulled away.

'Later.'

She was still smiling, but despair filled him. There would be no later, although he hadn't yet summoned up the courage to tell her. He had to get home to his wife – 'no excuses this time' – and he was already nearly two hours late. It was his wedding anniversary, for the little that was worth. Not that Eve would mind if he had to go home. She never did, which was part of the problem. He wondered what she really felt, but knew better than to ask. He was sure he wouldn't like the answer and pushed the thought away to the darkest recesses of his mind, where so many uncomfortable things lurked. Gazing at her, he felt like a drowning man.

She was still smiling at him. 'Come on. Hopefully this won't take long.'

She led the way, picking her way through the rubbish and builders' debris that littered the ground, and up the steps to the front door. She studied the row of bells for a moment.

'10B must be around the back,' she said, coming down the stairs again.

'Let me go first,' he said. 'In case he gives us any trouble.'

'He won't. Liam's a pussycat. He won't mind talking to me.'

'Pussycats can change their spots.'

'Not this one. He'll do anything for me.'

Not true, he wanted to remind her. As she well knew, Liam Betts had recently made himself scarce deliberately. Maybe he thought his cover was blown and had decided to leave town.

Eve crouched down and peered in through the grubby basement window. 'There's a crack of light under the door. Someone's definitely in there. Let's try around the back.'

The concrete path was slick from the recent rain and Jason nearly slipped as he followed it around to the side of the house. A tall wooden gate blocked the path, with barbed wire stretched above it. The gate appeared to be locked and he gave it a shove with his shoulder, but it still didn't move. She was at his side and he caught the smell of her perfume on the air. He wanted to close his eyes, bury his face in her soft, dark hair and lose himself again with her. It was all he could think about.

'There's got to be an entrance through there,' she said quietly.

It was clear, whatever the difficulty, she was not going to give up. 'I'll see if I can open it from the other side.'

Balancing precariously on a dustbin, he climbed up onto the damp wall that bordered the house, and edged along a few feet, before dropping down onto the path on the far side. Shielded from the light of the street, he couldn't make out anything. The narrow passageway smelled of damp and mould. As he stepped forwards into the blackness, he tripped over something that made a metallic clang on the concrete.

'Are you OK?' she whispered, from the other side of the gate.

'Yes. I just can't see.'

He pulled out his phone and switched on the torch. The gate looked solid, heavy-duty bolts top and bottom, with a shiny, new-looking mortice lock in the middle. He carefully slid open the bolts but it still wouldn't shift. It was locked. He also noticed a small peephole cut into the wood, with a makeshift metal flap. Somebody was keen on security. He shone the torch along the paved path that sloped towards the rear garden. A part-glazed door stood halfway along the side of the house, the number 10B crudely painted in white on the brickwork beside it. As he moved towards it, he heard the muffled throb of music and picked up the sticky, sweet smell of cannabis on the air. Again, there was no light showing inside. He decided to have a look around the back. His torch lit up a small, overgrown garden. The patio doors were closed, skimpy curtains pulled across. The fleeting shadow of somebody moved around inside and there were voices and laughter. He went back again to the side passage and rapped hard on the glass door panel. For a moment nothing happened, so he tried again. A light snapped on and through the rippled glass, he saw the flickering shape of somebody coming towards him in the corridor.

'Who's there?' A deep, male voice, foreign accent.

'Police. I'm looking for Liam Betts.'

'Nobody of that name here. Go away.' Eastern European; Russian, maybe.

'Look, we know he's in there.'

'I say go away.'

'We just want to talk to him . . .'

As he pulled out his warrant card, ready for the door to open, he was aware of a scuffling sound and a movement to his right in the garden. He turned, saw a face, heard the crack of gunshot, then another, felt a blow to his chest, followed by a sharp pain. He fell to his knees on the wet ground.

'Eve.' He tasted blood in his mouth. He tried again. No sound came out.

# TWO

A curtain of icy rain swept over the graveyard as the funeral cortége pulled up outside the church. It was barely midday, but the sky was iron grey. Eve ducked out of sight, quickly finding shelter under the dripping branches of an ancient yew tree. It was high up on a bank in a far corner, beside some ancient-looking monuments and the thick trunk and canopy provided a good shield from any prying eyes below. On another day, she would have liked nothing better than to wander around the graves, reading the inscriptions, thinking about the people buried beneath, imagining their lives, their loves, their deaths. 'Sometimes I think you feel more at home with the dead than the living,' Jason once said, when she was particularly wrapped up in a case. 'Somebody has to speak for them, and fight for them,' she replied. What he couldn't grasp was that for her the dead were ever present.

A hasty eight days after his headline-grabbing murder, the funeral had been billed as a quiet affair, for close family and friends only. Even so, a group of bedraggled reporters and cameramen were gathered around the main entrance gate and there must have been a good thirty vehicles clogging the parking area outside and overflowing down the narrow lane, testament to the fact that Detective Sergeant Jason Scott had been well-liked. The church was on the outskirts of the village, within commuting distance of London, it felt prosperous and secure. It was a postcard-pretty, roses-around-the door sort of village; everything clipped and tidied to within an inch of its life. The sort of place where people cared what colour you painted your front door, or if you parked your car in the spot outside their house, or put your bins out on the wrong day. It would drive her mad to live somewhere like that. She liked the transience and anonymity of London, where you could be married, or divorced, or dead, for months before your neighbours found out. She had never given much thought to where Jason lived, with Tasha and their young daughter, Isabelle, but she had certainly never imagined him in such a place.

It seemed so at odds with his easy-going, unfussy nature. She assumed that Tasha had chosen the location, as with most things, according to Jason. All Eve remembered was his complaining about the long daily commute to the office and how tired it made him. With a pang of sadness, it struck her how little she had known about him, or had wanted to find out.

The occupants of the cars collected in a subdued huddle in the road, sheltering under umbrellas. Eve spotted several of her work colleagues and pulled in even more tightly against the tree, watching as Jason's coffin was lifted out of the flower-laden hearse and carried up the steep flight of stone steps into the graveyard. She had been dreading that moment, wondering how she would react. But in the event, she felt nothing more than sadness and a weary acceptance. Tasha led the procession, her face downcast and veiled, leaning heavily on the arm of Jason's close friend and best man, DS Paul Dent. A middle-aged woman, who looked like her mother, followed closely behind, holding on tightly to the hand of a little blonde-haired girl. Isabelle: the reason why Jason had married Tasha. The *only* reason, Jason had insisted on more than one occasion, as though it mattered. He had brought Isabelle into the office before Christmas the previous year, while Tasha was off doing some shopping, and had proudly showed her off to everyone. When Tasha came to collect Isabelle a little later, the tension between her and Jason had been palpable. He had been seeing somebody else even then, Eve thought. She certainly hadn't been his first affair, which had made things easier from her point of view. She had no desire to break up any marriage, although she was intrigued to know why he seemed incapable of being faithful. Not long after they had started seeing one another, she had asked him about it, but he had mistaken her curiosity for something more. 'Don't think about it,' he said, cupping her face in his hands and tilting her chin up to meet his gaze, before kissing her. 'It's all in the past. There's nobody else – nothing matters, but you.' She hadn't needed, or wanted, the reassurance, something he couldn't understand.

She took a deep breath and exhaled, remembering the look in his eyes. She missed him – missed the touch of him, the smell of him, his sheer physicality more than anything. Because of her, he was no longer there. Again she pictured the scene at the house in Park Grove. What neither of them had known was that it had been under surveillance by a team from SCD9, the Met's Organized Crime Command. Hearing gunfire, the officers had rushed out of their van parked somewhere along the street, smashed down the wooden gate and found Jason lying unconscious in a pool of blood on the other side. Calling for backup, they had left her with him while they searched the flat and garden. She had cradled him in her arms in the passageway, holding him as close as she could, whispering to him, telling him to hang on, although she knew it was useless. The bullet had passed through him like a shaft of ice. How cold he felt, how heavy. The smell of his blood filled the dark, narrow space. Her hands were slippery with it; it was in her hair, on her clothes, on her lips. She was alone with him for less than ten minutes, but it had seemed an eternity. By the time the paramedics arrived, he was dead. Only that morning they had been lying in bed together in her flat, his arms locked around her as he tried to stop her from getting up, laughingly hoping to persuade her to call in sick and spend the day with him. If only she had listened.

As she squeezed her eyes tight shut for a moment, shaking her head vigorously as she tried to force the image of him from her mind, her phone vibrated in her pocket. She pulled it out and saw the words:

> *Are you ready to talk, Eve? I told you I'm here to help. John.*

She didn't know who John was, but it was the fifth text she had received from the same number in the past twenty-four hours. So far, she hadn't responded. But he appeared to know exactly what had happened at the shooting in Park Grove, the errors she had made, as well as various details that hadn't been released to the press or to her general work colleagues. Even so, she assumed it was yet another journalistic ploy, or somebody else, maybe one of her colleagues, trying to wind her up. Why would 'John', whoever he was, want to help her? As she stared at the screen, wondering whether or not to text back and tell him to leave her alone, another message came through:

> *You know you were set up, don't you?*

'Set up'. She stared at the words for a moment. Who was he? What did he want? The idea of a set-up had occurred to her, but she had dismissed it. The tip-off had been a good one, from a reliable source, Jason had assured her more than once. Like a child bearing a gift, he had been delighted to offer her what he thought she wanted. All that was ever on his mind was to please her. She had trusted him and had taken it at face value, being so keen to get hold of Liam Betts that she hadn't questioned him too deeply about where the information had come from. But it was clear that Betts was a decoy. He had never been at that address, or anywhere near it. Had somebody deliberately planted the information, knowing how she would react? If so, why? Did they want to wreck the surveillance operation or get at her? Her attempts to find out more had been thwarted. She was suspended, pending an internal enquiry and disciplinary hearing: locked out of the on-going investigation. Nobody would talk to her. In the end, she had tried to convince herself that she and Jason had just been in the wrong place, at the wrong time. But instinct told her it wasn't that simple.

As she tucked the phone away in her pocket, she heard someone call out her name a little way off behind her. She turned and saw a man coming towards her along the public footpath in the adjoining field, picking his way slowly and carefully over the heavy, wet ground, as though unused to the outdoors. The hood of his baggy, brown jacket was pulled down low over his brow against the rain and she couldn't make out much of his face, but he waved.

'Hey, Eve,' he called out, before scrambling untidily over the low wall separating the field from the graveyard. As he waved again, she recognized the familiar pudgy features of Nick Walsh, a reporter from one of the tabloids. *Shit.* Too late to hide now.

He came up to where she was standing, panting heavily, his freckled face bright pink. 'God . . . I'm unfit,' he said, between breaths. The rain was dripping off the edge of his hood onto his cheeks, his trainers were caked in mud and his jeans were soaked to the knee, but he didn't seem to care. 'I just need a few words. That's all.'

'Piss off, Nick. Now's not the time or place.'

'When is?' He put his hands on his hips and bent forwards for a moment, looking up at her expectantly. 'I can meet you anywhere . . . any time. Whatever you like.'

'I told you before to leave me alone.' She was inclined to say something a lot sharper, but depending on how the enquiry went, there might come a time when she would need Walsh, or someone like him, to put across her side of the story.

He stood up, his broad chest still heaving. 'Do you blame yourself—'

He wasn't particularly tall, but he had a powerful voice and the words resonated in the quiet of the churchyard.

'Shut the fuck up.'

'Sorry,' he said, smiling. 'Jason Scott's death. They say . . . it was your fault. That you shouldn't . . . have gone there with him.'

She gave him a hard stare, although he was only saying to her face what others were whispering behind her back, as though she had ever tried to pretend otherwise. Nowhere, not even in the darkest corners of her heart, had she attempted to justify what had happened, let alone delude herself into thinking someone else was responsible.

'You're wasting your time. I've got absolutely nothing to say to you.'

'Come on, Eve. Give me a break, will you?'

His voice boomed out and a series of shouts pierced the air from below, accompanied by a long, shrill wail. Eve looked over towards the church where Tasha stood, with her arm raised high, pointing up at Eve and Walsh, the sea of faces that surrounded her all looking in the same direction. Even though the wind drowned out most of her words, the gist was clear. A series of brilliant flashes erupted from the cameras down by the gate and she collapsed into Paul Dent's arms.

'That'll make a nice spread,' Walsh said grinning. He took out a pack of cigarettes from his pocket, cupped his hands against the wind and lit up. As he took a drag, he edged closer to Eve. 'So tell me, when's the disciplinary hearing?'

'Piss off.'

Not caring if Walsh followed her, she was about to strike off back across the fields, when her boss, Detective Superintendent Nigel Kershaw, broke away from the group below and started striding up the hill towards her. She backed away from Walsh, wanting to put some distance between them.

'You'd better go. There's nothing for you here.'

He was still smiling. 'Come on. They've hung you out to dry. You don't owe them nothing. What's going on?'

'I don't know any more than you do. Probably less, in fact.' With a glance towards Kershaw, he leaned towards her. 'Why don't you tell me quickly what happened, in your own words?'

She shook her head. 'There's nothing to tell.'

'That's not what I hear. My sources say you shouldn't have gone to that house.'

'No comment.'

'Is it true you and Jason Scott were more than just good friends? Would you care to comment on that?'

She folded her arms tightly across her chest and shook her head. 'I told you before. You're wasting your time.' She spoke as loudly as she dared. Kershaw had come up behind Walsh and she hoped he had heard.

'Hop it, Walsh,' Kershaw said. 'You're on private land. DCI West has nothing to say to you.' He was a big man, with a deep and gruff voice and a thick South London accent, and he towered over them both.

Walsh looked unfazed, but gave a slight shrug and held up his hands. 'No problemo.' He glanced over at Eve. 'I'll call you,' he said, making the sign of a phone and pointing his finger at her as he turned away. He pulled the peak of his hood over his face and, shoulders hunched, started ambling down the hill, whistling, towards the main entrance.

'Right, Eve,' Kershaw said. 'You better come with me. There's another gate just over there. Let's go and find somewhere quiet to sit down. We could both use a drink.'

# THREE

They walked together without another word into the village, Kershaw's large black umbrella sheltering them both, his driver following slowly behind in the car. It was the first time she had seen him on his own since she had been suspended and the silence was awkward. Their working relationship had been relatively good, as far as it went, but the idea of a quiet drink, just the two of them, had an ominous feel.

The Cricketers' Arms was the first pub they came to and she followed Kershaw inside into the main bar, which was still almost empty.

'What'll you have?' he asked, as he placed his dripping umbrella in the stand by the door.

'Coffee, if they have it, please. With a little milk.'

'Nothing stronger?'

'No thanks.'

'Of course, I forgot, you don't drink.'

She was surprised that he remembered, although in the after-hours heavy drinking culture of the Met, a non-drinker stood out like a beacon. He strode up to the bar, while she chose a table by the open fire. She caught sight of herself in the oval, brass mirror above the mantelpiece and grimaced. Her hair had been turned into a mass of stupid curls by the rain and her face looked pasty and drawn, with dark shadows under her eyes. She took a rubber band out of her bag and scraped back her hair, applied a thin layer of lipstick to her dry lips, then turned her back to the fire, trying to soak up as much of the meagre heat as she could. Seeing Kershaw returning with their drinks, she pulled up a chair and sat down.

'This should warm you up,' he said morosely, plonking a cup of milky coffee in front of her. 'You look drowned.'

He put a full tumbler of what looked like whisky and soda down on the table and sank heavily into a leather armchair opposite. He ran a hand quickly over his thick, greying hair, and leaned back in his seat. He loosened his tie and undid his top button.

'That's better.' He reached for his glass, took a mouthful, then shook his head. 'I never dreamt you'd come to the funeral, otherwise I'd have said something. You must've known it was a bloody stupid thing to do, surely?'

His roughly hewn face, with its square, pugnacious jaw, glowed in the firelight. Although he spoke quietly, she sensed anger close to the surface and made no reply. With Kershaw, silence was often the best policy. Let him run, get things off his chest and eventually he'd calm down. He stretched his long legs out in front of him and gazed into the flames for a moment, then glanced over at her.

'Why come here, when chances are you'd be seen? I've been trying to cool things down, put the lawyers back in their sodding boxes, keep everything under wraps and let the grieving widow have her day. I've done everything I can to limit the fallout to you, and to us. Then you turn up, with that effing reporter in tow, and all hell breaks loose again.' He took another large gulp, then caught her eye again over the edge of his tumbler. 'You're reckless. Like you just don't care about the consequences. Either to yourself or anybody else. Same with the shooting. You have to take everything to the bloody line. All the bloody time.' He sighed heavily, still looking at her. 'You baffle me, Eve. You know that? You could've got yourself killed.' He raised his eyebrows, as though expecting a reply.

What could she say? The thought that *she* might have been killed, meant nothing, but he wouldn't understand. She had worked for him for nearly twelve months and had always found him fair and relatively straightforward to deal with. From what she had heard, he had stood up for her, as far as he could, after the shooting and she wished things hadn't turned out this way. Although barely fifty, he was heading towards retirement in a few months and had been anticipating a smooth ride. Instead, he and his team were now under the spotlight of a major internal investigation, with all the ensuing questions and political ramifications. She had compromised him and for that she was sorry.

'Nick Walsh is nothing to do with me. I haven't talked to him or anyone else and I had no idea he'd follow me here.'

He leaned forwards. 'Don't be so bloody naïve. They're all over this like the pox, trying to dig up the dirt. I don't need you giving them more ammo by creating a scene.'

'*I* didn't create a scene. I didn't mean for anyone to see me.'

'Really?' He slammed his glass back down on the table, making the teaspoon on her saucer jingle, and looked at her searchingly. 'Did you think you owed it to Jason to be there, is that it? Is that why you came?'

'Owed?'

'Felt you ought to be here.'

'There's no "ought" about it.'

'Why, then?'

She met his eye. Did he really imagine that she could have sat at home, on her own, while the funeral took place, as if it had nothing to do with her? As if Jason had meant nothing to her? Standing in the churchyard, seeing Jason's body carried high on the shoulders of his friends and fellow officers and put in the ground, mattered. The image of it would stay with her forever, along with the knowledge that it was her fault.

He was still looking at her. 'Well?'

'I just wanted to say goodbye. That's all.'

The contours of his face softened a little. 'Whatever you felt for Jason, you must've known it was a bad idea, with his wife and family there, with the press and all that shit.'

Jason's marriage had been a sham and most of the people there, including Kershaw, knew it. But there was no point arguing.

'I told you, I didn't think I'd be seen.'

Kershaw narrowed his small, brown eyes and shook his head. 'You just don't bloody well care. That's the problem.'

He scraped back his chair a couple of feet away from the fire, which was burning well now, the flames leaping high up the chimney, and took out a dazzling white cotton handkerchief from his breast pocket and mopped his brow.

'Are *you* alright?' he asked, carefully refolding the handkerchief and tucking it back in his pocket.

The question took her by surprise, as well as the note of concern in his voice. 'About Jason, or the enquiry?'

'I meant about Jason, but either will do.'

'I'll be OK. About Jason, that is.'

He was looking at her searchingly and she saw confusion in his eyes. She ought to feel more, demonstrate more, but the perennial numbness was there. She couldn't cry or grieve in the way he expected, although she felt a deep, gaping pit of guilt and she missed Jason more than she cared to think about.

He leaned forwards towards her. 'Are you having counselling?'

'They gave me a number. But I don't need it at the moment.'

She could tell from his expression that she still wasn't reacting the way he expected, but she wasn't going to pretend. She didn't need therapy. She had had enough of it to last her a lifetime, although Kershaw wasn't to know. What was the point of examining and re-examining every detail, reliving each terrible moment, when all she wanted to do was to forget? Whatever the experts said, endless picking away at a wound prevented it from healing. There were better ways of dealing with grief and pain and guilt. She would manage on her own.

'You sure about that?'

'Really, I'll be fine,' she said firmly, hoping he would stop probing.

He stared at her, then gave a curt nod in reply and sank back in his chair, eyes fixed gloomily on the fire.

'Is there any news about the shooting?' she asked after a moment. It was all that mattered.

He picked a white thread off his suit trousers, examined it between his fingers, then dropped it onto the floor. 'Nothing concrete yet. We found the weapon a few streets away. Ballistics have linked it to an on-going investigation in Hoxton with Eastern European connections. But that's no surprise. We've had to release the girl who was with them in the flat. She doesn't know anything. The chief suspect got clean away, along with two other men. We think they're all part of the same Ukranian mob.'

'What about Liam Betts?'

'Nobody's seen hide nor hair of him.'

'He was never there.'

He jerked his head around towards her. 'Of course he bloody wasn't. Your info was shit.'

'It's more than that. I think it was a set-up.'

'Come again?'

'Someone set me up. Someone deliberately planted the info that Betts was going to be at that house, knowing that I'd fall for it and walk into the middle of whatever was going on.'

He frowned, as though it wasn't what he wanted to hear. 'Really? This what you're going to say at the disciplinary hearing?'

'Yes.'

'Unless you got proof, it's not going to fly.'

'I'll get the proof.'

He shook his head. 'It doesn't alter the fact that you went against orders trying to find Betts.'

'But I'm sure Betts knows something about the Highbury shooting.'

'And I told you to bloody well leave Betts alone.' Kershaw's voice carried across the room and a couple of people looked around.

'That was to do with something completely different. As you know, I tried several times to get hold of you.'

He glanced over at the bar, where a couple were having a heated discussion. His phone had been switched off for a quite a while. It wasn't the first time that he had been unaccountably out of contact. The rumour was that he had a mistress, who he was seeing on a regular basis during office hours and after. If necessary, she would make sure it came out at the disciplinary hearing why she hadn't been able to get hold of him. The Met had been her world for nearly fifteen years and she wasn't going to let it go without a fight.

'When I couldn't find you,' she said pointedly, 'I asked Superintendent Johnson and he gave me the OK.'

He looked back at her angrily. 'He says he didn't.'

'He's lying.'

'Why would he do that?'

'To cover his arse, like he always does.'

'There's nothing on record.'

'There wasn't time.'

He took a small bottle of pills from his jacket pocket, swallowed a couple, and washed them down with the remains of the whisky, then he banged the glass down on the table in front of him.

'You say Jason gave you the info, but you've no idea where he got it from, right?'

'Yes, but I intend to find out. And whoever did it, needs to pay.'

'You'll do no such thing. You leave it alone. You're in enough trouble as it is.'

'So it doesn't make any difference if I was set up? It certainly does to me.'

He leaned forward towards her across the table. She could smell the whisky on his breath.

'OK. Maybe someone wanted you to fuck up, or maybe they wanted to screw up the surveillance operation and they used you as bait, but it all sounds farfetched.'

'Doesn't mean it's not possible.'

'But you have no idea where the info came from, do you?'

'No. Not yet.'

'Look at it this way – the way the panel at your disciplinary hearing will look at it. You go off on a fool's errand in search of an informant who's officially off limits, who you've been told to leave alone—'

'As I said, I tried several times to call you and I got clearance to go ahead . . .'

He shook his head angrily. 'You take with you a fellow officer, your subordinate, a married bloke, who—'

'My relationship with Jason's irrelevant.'

He held up his huge hand. 'Let me finish. I'm making no moral judgements here. Jason Scott was no saint, but you were his superior and it doesn't help your PR. So, you take your sergeant with you and together you blunder into the midst of a major potential drugs bust. Two months' worth of expensive surveillance down the toilet, chief suspect's out the door and probably out of the country too, and your sergeant dead. And now *I've* got to take the flak from above.'

'I wasn't to know.'

'Yes you bloody well were. As I said, you just don't care. That's your problem, and now it's bloody well mine too.' He glanced at his watch and stood up. 'You have to put up your hand and take the blame.' He stabbed the air with his index finger several times for emphasis. 'Don't go wasting your time and energies on some fanciful idea that you were set up. And keep out of the bloody limelight. I'll do all I can to support you, but don't go pulling any more stupid stunts like the one today. Right?'

# FOUR

Eve pulled up in a space outside the house where she lived in Hazel Avenue, just off the Uxbridge Road. She switched off the engine, gathered up her things and hurried up the steps to her front door. The building was four storeys high, in the middle of a terrace of almost identical late-Victorian houses, almost all of which were divided into flats. Inside, the common parts had recently been redecorated and the hall smelled strongly of fresh paint and new carpet, which blotted out the dank odour from the street. She collected a couple of pieces of post from the mat, put the rest on the small shelf above the radiator and climbed the several steep flights of stairs to her flat at the top. She didn't mind the walk up and had chosen the flat because it was more private, with nobody clattering around above her, no footsteps thudding past on the stairs. The tenant immediately below was often away and the only noise to disturb her was the occasional pigeon up on the roof, its cooing carried loudly down the chimney.

As she reached the top landing, she bent down and checked the small strip of invisible tape that she had stuck across the bottom of the door and the frame on her way out. It was still in place. It was something she had been doing for years and it had become automatic. She often told herself she was being irrational, that she had no need to worry any longer, but at the back of her mind was still the idea that one day it might save her life. Reassured that it hadn't been touched, she peeled it off and let herself into the flat. It was light and airy, with a sitting room and galley kitchen at the front, and a bedroom and bathroom at the back, overlooking a drab patchwork of concrete yards and muddy gardens. She kept the blinds drawn most days, as much for privacy from the houses opposite as to shut out the view of other people's lives. The flat was rented and had come fully furnished in a bland, functional way, with inoffensive carpets and neutral colours and furnishings. She had added a few touches here and there: some olive-coloured silk cushions to soften the hard, angular sofa, a large glass vase for fresh flowers, which sat in the centre of the round dining table and a new, very expensive coffee maker after her old one had broken. There was nothing characterful, or memorable, or even particularly pleasing about the space, but it didn't bother her. It was comfortable and she had everything she needed, although even after ten months, she still had the feeling of being in transit. Nowhere had ever really felt like home. The solitude was what was important, the ordered predictability of living on her own. She hated sharing it with anyone, even for a short time. She didn't need someone to come home to, to worry about where she was, to question her about her day, or even just fill the space with the basic warmth of another human presence. It felt just fine as it was. Jason had commented on several occasions about the lack of personal things. He wanted to know more about her and he said the place gave nothing away. It was 'like a hotel'; she didn't see anything wrong in that. It wasn't 'homey' he said, by which she gathered he meant it lacked colour and clutter and endless useless possessions. She had tried to explain that she didn't like bright colours and that objects, knick-knacks, meant nothing to her. She didn't need any mementos either, anything with a connection to the past, that would twang her heartstrings each time she saw it and make her want to curl up inside. It was one of the many things he hadn't understood.

She turned on the overhead lights and carefully unlaced her muddy boots, putting them in the kitchen sink to clean later. She stripped off her wet clothes down to her underwear and hung them over a couple of chairs next to the radiator in the sitting room. For a moment, Jason's presence filled the room. She pictured him sprawled on the sofa just ten days before, a glass of red wine warming in his hand as he discussed the ins and outs of the case they had been working on. Work was the main thing they had in common, as far as she could tell, although maybe that was unfair. What had started as just a bit of fun had somehow morphed into something more, at least on his side. In the short space of time they had been together, she had gone out of her way not to know him, to keep him at arms-length, and yet somehow a small part of him had wriggled its way in and was still there. Death played tricks with the mind. She hadn't loved him and yet the shock of what had happened, losing him so suddenly, so violently, had awakened all sorts of uncomfortable thoughts. For no reason, she would hear his voice, little snippets of conversation burbling away and odd images kept popping unexpectedly into her head, catching her unawares, making her wish he were still there. The framed photograph of him, which he had presented her with one evening, stared down at her from the top of the small bookcase where he had put it. All the things that had so attracted her to him – his youth, his warmth, his energy and his easy-going smile – were so plain to see. It pained her to look at it.

He had been keen to have one taken of the two of them together, but she repeatedly refused and he had become angry. 'You're so bloody secretive, Eve. I want to know everything about you. Everything.' He had pulled her towards him, almost shaking her. 'Don't you want pictures of the people you care about?' No. She wanted to say, They're in my head, they're wrapped tightly around my heart, they're with me all the time.

He had made very little physical impression on the flat and she was glad of it. She had disposed of the few personal things he had left behind: a couple of work shirts, a pullover, a toothbrush and a razor. She had also deleted every contact with him on her phone. It was easier that way, nothing to snag uncomfortably on the order of her day and give a stab of regret. She crossed the room to the bookcase and picked up the photograph. With one last glance, she put it away face down in the bottom drawer of her desk.

It was too late in the day for coffee, not that she expected to sleep well that night. Instead, she made herself a strong cup of tea with milk and took it over to the large window, which over-looked the street. As she did most nights, she opened the blinds and stared out at the darkening skyline, with its roofs and chim-neys and glittering lights, the white glow of Wembley Stadium just visible on the foggy horizon. But the sense of peace she usually felt was absent. Everything had been turned upside down by what had happened in Park Grove. Somehow, she had to find out how Jason had heard that Liam Betts was supposedly staying at the house. Had he made a mistake? Or had somebody given him false information? Before joining the murder investigation team, he had worked for several years in one of the Met's organized crime squads. It seemed likely that that had been the connection. But so far, her contacts had drawn a blank. She had also tried speaking to Jason's close friend, Paul Dent, a few days before the funeral. He still worked in the same unit, but he had been particularly defensive when she asked him if he knew where Jason's informa-tion had come from. It wasn't from anyone there, he had said categorically. It was clear from the way he spoke that he blamed her for the problems in Jason's marriage, as well as his death. Having seen him at the funeral at Tasha's side, she realized it was pointless pursuing it any further.

She was about to pull down the blinds when she saw a large,

dark-coloured saloon car pull up in the street outside her house. A similar-looking car had been on her tail all day, taking little trouble to conceal itself. She had assumed it was press-related, although it looked far too up-market to be anything to do with Nick Walsh. A moment later, a man got out from the back, glanced up at her window, then climbed the stairs to the front door and rang her bell. She closed the blinds and turned away. She didn't want to speak to anybody. He rang the bell again, this time leaning on it for several seconds. He must have seen her from the street and wasn't going to give up. She went into the hall and picked up the intercom receiver.

'Yes?'

'Miss West? I'd like to speak to you please.' His voice was crackly and distant over the intercom, the thick London accent still audible.

'Who is it?'

'My name's Alan Peters. I have a message for you.'

'Who from?'

'I can explain. May I come up?'

'No. I'm busy.'

'I'd rather not talk to you about this out here in the street.'

'Then you'll have to come back another time.'

'You received some text messages today from my client . . .'

Texts? She hesitated. 'Is this someone called John?'

'That's right. He wants to get in touch with you. He wants you to know that he can help you.'

'I don't need anybody's help.'

'I think you do, Miss West. It really would be easier to speak face to face.'

She stood for a moment in silence, wondering what to do. *You were set up.* The words in the text had hooked her, playing on her own suspicions. Was it possible he knew something?

'Give me a few minutes,' she said.

She hurriedly threw on a pair of jeans and a pullover, then went downstairs. She opened the front door a few inches, wedging her bare foot behind it, her hand on the edge ready to slam it shut. A small middle-aged man, with glasses and thinning silver hair stood on the step below. He was smartly dressed in a beige mackintosh, with a dark suit and tie just visible beneath.

'You may remember me from a couple of years ago, Miss West. As I said, my name's Alan Peters.' He enunciated each word clearly, as though trying to make a point. He held out a card, which she took. *Alan Peters. Associate. Mercantile Partners LLP.* A City of London address. She stared at him, but couldn't place him.

'Who's John?'

'John Duran.' He gave a tight, little smile, as though she should have known all along.

The mention of the name almost made her start. She had hoped never to hear it again. She opened the door a little wider to get a better look at Peters. His eyes were sharp and alive behind his steel-rimmed spectacles, his mouth still puckered by some inner joke. Perhaps he was amused by her bewilderment, enjoying the impact that Duran's name still had on her. She saw a huge number of people on a day-to-day basis and there was nothing particularly memorable about Peters, but she suddenly placed him. He was John Duran's solicitor, an unpleasant, little terrier of a man, who had been involved from day one of Duran's arrest for murder right up until his subsequent conviction.

Duran, however, was someone she would never forget. He ran a small off-shore investment bank, with a London office close to Fleet Street. It was the legitimate front for some well-known Eastern European crime families. According to the Met's Organized Crime Command, he was the real criminal mastermind, the facilitator and fixer, managing their affairs and investments and laundering their money. He had been under long-term surveillance for well over a decade but no charges had ever stuck. Then a couple of years before, the body of one of his known associates, Stanco Rupec, had been found dumped on a stretch of grassland opposite the Old Bull and Bush pub, near Hampstead Heath. Rupec had been bludgeoned to death, his head and face beaten to a pulp. The crime scene photos had been some of the worst she had ever seen. CCTV footage recovered from two days previously, timed at around one in the morning, had captured Rupec's blue Mercedes driving at speed along Haverstock Hill, pursued by a black Jaguar belonging to another of Duran's entourage. The Mercedes was later found abandoned a little further along, just after Belsize Park Tube station. Neighbours had also reported hearing shouting around the same time, and some sort of a scuffle going on outside some nearby garages, but it had been a Saturday night and when the local police finally turned up, there was no sign of anybody. Appeals for witnesses finally produced a minicab driver who claimed to have seen a man being attacked in a street just off Rosslyn Hill, not far away. As luck would have it, the minicab had been fitted with both a dashcam and a rear-view camera, which together had captured a good part of the assault. Stanco Rupec could be seen running, then tripping over something. He held up his hands as he fell backwards. Even though there was no sound on the recording, it was clear he was screaming and begging for his life as Duran caught up with him. The blows rained down without even a momentary pause as the taxi drove past and accelerated away. Duran, himself, was clearly identifiable as the man wielding the crow bar and he was arrested and charged with murder.

Eve had been the senior investigating officer on the case. It was unclear why Duran had risked so much to attack Rupec out on the street, in plain view. Why he had done it himself, rather than leave the job to one of his many associates, was also a mystery. She had watched the video footage several times and had been struck by the degree of violence. The repeated blows were far more than would have been necessary to kill Rupec. It looked like an act of rage. Yet the emotion and lack of self-control were wholly inconsistent with everything that was known about Duran. He had never got his hands dirty before, certainly never been caught with blood on them. It had to be something very personal. But despite repeated questioning, no matter what interview tactics were thrown at him, he remained extraordinarily calm and inscrutable, steadfastly refusing to comment on his motivation. She could still vividly remember the hours spent either watching from a distance or locked away with him in a series of windowless, stiflingly hot interview rooms. The closeness and intensity of the experience had been characterized by the overpowering smell of the Paco Rabanne cologne, which he habitually wore. One of her mother's classier boyfriends used to drench himself in it, but the smell was now indelibly associated in her mind with Duran.

Nor could she forget the sight of him later at his trial, at the Old Bailey, where he had sat almost motionless and upright in the dock for hours, his face an impenetrable mask. He was over fifty, but his natural hair colour was still black and his sallow skin almost unlined. He had taken to shaving his head shortly before Rupec's murder and the five o'clock shadow of hair, with its pronounced widow's peak, covered his scalp like a dark cap. Most defendants adopted some sort of a pose, whether defiant, shell-shocked, sorrowful, scared, or simply bored. Duran's eyes never left her as she gave evidence, but no flicker of emotion crossed his face at any point. It was as though he were just an observer, listening to somebody else's trial. She would have given a lot to know what was going through his mind, what he really felt and, in particular, what had driven him to kill Stanco Rupec.

'John Duran's still safely behind bars at Bellevue,' she said. 'Hopefully for the next twenty years or so.'

'Mr Duran is still at Bellevue . . .'

'Why's he texting me?'

The fact that, locked away in a category 'A' high security prison, he had access to a mobile phone was not much of a surprise. There had been much in the media about drones being used to deliver all manner of contraband over prison walls, including drugs, phones and weapons, in some cases, directly to a prisoner's cell. Even without the help of new technology, old-fashioned corruption of prison staff could still buy you most things, particularly when you were as rich and powerful as Duran.

'He wants you to know that he doesn't bear you any ill will. He's been following recent events and is aware of your situation . . .'

'It's got nothing to do with him.'

'Mr Duran has some information that might be of interest to you.'

'I don't need anything from him.'

'He has evidence that you were set up. You can do what you like with it, but you'd be wise to listen to what he's got to say.'

She stared at him. 'What's the price of this information?'

'Mr Duran doesn't want any money.'

'But he wants something.'

'He just hopes that in return, you may be able to do him a favour.'

'A favour? For John Duran? I might as well kiss my career goodbye, or what's left of it.'

'It's nothing illegal. You have my word.'

'And that's worth something, is it?'

'Don't shoot the messenger, Miss West. You have the disciplinary hearing coming up. From what I hear, you're likely to be sacked, or at best forced to resign. Don't you at least want to find out who sent you and your dead lover to that house in Wood Green?'

His bluntness didn't shock her, even though it wasn't pleasant hearing it from him. In the days following the shooting, she had more or less accepted that the likely outcome would be that she would have to leave the Met. Whatever she felt about being thrown out, there was little she could do about it. But maybe if she could prove she was set up, they might take a more lenient line. If nothing else, she needed to find out for herself and make sure that whoever had done it was made to pay. Given Duran's connections in the Eastern European criminal world and what Kershaw had said about the Ukrainians in the flat at Park Grove and the broader Eastern European connection, it was easily possible that Duran might know, or could find out, something about what had happened. Why he wanted to help her, after she had been instrumental in putting him away, was another question. But it didn't matter for the moment. She needed to find out more.

'What sort of favour are you talking about?' she asked, still watching Peters closely.

His expression gave nothing away. 'You should speak to Mr Duran directly. He can tell you a lot more than I can.'

'Speak to him? What, at Bellevue?'

'Yes. If you'd like to go ahead, I'll sort out the visiting order straight away. Visiting hours are from two until four. The car can collect you tomorrow at midday, if that's convenient.'

# FIVE

Duran's driver dropped Eve outside Bellevue Prison, near Reading, just after one p.m. the following day. Built in the 1990s, surrounded by a series of high, faceless perimeter walls, it was a brutal, modern building, which stood out uncomfortably in the otherwise semi-rural landscape. She checked in at the visitor centre, which was next to the entrance, leaving her bag and personal belongings in a locker, then made her way to the main building, where she joined the shuffling, fidgeting queue of other visitors. The majority were women, either on their own or with children, the odd suited lawyer or other official visitor sticking out like a sore thumb in their sober work clothes amongst the colourful, noisy melee. The process was very slow and thorough and it was well over half an hour before she was shown into a small, brightly lit interview room. It was divided down the middle by a low wall and a glass partition, with a table and chairs on either side. She was pleased not to be in the main visitors' hall down the corridor. She had no desire to be seen by anybody visiting Duran.

She had just sat down when the door on the opposite side of the room opened and Duran entered, followed by a prison guard. His appearance shocked her. When she had last seen him at the Old Bailey, he had been a tall, very striking-looking man, but she barely recognized him. His face was gaunt, with deep shadows under his eyes, and his skin had an unhealthy yellow tinge. He had lost a lot of weight and his shirt hung from his broad shoulders, his trousers also very loose. Instead of the brisk, forward thrusting walk she remembered, he stooped, moving slowly and uncertainly, almost shuffling, like an old man. For someone who had previously taken so much trouble with his appearance, who cared so much about every detail, it was particularly striking.

He sat down stiffly opposite her and folded his hands on the table in front of him. As her eyes met his, she felt the familiar chill. 'Nice to see you, Eve. I'm glad you decided to come.'

The words came over clearly via the microphone, as though the glass partition wasn't there, his voice deep and a little hoarse, the tone flat and measured and without accent, just as she remembered it. There was no smile, or change in his facial expression.

'Forget the pleasantries,' she said, suddenly impatient. 'Let's get to the point. You say I was set up.'

Duran gave a slight nod. 'I can give you the evidence. It wasn't hard to get . . .'

'But I hear you want something from me in return.'

'Always so direct.' There was a pause while he unashamedly

studied her. 'You're looking very well, Eve.' There was a flicker of a smile, which felt like an insult.

'That's more than I can say for you.'

'Prison life doesn't suit me. But that's not why I wanted to see you. Do you believe in justice?'

'What sort of a question's that?'

'Humour me.'

'Yes, of course I do.'

'But you accept that the justice system is fallible?'

'Are you trying to tell me now that you didn't murder Stanco Rupec?'

Duran stared at her for a moment, his black eyes glassy, the dull glimmer of light behind them unreadable as always.

He gave a faint, weary sigh. 'No. This is not about me. There's a man here at Bellevue, who's in for a crime he didn't commit . . .'

'That's what they all say.'

Duran held up his hands and she noticed that even his palms had a yellow tinge. 'Not me. You need to hear me out. I did what I did and I'm prepared to pay the price, which is why I'm not bitter, at least not as far as you're concerned. You were just doing your job. But Sean Farrell is not a murderer. He was stitched up, and the real killer's walking around a free man.'

'What's any of this got to do with me?'

'His case is being reviewed in a few weeks. He's been through ten years of hell in this dump just to get this far. This is his one final shot to prove he's innocent, or at least show that the investigation was flawed. He's got some people working on his behalf, but they're just skimming the surface. They need help. Unless something else comes to light very soon, his application will be turned down. And then that's it for Sean. All hope gone. That's not justice.'

His words spoke of passion but the delivery was flat and without energy. As far as she knew, he didn't have an altruistic bone in his body and she couldn't fathom why he was interested in somebody else's cause.

'Why do you care?'

'Because I believe he's innocent. I've talked to him at length in here, made some preliminary enquiries myself, and I'm convinced he didn't do it. The police cocked up. This wasn't the Met, I hasten to add, so you don't need to defend them. It was somewhere out of London, in the Home Counties. They had him in the frame and they tried to make the evidence fit. They were just plain lazy and his lawyers were no better. They just wanted a quick fix, tick the box and move on. Problem is, they got the wrong man.'

'Shit happens. It's tough. More to the point, why are you bothering to get involved?'

He shifted in his seat and took a deep, rasping breath. 'Because it interests me.'

'Are you saying the justice system's corrupt? Is that your angle?'

Duran inclined his head. 'In some cases, without a doubt. In this instance, I suspect it was incompetence more than anything else, but they don't give a flying fuck. Their necks aren't on the line. They can go home at night to their families and their cosy little beds and put it all behind them. The only one who pays for their shoddiness, day in and day out, is Sean.'

She almost smiled. It was ironic hearing him take the moral high ground about the justice system, or its failings. He had been successfully dodging around it for years, but she let it go. He had a point, not that she would dream of saying so. Occasionally, she had seen at first hand fellow officers taking short cuts with cases. It was usually due to laziness, or over-work, or occasionally, as he said, incompetence. If it was true for the Met, who had the greatest number of murder cases to solve each year, it was even more so for a smaller, more rural police force, where murder was a much rarer occurrence. A murder investigation was always high profile and hampered by all the usual media focus and hype. Under the constant pressure to get a result as quickly as possible, errors might be made. Sometimes, it made even the best officers blind to what was in front of them. Although there was no excuse, it happened. But she reminded herself she was there to find out what he knew about her case. That was all.

'As I said before, what's any of this got to do with me?'

Duran inclined his head a little towards her, holding her gaze unblinking. The room was overheated and airless and she suddenly felt a little giddy. His dark scalp and forehead gleamed with perspiration and the whites of his eyes were bright yellow. He looked very ill. Maybe he was in pain, which would explain

his stiffness. She couldn't smell him through the glass but she
wondered if he still wore Paco Rabanne, if he was allowed such
luxuries in prison, then decided that, like access to a mobile
phone, it was something he would make sure of.

'I like the way you handle things,' he said quietly. 'You treated
me with respect and courtesy, unlike many of your colleagues.
I don't forget these things. What happened to you wasn't
right. I'll help you sort it, so you come out on top. But I'd like
you to do something for me in return. You've got time on your
hands until your hearing. Maybe you can use that time to help
Sean, see if you can turn up anything new that the others have
missed. That's all I ask.'

His request took her by surprise. It was the last thing she had been
expecting. She shook her head. 'Why don't you just hire a PI?'

'I could do, of course. Anything's possible, even from in here.
But you'll do a much better job. You're top-notch, Eve. You've
got all the necessary experience *and* you understand the system
from the inside out. If anyone can spot a flaw in the process,
you will. I'll pay you generously for your time . . .'

She felt the colour rise to her cheeks. 'I don't want your
money.'

'I'd forgotten how proud you are. I didn't mean to insult you,
but your reputation is trashed and you're likely to lose your job,
from what I hear. Money aside, that must matter a lot to you.'
He let the sentence hang. 'That's why, like it or not, you need
my help. I can give you the proof you were set up, who did it,
and why. It will stand up in any internal proceedings, or court
of law, if you decide to take it that far, and if you still don't get
what you want, the newspapers will love it, if you sell your story.
You can also have the satisfaction of helping an innocent man.'

She stared at him for a moment. Much that she'd like to believe
him, it all sounded hollow.

'Have you got religion, or something?'

The faintest of smiles appeared on his thin lips. 'What, me?
Of course not. I'm an atheist and proud of it.'

'What's your angle, then? Is it personal?'

He had no wife, children or other dependents, from what she
could recall, no significant other, male or female, to share the
huge, gated house in North London, with its indoor and outdoor

swimming pools, sterile works of art and expensive furnishings. She remembered from her visit, when they had searched his house, how it all felt like a film set, not somewhere actually lived in. She had wanted to see his home to get a better feel for the man, but she had been disappointed. Even the most personal of spaces, his bedroom, his bathroom and his huge, mirrored dressing-room, with its walnut panelled wardrobes, filled with tailor-made suits and sober, top of the range classic clothing, lacked personality.

Duran leaned back in his chair, stretched his shoulders and sighed. 'You're so incredibly suspicious, Eve. Although I guess I don't blame you. I met Sean for the first time here in Bellevue. Other than that, I can honestly say I have no personal connection, either to him or to Jane McNeil, the murder victim. You know, she'd have been just a few years older than you are now, if somebody hadn't stolen her future from her. Think about that.'

'Why, then? Why are you bothering yourself with someone else's problem? It's not like you and it doesn't add up.'

'Curious, lovely Eve. You just can't let things drop, can you? They keep worrying away at you, all these little mysteries, all these little inconsistencies. Like why I killed Stanco. I remember how you went on and on about it. It was so important to you. I understand you so well, you know. I'm just like you. I hate mysteries too. We both need to understand, put everything neatly away in its box, have everything explained to our satisfaction, so we can sleep at night. Do you have problems sleeping at night? I bet you do . . .'

He was taunting her now, closer to the truth than he could imagine. 'Don't try and analyse me,' she said sharply and stood up. 'If you're not going to explain yourself, I'm off.'

He held up his hand. 'Wait. Don't go, Eve.' His voice was suddenly loud and rasping. It woke up the guard, who had been standing motionless with his back to the wall, arms folded, in some sort of reverie throughout the interview.

'Are you done, Mr Duran?' the guard asked, the 'Mr' said without any hint of irony, the tone full of respect.

Duran looked around. 'It's alright, Dave. Just a few more minutes.' It was as though he were talking to his manservant. Duran looked back at her and leaned forward across the table.

'Please.' He spoke quietly, almost mouthing the word as though ashamed of it. There was an unusual light and eagerness in his black eyes. She had never heard him say 'please' before. It struck her forcibly that, in spite of his apparently uninterested manner, it mattered a lot to him, for some reason. Intrigued, still holding his gaze, she sat down again.

'If you really need an explanation, I'll give you one,' he said. 'I'm ill. Very ill indeed, as you can see.' He gestured vaguely towards his skeletal frame. 'The doctors have given me just a matter of months at most. I've been thinking about things a lot in here and I'd like to help some people, while I still can. Sean's one of them. You're another.'

Was he really dying, she wondered. Was that what this was all about? Based on the strange colour of his skin, it had to be his liver, or possibly his pancreas. Either way, from the little she knew, the prognosis wasn't good. Would somebody like him ever have regrets and want to make amends for the terrible things he'd done and the lives he'd ruined? Part of her wanted to believe that he could help her, but part of her, an important part, still mistrusted him. There had to be a catch.

'Say I agree to help. What if I can't find out anything? Or what if I find out for sure he's guilty?'

Duran sat back in his chair and spread his hands. 'All I ask is that you just take a look. Follow the evidence wherever it leads. If he's guilty, so be it. I'll let you have everything I've got on the case. Alan Peters can get the files over to you. You can then talk to Sean and take it from there. If you find out something that helps his case, great. If not, it's OK. And if he's guilty, that's OK too. All I care about is the truth. I want justice to be served. You do your best and I'll honour my side of the bargain.'

It was as though they were having an ordinary, everyday conversation and it struck her how surreal it all was.

'Will you, though?' She studied his face, trying to read something – anything – from his expression, but it was hopeless. 'Maybe you're just spinning me a line.'

He gave an almost imperceptible shrug and sighed, like a teacher confronted with a slow-to-learn pupil. 'What have you got to lose, Eve? You're up shit creek without a paddle, as I see it.'

It was galling hearing it from him, of all people, but she

couldn't disagree, not that she would let it show. The doubts still lingered. 'You're asking me to take a lot on trust. How do I know that your information's any good?'

His face hardened. It pleased her to see that at last she had touched a nerve, even if it was only his pride. 'Do you really think *my* intelligence would be *bad*? Information is power in both our worlds. I'm not only well connected, I'm very, very thorough. My contacts are excellent and I do in-depth research on people who interest me. Sometimes it throws up something useful.' He moistened his dry lips with his tongue and she caught a glimpse of glistening white teeth. 'Take you, for example.'

'Me?'

'Yes. I know a lot about you, about your hippy foster parents down in Lymington. They were most forthcoming.'

The words shocked her. There was nothing about her background in the police HR records, as far as she knew. She wondered what lies, what shameful pretext Duran had used to get the information. Had he sent somebody down to Lymington to talk to her foster parents, Robin and Clem Jackson, maybe pretending to be a journalist, or somebody doing research? She had last spoken to them immediately after the shooting, to let them know that she was alright. They hadn't mentioned anything at all suspicious.

'What the hell are you talking about?'

'You certainly struck gold with them; they're decent people. I wasn't so lucky with mine, I can tell you, although that's another story, for another time. But as I said, we have a few things in common, you and I.'

'How dare you speak to them. When was this?'

'When you first arrested me, of course. I wanted to find out everything I could about you.'

She pictured the cheerful, orderly little house in Lymington where she had lived for five years. She had indeed been lucky to be placed with Robin and Clem, the last in the very fortunate line of children to be fostered by them once their own brood of four had grown up and left home. The thought of such an intrusion on them, as well as on her private world, filled her with anger, as well as the idea that somebody had tricked them. They were too good, and kind, and trusting to be treated that way.

Nothing, nobody, seemed to be beyond Duran's reach. Who else had he spoken to? What else did he know?

She remembered a little of his background from the thick file that had been sent over from Organized Crime when he was arrested. Half Dutch, half Serbian, he had been born and brought up in the UK by his mother, who had been working in London as an au pair. Nobody knew what had happened to the father, but the mother had been killed in a hit-and-run accident when he was five, and Duran had been put into a series of foster homes. Somehow, he had later emerged with a top law degree, then qualified as an accountant, and had anglicized his surname from Duranovic to Duran. He had wanted to conform to some self-imposed ideal, even to the point of taking elocution lessons from a well-known stage voice-coach to remove any trace of his South London accent. In some ways, Eve understood. She had spent most of her life trying to blend in. When she moved down south to Lymington, she had worked very hard to eliminate any trace of her northern accent, a peculiar amalgam of the various places she had lived before. She couldn't afford to stand out. After so many years, she had forgotten what her real voice had sounded like. But Duran's need to transform himself was based on insecurity, as well as vanity. She refused to accept that there were meaningful parallels.

'So you've been spying on me. You must be desperate.'

'I like to know who I'm dealing with, that's all. The devil's always in the detail. I know what you did at uni, where you lived, what sort of student you were, what you liked to eat, the friends you made, the boys you shagged, and the same goes for your career with the Met and poor Detective Sergeant Jason Scott.'

'That's enough.'

He held up his hand. 'I'm just telling you this because I want you to understand that finding out who set you up, and why, was a piece of piss. I want you to have faith in me.'

Anger and humiliation hit her in waves. If the glass hadn't separated them, she would have hit him. Again she sensed his ego, what he said full of bravura and possibly exaggeration. She pushed the chair away and got to her feet.

'Faith in *you*? How dare you pry into my life like this. You know nothing about me.' She turned to go.

'Not nearly as much as I'd like, it's true. Your middle name's

Charlotte, isn't it?' he shouted after her. 'Eve *Charlotte* West. Funny that a three-day-old baby by the same name died on 25th August 1984, in Selly Oak Hospital, Birmingham.'

The words struck her like a blow. Her stomach lurched, the heat rose to her cheeks and it was all she could do not to make a sound or movement that would give herself away. Thank God her back was to him. It was a moment she had been dreading for years, the sharp, vicious tug at the thread that held her whole life together. She had prepared for it over and over again until she was sure she was pitch perfect, but nothing could quiet the thumping of her heart. At least he couldn't see or feel it.

She turned to look at him. 'It's a common enough name.' She heard her voice clear and steady.

A flicker of doubt crossed his face. 'Not *that* common,' he said, narrowing his eyes, still studying her intently. 'Anyway, you also share the same birth date. If I didn't like you so much, I'd say you'd stolen her ID. The key question is why. Who are you, Eve? I mean, who are you *really*?'

The blood was deafening in her head, but she held his gaze. 'What's the point of all of this?'

He sucked in his breath and nodded. 'You're class, Eve. You're wasted on the police.' He pushed his chair back and slowly stood up, holding out his hand towards the glass, as though he were asking for hers. His eyes glittered. 'I want you to know you can trust me, that's all. If you do me this one favour, your little secret's safe with me.'

# SIX

E ve walked slowly out of the room and back through the series of corridors and security checks to the main entrance. She wondered if he had planted spies to observe her and she decided to take no chances. There must be no signs of her inner turmoil to be reported back. Her footsteps echoed distantly on the lino and she felt as though she were sleepwalking, as she went over and over in her mind what Duran had said. 'If you do me this favour, your secret's safe with me.' How much did he know? Could he really have found out something material? The more she thought about it, the more it seemed unlikely. The fact that she shared somebody else's name and birth date could be dismissed as a coincidence. But in trying to blackmail her showed he was desperate, for some reason. Maybe she could play it to her advantage. Again, she kept coming back to why he had decided to take up Sean Farrell's cause. Had he really had some sort of Damascene conversion? She doubted it. 'It is better to reign in hell than serve in heaven,' Duran had once said to her, in one of his more forthcoming responses during his interrogation. At the time, she wondered if he had actually read Milton, or knew where the quote came from, or if it was something he had picked up second-hand, just liking the sound of it. But he was right about one thing. 'What have you got to lose?' he had asked. What choice *did* she have? There was a good chance he might know who had set her up, and why. Even if he didn't, or if she did what he asked and he then reneged on the deal, she would be in no worse a position than she was now. If he honoured his side of the bargain and gave her the information she needed, it might change everything at the disciplinary hearing. Also, whoever had done it would be made to pay. On balance, it was a risk worth running. Apart from anything else, she needed to stop him delving any further into her past.

She collected her belongings from the visitor centre, went into the ladies, checked to make sure it was empty, then locked herself in a cubicle. She closed the lid of the toilet, sat down and took out her phone. Was there any way Duran could find out her true identity? She was wondering whom to contact, who could possibly know, when the phone vibrated in her hand. She checked the screen. No caller ID. When she answered, she heard Alan Peters' flat, nasal tones at the other end.

'Where are you, Miss West?'

'Still at Bellevue,' she said, although she imagined he knew this. Duran's chauffeur, would have told him that she hadn't yet come out. 'Just getting my things from the visitor centre.'

'I understand you've now seen Mr Duran. Would you like the papers sent over to you?'

She took a deep breath. She had no choice, she told herself again. 'Yes.'

'When will you be back home?'

She looked at her watch. They would soon be hitting the beginning of the rush-hour traffic. 'Say a couple of hours.'

'There's somebody you should talk to. His name's Dan Cooper. He's a journalist and he knows a lot about the case. He works for a charity called 4Justice. It was set up by Cooper and his ex-partner, Kristen Harris. She's another journalist. They investigate miscarriages of justice and they've had some notable success.' He reeled off a few names, a couple of which were familiar. 'It's all linked to a TV programme of the same name on Channel 4. Luckily for Sean, they've taken up his case. I'll fix up for you to see Cooper first thing in the morning.'

'What if he finds out I work for the Met? This is a very sensitive time for me, with the disciplinary hearing coming up. I can't afford for word to get out that I'm doing anything like this.'

'If anyone asks, just say you have a *personal* interest in the case,' Peters said. 'That's allowed, isn't it? There's been all sorts of stuff in the papers, as you might've seen. Maybe it's piqued your curiosity. Nobody's going to blame you for offering to help free an innocent man.'

She said nothing. He made it sound so easy and reasonable but she knew how her superiors wouldn't view it that way, if they found out. But what choice did she have? She would just have to be careful.

'As far as Mr Cooper goes,' Peters continued, 'I'll make it very clear you're acting in an unofficial, voluntary capacity. The charity's short of funds and we've made a small financial donation to help oil the wheels temporarily. Cooper will be told to cooperate and to be discreet. To be honest, the way things are going, he should be grateful for any help he can get. But any problems, you just let me know and I'll have a word with him. You can then go back to Bellevue tomorrow afternoon to meet Sean Farrell.'

The files from Peters arrived by courier just after eight that evening. The sealed box contained a large, thick, black ring binder, labelled *Jane McNeil Murder*, as well as a bulky brown envelope, shaped like a small brick. Even without feeling through the paper, she guessed what was inside. She held it in her hand for a moment, loath to open it, then tore open the flap and pulled out a block of new fifty-pound notes, with a yellow sticky note attached, in Peters' handwriting: *£10,000. For expenses. AP.* It was way more than what was reasonable for a couple of weeks' work, plus expenses, and it stank of a bribe. She took a photograph of it with her phone, as well as the note, in case she ever had to explain. She wouldn't take a penny of Duran's money, over and above what was needed for expenses. There was also an old-style Nokia phone, still in its box. The yellow sticky note attached to it said: *Use this if you want to call me or Mr Duran. Numbers are pre-loaded. It's untraceable.*

She made a pot of mint tea, sat down on the sofa and picked up the file. The first page was a large, A4-sized colour photograph of a young woman, slotted into a plastic sleeve. In spite of a pair of unattractive, heavy-framed spectacles, Jane McNeil had been nice-looking in an unremarkable way, with small, neat features and shoulder-length, wavy, dark-brown hair. She was slim, dressed in jeans and a fitted denim shirt, but her body language was awkward, arms folded tightly over her chest, her smile shy and forced, as though she was unused to posing for the camera. A photocopied press cutting had been tucked behind the photograph.

*The semi-naked body of Jane McNeil, 27, was discovered in the West Woods, near Marlborough, on Friday evening, thirteen days after she was last seen at a party on the nearby Westerby estate. She was found in a densely-wooded area, half a mile from the main car park. Someone, presumably her killer, had attempted to burn Miss McNeil's body. Although thirty officers from Wiltshire Constabulary have been involved in the inquiry, questioning locals and Miss McNeil's former boyfriend, nobody has yet been able to shed any light on how her body came to be there, according to a police spokesperson. 'One theory we are looking into is that she may have been out jogging, as she liked to keep fit. But it's early days and we are keeping an open mind.' Det Supt John Hamill, who is heading the inquiry, yesterday renewed an appeal for anyone to come forward who may have seen Miss McNeil between the evening of Saturday*

*6th December and Friday 19 th December, the day her body*
*was found. 'We are talking to her family, friends and*
*colleagues and anyone else who may have relevant informa-*
*tion, in an effort to find out more about her,' he said. 'It's*
*an ongoing process and will take many days. It is far too*
*early to comment on a possible motive. We would like to*
*hear from anyone who has information relating to this*
*investigation and we hope that by releasing a photograph*
*of Jane, it will jog the memories of anyone who may have*
*seen her prior to her death.' The surrounding area was*
*sealed off by police yesterday. Further tests are still being*
*carried out to determine the cause of Miss McNeil's death.*

She skimmed through the first few pages, which were enough to
give her the gist of what had happened. Jane had worked as an
administrative assistant in the office of Westerby Racing and had
lived in a cottage on the Westerby estate. The timeline was clear
and straightforward. On Saturday, 6th December, shortly after
nine a.m., she had visited a gym, just outside Marlborough.
According to the security system, which required an electronic
log-in and log-out, she was there for just over an hour and a half.
Her ex-boyfriend, Sean Farrell, belonged to the same gym and
he arrived there around ten thirty. Several witnesses at the gym
described overhearing an argument between the two. Between
one p.m. and six p.m., Jane was at the Westerby Racing client
Christmas party, serving drinks and canapés to their clients, as
well as helping to clear up afterwards. According to several
people who were there, she left before the end, claiming she had
a headache and was going home, although nobody saw her leave.
The last recorded call from her mobile phone was made from
the Marlborough area to her mother, at 7.16 p.m. that evening.
  A work colleague of Jane's, Annie Shepherd, drove past the
cottage where Jane lived just before seven p.m. that evening and
noticed a couple of lights on inside. When another woman, Susan
Wright, went past half an hour later, the lights were all off. She
also said that she saw a man hanging around Jane's cottage,
peering in through the windows and hammering on the door. It
was dark, but she thought he was Jane's ex-boyfriend, Sean Farrell.
When Jane failed to arrive for work on Monday morning, Melissa

Michaels, the daughter of the owner of the Westerby estate, went over to the cottage to see if she was alright. One of the ground floor windows at the back of the cottage had been forced open and a pane of glass broken. There was no sign of Jane, or her car, and she called the police. Just over two weeks later, a couple of women out hacking in the West Woods with their dogs discovered the partially burnt and decomposed remains of a woman's body. It was tucked away in a gulley behind a fallen tree trunk, covered by a pile of dead leaves. The body was later identified as belonging to Jane McNeil. Her car was eventually found in a pub car park next to the Kennet and Avon canal, about two miles south of the cottage where she lived. The only recent prints in the car were Jane's, although a partial fingerprint belonging to Sean Farrell had been found on the inside of the passenger doorframe. There was no means of saying when the fingerprint had got there, but the absence of any other prints was odd.

Further down the page, Eve found a handwritten note to say that Jane had taken the car to be professionally cleaned a few days before she disappeared. The police assumption was that either Jane had driven herself to the pub to meet somebody, presumably Farrell, or that whoever had driven it had either wiped it clean afterwards or had worn gloves. Farrell's defence was that he had been in Jane's car countless times when they were still seeing each other and that the print had been missed by whoever had cleaned the car earlier that week. Nobody at the pub recalled seeing the car arrive, or either Jane or Farrell there that night.

Judging from the press clippings, Farrell had been a suspect right from the start, but there was nothing unusual in that. Strangerkillings were very rare, and in all crimes of violence against women, particularly those with a sexual motive, the obvious place to start was with men known to the victim. The autopsy summary gave the cause of death as undetermined, but of particular interest was a note relating to the presence of seminal fluid on the victim's thigh, although there hadn't been sufficient biological material to develop a full DNA profile. Ten years on, there had been a huge advance in the sensitivity and scope of DNA profiling techniques. Had this been a cold case review, re-testing the exhibits would have been a priority. But with Farrell convicted, the case was closed. Somebody – it looked like Alan Peters' writing – had also made a handwritten note on the page saying: 'See biologist's evidence'. Attached to the back of the pages was a passage from the transcript of the trial. The biologist who had analysed the samples taken from the body had given evidence to the effect that the few sperm that had been recovered were all 'deformed'. 'A couple of the spermatozoa have two tails, some have bent heads, or twin heads,' she had noted. Again, written by hand and outlined with a highlighter were the words: 'Sean Farrell had a vasectomy. No sperm should have been found, deformed or otherwise'.

Eve turned to a short section labelled 'Prosecution Case', which contained a summary of the evidence against Sean Farrell. It also contained what looked like copies of documents taken from his official police file, which were not in the public domain and she wondered who Duran or Peters had bribed in order to obtain them. She also found annotated transcripts from the trial, both from the defence and the prosecution. She wondered if Duran himself had made the notes, or if he had had someone else review the file. The case against Farrell hinged on a motive of jealousy. A couple of months before the murder, Farrell had made a scene in a bar where Jane was having a drink with another man. Jane had also made a complaint to the local police about Farrell stalking her, although it appeared he had been let off without a caution. Taken together with the argument at the gym just before she disappeared, the witness sighting of Farrell outside Jane's cottage that evening, and other information gathered from Jane's work colleagues and Sean's ex-wife of ten years, Farrell seemed an obvious fit.

On the Sunday morning after the Christmas party, Farrell had been seen by a neighbour carrying a large, heavy-looking roll of carpet out of his house and struggling to load it into his van. This was instantly viewed as suspicious, even though various friends of Farrell's told the police that he had been doing up his cottage over the previous couple of months, with a view to selling it. Although he said he had taken the carpet to the dump, it was never found. Apart from that sighting, Farrell had no alibi either for the Saturday night or for a large part of Sunday, the twenty-four-hour window of time during which it was assumed that Jane had been possibly abducted, and murdered. When questioned two weeks later, he had given misleading information regarding his whereabouts on the Sunday morning, saying that he had to visit his mother, who was ill. It turned out that this had been the previous weekend. When this was discovered, he had claimed unconvincingly that he had 'got confused and had mixed up the weekends'. From the police point of view, he was now a proven liar. Whilst Eve understood why they had seen this as further proof of his guilt, in her own experience perfectly innocent people made mistakes about dates and times when put on the spot, particularly in a formal interview situation. Also, not everybody had perfect recall of what they had been doing even a week before, let alone two or longer. But on top of everything else, it was damning for Farrell. It was not clear from the file if there had been any other suspects and, if so, who they were.

The final section was labelled 'Defence'. The police mugshot of Farrell taken at the time of his arrest showed a man in his mid-to-late thirties, a broad, fleshy face, with regular features and thick, short, fairish hair. He looked shell-shocked, with the drawn, exhausted expression of somebody who had been put through the mill. She wondered how long the process of questioning had taken before he was formally charged. The psychological assessment had painted him in a positive light, but the defence case, as it was, appeared to have rested entirely on the absence of direct evidence linking Farrell to the crime or the deposition site. The actual crime scene itself had never been identified. Based on what Eve had seen so far, it was surprising that the CPS had managed to get a conviction and she wondered if Farrell had come across poorly during the trial. Given what Duran had said, it was more likely that the defence team had failed to bring out, in any meaningful way, the absence of direct evidence against Farrell. Instead, they appeared to have lost the case because the jury had accepted the picture painted by the prosecution of Farrell's poor character. At the end were a few sheets of paper containing the logs for both outgoing and incoming calls covering the four weeks up to the Monday morning when Jane McNeil was reported as missing. This also included some voicemail transcripts. She flicked through them but nothing stood out as particularly interesting. Also, without knowing who the people were behind the names, it all meant very little. The file was better than nothing, but it was hardly comprehensive and she wondered whether information had been left out deliberately, or if it was all Peters/Duran had been able to put together. Hopefully, she would learn more from Dan Cooper.

She felt suddenly tired. She had read enough and went into the bedroom, pulled the curtains tightly shut across the blinds and switched on the shower. As she undressed, she had a sudden image of Jason, lying on the bed, looking up at her in the dimly lit room. 'Why is it always so dark in here? You can't tell if it's day or night. I want to see your lovely face.'

'I can't sleep if there's any light,' she had replied, although that was only the half of it. Sleep, or not sleeping, had been an issue for many years. Even the smallest pinprick of light was a disturbance. She had fitted special blackout blinds behind the curtains and bought the most comfortable bed she could afford, but it still wasn't enough. She had tried everything, from hypnotherapists to special sleep clinics and cognitive behavioural therapy, some more effective than others for a temporary fix, but it had all been a waste of time. Nothing had come close to curing her insomnia. It was why she usually preferred to sleep alone. As with everything else, the problem was in her head and nothing could fix that. When she did manage to fall asleep, the nightmares would often come, so vivid and desperate that when she woke up she was bathed in sweat, struggling to remind herself that they were only dreams. 'You sleep fine when I'm here,' Jason had said. He was right and it had surprised her. He had been her short-term therapy and, for a change, she hadn't needed the nightly pills. It was why she put up with his being there all night. She could curl up close and warm in his arms and, for a moment, imagine she was somewhere else.

She showered quickly and got into bed. She opened her laptop and found the 4Justice website. It was impressive, with a digital counter at the top, showing the number of cases they had been asked to investigate since the unit had been set up seven years before. There were links to a huge number of press articles on a range of subjects associated with miscarriages of justice, from a variety of renowned contributors. One page documented a list of cases that 4Justice had taken up, some with links to video footage. In many instances, a successful result had been achieved, with the sentence quashed and an innocent person having been released from prison. The advisory panel included a number of well-known forensic specialists, QCs, criminal law solicitors and journalists, including Dan Cooper and Kristen Harris. It seemed that, as well as Duran, Sean Farrell had the angels on his side. Could they all be wrong?

# SEVEN

I t had started to rain again and the morning traffic was almost at a standstill, backed up all the way along the Earls Court Road as far as the junction with the Cromwell Road. Eve cursed herself for leaving her umbrella at home and made her way as quickly as she could along the crowded pavement. The offices of 4Justice were in a shabby, four-storey building, not far from the Tube, the front door sandwiched between a Betfred and a Starbucks. The paint was scuffed and peeling and some-body had chalked the words 'out of order' against the small row of ancient-looking bells. A waft of warm doughnuts from one of the nearby shops momentarily filled the damp air and she suddenly felt hungry. Hopefully, the meeting wouldn't take long. Sheltering under the narrow overhang above the door, she took out her phone and dialled the office number. After several rings, a woman's voice answered. Repeating herself loudly several times over the noise from the street, Eve explained who she was. After a pause, she caught the words 'first floor' and the door buzzed open. The hall inside was poorly lit and smelled strongly of damp. Piles of dusty, unopened post lay on the threadbare brown carpet, next to a plastic recycling bin over-flowing with unwanted fliers. A sign saying '4Justice 1st Floor, Exotica Travel 2nd Floor' was pasted on the wall, with a large, black arrow drawn in marker pen pointing up the stairs. Peters had said that the charity was short of money, but after the impressive website, she had been expecting something a little more salubrious.

As she reached the first floor, the door on the landing opened and a stocky young woman, with short, spikey, black hair, appeared behind it.

'I'm Zofia,' she said, holding out a very firm, cold hand. She was dressed head to toe in black, her eyes heavily outlined in black as well. 'Dan's tied up at the moment. You can come in and wait.' Her Polish accent was strong.

The office was spacious and light, with a large sash window overlooking the street. Shelf-lined walls were stuffed with files and books and the noticeboard that hung over the Victorian marble fireplace was papered with a variety of press cuttings and photographs. A mishmash of tatty tables and desks had been pushed together to form a block in the centre of the room, which was laden with computers and more files and papers.

Zofia pointed towards a sofa under the window. 'You can sit there,' she said offhandedly, before returning to her desk and tucking herself behind it, her face hidden by a large, leafy pot plant.

Eve took off her wet coat and hung it on an empty hook by the door. Moving a collection of files and newspapers to one side, she sat down on the sofa. A few minutes later, a door at the back of the room opened and a tall, thin man emerged, a cloud of cigarette smoke following him out into the office. She recognized Dan Cooper immediately from the images on the website, although his face looked more gaunt and he had grown a rough sort of a beard. As he closed the door behind him, Eve caught a glimpse of a darkened room, with what looked like an unmade camp bed pushed up against the wall.

'You're here about Sean Farrell, right?' He ran his fingers quickly through his thick, brown hair, peering at her through narrowed eyes, as though dazed by the daylight. His voice was croaky and he spoke slowly as though every word was an effort. His frayed jeans hung low on his hips, pulled together loosely with a silver-buckled belt, an old denim shirt half tucked in at the front and open to his mid chest, the buttons done up incorrectly. It struck her that he had just hauled himself out of bed and dressed in a hurry on hearing her arrive.

'Yes.'

'You're with the police.' The tone was hostile.

'I'm not here in an official capacity.'

'Why *are* you here, then?' He met her gaze defiantly, his eyes an intense, watery blue.

It was all very well for Peters to assume that Dan Cooper would do what he was told and cooperate, but experience had taught her otherwise.

'I've been asked to help,' she said quietly, aware that Zofia had stopped tapping on her keyboard and was no doubt listening.

Dan shook his head dismissively. 'We don't need any help. Thanks.'

He was frowning and his hand shook a little as he reached in his shirt pocket for his cigarettes and lit up. The night before, she had read various articles he had written and watched a short video clip on the 4Justice website of him talking about a different case, which he had investigated and where they had succeeded in overturning a guilty verdict. He had all the vigour and clarity of a successful campaigning journalist and when she Googled him, she saw that he had won a number of journalistic prizes and accolades. He had had a promising career in mainstream journalism and she wondered what had taken him off on a detour into charity work. She also wondered what had gone wrong. Peters had mentioned Kristen Harris as being his ex-partner but it wasn't clear if he had meant it in a romantic, as well as a business, sense. Out of curiosity, she had watched a couple of other short clips from a TV programme presented by Kristen, highlighting a recent 4Justice case. She was good-looking, in an offbeat way, with long, wavy, dark hair and shiny red lips. Her presentation was slick and professional and she seemed very sure of herself as she talked and smiled at the camera. But it was all a bit over the top, a little too knowing and self-serving, Eve thought, given that Kristen was supposed to be presenting a programme on the serious issue of a miscarriage of justice, which had ruined somebody's life, rather than *The One Show*. By contrast, Dan Cooper had come across as earnest and genuinely passionate. Based on the little she had seen, she knew which one of them she would rather have as an advocate. But the man in front of her seemed to be falling apart and she understood why Duran thought he might need help.

She got to her feet, holding his gaze. 'Look. You may think you have everything in hand. I hope, for Sean Farrell's sake, you're right. But I have a job to do. I've been asked to take a look, as a favour for someone. Just in case I can turn up something. If I find anything, you can have it. What have you got to lose?' He made no reply and she continued: 'I've worked many, many murder cases—'

'Yes. Yes. I know exactly who you are,' he said, with a vague wave of his hand. 'But I still don't get why you're here.'

She shrugged. 'What I'm trying to say is, I'm used to dealing with this sort of thing and I understand how the system works. Maybe a fresh pair of eyes can be of use.'

'Why are you so interested in Sean Farrell?'

His expression was still sceptical and she gave him a hard stare in return. 'I'm *not*. I'd never heard of him until yesterday and, to be honest, I'd much rather go home and leave you to it. But as I said, I'm just doing a favour for somebody who, like you, believes Sean is innocent. That's all. I'm not here to spy on you. I'm not checking up on you. And I won't get in your way. But from what I hear, there's not much time to turn things around and Sean needs all the help he can get right now. I just need you to fill me in on a few things, then I'll go away and leave you alone. OK?'

He studied her for a moment, his full lips slightly apart, as though weighing things up in his mind.

'I thought Alan Peters had explained everything,' she said sharply, when he made no reply. 'Do you want me to call him now and put you on the phone?'

'He has. It just seems very odd, that's all. But I guess I shouldn't look a gift horse in the mouth, as they say. So long as you're not a Trojan horse.'

'I've told you who I am and why I'm here. I'm not going over it again.'

He sighed deeply as though it was too much trouble to resist any longer, slid out a chair from behind one of the desks and thumped down heavily onto it. He swung his feet up onto the desk, nudging aside a pile of papers with the heel of one of his ancient-looking cowboy boots, took a long, deep drag on his cigarette, then looked up at her through the smoke. 'OK. Fine. But be quick. I've got to go and see somebody in half an hour.'

He didn't look like a man with anything urgent to do. She sat down again and took out a notebook and pen. She wasn't leaving until she had what she needed. 'Before we talk about the case, can you tell me a little about Jane and what her background was, that sort of thing?'

He coughed, then looked round at Zofia. 'Can you get me a coffee please, Zofia. My throat's really dry and sore.'

Zofia shot him a sharp look, then rose from behind her desk with an audible sigh. 'What sort of coffee?'

'Black. Triple espresso. Maybe just a dash of hot milk. And something to eat. I'm absolutely famished.' He looked back at Eve and added as an afterthought: 'What about you?'

'I'm fine, thanks.'

'And some Hedex Extra,' he shouted after Zofia, as she grabbed her coat and strode out of the room. He swivelled back towards Eve. 'What were you saying?'

'You were going to tell me about Jane.'

He nodded slowly and half closed his eyes as though it was all an effort. 'She was an only child, born and brought up in a small village just outside Lincoln. Her father was an equine vet and she wanted to be a vet too, but didn't get the grades. She'd been working at the Michaels' yard for about six months.'

'Before that?'

'For a bloodstock insurance broker in Newmarket, I think.'

'So she was relatively new to the Marlborough area?'

'That's right. She wanted to work for a racing yard, or at least that's what her mother said. Reading between the lines, I think she also wanted to put some distance between herself and her parents.'

'You've spoken to them?'

'Just the mother. Briefly, on the phone and then about a year ago in person. She practically slammed the door in my face when she found out we were trying to help Sean. They're convinced Sean killed her.'

'Based on what?'

'What the police told them, I guess. They certainly don't want us digging it up all over again. They've been quite vitriolic, in fact.'

'I'm not surprised.'

She had seen it before and understood why they wouldn't welcome Dan's efforts. Families wanted closure so that they could grieve and then, if possible, move on as best they could with their lives. Jane's parents would want to believe that the police had got it right, that her killer was locked away behind bars for as long as possible, and that the murder of their daughter had been avenged. From their point of view, opening up the case all over again, with all the media attention and speculation, would reawaken the past, with all the endless wondering about who had killed their daughter, and why.

'What about other boyfriends?' she asked, watching Dan stretch his mouth wide into a yawn.

'Nothing serious for a couple of years, from what I was told. I don't think Sean was anything serious either, he just thought he was. That was the problem.'

'Tell me about the Westerby estate. I don't know the area and I know nothing about racing.'

'It's a big place and it belongs to the Michaels family. They're one of those horse racing dynasties and they've been there for several generations. When Jane McNeil was murdered, Tim Michaels was still in charge, but he died and it's now run by his son, Harry, and daughter, Melissa.'

'Is she the one who reported Jane as missing?'

'Yes.'

'Who lives on the estate now?'

'There's Tim's widow, Sally. Harry Michaels. He's divorced. Plus Melissa, her husband, and their children. I don't know who's in the main house these days, but there are a number of cottages dotted around the estate. I think a few are rented out, but the rest are occupied by the family or people who work for the Michaels, like the assistant trainer and people like that.'

'So Jane had one of these cottages to herself?'

'She was supposed to share it with two other girls, but they'd both left at the time of her murder, so she was there on her own.'

'A number of people seemed to be passing her cottage the night she disappeared. How easy is it to access the land?'

'Very easy, or at least it was. The whole place is covered in public rights of way and bridle paths, and anyone used to be able to come and go in a car, according to Sean. There are three or four entrances onto the estate and none were secured at the time Jane was murdered. You could just drive through. Even though it's private land, people used to use it as a cut-through from the A4 to avoid Marlborough town centre.'

'That must have made it very difficult for the police,' she said.

'I guess so. That's all changed now, since Harry Michaels took over. He put up security barriers everywhere to stop people driving through.'

'Tell me a bit about Sean Farrell. He was older than Jane, wasn't he?'

He reached forwards to stub out his cigarette and nodded. 'He'd been married before and had two kids. I don't know why the marriage failed, but his ex booted him out and it was all very acrimonious. She even gave evidence against him at his trial, saying he was prone to violent mood swings and was overly possessive and controlling. If you ask me, the mood swings were to do with having to live with her. I met her once. She's a right bitch.'

'How did he and Jane meet?'

'At the yard. He was the Michaels' farrier. By all accounts, he was pretty successful and looked after a number of racing yards in the Marlborough and Lambourn area. He and Jane started seeing each other quite soon after she started work there.'

'Let's get to the trial. What went wrong, in your view?'

He sighed heavily and shifted in his chair, rotating his shoulders as though they were stiff.

'A number of things. Sean was found guilty on the basis of circumstantial evidence alone. None of the forensic evidence gathered at the time indicated that he was her killer. There were fresh footprints in the mud around where the body was found, but they were too big to be Sean's, nor did they fit the boots of either of the two female riders who found the body. There was sperm on the victim's thigh, but Sean had had a vasectomy. You'd think that all the arrows were pointing away from Sean and not at him.'

'How did the police explain it?'

'They said the footprints could have been anybody's, even though the body was found nowhere near a footpath. Also, the prints were found directly around the body. But there were no footprints under it, so they must have been made after the body was dumped there, most likely at the same time. As for the sperm, the women's changing room at the gym was out of order, for some reason, so men and women were using the same place. The police had some ludicrous theory that the sperm must have come from a used towel or something. Or, that she had had sex with someone after the Westerby party and that Sean had seen this and flipped. But nobody knows who this other man is. The police certainly couldn't find him.'

'There were no other suspects?'

'Not that I'm aware of. I don't think they bothered to look very hard, once they had Sean in their sights. All of this should have been enough to create reasonable doubt in the minds of the jury, but the defence team were rubbish.'

'They must have had something else against him, surely?'

'A woman said she saw Sean near Jane McNeil's house on the Sunday night after the party at Westerby, but her testimony isn't totally reliable.'

'You mean Susan Wright?'

'Yes. She lived in one of the other cottages down the lane. She didn't even come forward for two weeks, as she was away on holiday when the body was found. She describes a man in a suit hammering on Jane's front door, but the physical description's vague, as he was facing away from the road and, at best, she could have only seen him in profile. According to his family, the last time Farrell wore a suit was at his father's funeral, yet she says she recognized Farrell in the headlights of her car . . .'

'So she knew him?'

'She worked with Jane and knew about their relationship, so maybe that was enough for her to make the association and think it was Sean. At any rate, it was pitch-black outside, no lights on inside Jane's cottage, and the porch light wasn't working either. I went down to Marlborough and walked past the cottage myself, just to check. It's set back from the road, up a bank, and there's a hedge at the front. Even with your lights on full beam, you'd be hard pushed to see much in the front garden at night.'

'You think she lied?'

He shook his head wearily. 'People often get things wrong, as I'm sure you know. Farrell said he went to the cottage earlier that evening to apologize for his behaviour at the gym, but Jane was still at the party, so it's possible that Susan Wright did see him and made a mistake about the time. Alternatively, it was someone else she saw, who was also looking for Jane. Someone had tried to break in through one of the back windows, but Sean's fingerprints weren't found on it. So the prosecution said he must have worn gloves. But that would imply premeditation, which just doesn't fit with his hanging around outside in full public view. He's also not the pre-meditating type, based on what I know of him.'

'Was there anything else to link him to the cottage?'

'They found some partial fingerprints that might have been his inside the house, but they were old and smudged and could easily have been left over from when he was seeing Jane. There's something else they tried to dismiss. Sean sent a text to some woman he'd just started seeing around about the time he was supposedly outside Jane's house. The call was logged in the vicinity of his home, which is about ten miles away. The technology wasn't as accurate then as it is now, but he couldn't have been in both places at once. The prosecution said he had someone else, some sort of an accomplice, send the text and help him deal with the body, but they weren't able to find any evidence that there was such a person. And why would anyone want to help him kill Jane? It just doesn't add up.' He looked at her challengingly.

She had to agree; it all sounded farfetched. 'What about the woman who saw him loading a piece of carpet into his van on Sunday morning?'

'He doesn't deny doing it. He says it was an old piece of carpet he took out of his living room, which he then took to the council dump. The police, of course, imagine it was either covered in blood or something, or that he used it to transport her body. Just because they weren't able to find it, it doesn't mean he was lying. The dump is used for recycling all sorts of household stuff and people just go and help themselves to whatever they want. The simple explanation is that somebody took it. Also, if you were going to hide a body in woods, why go there on a Sunday morning, when every man and his fucking dog are out walking around? How the hell was Sean supposed to have got the body from the car park to the dumpsite, which is half a mile away, without being seen? Jane was small and light, I grant you. But even so . . .'

'He could have taken it there some other time.'

'But then he would have had to store the body somewhere, either in the back of his van or somewhere else. The police found absolutely no evidence in the van and despite looking very hard, they failed to turn up any proof that he had a lock-up somewhere else, or had used a friend's place. They examined Sean's house, his clothing and bedding and his garden but there was no evidence of any blood or body fluid, or anything to suggest that Jane had been killed at his house, or that her body had been there at any point. That's why the prosecution came up with this stupid accomplice theory.'

He waved his hand in the air for emphasis and she sympathized with his frustration. The way he was spinning it, the case against Farrell seemed incredibly tenuous and she wondered why the police had been so persistent. There had to be something he wasn't telling her.

She caught his eye. 'You think the police fitted him up?'

'They needed a conviction and they had nobody else. The prosecution certainly made a great deal of the jealousy motive. But I guess it was all they had. And Sean had done a couple of stupid things, like follow Jane to a bar when she went out for a drink with another man and he made quite a scene. He'd had a few drinks and said some stuff he shouldn't have done. But there was nothing violent.'

'Jane made a formal complaint to the police about his stalking her.'

'It was followed up, but no action was taken.'

'Why was he so angry?'

'He felt unfairly treated. They went out for about three months. Apparently, she thought he was getting too heavy, and tried to cool things off.'

'That's code for possessive, isn't it?'

'Maybe from a female point of view.'

Eve picked up the bitterness in his tone and wondered if he was speaking from personal experience. 'So Jane dumped him?'

Dan nodded. 'Sean says it all happened out of the blue. One minute they'd been talking about going on holiday together, the next, she wanted nothing to do with him.'

'This was when?'

'A few months before she disappeared.'

Although a few months were often enough to get over somebody, feelings weren't always so easily switched off. Some people could keep an obsession going for years. 'What about at the time of the murder? Was he over her by then, do you think?'

He shrugged. 'In my view, he'd come to terms with the fact

that she was a lost cause. As I said, he'd started seeing somebody else and, by all accounts, it was going well. I questioned him hard about this, I assure you. He said he'd moved on and I believe him.'

He spoke emphatically, but she wasn't convinced. He might know the ins and outs of the case better than most, he might also have a good journalist's instincts for the truth, but after the length of time he had invested in supporting Farrell's cause, he was hardly impartial and maybe he had allowed things to colour his judgement.

'So what was the argument at the gym about?' she asked.

'Jane saw him come in and she flew off the handle. She made a real scene and accused him of stalking her. He says he wasn't, that he didn't know she was going to be there at that time and that it was stupid trying to avoid one another. He said he had every right to go to the gym. In fact, he'd been a member there longer than she had. This all took place just outside the changing rooms and a number of people witnessed the argument. Nobody disputes his version of what he said, but it was clear that Jane didn't believe him. Nor did the police.'

Eve was silent for a moment. Even if Sean Farrell were innocent, it was likely Jane had been killed by someone she knew. The police hadn't found anyone, so either it was somebody she had recently met, whom she hadn't mentioned to her friends and work colleagues, or else it was someone she had come across casually, maybe in a bar, or a shop, or on the street as part of her daily life. Had she been abducted, or had she gone willingly with whoever it was? Without knowing more of her character and day-to-day patterns, it was impossible to make any assumptions. It felt like looking for a needle in a haystack and she was suddenly struck by the lack of information and backup, compared to what she was used to.

'I have a copy here of her phone records,' she said, opening her bag and pulling out the file Peters had given her. She took out the sheet of paper with the call log and list of names, and passed it to him. 'Can you tell me who these people are?'

He studied it for a moment, then looked up at her. 'Where did you get this?'

'I can't tell you, I'm afraid.'

He shook his head irritably and passed the sheet back to her.

'Stuart Wade and Lorne Anderson both had several horses in training with Tim Michaels.'

'Why would they be calling Jane?'

'Trying to get hold of Michaels, probably. Or maybe something to do with the party.'

'Was it normal for her to use her personal phone for work?'

'Dunno. Holly Crowther's the girl she shared the cottage with. She was one of the Michaels' riders.'

'Where's she now?'

'Again, I don't know. She was sacked a few days before the party – no idea why.'

'Well, according to this, she texted Jane on the Friday, asking to come over and collect her stuff.'

He sighed. 'I imagine the police contacted her, but she wasn't called as a witness at the trial.'

'Even so, it would be good to talk to her. She must have known Jane relatively well, if they lived together. What about the other girl?'

'Grace Byrne? She went back to Ireland. I've got one of my researchers looking for both her and Holly.'

The way he spoke, he gave the impression that he had a team of people behind him, but she remembered what Peters had said about the charity's lack of resources.

'Do you mean Zofia?'

'No. She works here voluntarily. She's a graduate law student, in the middle of her PhD. We employ a professional PI from time to time, to chase down leads.'

Good PIs didn't come cheap and she wondered how he found the money to employ one, given the charity was short of funds. Speaking to Holly and Grace was a priority and she made a mental note to follow it up herself.

'OK. So who was Jane close to? Did she have anybody else she might have confided in?'

He shrugged. 'Apart from the girls she shared with, maybe someone in the office. But she was new to the area. I don't think she knew many people.'

Eve looked down at the list of names on the call log. 'Who is Kevin Stevens? He left a couple of messages asking her to call.'

'He was a freelance reporter, did quite a lot of work for the *Racing Post*. Again, it's another connection on the PI's list of things to check out.'

'You said he "was"?'

'Kevin Stevens was the victim of a hit-and-run. It happened a couple of months after Jane died. There's no evidence they ever actually met. I spoke to Kevin's editor at the *Post* and he said it could be something quite routine, like his wanting to interview Tim Michaels. Jane looked after his diary and made all his appointments.'

'But surely they'd ring the office phone, not her mobile?'

He offered another shrug in response.

'Have you talked to Kevin's family?' she asked.

'No,' he said, suddenly defensive. 'We don't have the resources to follow up on everything. Our job is to raise enough questions about the conviction to overturn it, rather than find the real killer. That's the police's job, or it should be.' He glared at her, as though she were responsible for all the failings of the system.

She held his gaze for a moment, wondering why, even in spite of what he'd said and the genuine passion in his voice, things still didn't add up. Given the lack of direct evidence linking Farrell to the murder, or evidence pointing in a different direction, it wasn't clear why he had been the only real suspect. Something was missing.

'OK. I agree the evidence against him is circumstantial, but unless the police were beyond incompetent, there must be something else to make them so sure Farrell did it. What have you left out?'

He glanced away, reached for his cigarettes, then lit another. 'There is something, although it's not really relevant.'

'I'd still like to hear it. I need the *full*, unedited picture, if I'm going to be of any help.'

He looked up at her. 'OK. When Farrell was in his early twenties, before he got married, he was arrested on suspicion of raping a woman. He admitted having sex with her, but claimed it was consensual. The police decided not to charge him. Twelve years later, when his marriage was on the rocks and his wife had booted him out, he was again charged with rape. A twenty-year-old woman he met in a nightclub in Swindon claimed he had followed her out of the nightclub and had raped her. Again he said she had agreed to sex, but this time he was remanded in custody. However, when the CPS examined the CCTV footage from the nightclub and street outside, they decided there was no chance of a conviction and the charge was dropped. Obviously, none of this came out in court, but I'm sure it coloured the police's and the CPS's view that they had the right man. As a result, they didn't bother to look for anybody else.'

She stared at him, amazed. 'So the man has a background of sexual violence. You seriously think none of this is relevant?'

'No. I don't. Innocent until proved guilty, isn't that what it's supposed to be?'

She exhaled loudly, still holding his gaze. What else was he holding back? 'Well, I disagree. I'd call it interesting and very relevant, in the circumstances. Once, I could dismiss, but twice? You could say there's a pattern beginning, particularly given the allegations of stalking Jane made against him.'

An angry fire filled his eyes. 'There's no fucking pattern. The police checked everything.'

She shrugged. 'Were there other incidents we don't know about, that maybe weren't reported? Did you bother to check?'

'It means nothing,' he said hoarsely. 'Sean's not a rapist. He was never charged.'

She shook her head wearily. Even if Farrell hadn't been charged or convicted of a sexual offence, such a background was hardly the norm. Without knowing the details, it was impossible to tell what it might mean, but to dismiss it as irrelevant was missing the point. Dan was as bad as the rest of them, she thought, not mentioning Farrell's background until pushed, trying to skew the evidence Farrell's way, even in conversation with her. Everybody always had an angle and Dan had probably invested so much time and effort in his belief of Sean Farrell's innocence that he, too, had lost all objectivity and couldn't see things straight. She had heard enough for the moment. She got to her feet and picked up her bag.

'Have you tried to get the exhibits retested?'

'Of course. But, as you know, there's no right in this country to retest the evidence and there's no consistent policy either from one police force to another. It's basically a postcode lottery.

Wiltshire Police, as they're now called, have refused on the basis that the defence team had full access at the time. It's possible the exhibits don't even exist any longer, or they can't lay their hands on them, which may be why they're trying to withhold them.'

'What do you mean? They are required to keep them safe.'

'Try telling that to another innocent man we're trying to help. I won't go into the details, but the sodding Hampshire constabulary have either lost all of the exhibits or deliberately destroyed them.'

He looked at her meaningfully, as though somehow again she were to blame. He was right. Although the Home Office guidelines stipulated that exhibits must be kept for thirty years, evidence did go missing occasionally and it could have disastrous consequences. Unacceptable though it was, what could she say? Human error happened in all walks of life, even the police.

'Going back to Sean Farrell,' he said, 'it doesn't matter that the defence team was beyond incompetent and that science has moved on leaps and bounds. As far as the police are concerned, the ship has sailed.'

'What about the Criminal Cases Review Commission? Isn't that what they're there for?'

'Supposedly. They're our last hope, but they're basically useless,' he said emphatically, with a dramatic sweep of his hand. 'They'll only send a case back to the Court of Appeal if there's what they call "new and compelling evidence" that the conviction was unsafe. Rather than champion cases like Sean's, they seem to be totally in thrall to the Court of Appeal. And *they* are very unwilling to quash convictions and go against a jury's verdict. Less than one per cent of appealed cases get overturned.'

'Why do you say the CCRC is useless? I thought they have the powers to request whatever they like from the police and the CPS.'

'In theory, yes. Problem is, they're completely swamped with applications and massively under-resourced. So they're looking for any excuse to turn people down. Just to give you an idea, out of the five hundred or so cases they reviewed last year, they sent only about thirty back to the Court of Appeal. That's all.'

She wasn't aware of the statistics, but if what he said was true, it was a depressing picture and she wondered how he coped, working with such poor odds. 'Isn't there anything you can do?'

He nodded wearily. 'Basically, we have to do the CCRC's work for them and present them with the evidence on a plate. Which is what we're trying to do for Sean. But if we aren't allowed to retest the exhibits, and for whatever reason they don't think it's worth doing themselves, there won't be any "new and compelling evidence" and they'll turn us down. Catch bloody twenty-two. It's no fucking way to run a criminal justice system.' He thumped the table hard with his fist. 'From what I hear, we have just a matter of a few weeks to come up with something before they decide on Sean's application.'

She saw the despair in his eyes and was reminded of Duran's original question to her in Bellevue: 'Do you believe in justice?' She had answered so quickly in the affirmative, but it was an un-thought-out, automatic response. The justice system was far from perfect. In her opinion, at the very least it sounded as though a forensic re-examination of the evidence was merited in Farrell's case. But without cooperation from Wiltshire Police, the CCRC was Farrell's last hope. Based on what Dan said, and the little she herself had picked up from the media, it wasn't an option that filled her with much confidence either.

She moved towards the door, then turned around to face him. There was something she had to clarify, if only to satisfy her own curiosity. 'One last question. Do you really believe Sean Farrell is innocent?'

He looked surprised. 'Yes. Of course.'

The response was quick and emphatic, but it still didn't convince her. Before she had a chance to say anything else, the door to the office opened and Zofia came into the room carrying Dan's coffee and a paper bag. Dan stabbed out his cigarette violently in an empty mug on the desk beside him and slowly got to his feet.

'We won't take on a case unless we're pretty certain,' he added. 'We have hundreds of prisoners contacting us each year, but, as I told you, we have very limited resources. We have to be very careful to focus on the cases where we can help most, where we can add value to what has been done before and where there's been an obvious miscarriage of justice.' He spoke vehemently, the irritation in his voice clear.

'Everybody gets it wrong though sometimes, don't they?' Eve said. 'Has it never happened to you?'

There was a beat before Dan replied, a quick, subtle movement of his eyes towards Zofia, which told Eve everything.
Then he gave a grudging nod. 'Yes. We've got it wrong a couple
of times. But I'm absolutely convinced this time. Sean Farrell's
innocent.'

# EIGHT

Dan watched Eve go, listened to her footsteps on the stairs,
followed by the distant thud of the front door.
        Zofia thrust his coffee and a paper bag at him. 'I got
you a couple of croissants. That's all they have left. The painkillers are in there too. What's she talking about? Does she think
Sean's guilty?'

'No. She's just kicking the tyres.'

'Why do you have to speak with her?'

'Because I do.'

He yawned, sat down again and reached for the coffee, burning
his fingers as he peeled off the plastic lid. He felt too weary to
explain, although he didn't blame her for being suspicious. Where
she came from, the police were mostly corrupt or incompetent,
or at least so she said. But he didn't like her telling him what to
think and what to do.

He took a swig and downed a couple of pills. He hadn't slept
at all well and felt nauseous. If Zofia hadn't been there, he would
have gone straight back to bed. Eve had been more than thorough.
His first instinct was to dislike her. He resented her irritatingly
professional, probing questions, but reluctantly he had to admit
she seemed to know what she was doing. She had also picked
up on his weak spot. Was Sean Farrell really innocent? He had
gone over it all in his mind again and again until he was convinced
that he was right, but his previous two mistakes had made him
wary. Was Sean Farrell really innocent? He still thought so. He
had been sure of it in the beginning, but the passage of time,
and the increasing pressure of the looming deadline to turn up
something new, which might, or might not exist, had eroded his

confidence. The doubt was doing his head in. He was battle-scarred and weary; in no fit state to do battle at all, if he was honest. He had lost all feel for the case. At the very least, Sean's conviction was unsound, based on the lack of direct evidence and the bungled defence, but that was not enough. He wanted so much to believe in Sean. He was ninety-nine per cent sure, but the other one per cent was keeping him awake at night. He needed to speak to Kristen, but she wasn't returning his calls.

Zofia was staring at him disapprovingly. 'What does she want?' she asked.

'To help, I guess. At least that's what Alan Peters said.'

She spread her hands. 'But why?'

He shrugged. 'I don't know. It doesn't really matter. He's paying her, not us.' She was still staring at him. 'What's your problem? We need all the help we can get.'

'What do you think of her?' Her tone was matter-of-fact as usual, but the remark was loaded, accompanied by a sideways glance, as she crossed the room to her desk.

'What do you mean?'

'She's very pretty, isn't she?' She peeled off her coat, swung it over the back of her chair and sat down.

He was aware of her eyes again upon him, searching and critical. Even without her, the voice in his head was saying the same unspoken things: You're a fool if you think Kristen will take you back. You've blown it for the last time. She's gone for good. Wake up. Get real. Pull yourself together. Sean Farrell deserves better than you can give. Yes, Eve's more than pretty. Almost as beautiful as Kristen. But it wasn't the sort of beauty that brought peace or happiness or pleasure, in his experience.

'I hadn't noticed,' he lied.

'Really?'

'Actually, I don't think she's very pretty, so shut up about it. It's irrelevant anyway what she looks like.' Did Zofia really think that he would allow a woman's looks to cloud his judgement? Anyway, the last thing on his mind was sex.

'If you say so.' Zofia turned back to her screen.

'Have you managed to track down Mickey?' he asked sharply.

'No. He's not answering his phone. I leave messages for the last three days but no reply.'

'Shit.' He banged his fist on the desk.

Zofia looked around. 'If he wants his pay, he will have to come in sometime.' When he didn't answer, she leaned forwards, eyes narrowed, and peered at him. 'Dan? When you last see him?'

'Last week. I bumped into him outside the Tube. He was on his way over here but I was running late and couldn't stop.'

'You give him money?'

He left the question unanswered for a moment, then closed his eyes and nodded wearily.

'Dan, how could you? I tell you not to trust him. Kristen never gives him money unless job is done. You know this.'

He let her words wash over him, then opened his eyes and blinked several times. They felt sore and dry. 'Yes, but we owed him some. And, as you damn well know, Kristen's not here any longer.'

'No we don't owe him. We are up to date. I keep record.'

'Well, he said we did, plus he needed some float for travel and expenses, and you weren't here. Anyway, when he's good, he's very, very good. He finds things out like nobody else. He's a wizard.'

She rolled her eyes. 'He's a *drunk* wizard. He's no good now, Dan. He smell of drink when I last see him. I tell you this many times. Why you give him money?'

He sighed. Like all real geniuses, Mickey was erratic and needed tight management.

'He said his mother was in hospital.' It sounded so lame. 'He also said something about going to the races. To do with Jane McNeil.'

'Jesus, Dan. Are you born yesterday? How much you give him?'

'Five hundred.'

'Jesus.' She waved her plump hand in the air. 'You totally crazy, Dan. In future, you let me deal with Mickey, please. I take care of him.' She made a gesture of slitting her throat.

He closed his eyes again and sighed deeply, as much out of exhaustion as for the physical relief of expelling the stale air from his lungs. His head was still throbbing and he felt like shit. The last thing he wanted to do was trail around London looking for wherever Mickey had gone to ground, then try to extract the money from him. If he still had it, which was doubtful.

'OK. OK. I agree it was a mistake.'

'You need to find him, Dan. *Now*. We need this information *now* and maybe we get some money back. You want me to come too?'

# NINE

' I swear to you, I didn't kill Jane,' Sean Farrell said, for the third time, holding Eve's gaze as though his life depended on it.

'I believe you,' she repeated, just to shut him up. She also wanted to placate him, so that he would talk to her openly, but underneath, she was far from convinced. In the back of her mind was what Dan had told her about the charges of rape, even if nothing had come of them. According to statistics, two women a week were killed in the UK by their partners, or former partners, one fifth of all homicides each year.

They were sitting opposite one another in the main visits hall at Bellevue Prison, just a table between them. The cacophony of noise and smells was distracting. She had no idea why they hadn't been given a closed room, like her interview the previous day with John Duran. Maybe Farrell was considered less of a security risk. Or maybe Duran had the power to request such a thing. But the place was full, Farrell was quietly spoken and, against the background buzz of voices, she had to strain to hear what he was saying. He was at pains to emphasize his innocence but she could tell nothing from his words and body language. It had been over ten years since his arrest and his lines were too well rehearsed. It was impossible to know if he was speaking the truth. Even with newly arrested suspects, she had long since given up trying to intuit innocence or guilt from a face-to-face interview. Some people were great actors and liars, others were not. And some, totally innocent, appeared guilty as hell. It was difficult to read anything much from body language, or the look in someone's eye, or the fact that their hands were sweating, or that they were crying. The evidence spoke louder and more reliably than any human could. The only thing she could say in Sean Farrell's case was that the evidence was sorely lacking. Until she had a clearer, fuller picture, she was making no assumptions. But if he wasn't guilty, who was?

She leaned forwards towards him, placing her hands flat on the table in front of her. 'I'm sorry to make you go over all of this again, Sean, but we need to come up with something new. If you were trying to find Jane's killer, where would you look?'

The fire died in his eyes. Maybe he had thought that just saying he was innocent would be enough, or maybe he realized he had failed to convince her.

'I don't know,' he mumbled.

'Come on. We need to find something.'

He shrugged, as though it were all meaningless, and shook his head. 'There's nothing new.'

His voice was surprisingly deep with a light, West Country accent. Even though he was seated, she could tell he wasn't particularly tall, with broad shoulders, short, muscular arms and strong, workmanlike hands, which he kept clasped tightly in front of him. The shell-shocked man in the police mugshot from ten years before was barely recognizable. His short hair was now thinning on top and almost entirely grey, his face and neck thickened, the strain of prison life and his various appeals showing clearly in his exhausted eyes and the deep lines of his face. He had one final chance to prove his innocence and it was probably all that was keeping him going.

'So where would you be looking, if you were me? You must have some idea, after all these years. I imagine you've been thinking of nothing else.' If you're innocent, she wanted to say.

His face hardened as though he read her mind. 'I told the police she was seeing someone else, but they wouldn't believe me. That's where I'd look.' He started to drum his fingers impatiently on the table.

He was like a stuck record, the same version being trotted out over and over again. He had been dumped. He had done nothing wrong. It had happened without warning. Rather than admit the possibility that Jane had just had enough of him, he was still fixated with the idea that there must have been somebody else.

Maybe he was right. She reminded herself that seminal fluid had been found on Jane's thigh and that it wasn't Farrell's.

'Forget what you've told everybody in the past. As I said, I'm looking at this completely fresh. I know you were feeling very hurt by the way she treated you. You followed her around on a few occasions, didn't you? She even made a complaint to the police.'

'Doesn't mean I killed her,' he said belligerently.

'Who did you see her with?'

'Just Holly and Grace, mostly.'

'Anyone else?'

'A woman from the office. She was a bit older. I think her name was Annie, but I don't think they were great mates.'

'What about men?'

He shrugged. 'I don't remember.'

'What about the man you saw her with in the bar in Marlborough, where you made a scene?'

'Don't remember his name, but the police checked him out. They told me he had an alibi.'

She made a mental note to speak to Dan Cooper again to make sure he had double-checked this. 'OK. Tell me what Jane was like? Tell me everything you know about her.'

He frowned, as though not knowing where to start. 'I dunno.'

'What was so attractive about her?' she prodded.

He gave her a blank look. 'She was nice-looking.'

'I meant her personality.' He looked puzzled, as though it wasn't what he had been expecting. Maybe in his book, looks were everything. 'Was she lively, easy to talk to?' she continued when he didn't say anything.

'She was quite quiet to start off with, a bit shy, but friendly when you got to know her. I used to see her at the yard a lot and we just got talking.'

'What did you talk about?'

'The horses, I suppose. And racing. It's hard to remember, now. So much has happened.'

'What were her good points? Was she clever? Funny? Silly? Tidy?' He had gone out with her for three months; there must be something useful buried in his unconscious. If nothing else, she needed to understand Jane McNeil better.

This brought a weak smile. 'She was very tidy, I'll give her that. Liked things just so and neat as a little pin, never a hair out of place. But she gave herself airs and graces, like she was something special. Lady Muck, I called her sometimes. Miss La-di-da. She liked her breakfast in bed. Liked me to bring it to her, like a bloody servant. And she was sharp. A lot sharper than me, at any rate. She knew what she was up to, if you know what I mean.'

'No, I don't. Can you explain?'

He rubbed his chin for a moment. 'She was full of ideas of what she wanted to do and she knew her own mind. She told me she had a plan. To be honest, I wasn't sure where I fitted in.'

'How do you mean?'

'Well, her parents had money, or so she said. She didn't like being seen in my van, I can tell you. If I was taking her out, it had to be the car and it had to be clean before she'd get in it. She told me she wanted to be a journalist, and write about racing and stuff to do with horses. She said she wanted to be on TV. That's why she was working in a racing yard, to get background experience.'

'Anything else about her?'

He frowned again, as though he didn't see the point of it.

'Anything at all?' Even the clearest memories faded with time and she didn't want to push him and make him feel that he had to come up with something. But she wasn't learning anything much from him.

'She was real nosy,' he said, after a moment.

'In what way?'

'You know, always asking questions.'

'What sort of questions?'

'She wanted to know about the other yards where I worked, for starters.'

'Why would that be?'

He shrugged. 'Search me. People used to tell her things.'

'Her friends?'

'The people she worked with, mostly. She used to tell me some of the stuff she'd heard around the office and I was gobsmacked. But that's women for you, I guess.'

'Can you remember anything in particular?'

'It was right silly stuff, but she found it funny. You know, stupid gossip, like who's shagging who, who had too much to drink, who's got money problems. That sort of thing. She was quiet and kept her head down and people just talked in front of her. One of the girls in the office split up from her husband and Jane knew before anyone else. I told her more than once to keep her trap shut. Telling tales gets you into trouble. But she said she didn't gossip, she just listened and she couldn't help it if people said things they shouldn't.'

'Was she particularly friends with anyone?'

'Not really. She didn't like the girls she shared with.'

'Why was that?'

'She said they weren't very nice. I'd say she preferred male company to women.'

Blackmail was as good a motive for murder as jealousy and she made another mental note to check with Dan Cooper if this aspect had been checked out. 'Did the police ask you about any of this?'

A look of anger crossed his face and he folded his arms tightly across his chest. 'They weren't interested in what I thought of her character, or anything else much. Apart from my being jealous, and stalking her, and all that shit.'

'Well, I am. You went out together, what, was it three months?'

'More or less.'

'It's enough time to get to know someone. What did you think of her?'

Again a blank, taciturn look. 'What do you mean?'

'What was she like, as a woman, I mean? Was she nice? Was she kind? Was she a warm and friendly type? Or was she selfish, just thinking of herself?'

His face hardened. 'You mean like most women?'

She sighed. 'OK. So from a man's point of view, was she a flirt? Was she a tease? Or was she the sort of girl to sleep around? Was that the message that came across?'

He stared at her sullenly. 'She wasn't a tart, if that's what you're getting at.'

'Look, I'm sorry if you don't like this, but it's important.' She decided she had to spell it out for him. 'Traces of seminal fluid were found on her thigh. We know it didn't come from you, so there had to be somebody else. Even though her body was in a pretty bad state when it was found the pathologist's report said there were no signs of her having been raped, so we must assume the sex was consensual. What I'm really getting at is, was she choosy who she slept with, or was she an easy lay?'

He looked down at the floor for a moment, rocking back and forth slowly in his chair, then he met her gaze. 'She wasn't easy. Took me several weeks to get her to go out with me, and more than that to get her into bed. I had to get her drunk. Tell you the truth, I'd almost given up on her.'

She smiled, wanting to encourage him. 'Thanks. That's very helpful. So what did the two of you used to do together?'

'We'd go to the gym, or to the Horse and Groom near where I live. Sometimes we'd go out for a meal, but during the week we mostly stayed in and watched TV. I used to have to cook for her, she couldn't even boil an egg.'

'Did she like going out?'

He nodded.

'Did she like expensive things and presents, or did she save her money?'

'All women like that stuff, far as I know, and she weren't no different. I took her to Bicester Village once, as a treat. I was going to buy her something nice, but before I had a chance, she'd blown eight hundred quid on a handbag and another couple of hundred on a pair of shoes. I kept my money in my wallet after that.'

'Where did she get the money? Her salary at the racing yard couldn't have been that much.'

'Search me.'

'I know it's a long time ago, but do you recall how she paid for them?'

He looked blank for a moment, then said, 'Cash. I remember now. I thought she was stupid carrying so much in her bag.'

'You weren't curious where she got it from?'

'I asked her. She said she won it on a horse.'

'And you believed her?'

He looked blank again, as though it was all too long ago.

'Did she often have a lot of cash on her?'

He sighed. 'Don't remember. It was usually me paying, not

her.' He rubbed his chin again, then added, 'Maybe her dad give it her. I told you, he was rich, or so she said.'

'Did you ever meet her parents?'

He shook his head. 'She told me she didn't get on with them.'

Eve looked at her watch. She had been there nearly an hour and it was time to go. There was nothing remarkable about Sean Farrell and nothing likeable either. The flickers of stubborn, macho cockiness were particularly off-putting. Maybe it was because she was a woman and that was his default response even after ten years in jail. But the members of a jury were only human and she imagined how he might have come across badly in court. She still had no idea whether he was innocent or guilty, but it didn't matter for the moment. She merely had to go through the motions for Duran and she had managed to learn something new about Jane McNeil. What Farrell had said about Jane's nosiness, and the cash that she had flashed around, offered up a new possible motive for her killing. But what intrigued her more than anything was why Duran had taken up Farrell's cause in the first place. From the little she had seen of Farrell, and what she knew of Duran, she couldn't imagine them getting along as people, chatting over a cup of tea and a biscuit, or fish and chips, in the prison canteen. Yet not only had Duran been inspired to donate money to the Farrell cause, he appeared to have embraced it wholeheartedly. For someone whose motives had previously been entirely selfish, it was out of character. There had to be something more and she was determined to find out what it was.

# TEN

It was past five in the afternoon and already dark when Dan finally stood outside the house in Kilburn where Mickey Fraser was apparently now living. He and Zofia had started by driving to a house in Tooting, which they had on file as Mickey's home address. But Mickey hadn't been there for almost a year. It seemed that he moved flats every few months and they had driven from Tooting, to Clapham, to Cricklewood, asking for Mickey at every one, and had finally been sent to 20b Acacia Grove, Kilburn. This had taken up most of the day. The Kilburn address at least seemed promising; a woman at the Cricklewood house said that Mickey had called her only a few weeks before about forwarding some post to him there. Dan had insisted on Zofia going back to the office after that. He felt angry and disappointed in Mickey and he wanted to speak to him on his own. Mickey had been tasked with tracing Jane McNeil's former housemates, Grace Byrne and Holly Crowther, as well as following up on the dead racing journalist, Kevin Stevens. He couldn't wait for Mickey to decide to resurface in his own time; he needed to find out how far Mickey had got, particularly with Eve now on his back.

Mickey's house was halfway along a terrace of tall, Edwardian red-bricks, most of which had been converted into flats with the front door up a steep flight of stairs. He pulled out his phone, switched on the torch and shone it over the dirty line of bells. A small, grubby card pinned to the top stated that flat B was in the basement. He went back down to the garden and found a short, narrow flight of stairs leading below, hidden behind a line of overflowing communal bins. Although basements were cheap and private – two reasons why they might appeal to Mickey – like a scurrying creature of the dark, it was appropriate that he would live in such a hellhole. He put his hand over his mouth, trying to block out the stench, as he carefully made his way down the slippery steps. The curtains were drawn, no light on inside, but that meant nothing. Mickey was probably sleeping off one of his periodic binges. It was dark at the bottom and it smelled even worse. The front door was tucked away deep under the stairs, in shadow from the streetlight above. Using his phone torch, he found the bell. He rehearsed in his mind what he was going to say if Mickey appeared and pressed it long and hard. He heard the buzz inside, but nobody came to the door. Music and voices drifted down from one of the flats above, but although he waited a good minute or so, no sign of life came from Mickey's flat. Just so that he could tell Zofia that he had made sure, he thumped his fist loudly on the door, calling out Mickey's name. He felt the door give a little under the weight of his hand and, in the pale wash of light from his phone saw that it had opened a crack. It seemed to be unlocked. He put his shoulder against

it and shoved and this time it swung open, banging loudly against
the wall behind. If Mickey was at home, he must have heard.

Dan reached inside the doorjamb and fumbled until he found
a light switch. He flipped it down, but no light came on.
Tentatively, he shone his phone inside and saw a little bathroom
to the left, under the stairs. Fumbling in the dark he found the
light cord and pulled it, but that didn't appear to be working
either. To the right was another door. As he pushed it open and
stepped inside, a waft of cold, damp air greeted him. It had a
musty smell, as though nobody had opened a window in a long
while. He shone the dim light slowly around the room, illuminating a kitchenette along one wall, the counter clean and tidy,
nothing in the sink or on the small draining board. He turned
the wash of light on the other side of the room, where an old
sofa and an armchair were grouped around a TV. The walls were
bare and the carpet was cheap and threadbare, as were the flimsy,
patterned curtains. It all had a transient feel and he wondered if
Mickey actually spent any time there. If he didn't, where was
he? A printer stood on top of a filing cabinet, next to the chim-
neybreast, on the other side of the room. The drawers were
hanging open and, as he crossed the room to take a better look,
he saw that the carpet behind the sofa was covered with a mess
of files and papers. It looked as though somebody had been
searching for something in a hurry and a lamp had been knocked
over and lay on its side in the middle. He picked it up, placed it
on a side table, and clicked the switch. But it, too, was dead.

Wondering if Mickey had had some sort of a drunken tantrum
in the dark, he called out, 'Hello, Mickey. It's Dan. Are you
there?' No reply.

A narrow corridor led from the room to the back of the house
and what he assumed was the bedroom. He called out again,
hoping to wake Mickey, if he was there. Again, no answer. He
imagined Zofia at his shoulder, whispering in his ear. *Go on,
Dan. Don't give up now. He must be in there. Maybe he's ill.
Maybe he needs help. What if he's hiding from you? £500 is a
lot of money.* He knocked at the bedroom door, put his hand on
the handle, then pushed it open.

The first thing that hit him was the stink. Urine. Vomit. Something
even more unpleasant. The stale air was thick with it and it caught

in the back of his throat. He wanted to retch and clamped his jacket sleeve over his nose and mouth as he shone the torch into the room. The small double bed stood at an odd angle away from the wall and clothes had been pulled out from the little chest of drawers and strewn around all over the floor.

It took him two steps to find Mickey. He lay on his side, on the floor behind the bed, naked apart from a pair of tight blue underpants, his hands and feet tightly shackled behind him to a kitchen chair. A pool of thick, dark liquid surrounded his head like a halo and his eyes were open, as far as Dan could tell from the swollen, beaten face, which was smeared with dried blood. His mouth was stretched wide, stuffed with what looked like a rolled-up sock, the toe poking out between his lips. Blindly, Dan staggered out of the room, through the sitting room, and into the bathroom. His phone clattered to the floor, as he fell to his knees and vomited into the toilet bowl. The smell from Mickey's bedroom still filled his nostrils and his head was throbbing. He felt hot and cold all at once, the nausea coming in waves. He couldn't focus. He couldn't think. His first reaction was to run, but he couldn't even stand up. Was Mickey's killer still in the flat? He didn't think so. The blood was dark and several hours old at least. When had it happened? He couldn't get the smell of it out of his mind. He vomited again and closed his eyes, the image of Mickey still in front of him.

Eventually, the nausea began to fade. He sat back on his heels and felt around the cold floor in the darkness for his phone. Finding it, he switched the torch back on and pulled himself up to his feet. He had to clear his lungs. He stumbled back to the front door and yanked it open, letting in a wet gust of air from the street. He stood just inside the door for a few moments, breathing in and out to calm himself. His head was throbbing worse than ever. Somehow he had to work out what to do, but he couldn't think clearly. He needed painkillers. He went back into the bathroom and shone the torch around the tiny room. It appeared to be untouched by whoever had been searching the flat and he was surprised, given Mickey's usually dishevelled appearance, how orderly it was, with just the basic essentials neatly lined up on a shelf above the basin. A small, mirrored medicine cabinet hung over the bath, half hidden behind the shower curtain. There was nothing in it apart from some spare razor blades, a jar of Vicks and a large plastic tub of Advil, which he assumed was left over from a recent trip Mickey had made to the US. It would have to do.

Hands shaking, he fumbled with the childproof cap. As he finally wrenched it off, the bottle slipped from his fingers and fell to the floor, spilling a mass of small red pills around him that bounced like beads on the tiles, along with something else that made a click as it dropped. He shone the torch over the floor and eventually found what he was looking for lurking behind the basin. He picked it up and studied it. It was a little, red memory stick, almost the same colour as the pills. 128GB. For Mickey to have hidden it so carefully, it must be important. He slid it into his jeans pocket. Mickey had been a secretive sort and he imagined him having a whole host of little hiding places dotted around the flat. He wondered how many of them the killer had found – and how many Mickey had been forced to give away under torture. He downed a couple of pills with a handful of water and then splashed some more water on his face as he studied himself in the mirror, wondering what to do.

There was no point in running away. His prints were all over the flat. He had no memory of exactly what he had touched and he knew it would be impossible to get rid of them all. His prints were also logged on the national system, thanks to a charge of affray as a student, and it wouldn't take long for the police to link him to the flat. He would have to call them, as soon as he'd worked out what to say. He smeared some Vicks under his nose and went back into the sitting room for a final look. There was no sign of Mickey's laptop and he assumed the killer had taken it, along with any external hard drive. If Mickey's mobile was still around, it would be in the bedroom, but he couldn't face going back in there. He was feeling shaky again and was about to leave, when he noticed a piece of paper lying facedown in the out tray of the printer. He picked it up and turned it over. It was a printout of a race card from the *Racing Post*, showing the runners for the 1.50 at Ascot the previous Saturday. He remembered what Mickey had told him the week before, about needing some funds to go racing. 'For research purposes,' Mickey had said. He had only half believed him. He photographed it, then returned the sheet to the printer tray as he had found it. He had seen enough. He needed a drink. He would go and sit in the car, while he worked out what to do.

As he went outside, the cold night air hit him with force, along with another wave of nausea. He sat down on the steps outside Mickey's front door and put his head in his hands. His phone started to ring in his back pocket. It was probably Zofia demanding an update. He decided he would have to speak to her and pulled it out but he didn't recognize the number on the screen. He stared at it for a moment, then pressed the green button, putting it on speaker. A woman's voice, low in tone and English, was saying something he couldn't quite hear against the background buzz of traffic. He caught the name Sean Farrell, then the word 'prison'. It took him a moment to realize it must be Eve West.

'Hello? Dan? Are you there?'

The image of Mickey tied to the chair flashed again in front of his eyes. He cleared his throat, thinking he was going to be sick again.

'Dan, are you OK?'

He leaned back against the damp wall, taking several deep breaths of air. Then slowly, with difficulty, he held the phone to his lips and spilled out the gist of what had happened.

# ELEVEN

'Are you back at the office yet?' Dan heard traffic in the background but Eve's voice was clear this time over the phone.

'Yes. Just got here,' he said.

'Good. I'm just down the road. I'll be with you in five.'

It was just after ten o'clock at night. He had texted her as soon as he left Kilburn Police Station and she had replied, saying she was coming straight over. A couple of slices of thin-crust pizza from the Domino's down the road lay congealing in the open box in front of him. Unusually he hadn't been able to finish them. He felt too sick. He closed the box and stuffed it in a bin.

He badly needed a drink. He fetched a bottle of vodka from the back room, where he was sleeping, but it was warm. There was nothing worse than warm vodka. He walked upstairs to the little kitchen on the half-landing, which they shared with the other office in the building, opened the door of the fridge, looking for ice, but there was none and he remembered that he had forgotten to fill the ice-tray the previous night. Zofia was sure to have ice in her flat in the attic – she wasn't the sort to run out of anything. She had the place rent-free, for the time being, which was a lot better than most post-graduate law students could dream of. The least she could do was make her ice available, and her bath. But ever since he had moved out of Kristen's flat a few weeks before and set up camp temporarily in the back room of the office, Zofia had started to get territorial about the top floor. Wearily, with the bottle dangling from his hand, he climbed the stairs to the top floor and let himself into her flat, where he found several full trays in her kitchen freezer. He took a glass from her cupboard and added a handful of cubes. But as he tried to top it up with vodka, his hand trembled so badly, he had to put it down again. Maybe he was in shock. Perhaps that was what it was. Using both hands, he managed to fill the glass and slowly and carefully put it to his lips. It was the first drink of the evening and he took a large gulp. Christ, what a day. He leant back against the wall and downed the rest of it.

After speaking to Eve at Mickey Fraser's flat, he had gone to his car outside and dialled 999. The police took no more than five minutes to arrive, cars screeching to a halt, lights flashing like a series of Christmas trees. They had sealed off the area immediately outside the house, as well as a section of the street, much to the annoyance, as well as morbid curiosity, of some of the neighbours. On discovering that he was the 'Dan' who had made the 999 call, they had swiftly carted him off to the local police station for interview. He had also voluntarily allowed his fingerprints to be taken, along with a mouth swab, and had then been kept waiting for over an hour until a pair of plainclothes police – a very young man, with greasy skin, and a hatchet-faced woman – had arrived from somewhere else to question him. Although they had been relatively polite, it was clear that they viewed his presence in the flat as very suspicious.

'Are you a friend of Mickey Fraser's?' one of the detectives had asked.

'No.'

'What is your relationship to him?'

'There is no relationship. He just did some work for us from time to time. On a freelance basis.'

'Why did you go to the flat?'

'He wasn't returning our calls.'

'Is it normal, if someone works for you, to go over to where they live, if they don't return your calls?'

'I'd advanced him some money. I wanted to find out how close he was to being able to repay me.'

'How did you first meet Mickey?' they had asked. 'Who introduced you?'

He mentioned the name of his former editor at one of the Sunday magazines and imagined that he would be next on their list to call.

One question led to another in an inevitable downwards spiral and he felt increasingly uneasy. He was so tired, he started stumbling over some of the answers, which only added to their suspicions. He knew nothing about Mickey's personal life, or who else he had worked for, or what else he had been doing. It was the first time he had been to Mickey's flat in Kilburn, or to any of his previous addresses. He told them a little about 4Justice and the Sean Farrell case, and he was interested to see their curiosity cool a little. He sensed, with relief, that they considered a ten-year-old murder case, with a man convicted and in jail for the crime, to be a less likely reason for Mickey's murder than something else Mickey was working on. Dan clung to that thought as they continued to question him until finally they, too, appeared to have had enough.

He filled his glass with more vodka and, tucking the bottle under his arm, closed the door to the flat and carried his drink back downstairs. To his surprise, he found Eve already standing in the middle of the office, gazing around as though she were carefully taking in all the details.

'The front door was open,' she said a little sharply.

'I left it open to make sure I didn't lock myself out.'

'No. I mean the door to the street.'

He looked at her wearily. She had to make a point about

everything. Security was the last of his worries. 'Sometimes it doesn't shut properly, but maybe I didn't close it when I came in. OK?'

'Are you alright?' She gave him a cursory look as she peeled off her coat. It looked as though she was intending to stay for a while, which was not good news. She was wearing a well-cut, dark-grey trouser suit that emphasized the curves of her slim figure and he wondered why she was so smartly dressed at that hour.

'A little shaken, but not stirred.' He attempted a grin. It was just something to lighten the mood, but either she didn't get the reference, or wasn't taken with it, as nothing registered on her face. Did she ever smile, he wondered. That was the problem with beauty. It took itself far too seriously. Along with her handbag, which she had left on the floor under her coat, he noticed a small leather briefcase and remembered she had been to visit Sean Farrell. He held up the bottle of vodka. 'Would you like a drink?'

She shook her head. He sensed disapproval, which annoyed him. He plonked the bottle down on the floor and collapsed onto the sofa with his glass, legs stretched out in front of him so that he was almost horizontal. If he had known her better, he would have lain down properly on the sofa, but he was in danger of falling asleep. It probably wasn't a good idea to get too comfortable. Hopefully, he could get this over and done with quickly.

'I'm the chief suspect, of course, but they let me go,' he said, aware that he was slurring his words a little. It was more from exhaustion than the alcohol, but he doubted she knew the difference. 'Zofia's with them now, giving her side of things.'

Eve pulled up the chair from Zofia's desk and sat down in front of him, one leg neatly crossed over the other, as though it were another professional interview. 'So who did you see?'

He leaned forwards and fumbled in the back pocket of his jeans for a moment, but the business cards weren't there. 'I guess I must have left their cards on the table at the police station,' he said, stifling a yawn.

'If you remember the names, let me know. They'll be from one of the murder investigation teams at Hendon, so I should know who they are. You said you were in Kilburn?'

He nodded and flopped back against the sofa, stretching his

arms out on either side along the back for a moment and flexing his stiff shoulders. He suddenly felt too tired to talk.

'You went to the station there?'

'Yeah. It was only a few minutes away from Mickey's house. I spoke to various policemen. I don't remember what their names were. They kept coming and going. I gave them a statement. Told them Mickey had been doing some work for us. Then they let me go.'

'Anything else?'

'They said somebody might be over to see me again at some point tomorrow.'

'Please can you make a note of their names so I know who to speak to. I'd like to try and find out what's going on.'

'OK.' She made him feel a little foolish for having lost the cards.

'Do they have any idea when Mickey died?'

'They weren't letting on. They asked for my movements over the past week. That's all. I told them when I last saw Mickey . . .'

'Which was when?'

'Last Thursday. Midday.'

'So he can't have been dead that long.'

'No,' he replied, thinking that from what he had seen of Mickey's body, it looked pretty recent and fresh. Although the blood on Mickey's face had dried, the black liquid pooled around his head was still a little wet and sticky-looking.

'Where did you see him last Thursday? At his flat?'

'No. I've never been there before. I happened to bump into him in the street outside Earl's Court Tube. He was on his way over here. He wanted some money.'

'What was he working on for you?'

He sighed and was silent for a moment. The quick-fire questions were doing his head in. His brain was fogged. It was like being back at the police station all over again. What was the point? Didn't she trust him? Again, she reminded him of Kristen. Whenever Kristen wanted something, like a dog with a bone, she wouldn't let go.

As if sensing his doubt, Eve leaned forwards towards him and folded her hands in her lap, as she held his gaze.

'Please, Dan,' she said quietly, with an unexpected gentleness. 'I know you've had a really rough day and I'm sorry to bombard you with questions, but it's very, very important you tell me everything you know. I'm here to help. Really I am. We're on the same side.' The softness of her voice was a soothing balm. He wanted to close his eyes and just listen to her talk. 'If Mickey's death is anything to do with the Sean Farrell case, *I* need to know. The police need to know.'

'They didn't seem to think it was,' he said vaguely. 'Or, at least, that's the impression they gave.' Even as he spoke, he knew it sounded weak.

'They don't know enough yet to make that judgement. Nor do we.'

She unbuttoned her jacket, took it off and with an economical sweep of her arm, hung it over the back of her chair. As she did so, he caught a hint of her perfume, something sweet and heady. She was wearing a plain, white blouse, which hugged the contours of her upper body like a glove, leaving little to the imagination. He took a gulp of cold vodka, swilling it round in his mouth, enjoying the bite of it on his tongue and the back of his throat. He felt the vodka warm his blood, as he told himself that her fears were groundless. Mickey's death was surely nothing to do with the Sean Farrell case. Maybe if he quickly gave her what she wanted to know, she would go away. If he was going to get anything done tomorrow, let alone get through another police interrogation, he needed some sleep.

He yawned. 'He was looking into two things, specifically. I think I told you before. Maybe I didn't mention Mickey by name. He was trying to find Grace Byrne and Holly Crowther, Jane McNeil's housemates. He was also supposed to be speaking to Kevin Stevens' family.'

'Where had he got to?' she asked, a sudden urgency in her voice.

'Not sure. I know he tried to find the girls via social media but drew a blank. They probably got married and changed their names. I don't know what he did after that. The problem with Mickey is that he often used to go off on a tangent, do his own thing, then expect us to pay for it. Kristen – my ex-partner – my *business* partner . . .' The phrase sounded so hollow and awkward and he was sure Eve must have noticed. 'Well . . . she had several rows with Mickey about it. She kept him on a tight rein . . .'

'But you specifically asked him to look into this journalist, Stevens, and the two girls?'

He nodded, aware of her sharp, dark eyes still upon him. 'Yes. I did. Even so, I can't be sure where he was with any of it. One thing would lead to another. He didn't always keep us up to speed. He was a bit of an unguided missile. Brilliant in a way, but erratic. You never knew what he was going to turn up next. But it was usually useful and, occasionally, it was a real gem.'

'What was his background?' She was looking at him intently, as though every word was important.

He looked up at the ceiling for a moment. He had never really given Mickey much thought before, just accepted he knew what he was doing and let him get on with it. Why keep a dog and bark yourself, wasn't that the phrase?

'He was in his mid-to-late forties, I guess. Divorced. No family that I know of. At least he never mentioned any. He lived alone. Used to be with the Met, but he had a drink problem. Got done for drink-driving and was chucked out. This was before I was introduced to him. He had a few journalist pals, who gave him work, including my old editor. He always said Mickey was one of the best when he put his mind to it. Mickey was also cheap, compared to a lot of them, which is why we used him here.'

'So, you went to his flat. Tell me exactly what happened. All the details, please.'

He suddenly felt desperately tired and wondered how much longer she was intending on staying. 'The lights weren't working. Either a fuse was blown or somebody had tripped it deliberately. I had to use my phone to look around, so I may have missed something. But I'm pretty sure his laptop was gone. At least, I didn't see it anywhere. There was a filing cabinet in the sitting room. Somebody had been going through it in a hurry. There were files and paper everywhere.'

Her eyes lit up. 'He wasn't just untidy?'

'It was more than that.'

'Any idea where he might hide his stuff?'

He shrugged. As he glanced over her shoulder into the middle of the room, the little red memory stick caught his eye. It was sitting on the desk behind her, its metallic casing glinting in the overhead light. As his eyes rested on it, it almost seemed to grow in size, as though it were trying to get his attention. He looked away, focussing first on the ceiling, and then on the toes of his boots, then on the door to the office. If he told her about it, she would only tell him to hand it over to the police. Until he knew what was on it, he wasn't going to do that. He might not tell her about it at all, he decided. He wasn't sure he could trust her.

'I don't know,' he said, trying to appear casual as though it were a straightforward question. 'Or at least he never said anything to me about it.' He glanced up at her.

She was studying him, head a little to one side, lips slightly parted. Her wavy, dark-brown hair formed a halo around her broad face and he thought she looked like a beautiful Pre-Raphaelite Madonna.

'Let's hope he backed his stuff up to the cloud,' she said calmly. Was there a hint of irony in it, or was it his imagination?

He shook his head quickly. 'Unlikely. Mickey was old-fashioned and very suspicious by nature. He used to go on and on about Big Brother and hackers. He didn't trust technology and he was very secretive.'

She held his gaze. 'Even so, he must have had some sort of a backup plan.'

'It's possible.' He couldn't look at her anymore. He stared down at his glass, swirling the melting ice around until he was almost dizzy, listening to it clink against the sides.

'Well,' she said, after a moment, 'from the way you describe the state of the flat, it sounds like an amateur job to me. Or they were disturbed. It certainly wasn't at all methodical, the way we would do things if we were looking for something. Perhaps they didn't find what they were after.'

He looked up at her. 'But they tortured him. He must have told them whatever they wanted to know, surely.'

'Maybe. Maybe not. Hopefully, something will come to light and we'll know more soon.'

She shifted in her chair and uncrossed her legs, still looking at him. He wondered what she was thinking. It couldn't be pleasant, he decided. What must she think of him? Then he decided he didn't care.

'So why exactly did you go to his flat?'

Was she doubting his account? He sighed. 'I gave him some money last week. It was part payment for some work he'd done, plus expenses.' He decided to miss out the part about the sick mother. 'He said he needed to go to the races, to do with Jane McNeil.'

She arched her brows. '*Horse* races?'

'Yes. His last words to me were "Gotta see a man about a horse".'

For a moment, he pictured Mickey's chubby face, and the cheeky wink Mickey had given him as he tapped the side of his broad, fleshy nose before heading back down into Earls Court station. Then the image of Mickey as he'd last seen him came to mind again, the smell in the room, the pokey, seedy flat. What a place. What a way to die. If only he'd questioned him the other day, shown a little more interest. But he'd just handed over five hundred pounds fresh from the cash point and felt, yet again, as though he'd been scammed. Also, they were standing in the middle of the street, people milling around them, which made it awkward to pursue his questions. Mickey wasn't one to give up his secrets easily, at least not until he was ready. He probably would have clammed up even if Dan *had* pressed him, particularly after he had handed over the money. Of course, he should have held it back until Mickey told him what was going on, but hindsight was a wonderful thing. No point beating himself up about it. Zofia was there to do that.

'I found something at the flat,' he said after a moment. There was no harm in telling her, he decided, as a gesture of goodwill. Maybe then she'd take the rest of what he'd said at face value. He took his phone out of his shirt pocket, scanned through the photos until he found the one he wanted. 'This was sitting face down in the printer tray.' He stretched across and showed her the image of the *Racing Post* race card.

She peered at it for a moment. 'I can't see the details. Can you send me a copy?'

He texted it over and she got up and went to her bag and took out her phone as it chimed. She studied the screen for a moment, enlarging the image with her fingers, then scrolling down over it. 'Was Mickey a gambling man?' she asked, glancing over at him.

'Not as far as I know. At least he never mentioned it. And when we were discussing Kevin Stevens, he didn't come across as being the least bit interested in horse racing. In fact, now I think about it, I remember his making a remark about people being fools to waste time and money on the sport.'

'Nine runners, which means nine jockeys, trainers and owners, or syndicates,' she was saying. 'I wonder what he was after.' She was standing with her back to the window, one hand casually propped on her hip, studying her phone again. His gaze rested unchecked on the blatant curve of her breasts. It struck him how odd it was to be closeted there with her all alone, having such an extraordinary conversation, at such a late hour. He barely knew her. She looked over at him and met his eye. 'You left the original paper at the flat, I hope?' Her tone was suddenly sharp and he felt as though he had been slapped down, even though she couldn't have had a clue what he had been thinking.

'Yes. Don't worry. I put it back exactly how it was, face down in the printer tray.' *I'm not a complete idiot*, he wanted to say.

'Your prints will be on it, but you can explain that when they ask you. In fact, I'd mention it *before* they ask. It will add weight to your story . . .'

'It's not a *story*,' he replied forcefully. Did she really suspect him of having been involved in Mickey's death? Perhaps he was being overly defensive, but she was a policewoman through and through.

'Your account, I meant,' she said, in a softer voice, returning to her chair and tucking the phone away in her jacket pocket. 'The key question is, did Mickey make it to Ascot last Saturday and, if so, what was so interesting about that particular race? You should crosscheck all the names on that race card with the Sean Farrell files. You should also check up on what Mickey was doing regarding Kevin Stevens and the two girls, see how far he got. Just to make doubly sure there's no connection.'

He made no reply. It was something he had already thought of and he didn't need her telling him what to do, like he was a trainee. She clearly had a low opinion of him and he was tempted to make a pointed comment about what he'd read in the papers about *her*, concerning the North London shooting. But something in her expression stopped him. He saw, for the first time, genuine concern in her eyes. He still didn't understand why she was getting involved. Alan Peters had been a little vague on the phone, but reading between the lines, he assumed it was for money. It didn't make sense otherwise. In a way, it didn't matter if she were being paid, so long as she was straight with him.

'How was your meeting with Sean Farrell?' he asked, wanting to move on. Had Sean convinced her he was innocent? Or was she still as sceptical as before? Did it really matter what she thought? He was just being insecure, wanting reassurance that he was right about Sean Farrell, which was stupid. He should trust his instincts more.

'Interesting in a way,' she said flatly. 'Something came up that I wanted to ask you about. When you spoke to Jane's parents, did they mention giving her money, or paying off her credit card?'

He shook his head. 'I told you, I didn't get very far with them.'

'Sean described her as spoiled, with a rich daddy. Is that true?'

'I know very little about them, other than the fact that there was some sort of row and she decided she wanted to get away from them and be more independent. It's why she took the job at Westerby.'

'Did the police ever consider blackmail as a possible motive? It's just something Sean said about her being nosy by nature and interesting herself in other people's business. He also said she liked to spend money, that she had quite a lot of cash on her at one point.'

'I've never heard anything about that. Nor did it come out in any of the papers or interviews I've read. I imagine the police would have gone through her bank account and credit card statements very thoroughly.' He looked at her questioningly.

She nodded. 'I'd hope so. He mentioned another man, who Jane had been seen with in a bar. The police ruled him out, but I'd like to talk to him, all the same.'

'I think you mean Steve Wilby. Last I heard, he was working at the Mercedes showroom in Swindon. I spoke to him about six months ago, but he couldn't shed any light. He had an alibi . . .'

'I know. He still spent some time with her, though, and he was there when Sean made that scene. I'd be interested in his impressions of both of them. I'm going to drive down to Marlborough tomorrow, try and talk to a couple of people who used to know Jane, in order to get a more rounded view.' She was quiet for a moment, then added: 'Can you tell me a bit about the Westerby estate and the Michaels family?'

'I think I told you, Tim Michaels died a while back. The estate and racing yard are now run by his son and daughter. I've got some stuff on them, if you want.'

He struggled to his feet and went over to one of the book-cases. Scanning the shelves, he pulled out a dusty box file and took it over to an empty desk. He rummaged through it and, after a moment, returned to the sofa, handing her a foolscap folder.

'Here you go. There's a map of the area as well, and the woods where her body was found, which you might find useful. There's also a lot of stuff about the family and the racing yard on their website. I doubt if they'll talk to you, though. I think I told you, since Tim Michaels died, they've upped the security big time. They're very private. When I sneaked in to take a peek at Jane McNeil's former cottage, I was caught by Harry Michaels and marched off the property. As he was carrying a shotgun at the time, I didn't argue. Unless you go posing as a prospective owner, you won't get past the entrance gate.'

# TWELVE

B ack home, Eve lay in bed, in the dark. The room was getting a little chilly, the heating having recently gone off, and she pulled the soft, blue woollen throw Jason had given her over her legs for extra warmth. She had taken a sleeping pill but it hadn't kicked in yet. She felt wired, unable to relax, let alone sleep, thinking over everything that Dan had told her. Mickey Fraser's death had changed things. The fact that he had been tortured before he was killed, and his flat searched, seemed to point towards his having stumbled on some-thing of value to someone. Dan seemed to think it had nothing to do with the Farrell case, but she sensed it was what he wanted to believe, based on what the police had said. Without knowing what other cases Mickey had been working on, it was impossible to form a view. She needed to find out as soon as possible who in Hendon was handling the case, so that she could get more information.

Another thing was troubling her. Dan had been very prickly when questioned. She put his defensiveness down to his being tired and not fully trusting her. She was prepared to make allowances, given what he had just been through. But there had been something really odd about his manner at one point. She thought back to that particular part of their dialogue, picturing him in front of her for a moment, lounging back on the sofa, one long leg crossed over the other, the half-full tumbler of vodka waving around in his hand like a baton as he spoke. He had been struggling to stay awake, as he talked about what was missing from Mickey's flat and the chaos in the front room. What he said about Mickey's being secretive about his work and not trusting technology made sense. As a PI and an ex-cop, Mickey would have known how easily systems could be hacked and information corrupted or stolen. In his line of work, security was everything. Dan had been relaxed up until that point, looking as though he was ready for bed. But when she asked if Mickey had anywhere in particular where he hid his backups or more sensitive files, Dan's facial muscles tensed and he glanced away, his gaze darting here and there around the room. It was all over in a beat, but she knew what she had seen. The righteous man of principles was a *bad* liar, a really *crap liar*, as well as a hypocrite. The fact that he clearly thought he had got away with it, made it worse. Did he really think she was born yesterday? He had shown her the photo of the sheet of paper, which he had found in Mickey's printer, almost as an afterthought, or more likely a diversion. But she was sure there was something else. Whatever it was, she intended to get it out of him, one way or another.

She still didn't feel at all sleepy. She switched on the light and went into the sitting room where she had left her briefcase. She took out the folder Dan had handed her earlier and went back into the bedroom, where she spread the contents out on the bed. Along with an Ordnance Survey map of the Marlborough area, she found some printouts culled from the Internet, including a brief guide to Marlborough town, and Ordnance Survey maps covering the Westerby estate and the West Woods.

A copy of Tim Michaels' obituary was amongst the pages, along with a piece about his death from the *Racing Post*:

### TRAINER TIM MICHAELS FOUND DEAD IN APPARENT SUICIDE

*The horseracing world is mourning the death, in tragic circumstances, of successful trainer and former Grand National winner Tim Michaels. According to the police, Michaels, 63, was found dead, late on Saturday evening, at his home, Westerby Farm, the Group 1 winning training yard near Marlborough, Wiltshire. Foul play is not suspected. Family friend and trainer James Bracewell told the Racing Post 'Shock is the word that comes to mind – shock and deep sadness. Our thoughts are with Tim's wife, Sally, and his two children, Harry and Melissa.' Earlier in the day, Michaels had been at Doncaster, where he saddled three runners, including a second and a third . . .*

The article was dated just ten days after Jane McNeil went missing. It was bizarre timing, she thought. Could there be a connection? She Googled 'Michaels family racing' and found their website. At first glance, it was impressive, with a brief history of the Westerby racing yard and the Michaels family, who had been there for over a century. She tabbed through the various images of the buildings and stables, gallops and other facilities, photos of horses on the racetrack and at home, and many happy-looking owners celebrating winnings. Although she knew nothing about racing, it looked like a very successful, top-end operation.

She clicked on the entry for Harry Michaels, Tim's son and heir:

*Born in Windsor in 1975, Harry hails from a family that is steeped in racing history. His great-grandfather, Henry Michaels, was the trainer of no fewer than four Grand National winners, one of which he rode to victory himself. His grandfather, Andrew, and father, Tim, have both ridden and trained winners at the highest level. Harry grew up at Westerby with his sister Melissa. He was educated at the*

*Royal Military Academy, Sandhurst, and spent eight years serving in the Scots Guards before joining his father at Westerby Racing . . .*

His photo showed a nice-looking, dark-haired man, with a square jaw and a hard, determined expression. With his army background, she could easily picture him with a shotgun slung over his shoulder, marching Dan smartly off his land for trespassing.

Eve tabbed through to Melissa's entry:

*Melissa has a degree in Geography from Oxford and has been involved in racing at Westerby for over 10 years, having previously held roles in marketing and PR at Newbury and Epsom racecourses. She plays a key role at Westerby in many aspects of the business and, in particular, is responsible for organizing owner visits and entertainment, as well as other events at Westerby throughout the year. She is married to local Member of Parliament Gavin Challis . . .*

Gavin Challis. The name leapt out at Eve. She quickly scanned the photographs below, finding one that showed a smiling blonde-haired woman, her two small children, a brindle-coloured whippet and her husband. She peered closer. There could be no doubt. It was the same Gavin Challis. She hadn't seen him for almost twenty years. As she stared at the once familiar, handsome face, she remembered what Dan had said about how the Michaels were very private. 'Unless you go posing as a would-be owner, you won't get past the entrance gate.'

She leapt out of bed and marched into the sitting room. The box Alan Peters had sent her was tucked away on a chair under the small dining table. She dumped the block of money onto the table, removed the Nokia box, ripped it open and took out the phone. She switched it on. It appeared to be already fully charged and working. It had been years since she had used such a basic model, but it would do the job.

She stared at it for a moment, feeling the smooth, black plastic, struck by how light it was in her hand. She didn't like the idea of using it, but equally she didn't want to use her own phone to contact either Peters or Duran, in case anybody from the Met decided to check her phone records. Even though what she was doing was above board, it was easier if there was no trace of a connection. The name 'Mr Duran' and his mobile number were programmed into the phone book, along with Peters' details.

Like her, Duran probably wasn't asleep and if he was, she didn't care. She went into messages, selected Duran's name and typed two words: *Gavin Challis.*

Her finger hovered over the send button. There was something revoltingly intimate about texting Duran, particularly at that hour. But it had to be done. She pictured him in his cell, lying in a bed that was too short and narrow for a man of his frame, however skeletal. She consoled herself with the thought that the sheets would be rough and scratchy, and the mattress and pillow probably hard and lumpy for someone so used to luxury. Even if he had been allowed to bring in some of his own things to make life more comfortable, it wouldn't be the same. They didn't have Emperor suites in prison. He couldn't change the dimensions of the tiny room, increase the height of the oppressively low ceiling, or give himself a lovely view over Hampstead Heath, as he had once enjoyed at home. He would never see that again. He could have been happily tucked up between the fine, crisp, monogrammed linen sheets in his two-metre-square, four-poster in Highgate, if it hadn't been for his one moment of madness.

She thought back to his calm, impenetrable face in the prison interview room. He had fed her a mixture of truth and lies. She now knew exactly why he had chosen her and she was pleased she had found him out. It was nothing to do with her professional skills, or the way she had handled his interrogation. That had been a smokescreen of flattery. No doubt the connection between her and Gavin had come up in the research Duran had done on her when she had arrested him and charged him with murder. But it probably wouldn't get him anywhere. No doubt Gavin would refuse to see her, or speak to her, after what had happened. She took a deep breath, trying to calm herself. All that mattered was finding out if Sean Farrell was innocent or guilty. She pressed send.

Taking the phone with her, she went into the kitchen area to make a cup of tea. She had just switched on the kettle when she heard the chime of a text. She snatched up the phone from the counter and read the message. *Well done. You were impressively quick! That's why I chose you, you know. Not just because you were once Gavin Challis's lover.*

It was as though he could read her mind and she shivered.

# THIRTEEN

The early morning fog had lifted and the drive to Marlborough, heading west on the M4, was straightforward. After just over an hour, Eve turned south off the motorway, onto a fast-moving narrow road that zigzagged through windswept expanses of open countryside, before finally dropping down a steep hill into Marlborough town. The broad High Street was crowded with cars and shoppers enjoying the rare sunshine and it took a frustrating few minutes to navigate her way through it and out the other side towards Tesco's where, according to Gavin Challis's website, he was doing a drop-in surgery that morning for his constituents.

She parked as close to the front of the building as possible and, not bothering to put on her coat, sprinted the short distance to the main entrance. A tall, tinsel Christmas tree stood just inside the sliding doors and she realized, with shock, that Christmas was just a few weeks away. A huge poster of Gavin stood on a stand beside the tree, with the banner 'Come and talk to Gavin Challis, your local MP' plastered across the bottom. She hated reunions as a rule and avoided them wherever possible. There was usually a good reason why people lost touch. Other than shameless curiosity, what was the point of putting yourself through it, raking up trivial memories from a long time before, just to fill the awkward silences? But Gavin wasn't just an old acquaintance from school or university or work, somebody who had casually drifted out of her life. Looking at the huge image of him in front of her, she felt suddenly nervous, heart quickening, sweat pricking her palms as she wondered how he might react on seeing her. She had tried not to think about it before, tried hard to push it from her mind. It was likely he wouldn't want to talk to her and if he did, she wondered if he would say something sharp and rude. If so, she couldn't blame him.

A sturdy, middle-aged woman was planted beside the photograph, handing out leaflets as people went in. She directed Eve to the back of the shop, where another woman took Eve's name and told her to wait. Not long after, an elderly man emerged from one of the offices. The woman disappeared inside, then came out again a moment later.

'He'll see you now,' she said crisply. 'But he hasn't got long. He's supposed to be over at Devizes in twenty minutes.'

As Eve entered the room, Gavin stood up and came out from behind the small table he was using as a desk.

'My God, Eve. It really is you.' He was smiling, his face flushed with what seemed to be genuine pleasure, and she felt the colour also rise to her cheeks. He shook his head, rubbing his mouth with his hand as he studied her unashamedly. 'Christ, how time flies. But you look the same, you know. Life seems to have treated you well.' His voice was just as she remembered it, low and measured in tone. It was one of the many things she had liked about him.

'You too,' she said, glad that she didn't have to lie. His short hair was still thick and blonde as ever, with no signs of grey, and there were few lines around the open, bluish-grey eyes. But as she examined him, she saw that he had changed. The soft, beautiful boyishness of his late teens had gone and the lines of his face had hardened and were more defined and masculine. Some men got better looking as they matured and she decided he was definitely one of them. The physical distance between them felt suddenly awkward, but she didn't move, waiting to take her cue from him. Surely he must be experiencing a mix of emotions, not all positive, on seeing her?

'When I heard your name, I didn't believe it was you,' he continued after a momentary pause, smiling even more broadly. 'But I'm *so* happy to see you again after all this time. I've often wondered what happened to you and how you were.' He was still looking at her intently. He crossed the room, moving with his familiar, confident stride, and closed the door, then pulled out one of the chairs from the table and carefully placed it behind her. 'Please, have a seat.' She was relieved to find that he had lost none of his natural warmth. It would make everything so much easier.

He was wearing dark suit trousers and a cream-coloured shirt, open at the neck, the sleeves neatly rolled up to his elbows. He sat down on the edge of the table facing her, searching her face as though she was something precious he had lost and now found again.

'It's so good to see you,' he repeated. 'What have you been doing? Why are you here?'

'I'm staying in Marlborough for a few days. I'm looking into the murder of Jane McNeil. I don't know if you remember . . .'

He looked surprised. 'Of course I do. How could I forget? She worked for my father-in-law. I thought they caught the man – the farrier.'

'You mean Sean Farrell.'

'That's right. I'd forgotten his name. Isn't he still in jail?'

'He is. His case is being reviewed by the Criminal Cases Review Commission. They're making a decision in a few weeks.'

He looked puzzled. 'I heard you'd joined the police. Why are they looking into it all over again? Has something happened?'

'They aren't. This isn't for work. I'm just doing a favour for a friend, trying to see if I can turn up anything that might help Sean's case.'

'His mother contacted the local MP, my predecessor, trying to drum up some support for an appeal, but I heard it was turned down. He's still maintaining he's innocent, then?'

She nodded.

'Well, if he is, I wish him luck. If there's anything I can do to help, let me know.'

'Thanks. I know you're in a rush now, but it would be very useful to talk to you at some point. Unofficially, I mean. Were you living here when it happened?'

'I was based in London, but we were at Westerby most week-ends and I remember it all really well. We knew Jane, of course. She worked at the yard and lived in one of the cottages on the farm. Marlborough's a nice, peaceful, little town. That sort of thing doesn't happen in a place like this. Everybody was really shocked. My father-in-law also died around about the same time. It was a pretty bleak period for us all.'

'I'm sorry to bring it all up again.'

He shook his head. 'It's OK. It just takes me right back for a minute.' He met her gaze. 'How are Robin and Clem?'

'They're fine. I visit them every so often. I'll probably go for Christmas lunch, as usual.'

'I remember it was always such a party and it went on for hours and hours. Mum and I could hear you all through the wall and I used to long to come over and join in the fun. It was so quiet at home with just the two of us.'

She nodded, thinking of the delightful hurly-burly of Christmas lunch at the Jacksons, when friends and family of all ages were packed, elbow-to-elbow and knee-to-knee, along a series of mismatched tables and chipboard extensions, which were covered in red paper cloths, heaving with crackers and tinsel and candles. She could lose herself in the warmth and hubbub and they were the best Christmases she had ever had.

'Is Robin still making his wonderful concoctions?' He raised his eyebrows, smiling.

'He certainly is. He's still got his allotment and there's no fruit or vegetable he can't ferment or pickle or turn into alcohol. He says it's what keeps them both going. Clem says he's trying to pickle her.'

'I particularly remember his sloe gin. It was amazing. You and I got very drunk on it one evening, didn't we? Do you remember?'

He was looking at her, head a little to one side, waiting for her response and she nodded slowly. How could she forget? It was the first time they had had sex together. She wondered if he remembered too. It seemed so long ago. Another time. Another life, almost.

'How's your mum?' she asked, wanting to change the subject. 'Clem said she had to go into a home.'

A shadow crossed his face, and he glanced down at the floor momentarily as he nodded. 'I'm afraid she doesn't know who I am anymore, which I find very difficult. Sometimes she thinks I'm my father. At least it makes *her* happy, I guess.'

'I'm so sorry,' she said, picturing his mother, with her neat, slim figure and pretty face. Always perfectly turned out, not a hair out of place, even on her meagre income. Gavin was her late, only child, a 'gift from God', she always said. Her gorgeous, talented, golden boy, whom she loved more than anything on earth. How terrible that she could no longer recognize him.

'I go and visit her every few weeks, then spend the night on my boat. I keep it down at a marina on the Beaulieu river. Do you remember, I took you there once?'

She nodded. 'You worked there all summer, crewing for that man with the massive yacht. It was a lovely place, surrounded by woods.'

'That's right. We went walking for miles along the river, away from the marina, and had a picnic and went swimming.'

She had a stray memory of Gavin lying naked and deeply tanned beside her in the long grass by the riverbank, as they gazed drowsily up at the swallows soaring and diving in the bright blue sky. Sex with Gavin had always been good, even at that young age. It had been by far the most functional thing – at least from her point of view – about their relationship.

'Nothing's changed,' he added. 'It's still as lovely as ever.'

'So you finally got your boat?' she asked, wanting to move on. It didn't do to dwell on the past.

'Yes. She's a beauty. I don't get to use her much, but it's a good escape when family life gets a bit overwhelming. My wife, Melissa, doesn't like boats, or the sea, but the kids will love it when they're a bit older.'

'So you have children?'

'Two little boys.'

'When did all of this happen?' she asked, waving a hand vaguely around the room.

'Politics, you mean? Oh, just six months ago. There was a by-election, after my predecessor died suddenly. I'm still the newbie, getting used to things, trying not to put my foot in it.'

She had never been a rebel but she had also never been a joiner of anything. The idea of pinning her colours to one mast and wearing a label for all to see, in some attempt to define herself, was anathema. She had no need of causes or crusades and she had thought he was the same.

She peered at him. 'But when I knew you, you were never that interested in politics. If anything, I'd say the complete opposite. Plus, I remember very clearly your saying that most politicians were either useless, or corrupt.'

He smiled. 'I guess I've grown up a bit. I've realized that things aren't always black and white. Anyway, my deciding to go into politics didn't happen overnight.'

'I heard you became a barrister.'

'That's right. I met Melissa, at Oxford and we got married almost straight after we graduated. I got a pupillage in a good chambers and we moved to London. But she steadily became more and more wrapped up in her family's business. It's been based just outside Marlborough for donkey's years, and I found myself spending an increasing amount of time down here. Thanks to a friend of her dad's, I started to get involved at a local level and I guess one thing led to another.'

He made it all sound so easy, but it was a remarkable change for the postman's son from next-door, on the busy road on the outskirts of Lymington. 'Well, I guess I should congratulate you,' she said. 'You've come a long way.'

'We both have, at least superficially. Who'd have thought you'd be a police detective? Not me, for one. But I'm sure we're both still the same people inside. Some things don't ever change.'

He rubbed his chin thoughtfully and looked as though he was about to say something else, when there was a tap at the door. He glanced at his watch and sighed. 'Unfortunately, I'm afraid that means I've got to go,' he said. 'I'm late for another surgery, but why don't you come over for dinner tonight? You can meet Melissa, and we can chat about old times and whatever else you like.'

She hesitated. What harm could it do? She might actually learn something useful about the murder, which was why she was there. 'That would be nice, thank you.'

'Where are you staying?'

'At a pub on the High Street.'

'Well, come over about seven thirty, if that's not too early.'

He wrote down the address and brief directions on a sheet of paper, then stood up.

'Really good to see you again, Eve,' he said, looking her steadily in the eye. 'It's been way too long.' He opened the door and ushered her out.

As she walked into the noisy shop and made her way back to the car park, she could still feel the warmth of his gaze. He was the same, kind, generous-hearted Gavin that she remembered, straight as a die as always. What you saw was what you got; there was no side, no secret agenda. Twenty years was a long time, but she felt a gentle, tugging regret that she had let go of him so easily. At least he appeared to be genuinely happy to see her and didn't seem to want to punish her for what had happened.

# FOURTEEN

'It's fucking encrypted,' Dan said, looking around at Zofia. He pulled out Mickey's little red USB drive from his laptop and tossed it onto the desk. 'Who'd have thought technophobe old Mickey would know how to do such a thing.' He gave a deep sigh.

He had hoped the flash drive would provide a nice shortcut to finding out what Mickey had been up to. Instead, he was going to have to do things the hard way, try and follow Mickey's footsteps as best he could. And it wasn't as though he had lots of spare time. Two new cases had come in for review and Kristen still wasn't answering her phone. Did she care about 4Justice anymore? Or was she so wrapped up with the documentary she was shooting – and the fucking French cameraman – that seven years of hard work counted for nothing? Zofia could do an initial analysis and review, but she lacked the experience and he would have to double-check everything himself. How on earth was he going to find the time to play detective? That was the priority. Also, where to start? He had given Mickey the barest of information and had left it up to him. He sighed again with feeling. He'd slept badly, waking up several times worrying about what had happened to Mickey and the police interrogation. Maybe there was an easier way – the right way, his conscience was telling him.

'I think I should probably hand Mickey's memory stick over to the police.'

'You kidding me, Dan?' Zofia pursed her purple-stained lips.

Her eyes were pale, glassy marbles, her disapproval palpable. It angered him. The fact that they were running fast to barely standstill was not his fault. It was Kristen who had left them all in the lurch without any form of warning. Zofia was young and full of misplaced idealism. She believed that the police were the enemy and, based on her own experience back in Poland, he couldn't blame her. It was good to be a purist, but there was a time and a place. Sometimes you had to be pragmatic. Sean Farrell's case was all that mattered and if he couldn't get access to the information on Mickey's flash drive, he was sure the police could.

He rocked back in his chair, folded his arms and exhaled loudly. 'No, I'm not kidding. I shouldn't have taken it in the first place, or held onto it.'

She shrugged and spread her hands. 'So what you tell them? How you explain you find it?'

'I dunno. Maybe that Mickey left it here in the office, or asked me to look after it for him. Something like that. I can't obviously say I took it from his flat, can I? Not unless I want to be charged with something or other, and thrown in jail. That wouldn't exactly help Sean, now would it?'

'Then why you not tell them this morning?'

She had a point there. He wasn't thinking clearly. The best part of the morning had been spoiled, so far, by his being inter-viewed by a different pair of brisk-mannered detectives – this time two cropped-haired women, one tall and thin and flat-chested, the other big-breasted and short, both dressed in ill-fitting black trouser suits. They looked like Laurel and Hardy, but without the humour or pathos. They had arrived at the office at nine a.m. and had refused to go away and come back again, insisting, in the intolerant manner of people who got up early and had a lot to do, on waiting right outside his room while he hurriedly dressed. Eve had been right about them. They appar-ently hailed from Hendon and worked for a murder investigation team. This time he had made of point of putting their cards in a safe place, to give to her later. Maybe she could get more out of them than he could. Like a well-rehearsed double act, they had gone over the same old ground, poking and prodding each detail of his original statement. They had told him bugger all in return. Unlike the previous team, there had been little reaction, either positive or negative, to the idea that Mickey had been helping with the investigation of a cold case. Whatever their view, it would be difficult, after all of that, to explain what he was doing with Mickey's USB drive.

Zofia folded her arms across her ample chest. 'You talk to Kristen?'

He sighed. In her eyes, Kristen could do no wrong and he often wondered if she had some sort of schoolgirl crush on her, as he watched her water and feed and nurture the little plant Kristen had left behind on her desk. He had even heard her talk to it, as she wiped the dust off its leaves. She had no concept of Kristen's failings, but then why should she? All that was good about Kristen, her sharpness, her single-mindedness, her determination, her drive and ambition had made her the success she was. But they were negatives when it came to a romantic relationship, particularly anything long-term. He had played second fiddle for far too long. He supposed it was why he had lost her respect. He wondered why it had taken him so long to see it.

'I can't get hold of her,' he said. 'She's not returning my calls.'

Zofia nodded sagely. 'She's busy woman. Maybe I know someone who can help.'

'Who? You mean one of your on-again, off-again Goth boyfriends?' He pictured a sea of interchangeable, young male faces, of varying nationalities, all with dyed black hair and an attitude. 'Maybe someone you picked up in a bar, or a club, or on Tinder?'

Zofia smiled. 'Nothing wrong with Tinder, Dan. You should give it a try.'

'Maybe.' At least she had a social life, he thought, which is more than could be said for him. 'What I mean is, this is someone you *know*, someone you *trust*?'

'Of course. He do favour for me. He owes me. He know what to do.' She reached for the drive, but Dan shook his head.

'I can't let you have it, Zofia. Who knows what's on it and how important it is. Something may happen to it. Then what do we do? How the hell would I explain that? I'd better hand it over.'

He pushed his hair back off his forehead and wiped his brow. Even as he spoke, he felt sick at the thought, imagining the afternoon unfolding at the police station, with yet more suspicion and questions. Another day gone, no further forward and no other work done.

'You'd better get on with checking the names on that printout I gave you. If any of them tally with anyone to do with the Westerby racing operation, call me straight away.'

She raised her black-painted brows. 'You're bonkers. You really want to call police?'

He leaned back in his chair and looked up at the ceiling. The patch of damp from the floor above was getting bigger. Or was it his imagination?

'Not really.'

She held out her hand again, nodding her head emphatically. 'I don't lose it, I promise. I'm sure I get it unlocked. You gotta trust me, Dan.'

# FIFTEEN

E ve could smell Steve Wilby's aftershave from ten feet away and she kept her distance as he led her into his small glass box of an office at the back of the Mercedes showroom. He had been easy to talk to on the telephone and was now all smiles, keen to demonstrate his desire to help. It was his lunch hour, he had been at pains to let her know, as though he were making a big effort to be helpful, and he had got them each a cup of nice-smelling coffee from an expensive-looking machine in the showroom.

'Tell me about Jane McNeil,' Eve asked, as he pulled up a chair for her. 'You went out with her after Sean Farrell, is that right?'

Wilby nodded, sitting down behind his desk. 'Just a few times. That's all.' He moved a small pile of papers to one side so that the space in front of him was clear and folded his hands on the desk expectantly.

Working back, Eve assumed he must be in his early forties, although he didn't look it. Smooth, was how she would describe him, with short, well-cut, dark-brown hair, a pleasant, regular-featured face and nice, hazel eyes. His crisp white shirt had the company logo on the chest pocket, which he wore with a plain, navy-blue tie and dark trousers. Like Farrell, he was short, with broad shoulders and a muscular build, but there the resemblance ended. He had also worn a lot better and was generally in much better physical shape, but of course he hadn't spent ten years in jail. Eve noticed a thick silver wedding band on his finger and a happy-looking picture of a wife and two children on his desk. It was a future – whether or not Jane had wanted it – that had been denied her.

'How did you two meet?' she asked, sipping her coffee, which was nice and hot, with not too much milk.

'One of the women from the racing yard where she worked introduced us. I was at the local Honda dealer in those days and I sold her a car. We got chatting. She found out I was single and we ended up going out for a drink. There was a group of us, some blokes I worked with, and this woman. She brought Jane along, plus another girl from their office. I got talking to Jane and I ended up asking her out. The woman who introduced us was really narked that I fancied Jane, but that's life. It's funny, even though we only went out a few times, I still remember her well.'

'Probably because of all the stuff in the papers,' Eve prompted.

'Yeah, I guess. The pictures didn't do her justice. She had nice colouring and she was a pretty little thing, particularly when she took off her specs, although a bit on the skinny side for my taste. She had nice eyes too, come to think of it. One was blue, the other brown, like that actress . . . you know . . .' He looked up at the ceiling, then shook his head. 'It'll come to me in a minute. Jane was a little self-conscious about it, but I thought it was kind of sexy and—'

'The woman who introduced you, what was her name?' Eve interrupted, before he got too carried away down memory lane.

'I dunno, but I can tell you where to find her. She was behind the till at the Blue Cross in Marlborough a couple of Saturdays ago.'

'You mean the charity shop?'

'Yes. It's in the High Street. There was a toy in the window my little boy wanted, so we went in. Took me a minute or so to place her, but I never forget a face and she don't look that much different.'

'Can you describe her?'

'Scrawny, long, dark hair tied back in a ponytail, with a white streak at the front. A bit New Age, if you get my drift. She's got a tattoo of a bird, or something, on the back of her hand. I noticed it when she took my money. She's the one who tipped the cops off about me when Jane was killed, the sour old cow. Lucky for me I had a cast-iron alibi.'

He was observant, and precise, she noted, and she liked his direct manner. He would make a good witness in court. Hopefully his memories of Jane would be equally sharp. 'So what happened with you and Jane?'

He shrugged. 'As I said, we went out a few times together. I'd just finished with someone, and so had she, so we were both treading a bit careful, like.'

'The person she'd just finished with, was this Sean Farrell?'

'I think so. She never mentioned anybody else.'

'What did you do with her?'

'I took her out for a drink, then for a meal, and we went to the flics after work one night.'

'You slept with her?'

He met her gaze. 'Never got the chance. She started making excuses. Then she didn't return my calls. Didn't take me long to get the message.'

'Were you surprised?'

He shrugged. 'Yeah. It was all a bit sudden. I mean, I thought things were going real good.'

He spoke as though being rejected wasn't the sort of thing that happened to him often. When she had interviewed Sean Farrell in jail, he had come across as a bit cocky too, although in a more belligerent sort of way. There was also the weak physical resemblance. Everyone had a type, to a greater or lesser degree. For some it was purely a superficial thing, about a body shape or hair or eye colour. For others it went deeper and was about personality and finding somebody who would fit in a particular way. The fact that Jane seemed to be attracted to someone who was confident and full of himself, possibly reflected a lack of confidence on her part and the need for someone else to be in control. She wondered what had put Jane off Steve Wilby so quickly. As far as she could see, he was better looking and had more obvious charm than Farrell.

'So, you wouldn't describe her as easy?' she asked.

'Far from it,' he said emphatically. 'I barely got to second base. And that was after three dates.'

What he said tallied with Farrell's own account of his

relationship with Jane. It also seemed to rule out the theory of Jane's having had casual sex with somebody she barely knew, who had then killed her.

'But you were fine about it?'

'Sure. My heart wasn't broken, if that's what you're thinking. *C'est la vie*.' He drank some coffee, then put the cup noisily down in the saucer and leaned back in his chair. 'The police made a right song and dance about it, saying I was angry and wanted revenge, and all that, but it was a load of bollocks. I've been around the block a few times. Sometimes you get on with a girl and sometimes you don't. End of. Just move on. No big deal. There's always more fish in the sea.'

He spoke matter-of-factly, without any trace of rancour. The police had checked his alibi and there was no reason for him not to tell the truth after so much time. 'Did Jane talk about what was going on in her life, at all?'

He shrugged. 'This and that. She seemed pretty lonely, far as I could tell. She hadn't been around here that long and I don't think she knew many people. She didn't like the girls she was sharing with, that much I remember. Maybe she was a bit of a prude, but she said they were a right pair.'

'What else did she talk about?'

'The yard where she worked, mostly, and all the people there, and the clients. She was full of it, like it was the best thing since sliced bread, meeting rich and famous people. To be honest, she talked about nothing else. I'm not into the whole racing lark, so it went right over my head. I also thought she was way too impressed by it all. To be honest, I found it a bit of a turn-off.'

She remembered Farrell's description of Jane, how she gave herself airs and graces and how he had called her Miss La-di-da. Jane had had dreams of a career in TV, but she sounded naïve and impressionable, possibly easy for the wrong sort of person to lead astray.

'Tell me about Sean Farrell. I understand he made a scene one evening when you were out with Jane.'

He laughed. 'He sure did, the stupid git. I'd arranged to meet her in this wine bar in Marlborough, but she was late and I was already there, waiting. She was all in a fluster, when she came in, something to do with work, she said. Anyway, I got up to buy her a drink and while I was at the bar, I remember looking around and seeing this bloke standing over her, talking to her, waving his arms about, like he's conducting the traffic, or something. I thought he was a friend of hers come over to say hello, but when I get back with her drink, they're having a right old set-to.'

'You think he followed her there?'

'No doubt about it. The bar's down a side street, so he couldn't have just been passing and seen us through the window, like he told the police.'

'Do you remember anything that was said?'

'It was a long time ago. But the gist of it was, she told him she was a free woman and could see who the hell she liked. I had to give it to her, she didn't mince her words. He went apeshit after that. You'd think he was her husband, the way he was carrying on, effing and blinding, but she stood up to him. When she told me afterwards they'd only gone out together for a few months, I was totally gobsmacked. I remember thinking the man had a real problem. Anyway, I told him to shove off, but he wouldn't listen to me. I thought at one point he was going to hit me. I went and found the manager, but before either of us had a chance to do anything, she turned on him and was ordering him out of the bar. She knew how to handle herself, I'd give her that much. She told him exactly what she thought of him. Said some right strong stuff about what a loser he was. Then she said if he didn't piss off and leave her alone, she'd call the police.'

'She wasn't scared of him, then?'

'Not one bit. She treated him like he was a piece of dog shit on her shoe.'

'So she clearly didn't see him as a threat?'

He shook his head. 'No way, poor girl.'

Again, the image Wilby painted of Jane tallied with what Farrell had told her. Although still a shadowy figure, Jane came across as someone who knew her own mind, who certainly wasn't afraid to stand up to Farrell. Had she misjudged him?

'Remind me, when did the scene in the bar take place?'

'At least a couple of months before she was killed, maybe a bit longer.'

She thought back to the timeline of Jane's six months in Marlborough. She had met Farrell quite soon after arriving and gone out with him for nearly three months. She must have dumped him not long before meeting Wilby. In Farrell's defence, the wound was still very fresh and raw when he saw Jane in the bar with Wilby. The fact that he had followed Jane there, just proved he was jealous. Wilby's account tied in with other accounts of Farrell's jealousy and it was good to hear it at first hand. But although jealousy was a strong motive for murder, the gap between the incident and Jane's killing was a couple of months at least. As far as she knew, there were no other reports of Farrell's stalking Jane during this time. What had he been doing with himself? Maybe after what had happened in the bar and the things Jane had said to him, he had finally decided to leave her alone and get on with his life. Or was he still brooding over it all that time, the pressure mounting? If so, it seemed odd that there were no other recorded incidents until the one in the gym, the morning of the day Jane had disappeared, and the accounts of what had happened there were not consistent.

She met Wilby's gaze. 'Did you ever get the impression when you were with her that she might have been seeing someone else as well as you?'

He was silent for a moment, then he clicked his knuckles loudly one by one. 'I dunno. She was nice-looking, but she wasn't a knockout, or anything. The quiet ones can sometimes surprise you, but if she had someone else on the go at the same time she was seeing me, she kept it well to herself.'

Again, her impression was that he was telling the truth. Why would he lie, or hold something back, ten years on? He had nothing to gain. But instinct was telling her there had to have been someone else in Jane's life. Why else would a lonely, shy girl like Jane suddenly ditch Wilby? He was certainly several notches up on Farrell. Even if Wilby wasn't Mr Perfect, surely quiet, lonely Jane would have held onto him for bit longer if there was nobody else around?

'Was that the last time you saw her?'

'It was the last time we went out together. But I saw her once after that, in London.'

'When was this?' There had been no mention of it in the file Peters had sent over to her.

'Just a few weeks before she died. It was late morning. She

was standing on a street corner, talking to a man. I thought
he was her dad.'

'Can you describe him?'

He rubbed his chin thoughtfully. 'I gave the police a
description at the time, but it's pretty basic. All I remember is
he was an old boy, with thick white hair.'

'Was he short or tall? Fat or thin?'

'Nothing that stood out. He was in a suit, with a stupid bowtie.
He looked like a right dick.'

'You assumed he was her father because of the way he was
dressed, or was it the age difference, or their body language?'

He frowned. 'I dunno. It was just my impression. Nobody
young wears a bowtie, do they? He looked like a businessman.
With money.'

'Why do you say that?'

'The suit was well-cut. Expensive. I used to work in a posh
showroom in London in my twenties. I know what I'm talking
about. Who else would he be, if he wasn't her dad?'

'Her father was a country vet,' she prodded.

He shrugged. 'Maybe he was an uncle, or a godfather, or
something. They were just chatting. Not close together, or nothing.
She was smiling at him, though. Like she was pleased with something. It was all over in a flash. Maybe I missed something.'

'You're sure it was her?'

'A hundred per cent.'

'Did she often go up to London?'

'I remember her saying something about it one evening. Said
she was meeting up with a friend for lunch, I think. I just assumed
it was a woman.'

Perhaps successful vets from Lincoln wore expensive suits when
they went to London. Or maybe Jane had been seeing a much
older man. Was the cash that Farrell had mentioned related in some
way? If so, was Jane moonlighting as an escort on her days off?

'What was Jane wearing?'

'Nothing special. I mean, she just looked like Jane, with her
specs and ordinary clothes.' He smiled. 'She didn't look like a
hooker, if that's what you're getting at.'

'Thank you,' she said, pleased that there wasn't much that
escaped him. It added weight to everything else he had said.

'OK. Just to make sure, there was nothing at all intimate about the way they were together?'

'No. I'm sure I'd have noticed. I told you, I thought the man was her dad. I'm sorry. That's as much as I can tell you.'

'Understood.' The last thing she wanted was to push him too hard and make him say something for the sake of it. She drained the remains of her coffee, wishing she had time for another, and stood up. 'One last thing. Where was this?'

'The corner of Berkeley Square, right outside the Porsche garage. I always slow down and look in the window when I'm passing, which is how I spotted her.'

He got to his feet and walked her to the door. 'You know, I feel real bad about what happened to her,' he said, thoughtfully, holding it open. 'Not that I could've done nothing to stop it. But I never dreamt the bloke I saw in the bar with her would kill her. Now you're saying he's got an appeal going, or something?'

'That's right. He's always maintained he's innocent.'

He shook his head slowly. 'Well, he looked like a right nutter to me.' He turned to face her. 'Do *you* think he's innocent?'

She sighed. He had been straight with her and she didn't want to lie. 'To be honest, I really don't know. That's what I'm here to find out.'

# SIXTEEN

Kevin Steven's widow, Shona, stood in the doorway of her fifth floor flat in Pimlico, an apron covered in pink hearts tied around her ample middle, a limp tea towel in her hand. 'Look, I'm happy to tell you what I told the police this morning,' she said wearily to Dan. 'But they really didn't seem that interested. I don't want to waste your time.'

It was past six in the evening and she had just got home from the school where she worked as a supply teacher. On top of the fact that she spoke softly and quickly, a gale was whistling through the open corridor and stairwell and he had to crane his neck to hear what she was saying.

He shivered. 'Tell me anyway, if you don't mind.' He was impressed that the police had been to see Shona so quickly. At least it meant they were taking what he had told them seriously.

A door opened along the corridor and a man came out with a small dog and started walking towards them.

With a nervous look in his direction, Shona said, 'Maybe you'd best come in. I don't want to talk about it all out here.'

She ushered him inside, past an old bicycle that was blocking the narrow hall, and into a small kitchen at the back, overlooking two identical, charmless, mid-seventies housing blocks. The room was clean and tidy, the walls painted pale blue, with old-fashioned pine units and a little, white Formica table pushed up against one wall.

'Have a seat. Do you want a cup of tea? I was just making myself one when you rang the buzzer.'

'Thank you,' he replied, although he could do with something stronger.

'Mickey Fraser came to see me a few weeks ago,' Shona said, taking out a box of tea bags and a couple of mugs from a wall cupboard. 'He told me he used to be with the police and that he was a private investigator.' She looked over at him for corroboration.

She was in her late-forties, he guessed, with a pleasant, soft-featured face, thick, dark hair, threaded with grey and a worried look in her hazel eyes that he sensed had been there for a while. He decided to go carefully, not push too hard.

'Both are correct,' he said. 'What else did he tell you?'

'He said he was looking into an old murder case. That a girl was murdered. Was it ten years ago?'

'That's right.'

'And a man's in jail for it, who shouldn't be there.'

'All the evidence points to the fact that he's innocent.'

She nodded. 'He told me about your charity. I've seen one of the documentaries you did. Mickey told me that Kevin tried to contact the girl several times in the week before her death.'

'Her name was Jane McNeil,' he said, wanting to personalize things, in the hope of jogging her memory. 'She worked for a racing yard near Marlborough.'

Her expression was blank. 'Mickey mentioned he wanted to

know why Kevin called this girl several times. I couldn't help him, I'm afraid. I knew nothing about what Kevin was up to on a day-to-day basis.'

'Was your husband contacted by the police at the time of Jane's murder?'

'If he was, he didn't tell me. Maybe he wasn't calling her about anything important.'

It sounded as though Mickey had hit a dead end. 'Did Mickey ask anything else?'

She sighed. 'Not really. I could see he was very disappointed. He asked about what happened to Kevin's laptop, which gave up the ghost years ago, and his old files, which I also got rid of. There was nothing at all interesting in them, I can assure you. But I'd kept some of Kevin's old diaries and notebooks. I told him he could have them if he wanted, if he gave them back to me when he was done.'

'He took them away with him?'

She nodded.

He wondered if he had stumbled over them in Mickey's flat. 'The notebooks were for work?'

'Yes. He wrote everything up on his laptop, but he liked to take notes longhand, particularly if he was interviewing some-body. He also preferred a diary he could write in, rather than using his phone or laptop.'

'Can you describe the diaries and notebooks?'

She brushed a fluffy lock of hair off her face. 'They weren't anything special, just A5 size, red, with hardcovers. The note-books had wire binders, so he could rip out a page if he wanted. He always had the same thing, same colour. He was a real creature of habit.'

'How many of them were there?' he asked. He couldn't recall anything matching their description in Mickey's flat, certainly not in the front room. But maybe the police had found them when they searched the place.

'Oh, several years' worth,' she said, filling the kettle and switching it on. 'But Mickey was only interested in the most recent ones. They were all in a box on top of my wardrobe, gathering dust, so it was easy to put my hands on them. Do you have any idea why he was murdered? The police wouldn't say.'

'No idea. But I was the one who found his body. He was tortured, you know. It was pretty horrific.'

Her brown eyes opened wide. 'Goodness. The police didn't mention that.'

He was sorry to shock her but he wanted her to realize how serious it was, in case there was anything she might be holding back, or had forgotten to tell the police.

The kettle pinged and she filled the mugs with water.

'Is there anything else you think I should know?' he asked.

She glanced away, looking down momentarily at her hands. 'Well, before Mickey left, he told me he thought Kevin's death might not have been an accident.'

'Really?' He tried to hide his amazement. Had Mickey genuinely believed it, or was it just a line he'd given Shona, to get her to open up? 'Did you tell the police this?'

'They weren't interested.' She stabbed the teabags with a teaspoon, then took them out of the mugs and dumped them in the bin. 'Milk? Sugar? There's sweetener, if you want.'

'Just a drop of milk, please.'

She poured milk into the mugs and handed him his, then leaned heavily back against the counter and took a gulp of tea.

'What exactly happened to Kevin?'

'He was the victim of a hit-and-run. The view at the time was that it was an accident and they're still sticking to it. The autopsy showed he'd been drinking quite heavily. More than twice the legal drink drive limit, they said. So their assumption was that he just stepped out into the road, not looking where he was going. Maybe it's better for their statistics that way.'

'Where did this happen?'

'Very near here, on Ebury Street, just after closing time. He was walking home from the pub. He went there most nights for a bit of company, if I had work to do. There weren't any witnesses or cameras, unfortunately. Some passer-by found him lying in the road. There was blood all over the place and they called an ambulance, but by the time it came he was already dead. I asked the police who came here this morning if they thought Mickey's murder had anything to do with Kevin, or his death . . .' Her voice trailed off uncertainly. 'They were very polite, of course. But they said it was highly unlikely. I could tell they thought I'd been watching too much TV.'

He nodded sympathetically. The detectives he had seen had been equally sceptical about his suggestion of a link between Mickey's death and the Sean Farrell case. It was all history. Ten years was a long time and a man had been found guilty and was in jail. Why would any of it have something to do with the present?

'So you don't think Kevin's death was an accident?' he asked. He saw the answer in her eyes even before she replied and he wondered if Mickey had seen it too and had decided to exploit her vulnerability. He also saw the glint of a tear, which she wiped away quickly with her knuckle.

'No. I don't.'

'Can you tell me why?'

She sighed. 'Before Kevin died, he was working on something important, something hush hush, or at least that's what he said. He said it was going to be the making of him.'

'Did he tell you what it was about?'

'No. Just that he had to be the first to break the story, but he hadn't got quite enough evidence to go public.' She sighed. 'I have to say, I'd heard it all before. Kevin was a bit of a dreamer. He was always trying to get the big break, so I wasn't holding my breath. He'd been drinking more than usual and he'd become a bit paranoid, which worried me.'

'How do you mean?'

'He thought our phone was being tapped, for starters, then he thought someone was following him.'

'When was this?'

'The week before he died. I'm afraid I didn't believe him. But when he was killed . . .' She shrugged and looked at him mean-ingfully. 'There was no proof, of course,' she continued, wiping away another tear. 'And when I told the police, I could see they didn't believe me either. At least they had the decency to check the phone, but they said there was absolutely nothing wrong with it. I didn't bother telling the lot that came this morning anything about it. They'd just be thinking the same. Stupid woman needs to get a grip and move on with her life.'

His heart went out to her. Sometimes people didn't get over things and she'd been living with what had happened for the past ten years. 'Do you have any idea what was in the notebooks?'

'No, but he had one for each story he was working on, at least if it was anything important. They were all labelled on the front, with the date he started them, and some sort of title or description. All the old ones – the dead ones, as he called them – were stacked together with elastic bands, in date order, in the box. He was very organized that way.'

'What about his most recent notebooks? The ones he was using at the time of his death?'

'There were two of them. They were in his satchel, underneath his desk. I put them in the box with the others.'

'You didn't look through them?'

She shook her head. 'I felt too emotional and what was the point? The police didn't think it was important. I'd completely forgotten about them until Mickey came to see me.'

'So you don't remember anything about the notebooks?'

She sighed. 'All I remember is that they were on top of the pile when I gave Mickey the box. I took the lid off to show him what was inside. I remember the label on one of them. Kevin had used a thick black felt tip to mark them up. It said "Weston", I think, and Michael something, and another name. All I know is Mickey seemed very interested in it.'

'Could it be "Westerby" and "Michaels", as in the surname?'

'Maybe.'

'You don't remember the other name?'

She shook her head.

'And you really have no idea what Kevin's big scoop was?'

'Sorry. I'm a history teacher. I know absolutely nothing about the racing world.'

# SEVENTEEN

The Rising Sun pub occupied an old brick and timber building, overlooking a small churchyard at one end of Marlborough High Street. Eve had booked the last available room, which was at the front, on the first floor, above the main bar. The room was large and pleasantly warm, but as she turned off the lights for a moment and closed the blinds, the light from the streetlamp opposite leaked through. Even at that hour, when the bar was nearly empty, the sound of music and voices drifted up from below. She had packed her prescription sleeping pills and an eye mask, as well as downloaded some new sleep music on her phone, but it still wouldn't be enough. She would have to see if she could find somewhere else to stay in the morning.

She had been surprised at how well the meeting with Steve Wilby had gone. After seeing him, she had driven from Swindon back to Marlborough, finding the Blue Cross shop on the high street, a hundred yards down from the Rising Sun, on the same side of the street. She had spoken to an elderly man, who was busy stacking books at the back of the shop, and described the woman Wilby had seen a few Saturdays before. He seemed to know who Eve was talking about, but told Eve to try again in the morning when the manager would be in. Eve had then called Dan. He had no idea who the man with white hair Wilby had seen with Jane could be. But when she suggested he try and speak to Jane's parents again, he refused. 'No point', he said emphatically. 'I told you, she slammed the door in my face last time.' She decided that she would have to do it herself. He had at least given her the names of the two detectives from Hendon who had interviewed him that morning and she had left a message for the SIO in charge of Mickey's murder investigation, DCI Andy Fagan, whom she knew well.

She showered and changed into a clean pair of trousers and a shirt, taking time over her makeup to compensate for the fact that she had brought nothing special to wear. The written directions Gavin had given her earlier were clear and the drive to Westerby from the pub took less than ten minutes. The entrance was just off the A4, along a narrow lane, which led up a steep hill, past a public parking area to a pair of white, wooden gates. A smart-looking sign with the words 'Westerby Estate. Private' in large black lettering was fixed to the fence beside it. She got out of the car and, following Gavin's instructions, rang the bell marked 'Westerby Farm'. A moment later, the gates slowly parted and she drove through. Apart from the immediate area lit up by her headlamps, she could make out little on either side, except dark fields, with a few trees here and there, sweeping upwards to an almost empty skyline. The road continued to climb, then levelled out about half a mile further on, just before a fork. Her headlights picked up a silver Range Rover with new plates, which was parked to one side of the road, half up on the verge, lights dipped, engine idling. Two men sat in the front and even before she pulled alongside, she heard raised voices. She couldn't remember if Gavin had said to turn left or right and there were no signs. She braked and put down her window. A moment later, the driver's window was lowered and a middle-aged man with a square jaw and a full head of thick, greyish hair peered down at her.

'Can I help you, luv?' The voice was gruff and deep, with a northern twang.

'I'm looking for Westerby Farm,' she said, peering beyond him into the car. The man beside him, in the passenger seat, stared steadfastly out of the front window, as though he didn't want to be part of the conversation. A bit younger, dark hair, was as much as she could tell.

'Take the left-hand bend just in front of you. You'll find the house at the bottom.'

Before she even had a chance to say 'thank you', or ask anything else, the window slid upwards and the man looked away. Wondering who they were and what they were arguing about, she took the turning for the farm, keeping an eye on the Range Rover in her rear-view mirror until its lights were hidden behind the brow of the hill. A little further along, she came to another set of white gates, which opened automatically as she approached.

The house was at the end of a long, tree-lined drive. She pulled into the gravel turning circle at the front and floodlights came on illuminating the gabled brick façade. As she switched off the engine and climbed out of the car, the front door opened and Gavin came out into the porch. He hurried towards her and embraced her warmly, then ushered her quickly up the steps and out of the cold into a wide, stone-floored hall. A series of old racing prints covered one wall and a huge, bare Christmas tree stood at the foot of the small staircase, with a number of cardboard boxes stacked beside it. From upstairs came the squeaky sound of children's voices, coupled with the rapid thud of small feet.

'It's the boys,' Gavin said, with a brief glance upwards, as he took her coat and draped it over a chair by the door. 'They should be in bed by now, but Melissa picked up the tree this morning, and they've been waiting all day for me to finish work and do the lights. Would you mind giving me a hand?'

'Of course not.'

She heard whispers immediately above and, looking up, saw two small faces peering at her through the banisters. They were in pyjamas and had their father's blonde hair and blue eyes.

Gavin smiled. 'That's Sam on the left, and Frank on the right.'

'Frank? You named him after your dad.'

He nodded. 'He's just turned six. Sam's only four. Mum was still more or less mentally together when Frank was born. His having Dad's name meant a great deal to her.'

Upstairs a woman's voice called out and the boys ran off giggling. For a moment, she thought of her own little brothers, not much different in age, their small, warm arms looped around her neck, legs clamped tightly around her middle, fingers playing gently with her hair, as she carried them each in turn to bed to read them stories. How she missed them.

Gavin pulled a thick coil of lights from one of the boxes, unravelled the end, then plugged them in and switched them on, passing Eve the coil of green wire. It was studded with tiny white bulbs, which looked like tiny stars in her hands. He started at the bottom, looping them carefully around the base, then climbed up the step-ladder to reach the higher branches. As she followed him around, paying out the string, she became aware of the aromatic smell of the tree. Clem and Robin had always had a fake tree because Clem hated the idea that a tree should be cut down every year, just for Christmas. But her own mother had always insisted on having a real tree, as big as she could afford, or fit in whatever tiny flat they were living in. She had helped her decorate it every year with paper chains and ornaments they would make together. She remembered the smell of baking, the peculiar, soggy cakes and misshapen biscuits her mother insisted on making, mingled with the sweet smell of dope that permeated the little flat whenever her mother's occasional partner, Daz, returned to the fold. It was usually at Christmas, as though he liked a brief shot of family life at that time of year and to claim paternal rights over his small sons, when nothing else of interest was going on. Although she tried to capture again each detail and smell, each voice and laugh and intonation, more than twenty years on the images were dimming. Sometimes she didn't know how much was real memory and how much her own imagination.

Tears pricked her eyes and, biting her lip hard, she pushed the images away, forcing herself to focus on the minutiae of what Gavin was doing, on his strong hands, the crisp cuffs of his pale-blue shirt that peeped out from the sleeves of his jumper as he looped the string around the branches.

'What do you think?' he asked, turning to her when he had finished.

She stood back and studied the tree. 'You need a few more lights at the bottom, I think.'

He rearranged the string until he was satisfied. 'That looks better. I'll do the decorations after dinner.' He rubbed his hands together. 'Right. Let's go and get ourselves a drink.'

She followed him along a passage into a huge kitchen, which was on one side of the house. The room was very warm compared to the chilly hall and delicious cooking smells were coming from a series of pots on the large green AGA.

'Melissa should be down in a minute. What can I get you?'

'Anything soft would be great.'

He opened a cupboard and studied the contents. 'There's coke, elderflower or tonic, unless you want the boys' squash or Ribena.'

'Tonic is fine. Thanks.'

As he sorted out their drinks, Eve gazed around the room. It had a comfortable, lived-in feel, with faded, blue-checked blinds and pale, yellow washed walls, the old floorboards scuffed and worn over the years by many feet. In a glazed extension to one side, a long refectory table was already set for dinner. It was covered with a navy oil cloth patterned with gold stars, and a jug of water and a vase of daffodils sat in the middle. She counted four places and wondered who would be joining them. Just as Gavin handed her a glass, a small, slim woman with short, blonde hair entered the room. Eve recognized Melissa from her picture on the Westerby website. She stopped just inside the door, and stared at Eve for a moment, her mouth a little open, as though she had seen a ghost.

'Melissa,' Gavin said, giving her a pointed look. 'This is Eve.'

'Sorry,' Melissa said, recovering herself. 'Yes of course. My mind's somewhere else. I've just remembered something . . . something I've forgotten to do.' She spoke hurriedly and a little breathlessly, her small hand flapping in the air as though trying to brush her confusion away. 'So you're Eve? I've heard a lot about you. I gather you and Gavin go back a long way.'

Eve nodded. 'We used to live next door to each other in Lymington. We went to the same school.'

'I was a couple of years older,' Gavin said.

'It was a long time ago,' Eve added, hoping to reassure Melissa, if that was what she needed. She had no idea what Gavin had told her. 'We haven't seen each other for a very long time.'

'Gavin tells me you're here looking into Jane McNeil's murder,' Melissa said.

'That's right.'

'I remember Jane well. It was awful when it happened.' Her tone was a little flat and Eve had the impression she was just being polite.

'Is dinner ready?' Gavin asked.

'Yes,' Melissa said. 'We're just waiting for Harry, as usual.'

She went over to the AGA and, using gloves, took out a small stack of plates from one of the ovens and transferred them to the top of the island unit opposite. She opened another oven and removed a large, heavy-looking casserole dish. Her movements were quick and staccato and she had a harried look in her eyes.

Eve wondered why she was so tense and off-key. She had given little thought to what had happened to Gavin in the past twenty years, let alone to what sort of woman he had married. It was often impossible to understand the dynamics of attraction, let alone love, she reasoned. But seeing Melissa, she was surprised. She was perfectly nice-looking, pretty even, but there was something a little prim about her, in her pressed, unflattering jeans, sensible, flat shoes and crisp, long-sleeved, pink blouse, the buttons done up almost to the neck, as though nothing of her femininity should be on show. Perhaps that was what a wife ought to be, she thought, someone who wasn't going to set the world on fire, who wouldn't give a man sleepless nights.

'Harry's Melissa's brother,' Gavin said, pouring Melissa a large glass of wine and handing it to her. 'He's divorced and lives on his own in a flat above the office, so he usually eats with us, unless he's got a better offer.'

As if on cue, the kitchen door opened and Harry entered the room. She recognized him instantly from his picture on the family website. She was also sure he was the man in the passenger seat of the silver Range Rover.

'Hello. You must be Eve,' he said, striding over to her and holding out his hand. It was cold from outside and his handshake was very firm. 'I'm Harry.' He held her gaze unblinking for a moment.

She nodded. Genetics were extraordinary, she thought. Harry was not particularly tall, but he was muscular, with dark hair and a broad, strong-featured, very masculine face, while Melissa was like a pale, dainty, little bird. Even allowing for the differences between male and female, and the fact that Harry must be several years older than Melissa, she would never have guessed that they were brother and sister. Yet Gavin's little boys were like two peas in a pod, dead ringers for their father. Her own genetic heritage was equally a mystery. Her mother had had long, straight, light-brown hair, fair skin and greyish-blue eyes. Eve remembered how it used to upset her to be told she didn't look like her mother at all. She was the dark, little gypsy child, found under a bush, someone had once teased her. She remembered how much it had hurt her and how much she had cried about it, in spite of all her mother's attempts to soothe her. The phrase, and the sense of not belonging, had stuck in her mind all her life. She must have taken after her father, whoever he was. He had been long gone before she was born. But doubtless he had been another bad lot. Her mother's chief flaw had been to fall, time and time again, for the wrong man.

'Right, everybody. Come and sit down,' Melissa said briskly, carrying plates over to the table, Gavin following behind with various bowls and dishes. 'I'm sorry it's a bit rough and ready, but I didn't have much time today.'

'Eve, come and sit next to me,' Gavin said, pulling out a chair for her, as Melissa started dishing out some sort of pleasant-smelling stew.

Harry placed himself opposite. 'So how do you and Gavin

know one another?' he asked, adding a dollop of English mustard to the side of his plate.

'They were next-door neighbours when they were growing up,' Melissa said. 'I told you earlier.'

'I see,' Harry said, helping himself to some mashed potato. 'When was this?' He looked up at Eve.

'In our teens,' Gavin said.

'But you kept in touch?' Again he was looking at Eve.

'The last time I saw Eve was when I'd just gone up to Oxford,' Gavin replied, before she had a chance to speak.

'Did you go out together, or something?' Harry asked.

'I don't know what you mean by "or something",' Gavin said, spooning some peas onto his plate. 'We were very young. It was a long time ago.'

His expression gave nothing away, but his manner was off-hand and Eve had the impression that he wanted to dismiss it all as some crazy teenage thing that meant nothing, no doubt for Melissa's benefit. Even though it wasn't true, she was happy to go along with it for his sake.

'Are you married?' Harry asked, his pale, steady eyes meeting hers across the table.

'Don't be so nosey, Harry,' Melissa said sharply.

'It's a fair question.'

'If a blunt one,' Gavin said. 'You'll have to forgive Harry, here. He doesn't like to waste time with small chat.'

'I don't mind answering,' Eve replied. She had nothing to hide, or feel ashamed of, on that score. 'No, I'm not married. Never have been.'

'So you're single?' Harry asked, his gaze still on her, as though they were the only two in the room.

'Yes.'

Up close, Harry's face was a little weather-beaten, as though he spent a lot of time outside. A neat scar ran at an angle right across his cheek, puckering one side of his top lip, giving his mouth a slightly disdainful look. She wondered how he had got it. The dark colour of his hair made his pale eyes all the more striking and she had the impression that there wasn't much he would miss. She also had the feeling that he was deliberately needling Gavin, for some reason.

'Did young Gavin, here, break your heart?' he asked, with another faint smile.

'Eve's unbreakable,' Gavin said firmly, before she had a chance to answer. 'At least as far as I was concerned. Now, let's leave the lonely-hearts stuff to one side. Please, Eve, can you tell us about what you're doing here. We're all dying to know.'

It was a relief to get off the subject of her personal life. She gave them a basic version, leaving out John Duran, saying that she was just doing a favour for a friend, who was a supporter of Sean Farrell's cause. She mentioned 4Justice and Harry seemed particularly interested, asking a series of questions about the appeal, while Gavin and Melissa mostly listened. She wondered if he remembered Dan snooping around the cottage. If so, he wasn't saying anything.

'How did Jane get the job with you?' she asked.

'I've no idea,' Melissa said. 'Do you remember, Harry?'

He shook his head. 'Word of mouth, usually. Racing's a small world and we don't normally have to advertise, even for clerical staff.'

'But she wasn't local,' Eve said. 'As far as I know, she didn't have any friends in the Marlborough area.'

Harry shrugged. 'I haven't the foggiest. It was a long time ago.'

'She was probably recommended by someone Father knew,' Melissa said.

'Yeah, I think you're right,' Harry replied. 'He always liked to do things the old-fashioned way. A personal recommendation counted more than anything with him. He always said you could trust people more if you knew where they came from.'

He was again looking right at her as he spoke and Eve wondered if he was talking about her, rather than Jane. Once more, she was curious to know exactly what Gavin had said.

'So, what happened? You reported her missing?'

Melissa nodded. 'She didn't turn up for work Monday morning, which was unlike her. She'd been unwell at the Christmas party on the Saturday and had gone home early. When she didn't ring in sick on Monday, I was worried about her and went over to the cottage to check on her. Her car was gone and there was no answer, so I let myself in. First thing I noticed was a window had been smashed at the back. It looked like there'd been a break-in, so we called the police. To be honest, they didn't seem that worried. They said Jane wasn't a child and had probably just gone off somewhere. Apparently, people do all the time. They seemed pretty sure she'd come back.'

'Then what happened?'

'Father got the window repaired and we thought no more about it until the police came calling again.'

'What was Jane like?'

Melissa turned to Harry. 'You probably knew her best, didn't you?'

'I guess. I suppose I saw the most of her on a day-to-day basis, apart from Father.'

'And?' Gavin said. 'I think Eve wants a bit more than that.'

Harry leaned back in his seat resting his elbow on the top of the empty chair beside him. 'Well, she was quite quiet, but she seemed to be hardworking and pretty organized. She just got on with things, far as I could tell. She basically ran my father's diary and dealt with the race entries. If you come into the office tomorrow, I'll show you the set-up, if you like.'

'That would be useful,' Eve said, curious that Harry hadn't once mentioned Jane's looks. Both Farrell and Wilby had found her attractive, but to him, it seemed she was just another faceless person in the office, not a real girl with personality or appeal. 'Was she attractive?' she asked, wanting to get more of a reaction.

Harry stared at her. 'I really didn't think of her that way.'

She met his gaze, a little surprised. Somehow, it didn't ring true. He wouldn't have been that much older than Jane and few men she had ever come across failed to register whether a woman was attractive or not. From the little she had seen of Harry, he was certainly no exception and she wondered why he was so dismissive.

'Jane actually looked quite pretty, when she made an effort,' Melissa said a little hurriedly. 'Like at the Christmas party, the day she disappeared. I certainly remember your noticing,' she said, with a sideways glance in Harry's direction.

'Not my type,' he said sharply, leaning across the table towards Eve. 'And before you go getting any ideas, Eve, the police checked out my alibi very thoroughly.'

'Mine too,' Gavin said quietly, looking at Harry.

'Were you surprised when Sean Farrell was charged with her murder?' Eve asked.

Harry looked at her thoughtfully. 'I guess he must have been jealous. He'd only just taken over from my father's old farrier, who'd retired, so I didn't know him at all well. But he seemed pretty on the ball to me, with a good team of lads working for him. I remember Father saying we were lucky to get him.'

'So, he wasn't just working on his own?' Eve asked.

Melissa shook her head. 'There's too much to do. Farriers around here make a ton of money, if they're any good, with all the racing and event yards in the area.'

'What happened to the girls who shared the cottage with her?' Eve asked.

'The Irish girl, Grace, went home,' Harry said. 'She was very homesick and never really fitted in. Then she had a bad fall up on the gallops and decided to call it a day, but that was a good month or so before Jane disappeared. I've no idea what happened to her after that.'

'I thought there was another girl?'

'If you mean Holly Crowther, I had to sack her,' Melissa said crisply.

'This was the week before Jane went missing?'

'That's right.'

'Any particular reason?'

Melissa glanced at Harry before replying. 'She was a trouble-maker, that's all, although my father had a soft spot for her, which is why she lasted so long.' Her tone was dismissive, as though it wasn't important.

'He wasn't the only one,' Harry said meaningfully, returning Melissa's gaze.

'No and she'd had a couple of warnings before,' Melissa said sharply. 'I gave her a week's wages, which was more than she was due in the circumstances, and told her to get out.'

Eve looked over at Gavin but he seemed to be paying no attention to the conversation, busy scraping up the last few mouthfuls of stew on his plate. Perhaps he wasn't aware of, or interested in, the comings and goings of the racing yard personnel. Or perhaps he was too polite to say something. But it was clear from the interplay between Harry and Melissa that there was some sort of story behind it. Whether any of it was relevant to what happened to Jane McNeil was another matter.

'Do you know where she went?' Eve asked, looking at Harry. 'I'd like to get in touch with her.'

'Off to another yard,' Harry said. 'I had someone ring me up about a month later for a reference and then again someone else about six months after that, so she obviously didn't stay long in the first job.'

Melissa looked at him surprised. 'You gave her a reference?'

Harry shrugged and gave an apologetic smile. 'She was a good little rider.'

'You never told me,' Melissa said, clearly annoyed.

'There are a lot of things I don't tell you,' he said sharply.

'Where did she go after here, then?' Eve asked, as Melissa and Gavin got up from the table and started to clear away the plates and dishes.

'One of the yards in Newmarket,' Harry replied. 'I think it was Fred Foxley's. The other yard was somewhere up north, but I don't remember the trainer's name or if he's still in business. People come and go a lot in our world, it's all pretty casual, and ten years is a long time. Is it important?'

'Impossible to say. They shared a house with Jane for several months, so they probably knew her better than anyone.'

'Right. I can certainly give Fred a call in the morning, if you like, just to double-check. I'll also see if I can find out where Grace is now. My head lass is her cousin and they come from the same village.'

'That would be very helpful.'

'Do you really think Sean Farrell's innocent?'

'I don't know,' Eve said. 'The trial certainly raised some questions that weren't properly answered. I haven't seen all the documentation, but based on what I've read, I'm surprised they got a conviction.'

He looked thoughtful for a moment. 'You say there's some sort of a deadline?'

'That's right. We don't know exactly, but we think they'll decide in a few weeks' time.'

'Who will? Decide what?'

'The Criminal Cases Review Commission. They'll decide whether or not to refer his case back to the Court of Appeal.'

He frowned, as though it didn't make much sense. 'What if they don't?'

'Then that's it.'

'What, for good?'

'I'm afraid so.'

They sat around the table, talking for a little longer, but it was clear everybody was tired. Also, in spite of their curiosity, the discussion about Jane McNeil seemed to have put a dampener on things. Eve remembered again how Gavin had described it as being a bad time for them all, with the suicide of Tim Michaels. Maybe that explained it. There was so much more she wanted to ask, but it would have to wait for a better moment. She said goodbye to Melissa and Harry, arranging to meet Harry in the office the following morning. Gavin walked her outside to her car. The air was sharp and stung her nostrils and the beginnings of a frost had already covered one side of the car, glinting in the lights from the house.

'How long are you planning on staying?' he asked, as she opened the driver's door and climbed in.

'Hopefully not more than a few days, although there's quite a lot of ground to cover. I'd like to look around the estate in daylight, if possible? Just to get a feel for the location and where it all happened.'

'Of course. I can give you a guided tour tomorrow, if you like. I've got a load of constituency business to deal with, which will take up the morning, but I can make myself free in the afternoon. I was also going to ask you if you'd like a place to stay, while you're here? I discussed it with Melissa while you were talking to Harry. We have an empty cottage, which we sometimes rent out as a holiday let, or offer clients from overseas when they come over. I'd suggest you stay in the house with us, but the cottage would be a lot quieter, and more private. It's actually where Jane used to live and it's just down the lane from here.'

She thought about it for a moment. It would be much more convenient, as well as possibly useful, to stay on the farm, and certainly a lot nicer than being at the pub. 'I'm happy to pay you,' she said, thinking that it would be a good use for some of Duran's money.

He shook his head. 'Not necessary. It's not booked out until the week before New Year, so it's yours for as long as you need it, until then. Come over around ten tomorrow and Melissa can let you in.'

# EIGHTEEN

*Hi Eve, re: the race at Ascot that Mickey was interested in, there were two runners with connections to Westerby. No.3, My Favourite Boy, trained by Harry Michaels, owned by the Come What May partnership, and No.8, London Match, owner Mr Lorne Anderson. Anderson was a client of Michaels Senior when Jane McNeil was there. He's one of the owners who called Jane several times in the week before she died. Haven't checked any other races. Dan.*

E ve stared at the screen for a moment, memorizing the names, then tucked away her phone in her bag and got out of her car. Tiny flakes of snow wheeled like dust on the freezing wind, stinging her face. It probably wouldn't stick, but the temperature was several degrees colder than in London and the sharpness of the air took her by surprise. She zipped up her coat as far as it would go, pulled the hood over her head and put on a pair of insulated, woollen gloves she had bought at a petrol station. She had followed Melissa from the house and Melissa now stood waiting for her in the lane further along, a hat jammed down low on her head, and a long waterproof coat and boots.

'This is it,' she said briskly, as Eve approached, with a vague nod towards the whitewashed cottage that was perched on a bank above them. 'Do you need a hand with your things?'

Eve shook her head. 'I've just got a small bag in the car. I can bring it in later.'

'Coincidentally, this was where Jane used to live,' Melissa said, leading the way up the steep, slippery, brick steps. 'It looks completely different now, of course. We did it up a couple of years ago. It was a total tip when the girls were here.'

The cottage appeared to be old, with a pretty lattice-work wooden porch framing the apple-green front door. The front garden was tidy, an old, clipped, wavy hedge separating it from the lane, which was a good six feet below. Eve remembered what Dan had said about the witnesses who had driven past the cottage on the night Jane disappeared and she had to agree with him. She doubted whether anyone passing in their car at night would have had a clear view of somebody standing under the porch.

Melissa reached up onto the ledge above the front door and produced a large, old-fashioned key on a chunky, wooden fob.

'Was the key always kept on the ledge?' Eve asked, as Melissa unlocked the door.

'I imagine so. There isn't a duplicate.'

'Wasn't anyone worried about security?'

'It was a habit of my father's for all the houses, including ours. He hated the idea of locked doors. It's not like London around here, you know. You can leave your back door unlocked – even your front door – and nobody comes in.' Her manner was stiff and her tone a little off-hand.

'I thought somebody broke one of the windows at the back of the cottage, the night Jane disappeared?' Eve asked, following Melissa inside, wondering if she was usually so charmless. 'If the key was so readily available, why would they bother?'

Melissa shrugged. 'I suppose it means it had to have been somebody who didn't know about the key system.'

'But Sean Farrell must have known, surely?'

Melissa gave her a blank look. 'I guess so. Or maybe he was just being clever.'

The small, bright hall had a new-looking, quarry-tiled floor and smelled of fresh paint, but the air was almost as chill inside as out.

'I put the heating on an hour ago, but it takes time to warm up,' Melissa said, as though reading Eve's thoughts. 'The boiler's old and can be a bit temperamental sometimes. If you have any problems, just give me a call and I'll send somebody over to sort it. I'm afraid the Wi-Fi's not working at the moment. We've been waiting for days for BT to come and fix the line, but still no sign. You'll have to use your mobile, if you can get a signal, or come and use our Wi-Fi at the yard or the house. That's the kitchen,' she said, opening a door to the left. Eve glimpsed a small table and chairs under a mullioned window, blue-patterned fabric blinds and cream-coloured units. Everything looked clean and tidy and homely. 'I've put some basics in the fridge to start you off,' Melissa added.

'Thank you. Let me know what I owe you.'

Melissa shook her head quickly. 'Don't worry about it. You'll find everything else you need for cooking in the cupboards. It's pretty well stocked with day-to-day stuff. If you want anything else, there's a Waitrose on the High Street and, of course, you know where Tesco's is.' The remark was off the cuff, but Eve again picked up a sharpness in her tone. It was clear she wasn't happy with Eve staying there. What had Gavin said?

'The sitting room's this way,' Melissa said, pushing open another door, this time on the right.

Eve followed her into a large, low-ceilinged room, with windows both front and back, as well as a small side window, with a view of the woods beyond. Like the kitchen window, they were all lead-paned, with simple iron lever handles and no locks on either of them. Maybe there was no need for security, given that the cottage was on private land, but she wouldn't have been happy there for long.

Eve went over to the front and looked out for a moment across the road to the fields opposite. It was a bleak, windswept landscape, with few trees, the ground rising steeply in the distance towards an iron-grey sky. The farmhouse where Melissa and Gavin lived was hidden from view, down in the dip on the other side of one of the hills, and there wasn't another house in sight. She was struck by the sense of isolation. It was just the sort of spot she would have chosen for herself, if she didn't have to live in London, but if you screamed, there was nobody around to hear.

'If it gets really cold, you'll want a fire,' Melissa said. 'The stove chucks out a good amount of heat once you get it going and if you need more logs, there's a small store at the back of the house. There are three bedrooms and a bathroom upstairs. I've put you in the biggest one. It's to the left, at the top of the stairs. You'll find clean towels in the cupboard in the bathroom.

Let me know if there's anything else you need.' Again, her manner was off-hand, as though she were just going through the motions.

Eve turned to face her. 'Thank you. It's very nice. What a shame I'm only going to be here a couple of days.' She forced a smile, which brought a momentary lightening of Melissa's expression. 'Gavin said you rent the cottage out?'

'Yes, mostly in the summer, when Marlborough College summer school is going on. The clientele is very demanding, I can tell you. It's been so successful the last couple of years, we're going to do up another couple of cottages on the estate to rent out. It's very nice to get some extra income towards all the bills.'

As she followed Melissa back into the hall, Harry appeared through the front door. His face was red from the cold and he was warmly dressed in a heavy, green waterproof jacket and flat cap.

'Morning, Eve,' he said, hurriedly wiping a pair of muddy boots on the mat. 'Sorry I'm early, but do you mind coming now? I've got to shoot off in half an hour to watch one of our horses.'

'Now's fine,' Eve replied.

'You'd better follow me, then.'

'I'll lock up and leave the key where I showed you,' Melissa said.

Harry trotted down the steps to where an ancient-looking, iron-grey Land Rover Defender was idling in the middle of the lane. A pair of dogs were jumping up and barking loudly in the back. He waited until Eve had collected her car, then took off down the track. In spite of the water-filled ruts and deep mud, he drove fast and she struggled to keep up. Eventually, the road dipped down a hill, around some trees, and they arrived at a huge concrete yard where several horse lorries were parked, all painted maroon, with the Westerby Racing logo on the sides. The complex of buildings was large and impressive, with several modern-looking barns grouped around a collection of older redbrick buildings. Harry pulled into a space outside a small, Victorian gabled house and she parked beside him.

'This is Grace's number,' he said, as Eve climbed out of her car. He handed her a folded piece of paper. 'According to Siobhan, she's married with two kids, now, but still living in the same village and still riding.'

'In racing?' It suddenly seemed a very small, enclosed world. Maybe once part of it, you never left.

He nodded. 'It's got one of the best training yards in the Republic, so it's impossible to avoid. I also called Fred Foxley first thing this morning. He remembers employing Holly Crowther for a few months after she left here, but that's about it. He has no idea where she went afterwards.'

'There must be employment records.'

Harry shook his head. 'I asked, but Fred said she just rode for him on an ad hoc basis and helped out with some of the breakers. He paid her in cash, which is not unusual in our business. He also said he was pretty sure she had another job going somewhere else at the same time.'

The wind was less strong down in the valley but the air was still icy and she wished she had brought warmer clothing. She put her hood up again, pulling it tight around her ears. 'And you don't remember the name of the other yard that asked you for a reference?'

He held her gaze for a moment, then said, 'If it's really that important, I suppose I can make a few calls later, if you like.'

'I'd be very grateful.'

'OK. But as I said last night, people move around a lot in our industry. It's easy come, easy go.' It was clear from his expression that he thought it a waste of time. 'Even if I do find out where she went after Fred's, she'll be long gone by now.'

'I understand.'

He gave a curt nod. 'The office is in here.'

He opened the front door of the house and led her through a hallway into a tiny room where four women of varying ages sat at a bank of desks in the middle, all on the telephone. The walls were papered with photographs and other racing memorabilia and a series of ancient-looking filing cabinets ran along one wall, stacked with various trophies and awards. In the cramped space, the noise and hum of voices was intense. She wondered how anybody could concentrate.

'We moved everything around after my father died, but this is where Jane used to work,' Harry said. 'As you can see, it's pretty hugger-mugger and people have to share desks. That's my office, through there.' He waved his hand towards a door at the back of the room. 'It used to be Father's office, when Jane was here. My flat's upstairs. Nothing like living above the shop, to keep you on your toes.'

'Did anyone here know Jane?'

He shook his head. 'Nobody's been here that long.'

'Do you mind if I look around outside?'

'If you like, I can give you a quick tour of the yards before I go.'

'I understand that Jane was last seen at a party here,' she said, following Harry back outside into the cold.

'That's right. The owners' Christmas party. We do it every year. Always the first weekend in December. My father started the tradition. We put up a marquee in the indoor school over there.' He pointed towards one of the huge barns in front of them, just as a small string of horses and riders clattered past, heading towards the open entrance.

'So what happens at one of these events?' she asked, her eyes stinging from the wind.

'It's really just a jolly for the clients, as well as potential new clients, with some family and friends thrown into the mix. It's always packed. Apart from the fun and games, the main purpose is to show off the new batch of yearlings we buy at the sales and sell shares in them.' He strode towards another group of buildings and she had to push herself to keep pace with him.

'How many people are we talking about?'

'It varies, but usually a good two hundred or so. There's a sit-down lunch after the yearling parade. We wine and dine them well and it goes on all afternoon. It can get very lively, if you get my drift.' He looked around at her. 'We've got one coming up tomorrow if you want to come and see what happens.'

'That would be helpful, thanks.' She felt an outsider in a very alien world and, ten years on, the trail was stone cold. But at least she could soak up the atmosphere and get a feel for what might have happened the day Jane disappeared.

'I understand Jane was helping out at the party.'

'We use outside caterers, but all our staff lend a hand.'

'But she was taken ill and went home early.'

'So I'm told.'

'Do you remember what happened? Who she talked to before that?'

He stopped in front of a high wall, which acted as a windbreak, and turned to face her, hands jammed in his pockets. His face looked ashen in the hard, grey light and the scar on his cheek was livid.

'Look,' he said, as though trying to choose his words carefully. 'I'd really like to help, particularly if Sean Farrell's innocent, but this was all a long time ago. I can barely recall what went on *last* year, let alone ten years ago.'

'But I imagine you gave a statement to the police at the time.'

'Yes, of course I did. We all did. Not that any of us could add much. Father was still alive and running the show then, but it's always a scrum. I'd have been tied up with clients the whole day. I really don't remember who was there and who wasn't. If you come along tomorrow, you'll get the picture. Also, my father died shortly afterwards and that was all any of us could think of for a long while. I'm afraid Jane's death paled in comparison.'

He clamped his mouth shut and she realized she would have to let the subject drop. She didn't care if she upset him, but she couldn't compel him to talk. Again, the timing of Tim Michaels' suicide struck her as an odd coincidence. She would speak to Gavin later and see if his recollection was any better. Harry turned away and started marching towards the group of older-looking buildings.

'That's Old Yard over there,' he said, striding through a wide arch, under a clock tower, into a large, cobbled quadrangle. It was framed on all four sides by stables, with windows and lofts above. The soft, red brick was weathered and the green-painted stable doors were peeling in places. Most of the occupants were tucked away out of sight, although she heard the odd whinny and the air was filled with the tang of hay and manure and their pungent smell, whichever way she turned. People were coming and going, some with forks and wheelbarrows, others busy sweeping and clearing the ground with leaf-blowers.

'Is it always so busy?' she asked, watching as a small, dark-skinned man tied up a chestnut horse outside a stable.

He turned to face her again, this time smiling. 'The flat season's over, but there's never a quiet time. We've got sixteen horses in training for the jump season, plus all the yearlings to break. Work in a racing yard never stops.'

'Where do you find your staff?' she asked, hearing two girls talking to one another in a foreign language she didn't recognize.

'My head lass, Siobhan, is from Tipperary, and several of the riders are also Irish, but a lot of the yard staff are Eastern European and Mr Singh, over there, is from Rajasthan. They all live on site in the hostel we built after my father died.'

'How many horses do you have?'

'In this yard, just over twenty. This is where it all started, back in the late nineteenth century. As you can see, it's pretty old-fashioned. That's one of the tack rooms.' He pointed towards a huge, half-open metal door, studded with rivets. 'People are always trying to steal stuff, so it's alarmed. We have three yards in total. This, and Armandio Yard, which you can see through there, are the oldest.' He pointed towards another arch opposite, with an almost identical quadrangle beyond. 'It's named after my great-grandfather's Grand National winner. There's also an American barn on the far side, which my father built just before he died, where most of the horses are housed.'

'It's all much bigger than I imagined,' she said, following quickly behind.

'It has to be. We have well over eighty horses here in peak season, mostly for flat racing, which is my passion, although I still look after several of my father's old National Hunt clients. The gallops are about half a mile away, up on the Downs. We're lucky to have several different surfaces, including an all-weather Polytrack, which we use depending on the time of year. My father spent a lot of money improving the facilities and they're as good as any in the UK.'

Although he was giving her the sales spiel, she saw genuine pride in his eyes. The office was just ahead of them and she realized the tour was nearly over.

'Just one quick question. Were you by any chance at Ascot last Saturday?'

He stopped and turned around. 'Last Saturday? Yes. I was with one of our new owners and his wife. Why?'

'Do you remember seeing this man?' She pulled out her phone and showed him a photograph of Mickey, which she had found on one of the dailies' websites. She had no idea how recent it was, but if the Met had released it to the press, it had to be relatively current.

Harry glanced at it, then shook his head. 'There were several thousand people there. Who is he?' His expression gave nothing away, but she had the feeling he was lying.

'Just someone who was doing some work on behalf of the charity helping with Sean Farrell's appeal. I'd also like to speak to a couple of former clients of yours, if possible. Lorne Anderson and Stuart Wade.'

He frowned. 'Why?'

'They both called Jane the week before she died.' It was more than she wanted to say, but she couldn't see any way around it.

'There could be any number of perfectly legitimate reasons why. Surely the police checked this out at the time?'

She shrugged. 'Perhaps. I don't know.'

He still looked sceptical. 'Lorne Anderson took his horses away when Father died, but Stuart Wade still has a few with me. I can speak to him, if you want, although I'm sure he talked to the police. Actually, better still, he's coming to the party tomorrow. I'll introduce you and you can ask him yourself.'

'How do I get hold of Lorne Anderson?'

'No idea. Sorry. Now, I really must press on.'

'I imagine it's a very expensive business owning a racehorse,' she said, keeping pace with him as he started marching towards the car park.

'It can be, although a lot of our clients choose to participate as part of a syndicate. It's basically like a partnership. The syndicates usually own two or more horses, so it's a way of spreading your bets, as well as getting all the fun of ownership at a fraction of the cost.'

'Were either Lorne Anderson or Stuart Wade members of a syndicate?'

He shook his head. 'No. They're both sole owners. They've got a lot of money to invest. Lorne was a successful venture capitalist – I imagine he still is. And Stuart's in property.'

'Are all of your clients wealthy businessmen?'

'Lord, no. They come from all sorts of backgrounds, from plumbers and farmers and shop-owners, to footballers, golfers and actors. Lots of people are into racing, you know.'

For Eve, the world of racing conjured up polar opposites: on the one hand, men attired in top hats and tailcoats and women in colourful outfits and ridiculous hats at Royal Ascot, the images sprayed across the front pages of the tabloids every June; on the other, the seedy betting shops, reeking of a mixture of stale cigarette smoke and alcohol, full of desperate old men, where she had been dragged by one of her mother's boyfriends on her way home from school. Like any walk of life, there were many versions of reality, she imagined.

The clock in the tower chimed the hour and Harry glanced at his watch. 'Damn thing's running slow again. I'm afraid I've really got to dash now.'

He had said all along he was short on time, but he now seemed in even more of a hurry. Whether it was the mention of Mickey or one of the Westerby clients, she couldn't tell, but she sensed discomfort. They were almost back at the office when a canary-yellow Lamborghini burst through the gap between the barns and screeched to a halt in the middle of the parking area. A girl jumped out, hip-hop blaring from the car speakers. Without even bothering to turn off the engine or close the driver's door, she strode towards them.

'Why won't you return my calls, Harry?' she shouted in a shrill, nasal voice, the accent strong Northern Irish. 'I've left shedloads of voicemails. I need to speak to you right *now*.'

She was tiny and skimpily dressed, in jeans, high-heeled ankle boots and a green satin bomber jacket, apparently oblivious to the cold.

Harry held up his hands, palms towards her, like a policeman stopping the traffic. 'Sorry, Stacey. It will have to wait.'

'It can't fuckin' wait.'

'Can't you see, I'm busy?'

'I don't care.'

'Well I do. As I said, *I'm busy*.' He glanced meaningfully towards Eve.

'When, then?'

'I'll call you later.'

She came right up to him and put her hands on her hips. 'You said that before. I *need* to speak to you. It's fuckin' urgent.' A mass of strawberry blonde curls framed her pretty, freckled face, but her eyes were red and swollen and it looked as though she had been crying.

'*Not now*. Eve here's with the police,' he said forcefully. A flicker of surprise crossed the girl's face and she glanced over at Eve, then back at Harry.

'What's goin' on?'

'Nothing that concerns you. We're busy discussing an old murder case, that's all. I've told you I'll call you later, and I shall. This afternoon. I promise.'

'You'd bloody well better. Otherwise there'll be trouble.'

'I promise.'

With a toss of her curls, she stomped off back to her car and, giving Harry a final, meaningful look over her shoulder, climbed in and slammed the door. The tyres squealed angrily as she turned on the tarmac.

Harry turned to Eve with an apologetic smile. 'Sorry about that.'

'She seemed very upset about something.'

'She's got herself in a spot of bother, that's all,' he said.

She held his gaze, intrigued, wondering what their relationship was. Stacey could easily have been his daughter. 'She didn't react well to hearing I was with the police.'

'Stacey's a jockey,' Harry said, by way of explanation. 'She's just a bit highly strung.'

'So I see. What does she want so badly with you?'

'I don't mean to be rude, Eve. But it's none of your business.'

'Nice car.' Eve made a mental note of the distinctive personal number plate as it disappeared from view. The car looked brand new. The latest model, worth a couple of hundred thousand pounds at least. 'She must be incredibly successful.'

'She's a decent jockey, but it's her boyfriend's. He's a jockey, or at least he used to be.'

'Would I have heard of him?'

'Probably.'

Eve looked at him inquiringly, amused that he was being so cagey, still wondering what lay behind it. 'So? Who is he?'

'You're very curious, aren't you?'

'Yes.'

'I suppose there's no harm in telling you.' He mentioned a name she recognized.

'She's very young. He's old enough to be her—'

'When has that ever stopped anybody,' he said sharply. 'Anyway, she's older than she looks and knows exactly what she's up to. Now, I really must go.'

She followed him to his car. 'Just one more thing. Would you be able to give me the names of the members of the Come What May syndicate?'

Harry stopped again and stared at her for a moment, one eyebrow raised, as though it was on the tip of his tongue to say something very rude. Then he cracked a smile. 'Look, Eve. There are forty people in that syndicate. You don't honestly think you can gain anything by talking to all of them?'

'I didn't realize there were so many. I told you, I know absolutely nothing about racing.'

His expression softened a fraction. 'Of course not. Why should you? I'm sorry to be in such a rush and I really do want to try and help.' He put his head a little to one side and gave her an appraising, provocative stare. 'Look, why don't we have dinner this evening, if you're free? We'll have more time and you can then ask me whatever else you want. OK?'

# NINETEEN

It was nearly lunchtime and Marlborough's broad High Street was buzzing with activity. The lamp posts were festooned with unlit Christmas decorations in the shape of swans and the pavements below were crowded with shoppers. It appeared to be market day, the centre of the road occupied by a long line of stalls selling all manner of things from cheeses and other farm produce, to ornamental plants, Christmas wreaths, and fancy wicker baskets and dog beds. A queue of cars inched along on both sides of the street, some drivers holding up the traffic as they tried to find parking spaces, others gawping through their windows at the goods on display. It took Eve a while before she eventually found a parking space near the church at the far end, close to the Rising Sun. She got out, put on her jacket, and made her way slowly along the pavement, skirting around the little knots of mothers with pushchairs and groups of uniformed school children, who were gathered chatting outside the various cafés and shops.

A young man stood behind the till of the Blue Cross charity shop, sorting through some items of jewellery in a display case. She asked to see the manager, explaining that she was looking for Annie. He disappeared for a moment into a room at the back, then re-emerged, along with a middle-aged woman, who joined him at the counter.

'You came in yesterday, didn't you? I'm sorry but Annie isn't in today. Can I help?'

'It's personal. Is there any way I can get in touch?'

'If you leave me your name and phone number, I'll give her the message.'

'I'm only here for a couple of days,' Eve said, as the woman wrote down her number. 'So it's pretty urgent.'

'Can I say what it's about?' the woman asked.

'Just tell her it's about Jane McNeil.' There was no reaction in the woman's eyes to the name. Most likely she was new to the area. Marlborough was a small town and it was unlikely such a murder would be forgotten, even after ten years.

'Anything else?' the woman asked, as she scribbled the name down on the piece of paper.

'Say it's to do with Sean Farrell's appeal.'

As Eve repeated the name, the woman looked up. 'You know, I've heard that name before. There was a man in here about a week ago, asking for Annie. I'm sure he mentioned that name, or something very similar.'

'Can you describe him?'

'I'm sorry, I didn't really notice. We were quite busy at the time.'

Eve pulled the photo of Mickey out of her bag and held it up. 'Is this him?'

The woman peered at it short-sightedly, then nodded. 'I think so. He left a business card with me. He was some sort of private investigator. I passed it onto Annie when I saw her, but I've no idea if she called him back.'

Eve walked out of the shop and down the high street towards her car, wondering if Mickey had managed to speak to Annie, and if Dan had known about it, and had kept it from her for some reason. She was due to meet Gavin at two thirty at the cottage. She bought a coffee and a bacon and avocado sandwich from a café, went back to her car and switched on the engine, turning the fan up high to get rid of the mist of condensation that clouded the front window. She called the number Harry had given her for Grace Byrne but it went straight through to voice-mail and she left a message. As she reached for her coffee, her phone rang. The number on the screen was withheld.

'Just getting back to you about the Mickey Fraser case.' DCI Andy Fagan's deep voice crackled distantly over his hands-free. It sounded as though he was in his car, driving, or being driven, somewhere through the London traffic. 'I tried calling you a couple of times.'

Even over the phone, she could tell he was chewing gum, which had replaced a lifetime of smoking Silk Cuts. She pictured the perennially weary look on his pudgy face, the creased suit, the crumpled tie, spotted with yesterday's lunch. With three children under the age of five, and a wife who worked, she had no idea how he kept it all together.

'I'm not in London,' she said. 'There's next-to-no signal where I am at the moment.'

'Lucky you! It would be nice to be out of range for a few days. So what's your involvement in all of this, Eve?'

'Mickey Fraser worked as a freelance PI for the charity 4Justice. You've talked to Dan Cooper and I understand he filled you in about the Sean Farrell case, which has been referred to the CCRC—'

'I know all that,' Fagan cut in. 'What I don't get is, what's *your* angle?'

'I'm just helping out on an ad hoc basis, while I wait for my disciplinary hearing. It's better than sitting at home doing nothing.' It sounded weak, but it was the only explanation Fagan might buy.

There was silence for a moment, then Fagan sighed. 'Look, I'm really sorry about what's happened to you, Eve. It sounds like they've made a right cock-up. I just wanted you to know that you have my full support, whatever it's worth. Hopefully, they can sort it all out and you can get back to work, but if there's anything at all I can do to help, or you just fancy a drink and a chinwag at any point, you just let me know. OK?'

The warmth in his voice touched her. He wasn't the first of

her work colleagues to offer support and express his condemn-
ation for the way things had been handled. It was the main thing
that had kept her going since Jason's shooting. Not that it would
make any difference at the hearing.

'Thank you. I hope so too. Meantime, I need to know if you think
there's any link between Mickey's death and the Sean Farrell case.'

There was another pause and she heard the shriek of a car
horn over the phone, then Fagan said, 'You really think Sean
Farrell's innocent and there's a murderer walking free?'

'I've no idea. The best I can say for the moment is that, from
what I've read, the trial process looks flawed. The scientific
evidence was also inconclusive and, in my view, there are good
grounds, ten years on, for retesting the exhibits. Unfortunately,
the local police aren't being cooperative.'

'OK. Knowing you, I'm sure you're right. But I've spoken to
someone at Wiltshire Police and they put me in touch with the
Senior Investigating Officer who was running the investigation
at the time. He's retired now. It probably doesn't mean that much,
but he still seems to be well regarded. The bottom line is, he's
absolutely one hundred per cent sure they got the right man.'

'Of course he is,' Eve said flatly. Every cop she'd ever known
would declare he was a hundred per cent sure he'd put the right
man in jail, at least in public, or to his fellow officers. There was
too much professional pride at stake in a successful conviction,
especially a high-profile one. Even in the face of blinding evidence
to the contrary, some SIOs still refused to admit that they had
got it wrong.

Fagan laughed. 'Fair enough. I don't know the man and I'm
not ruling anything out at this stage. I'm happy to tell you where
we are, if you keep it to yourself. You know Mickey Fraser used
to be with the Met?'

'Yes.'

'I've checked him out and, personal problems aside, he was
apparently a good detective. He had a handful of cases on the go
apart from the 4Justice investigation, although most are pretty
run-of-the-mill stuff. We're chasing down all the leads, but so far
there's nothing out of the ordinary, apart from the Sean Farrell
case. However, Fraser's personal life was pretty colourful. He was
gay, into BDSM, and happy to pay for it. There was quite a lot

of traffic in and out of his flat, from what the neighbours say, and it seems he preferred them young. It's possible somebody got a bit over-keen, or maybe tried to extract some extra cash.'

'What about forensics?'

'Poor old Mickey wasn't great at housework. The place is awash with all manner of human DNA. Nothing useful's turned up so far.'

Fagan's tone was matter-of-fact and she couldn't read anything into it. 'So what do you think happened?'

'Difficult to say at the moment. According to the post-mortem report, he was beaten about quite a bit while he was still alive, but cause of death's a broken neck. They used plastic ties to bind him and a strip of the bed sheet as a ligature. There's no sign of sexual activity, although we found traces of cocaine all over the flat. My first impression, for what it's worth, is that it all has an improvised feel, rather than something pre-meditated.'

'I heard the flat had been ransacked.'

'Could be someone trying to make it look like a burglary, or searching for cash, or valuables. His phone and wallet and laptop were all gone. As far as we can tell, there wasn't much else of any value in the flat.'

She picked up a vagueness in his tone, as though he was trying to play things down, for some reason. 'Any idea when he was killed?'

'Monday, around teatime, we think. The neighbour on the ground floor heard some funny noises coming from below, when her kids got home from school. A witness has come forward, who lives further down the street, who saw someone come out of the basement around seven p.m., when she was on her way home. Unfortunately, it was dark and she didn't get a good look at the face, but the general description is of a youngish male, thin, not particularly tall, dressed in jeans, white trainers and a baggy, dark-coloured hoodie. She said he shot out of there like he was on fire, with his head right down, and ran off towards the Tube. He had some sort of a rucksack, she thought. We're checking all the cameras in the area and at the Tube station, as well as Fraser's call log, but nothing so far. We don't know who the boy is, as yet, but at least we have a better idea of the timeline.'

'Sounds like you think the killer was someone he knew, and nothing to do with the Sean Farrell case?'

Fagan sighed. 'Look, I'm keeping an open mind, but a ten-year-old case, with a guy in jail? What are the odds?'

Again she had the feeling that he was playing things down. 'So this puts Dan Cooper in the clear?'

'So it appears. His alibi checks out for the time in question, anyway, and there's no obvious motive. But he was the last person Fraser called from his phone, according to the O2 phone log. Fraser tried three times, in fact, between around two p.m. and four p.m. on the Monday, but Cooper didn't pick up. Do you have any idea why Fraser would be wanting to talk to Cooper so urgently?'

'Sorry, I don't,' she said, thinking back to her various conversations with Dan, wondering why he hadn't mentioned it.

'Cooper says his phone was out of juice and Fraser didn't leave a voicemail. Cooper also says he has no idea what the calls were about, but that Mickey probably wanted some more money. Is Cooper a friend of yours?'

'No. I've only met him twice, both times to do with the Sean Farrell case.'

Fagan gave a loud sniff. 'Do you think he's reliable?'

She hesitated. It was an odd question and she wondered what lay behind it. Apart from the recent brief episode of evasiveness, Dan had come across as relatively straight, at least in his dealings with her. But whether he had been totally honest with Fagan's team was another matter. 'I'd say he's pretty switched on, but he's a bit of an idealist. He's also under a lot of pressure. The charity's short of money and from the little I've gathered, his personal life's a mess and he has a drink problem. Whether he's telling you everything about what Mickey was up to, I can't say. I'm not sure if he's been totally honest with me either, but I have no concrete evidence to the contrary.'

'So you wouldn't know if he found anything in Mickey Fraser's flat when he was there, something he might be keeping to himself, perhaps?'

'What sort of thing?' she asked, curious that Fagan had reached the same conclusion.

Fagan sighed even more heavily this time. 'OK, Eve. There's something perhaps you should know. We've gone through all the papers strewn around the flat and put the files back together, but we found absolutely nothing to do with the Sean Farrell case, no file, no documents, no papers, not even an expense receipt, nada, which is very odd. He may have been shit as a housekeeper, but Fraser kept files on all of his cases, both current and old, and like the good cop he was, he was meticulous about his paperwork. So there ought to be a file for the Sean Farrell case, right? It was the biggest thing he was working on at the time. But we can't find one. We've been through Fraser's car, the rubbish, which luckily hadn't been collected yet, plus every other place we could think of, but sweet F.A. so far. Do you think Cooper took the file, for some reason? Is there something to do with the investigation he's trying to hide?'

Eve thought back again to her conversation with Dan two nights before. At the time, she could have sworn he was keeping something from her, but why would he take the file? Surely he must know what was in it.

'I don't know,' she said, after a moment. 'I honestly can't think what it might be. But then again, if Mickey's death was to do with his personal life, or someone trying to rob him, why would the killer bother to go through his files, and why take that one? Dan said they'd been thrown all over the floor.'

'Maybe Cooper made the mess in the flat and took the file to muddy the tracks.'

'I just can't see why he'd do that. At least, as far as I'm aware, there's nothing that 4Justice would want to conceal. They're a charity. What they do is above board.'

'I suppose so,' he said thoughtfully. 'But one thing I'm more or less sure of, there must have been a file. So either Cooper took it, or the killer did. If it's the latter, it means the Sean Farrell case isn't as dead as we think. Either way, I think you should be careful, Eve.'

# TWENTY

As Eve drove back along the drive to the cottage, she noticed a pale blue Mini parked in the middle of the lane outside. An elderly woman stood at the top of the steps in the front garden, shielding her eyes and peering in through one of the front windows. She was smartly dressed in a long, cherry-red coat and a silk scarf at her neck. Eve's first thought was that she was collecting for charity.

Eve parked in the side cut and as she walked back towards the cottage with her small bag of food shopping, the woman turned to face her.

'Are you Eve?' she called out in a shrill voice.

'Yes,' Eve replied, climbing the steps towards her.

'I'm Sally Michaels, Melissa and Harry's mother.'

Eve stopped on the step just below where she was standing and held out her hand. It wasn't taken. Sally was small and slim, with short, reddish-blonde hair, her face an older, harder, more heavily made-up version of Melissa's, with the same pale skin and large blue eyes, her expression equally unwelcoming.

'I've just got back from London. Melissa tells me you're staying here, something to do with Jane McNeil's murder. Is that right?' She was peering at Eve curiously, and Eve wondered what Melissa had said about her.

'Just for a couple of days, that's all.'

'I understand you're an old friend of Gavin's.'

'Yes.' Eve felt a few drops of icy rain on her face. 'Look, do you want to come in?'

'No, I do not. I came to tell you you're wasting your time. Sean Farrell's as guilty as they come.'

She was taken aback by the ferocity of Sally's tone and wondered what lay behind it. 'It's quite possible he is guilty.'

Sally's eyes opened wide as though she had been expecting a different response and her mouth sagged open. 'Why are you here then?' She waved a leather-gloved hand in the air. 'What's the point in dredging it all up again?'

'Just checking up on a few things, that's all.'

'But you think he's innocent, don't you?'

'No. I haven't come to any view, as yet.'

Sally stared hard at her. 'But you're looking for evidence to *prove* that he's innocent, aren't you? If so, you certainly won't find that here.'

'Maybe not. And I'm not looking for anything specifically. I'm trying to keep an *open* mind.'

Again Sally looked as though she had been prepared for more of an argument. It was the truth, after all, not that she owed Sally Michaels anything or had any intention of discussing things with her on the doorstep, let alone having an argument. Why it mattered so much to her, was another question.

Eve heard the sound of another car in the lane and, as she turned, saw a black Audi estate pull up behind Sally's car.

'Well, don't go causing any trouble,' Sally said sharply. 'We had enough of that last time.'

Not waiting for a reply, she pushed past Eve and marched down the stairs, just as Gavin got out of the Audi. With little more than a nod in his direction, Sally climbed into the Mini and drove away at speed.

'I see you've met my mother-in-law,' he said grinning as he came up the steps to where Eve was standing. 'Did I catch her being rude to you?'

'She basically warned me off, told me to mind my own business. She's convinced Sean Farrell's guilty and I'm just here to stir things up.'

'In more ways than one,' he said, still smiling broadly. 'Nicely so, I mean. Pay no attention to her. She has her head in the clouds most of the time.'

'She seemed very emotional about it.'

He nodded slowly. 'She means well, but she never really got over the shock of Tim's death and everything that followed. The discovery of Jane's body came almost immediately afterwards and she bitterly resented being questioned, and all of the police stuff and people trampling over the estate, when she was trying to grieve. I guess she can't face going through it again.'

If that was all, Eve had some sympathy for Sally, although it still wasn't good enough. Maybe she was being hard-hearted, but it was ten years on. Why was it still such a live issue? How many people would rather an innocent man be left to rot in jail – if that's what Sean was – than have the past raked up? It wasn't as though Jane had been Sally's daughter.

'Are you ready to go?' Gavin asked.

'I've just got a few things to put away in the fridge. Do you want to come in?'

He shook his head. 'I'll wait for you in the car.'

Five minutes later, she climbed in beside him. The car was warm, Classic FM playing on the radio.

'Where do you want to go?' he asked. 'I've done everything I needed to do today, so I'm at your disposal.'

'Could you give me a quick guided tour of the estate? I want to get a feel for the geography. I'd also like to see where Jane's car was left. It was in a pub car park south of Marlborough. I'd also like to go to the West Woods, where her body was found.'

'The West Woods are pretty big.'

'I've maps of the specific locations.'

He stared at her for a moment, as though he found it all a bit peculiar. 'Of course. If you think it will help. I imagine such things are normal to you, with what you do.'

'Yes.'

He put the car into gear and they drove away down the hill towards the stable yard. 'Did Harry show you around this morning?'

'He did. He was a bit pushed for time, but I get the general picture. He seemed very proud of the facilities.'

'The Michaels have been here for four generations. It's amazing, really, that it's survived this long. I wonder if either of my boys will want to get involved when they grow up.'

'Maybe they'll take after you.'

He smiled, but made no reply. She picked up a wistfulness in his manner and wondered what lay behind it and what ambitions he had for his children and if any of it concerned Westerby Racing. Perhaps he and Melissa didn't see eye to eye, or was she imagining things?

They drove up a steep hill and through fields on either side, with woods in the distance. Apart from a couple of cottages and a few barns, there was little sign of human habitation.

'Do you remember Jane?'

'Vaguely, more because of what happened than anything else. I was working in London during the week. I rarely ever went over to the office, unless it was to find Tim or Melissa.'

'What was Jane like?'

'Quiet and serious, from the little I remember, but I don't think I ever really spoke to her much. As you know, she was living in the cottage you're in now, with a couple of other girls. My only real memory of her was when they had a barbeque one evening in the summer, with some of the lads from the yard, and made too much noise. Tim got very cross and was threatening to sack them all on the spot. I had to go over and calm things down and tell everyone to go home. She seemed quite sober and together, compared to the rest of them and I got the impression she wasn't enjoying herself very much.'

They came to a small junction where he pulled up momentarily. The gates were in the middle of a small clump of trees, with neat post-and-rail fencing marking the perimeter. She could just make out the road beyond, with more bare, rolling hills sweeping upwards to the empty horizon.

'That's the back entrance over there, so you get your bearings, but the West Woods are in the other direction. It'll be easier to go out the front.'

'I understand people used to cut through here ten years ago,' she said, as a car zoomed past on the main road.

'Yes, there was nothing to stop them then. Tim didn't mind, but Harry put up barriers everywhere. I don't blame him for wanting more privacy, although there are bridleways and public footpaths all over the farm, which he can't control. But he's forever changing the gate security codes without telling anyone, which is a bit of a pain for those of us who sometimes have to catch an early train to London from Swindon.'

'Is he worried about security?'

'Some farm machinery and bits and pieces went missing from one of the barns a few times, but I think he's just territorial.'

The estate was larger than she had imagined and the road wound up and down over the hills, with wooden-railed gallops just visible in the distance near the top. The sky was heavy with cloud and it all had a windblown, desolate feel. It was also that time of year when everything looked grey and muddy and at its worst. The shortest day of the year was just over two weeks away and she felt the weight of so much unrelenting darkness for a moment.

Eventually they passed the turning to the farmhouse and came to the main entrance on the Marlborough side, where Gavin stopped the car again.

'Show me exactly where you want to go.'

She pulled the maps Dan had given her out of her bag and passed them to him. He studied them for a moment, then said, 'OK. The pub's about ten minutes away, off the Pewsey road. But it'll be getting dark soon, so we should go to the West Woods first.'

A freezing rain started to spatter the car as they crossed over the A4 and headed south over a small river and along narrow lanes through a couple of villages and open farmland.

'The woods are just up here,' he said. 'There are several ways in, I seem to remember. But I think we'll head for the main car park. It will be more sheltered there and probably quicker on foot to where you want to go.'

He turned off the lane onto a muddy track and almost immediately they were in the woods. The trees were tall, thickly planted on either side, and the high evergreen canopy cut out much of the remaining light. A minute later, the pine trees faded into a mixture of evergreen and bare, deciduous trees, and they came to a large clearing surrounded by huge beeches, the area underneath dotted with wooden picnic benches and tables. They pulled up alongside a couple of parked cars, but there was nobody in sight.

They got out and Gavin changed his shoes for a pair of wellingtons from the back of the car and put on a heavy waterproof jacket. 'Last time I was here, the bluebells were out. It looked absolutely amazing. Just a sea of violet everywhere, and sunlight. It must have been late April, or early May.'

'I prefer it like this,' she said. 'I imagine it's full of people in spring and summer.'

'And endless, bloody dogs.' He zipped up his coat and, glancing over at her, caught her shivering. 'You're going to freeze, dressed like that. Do you want to put my coat around you?'

'No. I'm OK. Don't worry.'

He looked at her as though she were mad. 'Are you sure you want to do this?'

A biting gust of wind blew her hair into her face and she could feel the cold through her jacket, but now she was there, she didn't want to give up. 'Really, I'm fine. I'll warm up once we start walking.'

He shrugged. 'Up to you.'

She sensed his reluctance. Given the weather, it was a lot to ask and no doubt he'd rather be tucked up in front of a fire somewhere. She consulted Dan's map, getting her bearings.

'It's this way, I think,' she said, pointing towards a wide track that led away uphill. 'Are you sure you want to come? I'm happy to go alone, if you don't mind waiting for me in the car.'

He shook his head and smiled. 'No. I'm more than happy to keep you company. It just seems such a strange thing to be doing, that's all.'

She realized it must be very odd for him to walk around some deserted woods in the middle of the afternoon, with someone he hadn't seen for twenty years, trying to find the spot where a murdered woman had been found. But for her, it was as normal as breathing. She needed to get a feel for the place. Ten years on, at almost the same time of year to the day, it probably looked little different. But the trail was cold and any traces of evidence long gone. The lack of freshness and immediacy was something she had never had to deal with in her years at the Met. It all felt incredibly distant. For a moment, she wondered if she were mad to have agreed to take on Farrell's case. It was also strange to be there with Gavin. He was part of a different world. Only a few days back, she would never have imagined that she would see him again, let alone that she would be doing something like this with him, particularly after everything that had happened between them.

They walked in silence for a while, following the series of tracks and bridleways marked out on Dan's map. The route was up and down, the ground soft and slippery beneath the thick carpet of decaying leaves. The air was bitingly cold but at least the trees offered some protection from the wind. She saw a couple of people out riding in the distance. Somewhere a man called and whistled to a dog. Otherwise they were alone, the only sounds coming from the crunching of twigs beneath their feet and the soft drip of moisture through the branches above. Eventually, they joined a bridle path and came to the point that Dan had circled on the map. Although it was a blown-up version of the local Ordnance Survey map, it still wasn't very detailed. According to Peters' report, Jane McNeil's body had been found about twenty metres off the bridleway, in a north-easterly direction. It had been concealed next to a small brook or gulley, under a pile of leaves, up against a fallen tree. The general picture had prob-ably changed little in the intervening years, but the specifics had done. The dead tree would have been removed and chopped for wood long ago, and others had fallen since. Without any other distinguishing features, let alone police tape to help guide her to the scene, it was impossible to know where the exact spot had been. The only observation she could make was that the killer had chosen a location well off the beaten track.

She pulled out her phone, wondering if there was some way to get a better reading of the location, but there was no signal. In a way, it didn't matter. Although tyre tracks had been found in the muddy ground near the body, both from a 4x4 vehicle and a couple of off-road motorbikes, it wasn't clear who had made them, or when. Even if Jane had gone there willingly, why bring her all this way to kill her? She agreed with the conclusion of the original investigation; it wasn't a place of execution. The woods had been just the dumpsite. The question was why there. They were more or less in the centre of the woods. Assuming that the killer had driven to the woods with Jane's body, either parking in one of the lanes on the perimeter, or in the car park, it would still have been quite a trek. Lugging a five-feet-five, hundred-and-ten-pound dead woman that distance, over that terrain, without being observed, was no mean feat. Perhaps the killer had managed to drive into the woods, skirting around the various heavy barriers she had noticed along the way. She also wondered if the killer had deliberately brought the petrol with them, or if it was an afterthought. Maybe, as the police had initially suspected, the killer had had an accomplice. Perhaps they hoped the body would never be found, or at least not until the spring, or even several years later. One thing was clear, the choice of location showed local knowledge and her gut feel was that the killer was someone Jane knew.

High up in the trees birds were calling to one another and she heard the rasping alarm of a blackbird, along with something else she didn't recognize. It was only mid-afternoon but the woods were already filled with a murky half-light.

'What are you thinking?' Gavin asked, from behind her.

She had forgotten he was there and turned around. He was standing a few metres back, under the dripping branches of a tree, watching her. His hair was dark from the rain and he looked pale and cold, chin tucked into the zipped-up collar of his jacket, hands deep in his pockets.

'Just that somebody knew these woods and went to a lot of trouble to hide Jane's body. I think they were very unlucky she was found so quickly.'

'Is this where it happened?'

'No. I'm sure she was killed somewhere else and brought here.'

He looked grave and shook his head slowly. 'It doesn't bear thinking about. I feel incredibly sad for poor Jane and her family all over again. But if you've seen enough, we'd better get going. It's going to be dark very soon and we'll have trouble finding our way out.'

# TWENTY-ONE

Zofia's bath was on the short side for someone of Dan's height – or anyone over average height – and it was as narrow as a coffin. The bath water wasn't as hot as he would have liked either, and there wasn't much of it. But it was all that was on offer, short of going to the local swimming pool and taking a shower there. Convenience was everything, after the day he'd had.

He had spent the morning with a group of law students at UCL, who were setting up an innocence project that might provide 4Justice with additional free research support. It was through the law faculty that Kristen had originally come across Zofia. In Kristen's absence, he was developing a good rapport with one of the female lecturers, who seemed interested in working together. Even though the students would need a great deal of supervision and he had the strong suspicion that the woman fancied him, which wasn't reciprocated, he badly needed help with sifting through all the potential new cases that were coming in. It was a laborious process. Many were hopeless from the start, not meeting the basic criteria that the charity had set out for applications. These could be thrown out straight away. But others required more work – often a great deal of work – before it was possible to assess whether or not it was worth spending further time and resources looking into them in greater depth. If a case passed this hurdle, the charity's advisory panel of experts would then review it, looking for the holes in the prosecution case and usually the holes in the defence that might be filled by proper research and expert input. If they agreed that a case had merit, it would then be taken on. This all took manpower and time – neither of which he had.

That afternoon he had been hunched over his desk back in his office, reviewing two cases that had been shortlisted from the latest bunch of no-hopers. Neither looked particularly compelling at first glance, but he still had to go through the motions and put together a considered response to the men's solicitors. He had already told himself that, with Kristen gone, he would have to cut right back on the number of cases he took on. He had a few journalistic contacts who were prepared to lend a hand from time to time, but without Kristen, it wasn't enough. Whilst he still believed, with all his heart, in the importance of the work 4Justice did, he had run through most of his savings and he couldn't carry the weight of it much longer on his own. They either needed a serious cash injection, or they would be forced to fold.

His shoulders and back were stiff and aching from the worry of it all and his head was spinning. Zofia was out somewhere, supposedly checking on how things were going with the attempt to hack into Mickey's memory stick, so at least he wouldn't be disturbed. He slid down in the bath until the water was lapping his chin, knees uncomfortably out in the cold, feet jammed under the taps. The light bulb that hung from the centre of the ceiling was covered in a pink gingham shade that was turning brown at the edges. The towels were also pink and fluffy, and bottles of bath oil and candles were dotted around the room on every available surface. He found it difficult to imagine Zofia lying in the bath, surrounded by a sea of scent and candlelight, let alone choosing anything pink. Maybe there was a hidden, soft, girlie side to her that he had missed, deeply repressed beneath the usually humourless, no-nonsense attitude and uniform of black. Thinking about it, it was almost kinky, like finding bondage gear beneath a nurse's starched uniform, except the other way around. A tumbler of ice-cold vodka, still viscous and sweet, sat reassuringly on the little wooden stool next to the bath, along with his phone. He closed his eyes, let his mind zone out. For a moment, he was back in the bathroom in Kristen's flat. Her bath was big enough for two and he imagined her coming in, peeling off her clothes and slipping in with him.

The ring of his phone brought him back to the present. He peered over the edge of the bath, glanced down at the screen and saw Mickey's name. He sat up, sending a wave of water splashing onto the old lino. Mickey Fraser, in stark white letters. It really was Mickey's number. Was it a joke? Then he remembered that Mickey's phone was missing, apparently stolen by the killer from his flat. He grabbed a towel off the rail above, hurriedly wiped his fingers and reached for the phone. But as he answered, the call was cut. For a moment, he wondered if he had been hallu-cinating. But the glass of vodka was still half full and it was his first that day. He checked the recent call log. Mickey's name was definitely there. For a brief, unreal moment, he thought again that he'd gone mad and that Mickey wasn't actually dead. Then he refocussed. He grabbed the vodka and took a large swig. Who has Mickey's phone and why were they trying to contact him? Was it the police, or Mickey's killer, or someone else? He took another gulp and emptied the glass, wondering if whoever it was would call back, but the phone stayed silent. Maybe his number had been dialled by mistake, but it meant that Mickey's phone was switched on somewhere. He opened his call log and pressed Mickey's name.

He expected the phone to be switched off, but it rang several times. Then a man answered.

'Yes?' The voice was deep and gruff. From the intonation, Dan could tell he was foreign.

He heard music in the background, something electronic, with a thudding beat.

'You called my phone just now. From Mickey Fraser's phone.'

There was breathing at the other end, then the man said, 'Wait.'

Muffled sounds followed, like a pocket call, with distant, inaudible voices. Then silence.

'Hello. *HELLO*. My name's Dan Cooper. You called my number.'

There was crackling at the other end, men talking in a language he didn't recognize. He heard the music again, then another voice.

'You Dan? You friend of Mickey?' It was very different in tone to the previous man's, younger and higher in pitch, but with a similar, thick accent.

'Yes. My name's Dan Cooper. I was a friend of Mickey's.'

'He tell me your name. I am Mickey's friend too. My name is Hassan.'

'Why do you have Mickey's phone? Why are you calling me?' Silence.

'Mickey's dead.'

There was another long pause, then the man said, 'I know. I am very sad. I need to talk with you.'

# TWENTY-TWO

'What will you have?' Gavin asked.

'Soda, ice and lemon, please.'

'Nothing stronger?'

Eve shook her head. 'I don't drink alcohol anymore.'

He looked at her enquiringly, then nodded, as though it was yet another strange thing about her to take in, and turned away towards the bar.

They were in the Bargeman's Rest free house, by the Kennet and Avon canal, where Jane McNeil's car had been found ten years before, tucked away in a corner of the car park. It was a picturesque spot overlooking the water. She imagined it would be packed with tourists in summer, although with the dark-brown stretch of canal outside and lack of greenery and flowers around it, it looked a little bleak and uninviting at this time of year. From the report Peters had given her, the police had formed no theory as to why the car had been left there, other than that Jane must have driven it herself. No fingerprints, other than hers and Farrell's, had been found inside it. The pub had changed hands twice in the intervening period and the woman behind the bar, who had a strong Geordie accent, said she'd only worked there for six months and had no knowledge about what had happened ten years before, nor knew anyone who did.

Gavin returned a few minutes later with their drinks. Seeing him walk across the room towards her, Eve was struck again by how extraordinarily handsome he was. She could see it objectively now, not coloured by complex teenage emotions, and was amused to watch as heads, both female and male, turned involuntarily in his direction as he crossed the room. He was heart-stoppingly beautiful. That was the right word for it. He should have been an actor, not a politician, she thought.

'Any particular reason you don't drink anymore?' he asked, sitting down opposite her.

There was no edge to the words, nothing more than a polite inquiry. Unlike so many people, Gavin said what he meant. His directness and lack of side had been one of the many things she had liked about him. Most people assumed she was a reformed alcoholic, which didn't bother her. But something about Gavin invited frankness, particularly in the bizarre situation they found themselves in. It was as though reality was suspended. She had to be on her guard not to give away too much. She had no desire to explain that, when he knew her, alcohol had been a means of escape from her 'demons', as Dr Blake, one of her psychotherapists, had called them, a man very fond of clichés. Later, she had tried all sorts of other mind-altering substances in the hope of blotting out the memories, but the release was temporary and, if anything, it made it all so much worse. The past became even more vivid and present and terrible. Sobriety was the only thing that seemed to work and make the shadows recede for a while.

'I found alcohol didn't suit me, that's all.' She met his gaze, hoping he wouldn't probe further. Alcohol had also been her only means of developing a relationship with him, allowing her to go far further than she might otherwise have done with what she had viewed at the time purely as an experiment.

He smiled good-naturedly and picked up his pint. 'Fair enough.'

'Can I ask you something, Gavin?'

'You can ask me anything. Anything at all.'

'Why did Tim Michaels commit suicide?'

He coughed, stared at her hard for a moment, then put his glass firmly on the table.

'Sorry, Eve. I really wasn't expecting that.'

The question was perhaps a little blunt and maybe he wasn't

comfortable discussing the Michaels family, but she decided to press ahead. If he wouldn't talk to her, who would?

'I need to check every possible angle.'

He raised his eyebrows, looking almost pained. 'Tim's death is an *angle*?'

She shrugged. 'I don't know.'

He wiped the back of his mouth with his hand and sat back in his chair. 'I guess I can tell you, if that's what you really want. If you think it will help.' Again he hesitated.

'If you don't mind.'

'OK. From what I know, Tim suffered from depression most of his adult life. He was a difficult man to be with at the best of times. He was a perfectionist and very exacting, some would say hard, on both himself and those around him. We only found out after his death he'd been having money problems for several years.'

'You surprise me.'

'I don't know the ins and outs, but racing's a fickle business and you're only as good as your latest results. He'd overspent on upgrading the facilities and then he had a few bad seasons, coupled with a run of bad luck generally, and clients started taking horses away. They said he'd lost his touch. As you've gathered, the family's been in racing for several generations and there's a lot at stake, not least personal pride. For him, a life outside racing was not worth living. Also, I guess he couldn't cope with the idea that he might be the one to lose it all.'

'What about the estate? Surely it's worth a lot of money, even if the business wasn't going well? He could have sold it, or rented it out, couldn't he?'

'Not an option. He'd have seen it as a complete failure and disgrace. Racing really was everything to him. Nothing else mattered. When he died, he left a load of debts and we discovered the property was heavily mortgaged. Luckily, Harry and Melissa managed to sell off quite a lot of land and some cottages and turn things around gradually, but it was a very difficult time.'

She looked at him, surprised. It was a very different picture to how it appeared from the outside, or at least to how Harry had briefly painted it that morning, although ten years was a long time.

'But it's OK now?'

'It appears to be. I'm not sure how good Harry is as a trainer, but unlike Tim he's great at schmoozing the clients, which goes a long way in this business.'

'Were you close to Tim?'

He shook his head. 'He wasn't a man who was close to anybody. He also didn't approve of Melissa and me getting married.'

'Really?'

He sighed. 'He thought we were too young, for starters. But the main reason was, I guess, he dreamed of his only daughter marrying someone very different, someone who understood and fitted in to his world.'

'Why does that matter?'

He smiled. 'The racing world's a bubble. If you're in it, it's all-encompassing. It's *all* that's important. It's difficult for anybody like you or me, on the outside, to understand.'

She felt instantly sorry for Gavin, a man who, in every respect, should be a son-in-law to be proud of. Then she rebuked herself. He didn't need her pity, although maybe it explained his decision to go into politics. Perhaps he was trying to show the Michaels, or the world around them, that he was good enough. At least Melissa went up in her estimation several notches, for standing up for what she wanted. Or maybe, like most women where Gavin was concerned, she just couldn't help herself.

'Take Harry, for instance,' he continued. 'Both his marriages failed because the women couldn't hack it, or didn't want to. It's quite typical, from what I hear.'

'Going back to Tim, were there any doubts about the verdict?'

Gavin frowned. 'Suicide, you mean? No. I don't think so. Tim left a note. Harry found it beside his body. It wasn't entirely coherent, but from what I understand, it was all to do with the money problems and his shame.'

'You saw the note?'

'No.'

'But Melissa did?'

'Honestly, I don't know. If she did, she never said.'

'But she accepted the verdict? There was nothing open to question?'

He looked troubled, as though a dark cloud had passed across his face. 'I assume not. I mean, it was a difficult time. We didn't really talk about it.'

What he said seemed so odd. Surely he should know everything Melissa had been thinking and feeling? Wasn't that what marriage was supposed to be about, the sharing of everything, your worries, your fears and deepest secrets? It was another good reason to avoid it, she had always thought. There was a large part of herself that she would never disclose to anyone. But if there was ever a man a woman could unburden herself to, share everything with, it was Gavin, she decided, wondering what had held Melissa back. Did the Michaels family have a secret they couldn't share with anyone, not even him?

'OK. This may seem another odd question, but is there any way Tim could have been having an affair with Jane McNeil?'

Gavin rocked back in his chair and laughed. 'You've got to be joking.'

She wasn't, but at least the question had lightened his mood again. 'Maybe her murder and his suicide are nothing to do with one another but . . .'

'You think maybe there's a link?' He shook his head, still smiling at her. 'Oh, Eve. You didn't know my father-in-law. He cared far, far more about horseflesh than female flesh, plus if he had been that way inclined, he would never have dared carry on with anyone on home turf, forgive the pun, under the eyes of my mother-in-law. You've met her. She'd have flayed him alive.'

'I'm sorry, but I had to ask.'

'Don't be sorry. I said you could ask me anything, and I meant it.'

'It's just that I don't believe in coincidence and I find the timing of the two events very odd.'

He rubbed his forehead. 'I'd never thought of it like that before. The weeks and months after Tim's death were a God-awful time and we had so much else to sort out, let alone think about. I'm afraid what happened to Jane was – it has to be said – peripheral.'

'The police never brought it up?'

'Not as far as I know. It's such an extraordinary idea. Melissa would've told me, I'm sure. She idolized Tim and she's quite old-fashioned. She'd have been very, very upset at the thought of him having an affair.'

Again, Eve had the sudden impression of distance between Gavin and Melissa, as though he were on the outside looking in. Tragedy made people close ranks and she imagined the wall of grief around the Michaels family. Maybe they had used it to hide behind, as well. Although it was an obvious lead for the investigation to follow, the police had Sean Farrell clearly in their sights at the time and possibly weren't looking at other avenues.

'Even so, what do you think?'

He shook his head thoughtfully. 'Jane and my father-in-law? Some sort of late-night office romance? It just doesn't fly. If anything, between you and me, I'd have said Tim was a closet queen. Like many of his generation, he was a very repressed man in all sorts of ways.'

'I picked up something between Harry and Melissa at dinner last night, when we were talking about Holly Crowther. What was that all about?'

'No idea, I'm sorry. I wasn't paying attention.' Gavin put his head to one side and looked at her quizzically. 'It's funny. Part of me expects you to be the same Eve I used to know, yet I also know that can't be. But you *do* seem just the same, in so many ways. I have to keep reminding myself that twenty years is a hell of a long time. There's so much I don't know about you.'

'It certainly is.' In more ways than one, she wanted to say. It was a lifetime. In a parallel universe, if things had been different, she might have been sitting there, married to him. It was a strange thought.

'Here, I've got something to show you.' He took out his wallet and pulled out a photograph. 'Do you remember this?'

The edges were a little dog-eared and the colour had faded, but she saw the two of them together sitting at a table somewhere. He was leaning in towards her, his arm around her, and they were both smiling at the camera. They looked so incredibly young, so happy. Yet she knew she hadn't been.

'Where was this?' she asked, handing him back the photo.

He tucked it away again, looking a little disappointed. 'Don't you remember? When you came to see me in Oxford the first time. Some American tourist took it for us with my camera.'

'Oh, yes. Some pub out in the country. It had really good food. You drove me there in your Dad's old blue Fiat. We nearly went into a ditch on the way back.'

He smiled. 'If I remember correctly, I was trying to kiss you. You say you've never married. Why?'

She could give him all the platitudes about not meeting the right person, but it wasn't the truth. She felt she owed it to him to be direct. 'I didn't want to.'

'Any serious relationships?'

She hesitated. There were all sorts of excuses she could make. The intensity of her job, the long hours, the emotional wear and tear. It all precluded anything long-term, particularly with someone on the outside, who didn't have a clue what being caught up in that sort of world was like. Also, in the feverish atmosphere of each new case, thrown so closely together for such long hours, it was easy for relationships to spring up, blaze briefly, then die down again when it was all over. It was almost a means of getting through it all. The truth was that it also suited her. She didn't need, or want, any ties. She wondered if Gavin had any idea from what he'd read in the papers that Jason had been her lover. Maybe that was what lay behind the question and he was worrying about the impact Jason's death had had on her, and what she might be feeling.

'Not really,' she replied. 'I'm perfectly happy as I am.' Certainly as happy as she ever could be.

Gavin seemed a little relieved and she realized her guess had been right. 'Well, I'm pleased to hear it. You certainly look very well.' Then he shook his head. 'I've often thought of you, you know. I remember that time so vividly. I often wish we could go back and . . .' He paused, then sighed. 'And do things differently.'

'But we can't.'

'No,' he said firmly. 'But I'm still sorry we ever lost touch.'

She said nothing, shocked by the polite dishonesty of the phrase. It was Gavin all over. They hadn't simply lost touch. The break had been sudden and violent and entirely her fault. She had been staying with him for a long weekend in his room at Oxford. He had seemed odd and uncharacteristically out of sorts, as though something serious was wrong, although she had no idea what was behind it. She remembered the feeling of silent, unexplained pressure building over the two days, like the change in atmosphere before a big, electrical storm. When he finally blurted out that he wanted to marry her, it took her completely by surprise. It didn't matter how young they were, he knew his own mind, he kept insisting. He wanted to be with her for the rest of his life. She could still picture herself, speechless, gasping for breath, the sense of panic rising inside, as images of what it all entailed flooded her mind. She had never given even a moment's thought to the possible consequences of their relationship before. It struck her that she had been sleepwalking all the way through it until Gavin said those words. She couldn't cope. Everything was closing in on her. She was being suffocated. She had to get away. She pushed past him and rushed from his room, almost falling down the narrow staircase. She ran blindly out into the sunlit quad and didn't stop until she finally reached the river at the back. She paused for a moment, staring out at the water, wondering if she should throw herself in. Then she sat down under a tree, put her face in her hands and wept. Gavin had eventually found her. Seeing him, standing over her, his face full of emotion and concern, panic took hold again. She didn't want him to touch her, or come near her. She had been living a lie and she couldn't carry on. She couldn't explain; she didn't even totally understand herself. She just needed him to leave her alone. She had quickly packed up her things and left. He had tried over and over again to contact her, but she had managed to avoid him, going out of her way to make sure she never crossed his path. She had then travelled abroad for a year to put some distance between them, before going to university. When she eventually returned, she heard he had got engaged.

She thought of A.E. Housman's lines from *A Shropshire Lad*, which had been a favourite of her foster-mother, Clem, a retired English teacher: '*Into my heart an air that kills, from yon far country blows, what are those blue remembered hills, what spires, what farms are those? That is the land of lost content, I see it shining plain, the happy highways where I went and cannot come again.*' The land of lost content. The air that kills. Clem had thought she was far too young to understand the concept. But she was so wrong. Nostalgia was pointless; it poisoned everything it touched. Also, what Gavin was romanticizing about was something that had never existed in the first place. It had all been a sham.

From nowhere, she had an image of him from twenty years before. They had been drinking in the pub near where they lived in Lymington and he had walked her home. It had started to rain and they had stopped for a moment under a bus shelter. She had felt quite high, happily so for a change, and before she knew it, he had pulled her towards him, bent down and kissed her. The feeling of that kiss had never left her, the desire, coupled with revulsion. 'Am I the first person you've kissed?' he had asked a few moments later, taking her hands in his and studying her closely, face flushed, emotion bright in his eyes. He wasn't making fun of her. She could feel the intensity of her teenage embarrassment and confusion even now. 'I hope I am,' he had said, not waiting for a response. 'I want to be the first for everything with you.' He was full of hope and enthusiasm and decency.

How could she explain? He hadn't been the first. She pictured the long-haired man dressed in leather, with the heavy, dark brows and piercing, deep-set eyes, the smell of stale sweat and tobacco that lingered around him, his fingers stained yellow with nicotine. He had sat down beside her on her pink Princess bed, pressed his hard, dry lips to hers and briefly slid his hand between her thighs before they were interrupted. His face, the look in his eyes, were burned on her mind, along with the tattoo of a hooded skeleton on his muscled bicep. He had caught her staring at it. 'It's the Grim Reaper,' he had said, in some strange, foreign accent. 'You like him?' He was grinning. 'It's why they call me Dr Death.'

Even after so many years, she felt the involuntary sting of shame, as though what had happened was in some way her fault. She shuddered, exhaled sharply and closed her eyes, hugging herself for a moment as she remembered the earthquake that had ripped apart her life, separating her two worlds. The BEFORE and the AFTER. She had managed to keep the two worlds precariously separate for so long, but the fault line between them was fragile and Duran's questions about her past had reopened all the old fears.

'Are you OK?' Gavin asked.

She opened her eyes and looked up at him, putting her hands

to her mouth for a moment as she struggled to focus, then hurriedly swept the hair off her face. She felt hot and sick. Pushing the sleeves of her shirt back to her elbows, she took a gulp of water.

'Eve?'

'It's just something I remembered. Something I'd rather forget.'

He looked alarmed. 'Nothing to do with me?'

She reached out her hand to reassure him. 'No. Of course not.'

He took hold of her hand and turned it palm upwards, examining the inside of her forearm and tracing the long, pink groove that marked her skin with his finger.

'I remember your scar,' he said. 'You always said you'd had an accident, but I never dared ask if it was true. What really happened? You can tell me now.'

She withdrew her hand and pulled down both of her sleeves.

'You had one on your shoulder too, quite a deep mark.'

'It's still there. It *was* an accident.' She could see he still didn't believe her.

'But you can't have been very old, if it was before I met you.'

'I wasn't. I was twelve.'

He looked at her for a moment as though he wanted to say something else, then glanced down at his watch. 'Christ, I didn't realize how late it is,' he said, getting quickly to his feet. 'I'm sorry. I'm late. There's so much more I want to talk to you about, but I've got to go. Melissa's out with her book club this evening and I need to collect the boys from a friend's house in twenty minutes and give them their tea. What are you doing later?'

She picked up her bag and coat and stood up. 'I'm having dinner with Harry.'

'Harry?' Although he covered it well, she saw the flicker of surprise.

'I want to pick his brains about a couple of his clients who were in touch with Jane the week before she disappeared.' Even as she spoke, she realized she didn't have to explain anything to anyone, not even him.

'Maybe another time, then,' he said affably. 'I'm afraid I'm heading back to London tomorrow night. I'm on a Commons select committee and there's an important meeting first thing

Monday morning. I probably won't be back here until Friday. I guess you'll have left by then?'

'Yes.'

'But Melissa tells me you're coming to the Christmas party tomorrow.'

'Again, all in the interests of the case.'

'Good. It's always a scrum, but maybe we can find a quiet moment together there.'

# TWENTY-THREE

D an checked his watch. It was well past eight in the evening. He had been hovering for quite a while outside the entrance to the Apple Store in Covent Garden, where the man on the phone had told him to wait. People came, people went. The store seemed to be a popular rendezvous point. But there was no sign of the man – the younger man, Mickey's so-called friend, who said his name was Hassan. Dan searched the faces around him, but other than a dark-skinned teenage boy in a navy-blue anorak, who glanced at him suspiciously before going inside the shop, nobody made eye contact. They were all doing their own thing, having fun, window-shopping, drinking and eating and not remotely interested in him. He felt like some sort of sad loser on a blind date standing there, and he was freezing, water seeping up from the cobbles through the soles of his boots where the leather had worn thin. There were so many people milling around, he wondered how Hassan was going to spot him. He ought to be wearing a green carnation pinned to his lapel, or have a copy of *Time Out* magazine tucked into his jacket pocket, or something similar. But in broken English Hassan had said it wasn't necessary, that he would find him. He said Mickey had shown him a photo of Dan on the 4Justice website. All Dan had to do was to keep his phone switched on and to come alone. Dan had been nervous about going there, knowing that it was probably a stupid thing to do. He ought to call the police and leave it to them. But something about Hassan's voice, in particular the way he said 'I am very sad', sounded genuine. He kept replaying the sentences over and over again in his mind, trying to hear a flaw or a false note, but there was none. He should trust his instincts, he kept telling himself. If the man really had been Mickey's friend, they should talk. There might be a simple explanation why he had Mickey's phone and maybe he knew something that could be of help.

In spite of the bitter wind and the recent rain, the piazza was crowded and the restaurants and bars were full with people waiting to sit down. A jazz band played loudly somewhere inside the covered market and a fire-eater was entertaining a large crowd in the middle of the square, beside a twenty-foot Christmas tree. A giant silver reindeer stood in front of the entrance to the market, rearing up on a sleigh filled with a heap of shiny presents, its throat outstretched as though calling to its friends in the sky. It was covered head to toe in white lights, with a sparkling red collar of bells around its neck, and looked like something from a Disney film. All that was missing was snow and a posse of elves coming around the corner singing.

The air was filled with wave upon wave of food smells, pizza, some sort of pungent, spicy, mulled wine, mixing with roasting chestnuts and fried onions, which conjured up burgers and hot dogs and other delicious things. He hadn't had much to eat since breakfast and was hungry as hell, but it would have to wait. He checked his watch again, as if somehow it would speed things up. Hassan was now a full twenty minutes late. He tried calling Mickey's number but it went straight to voicemail. Maybe he never meant to come. Perhaps it was some sort of wind-up, or a sick joke. He'd give him five more minutes then, sod it, he'd get something to eat and go home. He watched as a couple met up and passionately embraced just a couple of feet away. As they pulled apart momentarily and looked longingly into each other's eyes, he felt a sudden pang of loneliness.

His phone was ringing. He pulled it out and saw Mickey's name on the screen.

'Hello?'

Silence.

'Hello? This is Dan Cooper.'

More silence. He pressed it hard to his ear, trying to block out the noise around him, but he heard nothing. Had they hung up? He looked at the screen. The call was still connected.

'Hello? Are you still there?' he asked.

'Are you alone?' a man asked. It was the deeper, older voice, not the younger man who called himself Hassan, who had claimed to be Mickey's friend.

'Yes. I'm alone. Who is this?'

There was a pause, then the man said, 'You can call me Nasser. Do you have money on you?'

'What for?'

'I sell you Mickey's phone.'

Dan hesitated. Was this what it was all about, just some cheap ploy to extract cash? If so, he would call the police. 'I don't want to buy Mickey's phone. I just want to talk to your friend. The one who says he knows Mickey. Is he with you?'

'I want five hundred pounds and I bring you to him.'

'No. I want to meet him first and then I will think about giving you some money.'

There was a long pause. Dan heard familiar sounds echoing in the background, more or less the same sounds he was hearing through his own ears. Nasser must be somewhere nearby, no doubt watching him. He looked quickly around, scanning the crowd of people and met the stare of a youngish, dark-skinned man dressed in a silver-grey bomber jacket. He was looking straight at him but as he met Dan's eye, he looked away. There was no phone in his hand. Maybe he was wearing a headset. He then raised his hand to his mouth, took a large bite of something in a wrapper and turned his back on Dan.

'Hello?' Dan said. 'Are you still there?'

The man had been joined by a pretty, red-haired woman. She was laughing and saying something to him. They both seemed happy and relaxed and normal. He was imagining things. He looked around again, but there were so many people, it was impossible to single out anybody in particular.

'Hello?' Dan bellowed into the phone. 'Are you still there?'

'I'm here,' Nasser said. The voices in the background grew suddenly louder, as did the jazz. He must have moved inside the covered market. 'You tell anyone you come here?'

'No. What are you worried about?'

'I call you back.'

'I want to speak to your friend.' But the call had been cut.

Dan walked through the throng into the market. It was a dazzling sea of brightness and colour, with two more Christmas trees, one at each end amongst the crowded restaurant tables. The huge atrium was lit by thousands of small white lights. Evergreen garlands decked the railings of the first-floor balcony and giant sparkling silver and red baubles hung amongst the eighteenth-century lanterns from the high, vaulted ceiling. Music and voices, and the clatter of china and cutlery reverberated deafeningly around the space. He stood still for a moment, taking it all in, looking for any face turned momentarily towards his. But he saw nothing out of place. Nobody. He was about to give up when the phone in his hand vibrated. He looked down and saw it was ringing. Mickey's number again. He answered.

'Hello?'

'Walk out the market.'

'Which way?'

'Go to the church. I see you there.'

'See me where?' he shouted. But Nasser had hung up again.

The church. He must mean the one on the west side of the market, a large stone-faced classical box of a thing, with a rather brutish classical portico and columns at the front. He threaded his way as fast as he could in and out of the tables and shoppers and went outside into the busy piazza, where another huge, glittering Christmas tree stood in the centre. The church was almost directly opposite. A number of people were gathered in front of it, but nobody made eye contact. The clock on the portico above struck the hour. He waited for a moment, hands in his pockets, wondering what to do, then glanced back across the square towards the market. As he scanned the faces, he caught sight of the boy in the navy anorak again, standing beside the Christmas tree, looking straight at him. As Dan half-raised his hand, the boy turned abruptly away and disappeared into the crowd.

Dan was about to follow him when he felt a tug at his sleeve and a man brushed past with the words: 'Follow me.' It was the same deep voice as on the phone. Nasser was short – maybe five feet six at most – and thickset, dressed in a black ski-jacket and jeans. Dan didn't see his face clearly, but he had the impression of a band of tanned skin and dark eyes in between the beanie pulled down low on his head and the thick scarf wrapped around his neck. Like a skater on ice, he moved fluidly and fast, weaving his way expertly in and out of the people milling about, ducking around the little groups gathered around street entertainers, heading south towards the Strand. All Dan could see was the black hat bobbing up and down, turning this way and that, and he had a struggle to keep him in view. He was aware that he was being led away from the lights and the crowds. Again, he had the feeling that it was a set-up, but he would have to take a chance. He couldn't risk losing this one connection with Mickey.

There was a bellow up ahead, a deep bass voice, and the sudden shifting movement of people to left and right. He lost sight of Nasser's head in the melee. More shouting. Some sort of scuffle. Pickpockets, maybe. A heavily built man ran at full pelt into the piazza from the right and the crowd parted in front of him like long grass blown by the wind. Dan heard footsteps thundering up behind him. Another person ran past, knocking aside a female shopper who fell to the ground, bags spilling onto the pavement. More shouts, this time female and angry. There was the blast of a car horn and the screech of brakes in the street ahead, followed by a piercing scream. The crowds of people surged forward and he followed them, but it was impossible to see what was going on. He had lost sight of Nasser.

As he stood, wondering what had happened and what he should do, he felt somebody firmly take hold of his arm. He turned around and saw the pretty, red-haired woman from before.

'Dan Cooper. I'm DC Kelly. I need you to come with me.' She wasn't smiling now.

# TWENTY-FOUR

'Harry, go home,' Eve said, pushing Harry gently away with her fingertips as he leaned in to kiss her again. It was well past midnight and they were standing under the porch outside the cottage, the overhead lantern casting deep shadows on his tired face.

He was smiling, as though he still didn't believe she meant it. 'You sure about that?'

'One hundred per cent.'

She said it very firmly, not caring if he took offence. It was late and she wanted to go to bed. She also wondered why he hadn't made a move before, if that's what he wanted. He didn't strike her as the inexperienced, unconfident type. Her main interest in inviting him in for a coffee, apart from sorting out the boiler, which had stopped working, had been to see if he might eventually divulge something interesting. But he hadn't.

'That's a shame,' he said, still grinning broadly, his face close to hers as he gazed at her in an unfocussed sort of way, perhaps hoping she would change her mind. 'I know it'd be good.' When she said nothing, he gave a little shrug, stepped back and turned to go. 'Another time, maybe. I've really enjoyed this evening.'

He was a funny sight, jingling his large bunch of keys like a gaoler as he swaggered down the steps whistling, hair a little messed up, one flap of his jacket rucked up at the back from where he'd been sitting deep in an armchair for the past hour or so. Anyone watching would think that he had just got lucky, rather than been turned down.

He climbed a little unsteadily into the Defender, started the engine and rolled down the window. 'See you tomorrow. Twelve p.m. sharp and don't be late.'

He shouldn't be behind the wheel of a car, but she didn't want to give him any excuse to come back in. At least it was a private road, he couldn't injure anyone but himself, and he'd probably driven it blind on numerous occasions. He revved the engine loudly and, with a screech of tyres, took off down the lane. She watched the taillights bump along the pot-holed road, finally disappearing around the bend behind the trees and wondered if he was really quite as drunk as he was making out.

He had picked her up at the cottage at eight that evening and taken her to a nice restaurant on Marlborough High Street. He seemed rather perplexed when she told him she didn't drink; not that it seemed to inhibit him. He tanked back a couple of gin-and-tonics before dinner, and two-thirds of a bottle of red wine with the meal, and she had insisted on driving him back. After fixing the boiler, he accepted an offer of coffee, although clearly disappointed that there was nothing stronger in the house. He had stoked up the wood-burning stove in the sitting room and sat down in an armchair next to it, as though intending to stay for a while. She had chosen the sofa opposite, wanting to put some distance between them. She didn't want to encourage him, which she had the feeling would have been all too easy. It wasn't that he was unattractive – quite the opposite, in fact. He had the rugged looks that appealed to a lot of women and an economical, purposeful, athletic way of moving, which reminded her of Jason. But Jason's shadow still hung heavily over her; it was all far too fresh and raw. Also, alibi or not, Harry was too closely associated with the case and it was a line she had never crossed in the past.

More than once, she had caught a hint of something sharper beneath the light-hearted banter. She was aware of his watching her whenever he thought she wasn't looking, as though he couldn't quite make up his mind about her. Also, throughout the evening, she had the feeling that he was holding himself in check, maybe not wanting too much of his real self to show. She understood why he might be wary, but it put her on edge. He had, at least, given her one half-useful piece of information. He had found out that Holly Crowther had gone to a yard in Yorkshire, after the job in Newmarket. She had lasted there only a few months, before leaving because she was apparently pregnant. Nobody had a clue where she had gone from there. Apart from that, he seemed happier to ask questions, than answer them. He was particularly interested in her work for the police. He liked watching all the cop shows on television when he had the time, but he had never met a 'real-life' detective before, let alone a female one. Was it anything like on TV? But the endless questions were just a smoke screen. Underneath it all, she felt he couldn't work her out and was troubled by it. He had also asked her, more than once, how she came to be involved in the Sean Farrell appeal. He tried very hard to probe her connection with 4Justice, as well as asking about the man in the photo she had shown him. She refused to mention Mickey by name, or explain exactly what Mickey had been doing at Ascot Racecourse, let alone the fact that he had been murdered.

Just to shut him up, she had eventually said that Dan was an old friend and that he was the one who had brought her in to help with Farrell's appeal. She could tell from his expression that he didn't believe her, but he didn't pursue it. In return, he had talked a little about his two failed marriages and a lot about his family and the racing world, but she had the impression it, too, was just padding. At times, it felt as though they were engaged in some sort of fencing match. He was particularly evasive and sketchy about his clients, even those from ten years before, and particularly Lorne Anderson. However, he did confirm that Stuart Wade was coming to the party the next day and promised to introduce her to him. Alcohol affected people in different ways, but in spite of the considerable amount Harry had had to drink, there were times when he seemed quite startlingly sober.

There was one particular moment that she kept dwelling on. He had gone to the kitchen and got himself a glass. Sitting back down deep in the armchair by the fire, he had pulled out a large hip flask from his jacket pocket and poured out the contents. Even from across the room, she could smell the brandy and it made her feel a little queasy. He swirled the golden-brown liquid around thoughtfully, took a large swig of it, then peered up at her over the rim of the glass.

'Why are you here, Eve?' His voice sounded suddenly tired and a little croaky.

'I thought I'd explained.'

'No. I mean, why are you *really* here?'

'What do you mean?'

'It's nothing to do with Gavin, is it?'

The question took her by surprise. Did he actually think the whole Sean Farrell thing was a pretext for her getting back in touch with Gavin? It suddenly occurred to her that this might be what Harry had wanted to find out all along. If so, she was surprised it had taken him all evening to get to the point.

'Why do you ask?'

He was drawing hard on his umpteenth cigarette, watching her closely through narrowed, slightly watery eyes. 'You and he seem very close.'

'Not really. It was all a very long time ago.'

'Well, even though he tries to hide it, he's clearly very fond of you.'

'You're reading too much into things.'

'I'm just very protective of my little sister, that's all.'

He said it lightly, almost jokingly, but there was an undercurrent of something more serious and sharp beneath the remark. She wondered if he was asking for himself, or if Melissa had put him up to it, or if something else lay behind it. What exactly had Gavin said about their past relationship?

'How nice,' she replied. 'I wish I had a big brother like you.'

'You don't need one. You seem to know very well how to look after yourself.'

The only other time she had scratched the surface and provoked any form of genuine reaction from him in the whole evening, had been in the restaurant, when she had asked out of the blue: 'Could you explain race-fixing to me, Harry?'

She had done it deliberately, tired of all the empty chit-chat and not caring at all if she upset him. She had caught him completely off-guard. He was in the middle of sipping his wine and he coughed, spluttered and stared hard at her for a moment, then recovered himself and shook his head.

'Don't play the fool with me, Eve. It doesn't become you. You know exactly what it is.'

'Did you get hold of Stacey Woodward, then?'

He looked even more surprised, as well as angry. 'Yes, thank you.'

Maybe he had thought she wouldn't take the trouble to find out who Stacey was. But she had Googled Stacey's famous boyfriend earlier and found a picture of the two of them on someone's yacht in the South of France the previous summer, along with Stacey's full name. This had then led her to a piece from one of the tabloids entitled 'New Corruption Scandal Hits Horse Racing'. The article was dated just five days before. Stacey Woodward and two other jockeys, plus a trainer and three owners, none of whose names she recognized, had been charged with race-fixing by the British Horseracing Authority, the sport's regulator. The article went on to detail the charges, mentioning a lengthy investigation, which had exposed a 'wide-reaching conspiracy'. It appeared that the trainer and owners had formed a gambling ring and had paid the three jockeys to make sure that their horses didn't win. There was mention at the end of the article that the BHA investigation was still ongoing and that other charges were likely to be brought.

'She really is in a lot of trouble, isn't she?'

'What of it?' he said, sharply.

'Why does she want to talk to *you* so badly?'

'She just needs some friendly advice, that's all.'

'Really?'

He slammed his glass down on the table and stared at her. 'Eve, this has *absolutely nothing* to do with you, nor with why you're here.'

He looked as though he was going to get up and walk out if she pursued it any further and she let it drop. Curious though she was, particularly given his reaction, he was right: it had nothing to do with Jane McNeil's murder. That was all that was important. Not long afterwards, dinner over, he had called for the bill.

With the front door propped open wide to clear the haze of Harry's cigarette smoke, she went back inside, straightened and plumped up the seat cushions, tipped the contents of Harry's ashtray into the bin and put his coffee mug and glass in the dishwasher. She didn't want to have to confront any of it in the morning. She put on her coat, fished her phone out of her bag and went out to the far corner of the front garden, where she had found a signal earlier in the day.

There had been a missed call and voicemail from Andy Fagan while she and Harry were having dinner, along with a voicemail from Grace Byrne returning her call. There was also a text from Peters, asking if she was making any progress, plus an urgent one from Dan. *Something's happened. Call me. Dan*

She tried to call Dan but his phone was switched off. It was too late to call Grace back, but she pressed play and listened to Fagan's message.

'Hi, Eve. It's Andy. Can you give me a bell please, soon as you get this? Need to give you the heads up on something.' She picked up an urgency in his tone and wondered, with a sinking heart, if there was any connection with Dan's text.

She phoned Fagan but he, too, didn't answer. No doubt he was at home, tucked up in bed with his wife. She left a brief message explaining that she didn't have much of a signal and would try again in the morning, then stood for a moment looking out at the sky. There was a distant, yellowish glow on the horizon from the direction of Swindon, otherwise it was clear and black and full of stars.

She was about to go back inside when she heard a noise. It sounded like the snap of a branch and it came from the woodland area just beyond the cottage boundary. She stood still and listened. Silence. A cold winter moon had slid out from behind a patch of cloud. It was almost full and shone brightly on the frosty fields and garden below, but the woods were black and she couldn't make out anything beyond the perimeter. She heard another sound, some sort of hurried rustling in the undergrowth, followed by the crack of another branch. It could be deer, or maybe a badger, something largish and relatively weighty, but she wanted to make sure. Using her phone as a torch, she followed the path around to the side of the house where the hedge finished and a makeshift fence started, and shone her torch into the trees beyond. The beam of light was weak, but she picked up a movement.

'Who's there?' she shouted.

No answer. She grabbed one of the posts and climbed up onto the fence, stepping carefully over the barbed wire that ran along the top rail and dropping almost silently onto the stretch of rough grass on the other side.

'Hello? Who's there?' As she started walking towards the woods, she heard the crack of breaking branches, the noise now further away, moving swiftly up the hill in the direction of the main road. Even a large deer wouldn't make such a din. Someone had been watching her.

# TWENTY-FIVE

Eve woke early the next morning. She had barely slept, lying awake for much of the night listening to the wind in the trees and the sounds from the lane below. Occasionally a car would go past and made her wonder if whoever had been watching her had come back. What was the point of spying on her? What did they want? Her first thought was that it might be a journalist from London, still looking for an angle on the shooting, although it wasn't clear how they could have found her. If not, maybe it was something to do with the Sean Farrell appeal. Perhaps she had stirred up something unpleasant, which would at least mean she was heading in the right direction.

She opened the bedroom curtains and gazed out at the dark, misty fields opposite. Other than a couple of lights dotted here and there, it was difficult to see much beyond the lane. Somebody could easily have stood out there, watching her all night. Again she felt the isolation of the place and thought of Jane McNeil, on her own in the cottage for the last few days of her life, after the other girls had left. Had she minded? Had she felt nervous, or afraid? Had she any idea that she was in danger?

Eve showered and dressed quickly, wanting to go for a walk to clear her head as well as to see if she could trace the path that the intruder had taken. The cottage was chill and damp, the heating only just kicking in, with the old pipes rattling and groaning. But at least the boiler was still working. Harry could be thanked for that. Downstairs, when she made coffee, she could still smell his stale cigarette smoke lingering in the air. She wondered how he was feeling this morning.

As soon as it was light enough to see, she put on her coat and boots and went outside with her phone in order to get a torch from her car. There was a heavy mist and the overnight frost had turned the garden completely white. She walked around the house, checking the few small flowerbeds under the windows, but there was no sign that anybody had been there looking in. She went back into the front garden to where she had stood on the lawn the previous night with her phone. She could just make out the faint shape of footprints pressed into the stiff, white grass. Whether they were from the night before or that morning, she couldn't tell, but they looked far too big to be hers and they led towards a gate at the perimeter of the woods. An old, faded notice pinned to a tree beside it said: *Private. Keep out. Trespassers will be prosecuted.*

The gate was fastened by a long, lever catch, which was stiff and rusty and a struggle to open. The gate had to be lifted up on its hinges to pull it free and as she swung it back, it made a loud creaking noise. In the quiet of the country, it was as good an alarm as any and she was sure she hadn't heard the noise the previous night. Sheltered by the trees, the ground on the other side was soft and brown and free of frost. A large puddle of water had collected in a hollow in front of the gate, now covered in a thin, unbroken film of ice. She noticed a couple of partial footprints in the muddy ground around it, toes pointing forwards, as though somebody had recently stood there, looking over the gate towards the cottage. Judging from the size, they were a man's boots, with a deep outdoor tread. They could have been made by an innocent walker, but she took out her phone and photographed them just in case, using her own foot as a makeshift yardstick.

The cottage sat at an angle to the woods, facing across the road. Anybody standing at the gate would have had a clear view of the front garden, as well as through the side window into the sitting room. Thank God she had closed the curtains when she went in there with Harry, after dinner. The kitchen, her bedroom above, and the bathroom were on the other side of the house and she reassured herself that she had drawn all the curtains and blinds as soon as it got dark. It was a stroke of luck she had gone out with her phone to make calls after Harry left, otherwise she might never have known she had been being watched. A narrow, overgrown footpath led through the trees up the hill. The track was covered in a thick, soft layer of leaf mould, which deadened any sound, and although there were traces of footprints here and there, it was impossible to say when they had been made. None were clear enough to be matched to the other footprints. She followed the steep path until finally she reached the top. She climbed over a small stile and came out into the open. A heavy mist filled the air, softening the slowly brightening landscape. She could just make out the road that ran through the estate and the Marlborough-side gates in the distance. The public car park was just beyond, she remembered. Anyone could have easily parked their car there and climbed over the gates without being noticed, although why they had bothered to approach the cottage through the woods was another matter. Perhaps they were worried about being spotted in the lane or in the fields at the front, where it was more open.

She was about to go back down the road to the cottage to pick up her car, when she heard a series of high-pitched whistles. A moment later, a dog shot out of the mist and ran up to her, panting. It was some sort of a whippet, brindle-coloured, wearing a thick, red, leather collar, with a heart-shaped brass tag. As she bent down, it licked her hand as though looking for treats. She was just about to check the tag, when there were more blasts of the whistle and the dog took off back across the road, this time in the direction of the farmhouse.

'Hey, Eve,' a man shouted. The voice came from the direction of fields on the opposite side of the road. 'Over here.'

It sounded like Gavin's voice. Scanning the misty horizon, she could just make out the dark smudgy shape of somebody running towards her over the brow of the hill, beyond the gallops. She walked over to the track and waited. Gavin moved quickly and, a moment later, had crossed the gallops and was ducking under the rail beside her. He was wearing a black tracksuit, the bottom of the legs and his trainers soaked from the long grass. He unplugged a set of earphones and put his hands on his thighs, bending forwards momentarily to catch his breath.

'Didn't expect to see you up so early on a Sunday,' he said. 'You going for a run?'

He was breathing heavily, nowhere near as fit as he used to be, she noticed. It was what age and a desk job, as well as a comfortable, unchallenging home life, did to you. She had been a pretty fast runner, but nothing compared to him twenty years before. Looking at him now, she thought she could easily outrun him.

'Not this morning. I just needed some fresh air.'

He stood up, frowning as he studied her more closely. 'Are you OK?'

'I'm fine,' she said, deciding not to mention what had happened the night before.

In the strange, grey light his face appeared unusually drawn and he looked dishevelled, still unshaven, his blonde hair messy and dark with sweat. His eyes were particularly weary, as she met his gaze, and she thought he appeared troubled.

'What about you? Are *you* alright?'

His expression shut down. 'It's nothing,' he said a little sharply, still breathing heavily. 'I just haven't had much sleep, that's all.'

His tone was unusually brusque and she wondered why he seemed so on edge. She knew him too well to let it go. 'Nothing's wrong then?'

'No. I'm just tired. Melissa came home early with a headache and went to bed. I had a load of constituency emails to catch up on, then I ended up watching a couple of rubbish films until very late. Probably had a few too many whiskies as well. It's good to get out here and clear my head. But now the bloody dog's run off again.'

'I saw a brown-coloured whippet a minute ago.'

'That's the one. Snippet the whippet. Stupid name, but it's what the boys called him. He's Melissa's and he pays absolutely no attention whatsoever to me. I think he'd rather I stayed in London.'

'He ran off towards the house.'

'That makes sense. He's a practical sort. Now he's had his morning run, he'll be wanting his breakfast. He couldn't give a damn about me. I finally understand why Harry has Labradors. They do what they're told. He doesn't tolerate disobedience.' He glanced down at the torch in her hand then peered at her. 'Seriously, Eve. You look very pale. Is anything the matter?'

She didn't want to alarm him but she decided it would be better to explain. 'Like you, I also didn't get much sleep. I—'

'You enjoyed your dinner with Harry, then?' Again, the same sharpness of tone.

It struck her that maybe Harry had a reputation where women were concerned, not that it mattered. Whatever Gavin thought had gone on between her and Harry, she wasn't going to spell it out for him, let alone correct any misapprehensions.

'Yes, I did,' she said, holding his gaze. 'Something came up I wanted to ask you about. What exactly is race-fixing? I mean, I know what it is in general terms, I just want to understand the specifics. Why would anybody want a horse to lose?'

Gavin raised his eyebrows. 'May I ask why?'

Although surprised, his reaction was very different to Harry's the night before. 'Humour me. Please.'

He stared at her for a moment, then shrugged. 'OK, not that I'm an expert, of course. For starters, a trainer may deliberately pick a course that doesn't suit the horse – say it's too long or short or the incline isn't what the horse likes, so that it doesn't do well. It loses a few times, which means it then has a lower handicap when you then pick the right race and track, where it has a much better chance of winning.'

'That's not illegal?'

'No, not at all. Just tactically clever.'

'I'm talking about dishonest reasons to stop a horse. I presume it's so that another horse wins?'

'Yes, or again to keep the handicap down for another race in the future. There's also another reason. In the old days, you could only bet on horses winning or being placed, but thanks to Betfair you can now bet on a horse losing. With computer systems, it's a lot easier to spot if something funny's going on, but it still happens, from what I gather.'

'So how do you stop a horse?'

He was looking at her curiously, his head a little to one side. 'You can nobble it . . .'

'Dope it?'

'Yes, that's one way, although it's much easier to pick up these days, with all the checks. Or you can get the jockey to throw the race, maybe ride it out in front when it likes to come from behind, or just not try hard enough. There are all sorts of possible excuses for riding a bad race, such as the horse didn't feel right, or something along those lines. Racecourse stewards are always on the lookout for that type of thing, but of course it still happens and some things are very difficult to prove. There are jockeys who are not only very good at winning, but also losing, if you get my drift.'

'I assume it's all about money.'

'Of course. Where there's brass, there's muck. However glamorous racing appears from the outside, it's an intensely competitive and often cut-throat sport. The majority of trainers and jockeys make little money, if any. There's always somebody who'll be open to making a dishonest buck. Why are you so interested in all of this?'

'Just curious. Harry wasn't very helpful when I asked him about it last night.'

He shrugged again and looked away, as though it was unimportant.

'In fact, he seemed rather touchy about the whole subject. Any idea why?'

'No.' It was clear from his tone he wanted to leave it there.

'Do you have CCTV anywhere on the farm?' she asked after a moment.

He turned to face her again. 'CCTV? Why? Is something wrong?'

'Possibly.'

'There are cameras on the yards and around some of the barns. What's happened?'

'I think someone was watching me last night.'

He raised his eyebrows. 'Watching you? Where?'

'Someone was out in the woods just behind the cottage.'

'How do you know?'

'I heard noises. I think I saw someone.'

'What did they look like?'

'I just saw a movement, but I don't think it was an animal.'

'Probably poachers.'

The idea of poachers hadn't occurred to her, but from the little she knew, they didn't hang around. They didn't stand still at a gate, watching a house. If anything, it was more likely to be a would-be burglar, although there was nothing in the cottage worth taking.

'We've had a few problems recently. I'll mention it to Harry,' he said abruptly.

'I don't think it was poachers.'

He was about to say something else when, from nowhere, she heard a dull, drumming sound coming from the right. 'What's that?' she asked.

'You'll see. You'd better stand back.'

The noise was getting louder and they moved a couple of feet away from the railings, just as a string of horses and riders appeared from out of the mist at the bottom and came galloping up the hill towards them. As the group flew past, the ground shaking, sand and fragments from the track flying up in the air, she smelled the horses' sweat and felt the adrenalin surge of speed. Then they were gone, disappearing as swiftly as they had come over the brow of the hill and back into the mist.

Gavin looked around at her. 'Why would someone be watching you?'

'It's possible a reporter followed me here. They've been hassling me since the shooting in London. It could also be something to do with the Sean Farrell appeal.'

He frowned. 'Are you serious?'

'It's easily possible.'

'But why?'

'I don't know.'

'Do you want to call the police?'

She shook her head. 'I don't think so. Not at the moment, anyway. I can look after myself.'

'I'm sure you can, but you shouldn't have to. Really, don't worry. I still think it's more likely to be poachers, but if it happens again, we should call the police.'

# TWENTY-SIX

'So this mystery man calls you out of the blue from Mickey Fraser's phone. He tells you not to call the police and you trot along to Covent Garden, like a good little boy, to meet him,' the first detective said. He was the older of the two, maybe fifty, give or take a year or so, with an old-fashioned ginger brush of a moustache and surprisingly feminine, long-fingered hands. Even across the table, he smelled of stale cigarettes.

'Yes,' Dan said. 'That's what I said. He wanted some money.'

'In exchange for the phone?'

'I didn't want the phone. I just wanted to talk to Mickey's friend.' He had the impression that any form of payment for the phone of a murder victim was a major crime.

'But he thought you'd gone there to buy the phone. Yeah?'

'No. There was no mention of any payment when I spoke to him. As I told you, all I wanted was to talk to the man who said he was Mickey's friend.'

'But the other man thought he could get some money out of you?'

'I don't know what he thought, but I just wanted to talk to Mickey's friend. OK?'

'You didn't think it was just a wee bit *suspicious*?' the other detective chipped in. 'Did it *occur* to you that maybe the killer had taken Mickey Fraser's phone?'

She was a short, butch-looking Scot, with a surprisingly high-pitched voice and prim, thin lips, lined in an unpleasant shade of dark red. She had an irritating habit of emphasizing certain words and raising her eyebrows meaningfully at the same time. He couldn't decide which of the detectives he liked least.

Naturally it had occurred to him, but as he kept telling himself, the other man, the younger one, who had called himself Hassan had sounded genuine. There had been real emotion in his voice when he said the words 'I am very sad'. If he had killed Mickey, why would he bother to say that? There must be some other explanation. Both detectives were staring at him.

'Look,' Dan said wearily. 'If the killer had taken Mickey's phone, why would he try and sell it back to me? It doesn't make any sense.'

There was a heavy silence for a moment and he had the impression they knew something he didn't. The room was hot and stuffy, an unpleasant, sour smell hanging in the stale air. He didn't know if it was coming from him or the policemen. They had been at the station for most of the night and none of them had been home for a shower and a change of clothes. He was exhausted. The only consolation was that they must be too. He had managed to extract a cup of milky coffee and a soggy ham and cheese sandwich out of them, but that was all. He felt weak from hunger and lack of sleep and increasingly incoherent. They had taken away his phone. The room had no window and he wasn't wearing a watch. He had no idea what time it was, but based on his tiredness alone, he imagined it must be getting light outside now.

'The man said he was a friend of Mickey's,' Dan said. 'I just assumed Mickey had given it to him for some reason.'

'Which man was this?' Ginger asked.

'The younger one.'

He kept thinking about the two foreigners he had spoken to on the phone, one of them the short, swarthy man he had met in Covent Garden called Nasser. He had looked like the sort of hard, desperate person who would pull a knife on you at the drop of a hat. Hassan had sounded softer, more direct, or at least less grasping. Again, he replayed in his mind Hassan's words. He had seemed genuinely affected by Mickey's death, Dan was sure. Whatever line the police took, he had to trust his instincts. But what exactly was Hassan and Nasser's connection to Mickey? He had no idea what went on in Mickey's personal life, let alone why two such people would have his phone if they hadn't killed him. But he understood the importance of the phone to the police and their obsession with it. It was the one live connection to Mickey and possibly his murder.

He assumed that they had been tracking it, whenever it was switched on. On. Off. On. Off. It must have driven them mad. They had arrived at Covent Garden very quickly and it suddenly occurred to him in the car on his way to the police station that he must have been under surveillance, probably since the first call made from Mickey's phone to his. The thought made him shiver. He had a deep mistrust of all forms of authority, not least a self-regulating body like the police, with its track record of cover-ups, incompetence and corruption. No doubt there were good apples amongst the bad, and Eve appeared to be one of them. But the two detectives facing him would have fitted in well in *Life on Mars*. They were even worse than the previous pair who had interviewed him, lacking any form of finesse, let alone charm. Charm got you a long way in life, he'd always thought, or at least that's what his mother had repeatedly told him, and she was generally right about most things. Somebody needed to tell this duo that you catch more flies with honey. But they were of the school that believed you needed a whacking great mallet to crack a nut and, by the look of them, they were there for the long haul. He could see the day stretching ahead, the same tedious, repetitive questions. It was as though all 'suspicious' people – especially journalists – were tarnished with the same brush. They thought that if they bullied and threatened and wore you down enough, you would eventually cave in. But they were wrong, at least as far as he was concerned. He had been prepared to cooperate, up to a point. He wanted to find Mickey's killer as much, if not more, than they did. But he soon realized his mistake. He couldn't trust them to listen with an open mind to what he had to say. Faced with such an onslaught, his instinctive defence mechanism was to hunker down and lie where necessary. He couldn't even begin to imagine how they would react if he told them about Mickey's memory stick.

He met the woman's stony gaze. 'Anyway, why on earth would the killer be calling me?'

'Why on earth *indeed*,' she replied, with heavy sarcasm. 'Unless maybe *you* and this other bloke killed Mickey.'

This was a new angle. No doubt they had been working their snail-like way towards this all the time. Dan sat back in the chair, arms dangling at his sides, and stared across the small table at the pair of them in disbelief. It was so preposterous, he almost laughed, although humour was an alien concept in the police interview room. He'd tried to crack a few jokes earlier, just to lighten up the tone, but they were greeted with brutish silence.

At least there was one big truth to hang onto: 'I've told you before, I had nothing to do with Mickey's murder.' He said it with as much righteousness as he could muster, looking from one to the other.

Ginger folded his lily-white hands on the table. 'Just to get things straight, this man you went to meet in Covent Garden was Mickey's friend, right?'

He shook his head wearily. 'That's what he said, but he wasn't the one who called me when I was waiting outside the Apple Store. The voice was different. I told you this before.'

'He was called Nasser, right?'

'Yes. So he said.'

'Did you see the *other* man?' the woman asked. 'This Hassan person? The one you *say* was Mickey's friend?'

Dan sighed. 'No. I don't think so.' He thought of the boy in the navy jacket outside the Apple Store. Was he Hassan? He looked very young. He had glimpsed all sorts of other people in the crowd who might have been Hassan, but the more he chased the images in his head, the more they all started to resemble the older man who had taken flight. He was too tired to think about it any longer. Maybe if he let it rest – if they would let it rest – something might come to him.

'So you *know* what he looks like?' She had a sly look in her eye, as though she was onto something.

'*NO*. Don't twist my words. I told you, I never met him. I have no idea if he was there. The one who first spoke to me on the phone – the one who met me outside the church – was the older man who said his name was Nasser. Got it? You must know what happened to him? I saw your lot chasing him down the street. There must have been four or five against one. He can't have got away.'

The detectives exchanged glances but made no reply. Surely

they hadn't let the man give them the slip? Or maybe they were
trying to fool him. The piazza had been swarming with police. Of
course they had caught the fugitive – which explained the kerfuffle.
No doubt, they were grilling him in another interview room,
probably along the same corridor.

'Why don't you fucking well ask him? He's the one you should
be talking to, not me.'

Ginger moistened his lips. 'Problem is, Dan. We can't ask
him.'

'Why's that?' He looked from one to the other but couldn't
read anything from their expressions. It was as though they were
pregnant with some special knowledge, something that they
expected him to know too.

'And he *wasn't* carrying any ID so we have *no* idea who he
is,' the woman added crisply. 'You *sure* you don't know him?'

The exasperation rose in his throat. 'Just ask him, for Christ's
sake. He speaks fucking English.' He decided to say nothing
more and call for a lawyer. He should have done it a long time
ago instead of trying to cooperate. He stretched out his legs under
the table and folded his arms defiantly.

'Not any more he doesn't, Danny boy,' Ginger said. 'This
man, the one you went to meet, who you *say* you don't know,
who you've never met before—'

'I haven't,' he shouted. 'I don't know him from Adam.'

'Well, whoever he is, he's not talking to anybody any longer.
He's friggin' dead.'

# TWENTY-SEVEN

Eve glanced at her watch. It was nearly a quarter to one and
she was late for the Westerby Christmas party. The mist
had cleared and the frost had all but melted, but a chill
still hung in the air and the sky was overcast. The walk along
the lane to the yard at the bottom of the hill should have taken
no more than five minutes, but her progress was hampered by
the deep ruts and puddles, as well as having to frequently step

aside onto the muddy verge to make way for the last straggle of guests sweeping past in their cars.

She had been into Marlborough earlier to get some breakfast and had sat outside the coffee shop in her car with her cappuccino and croissant, listening to her voicemails and returning calls. Her barrister had phoned to discuss some details he needed for her disciplinary hearing. Again, she was unable to reach Grace Byrne and left another message. Other than that, there was nothing urgent, no further messages from either Fagan or Dan, and both of their phones were switched off when she tried to call. She was on her way back, just on the outskirts of the town when Grace called again. Eve pulled over and had sat talking to her for a good ten minutes, the conversation incessantly interrupted at Grace's end by the plaintive demands of her small children in the background. It was clear from everything Grace said that she hadn't like Jane. She described her as 'stuck on herself' and 'no real fun'. She added very little to what Eve already knew other than to say that Jane was always sneaking off somewhere, without telling her and Holly where she was going and they thought she 'had someone on the sly', although they had no idea who. She said she had told the police this, when they contacted her, but they hadn't seemed particularly interested as she didn't have any details. She also said she hadn't spoken to Holly since leaving Westerby and didn't know how to get in touch with her.

A variety of expensive cars were lined up on the verge for the last part of the way, spilling out into the parking lot beyond, alongside the maroon-coloured Westerby Racing lorries and the two shuttle buses, which had been provided to ferry guests back and forwards from Swindon station. The indoor school was housed inside a huge, modern, metal-clad barn. Melissa stood on the concrete paving just outside the entrance, wrapped up tightly in a dark overcoat and high-heeled boots, greeting the last few guests as they arrived. She nodded politely at Eve, but seemed distracted as she handed her a large, glossy programme. A huge crowd of people were already gathered inside and the noise was deafening. Champagne, Bloody Marys and other drinks were flowing freely, the party in full swing. The sawdust arena had been divided down the middle by a low wall of straw bales, with a row of seating just behind it, which was already fully

occupied, everyone else grouped tightly around watching the
yearling parade. The area at the back of the arena had been
enclosed by a white marquee and was set up with tables and
chairs ready for lunch. Harry stood in front of the bales, a mike
in one hand, an open programme in the other, his voice blaring
over the speakers as he announced each horse as it was led in
by one of the grooms. Judging from the numbers he was calling
out, it looked as though she had missed most of the action. Eve
took a glass of sparkling elderflower from one of the trays being
offered around and joined the back of the crowd. They were a
motley collection of people of all ages. Although a few were
smartly turned out, the majority were dressed for warmth in
heavy winter coats and jackets, hats and scarves and she didn't
feel out of place at all. Many of them seemed to know one another
and they drank and talked animatedly over Harry's commentary,
as they watched hundreds of thousands of pounds worth of
horseflesh circle gracefully around the arena. She spotted Sally
Michaels talking to a collection of people in the middle of the
throng and Gavin, at the back, with another group of guests. He
wore a dark suit and tie and was smiling and shaking hands, his
two little blonde-haired boys at his side.

'Here are my last five – last, but by no means least,' Harry
announced. 'And aren't they worth the wait, ladies and gentlemen?
Come on, Colin, I know you've been eying up the chestnut colt
all morning,' he said, pointing his programme at a stout, red-faced
man, who was seated on one of the rows of chairs at the front,
with his wife. 'Don't let Alison stop you getting your cheque
book out.'

Harry seemed relaxed and in his element, with no sign of a
hangover or tiredness from the previous night. Gavin had said
that he was great at schmoozing his clients and she had to agree.
He was a natural, joking and bantering good-naturedly with the
audience, outlining each horse's breeding, its individual qualities,
its genetic relationship to famous winners and occasionally giving
a relevant anecdote to keep the crowd's interest. He hyped each
horse's potential to the maximum and they were an exotic bunch,
one yearling coming from Kentucky, another from France and
another from Australia. To her untutored ears, Harry made each
one sound as though it were a dead cert for the Derby in a few

years. There was such a competitive buzz amongst the audience, the atmosphere was infectious. She'd read somewhere that racing was highly addictive, and a lot more expensive than class A drugs, and she could see why.

'Thank you very much to my head lass, Siobhan, and the rest of the team,' Harry said, once the parade was over, gesturing towards the grooms and the other members of staff who had gathered by the entrance to the arena. Then he turned to the audience. 'Thank *you* very much, too, ladies and gentlemen, boys and girls, for your *partial* attention. We'll now move onto the bit you all love most . . .' He paused for effect before bellowing, 'Lunch!'

The inside of the marquee was decked out in the maroon and cream Westerby Racing colours. A variety of multi-coloured racing silks hung on the walls of the tent, with a TV screen placed in each corner, silently replaying Westerby Racing's successes of the past year. There was a seating plan pinned to a large board at the front of the marquee and Eve found her name and allocated table. Her place was marked with a handwritten card and she sat down between Mike, an affable Australian businessman, there with his much younger girlfriend, and Marion, an elderly widow from the Midlands. Both owned horses, or parts of horses, trained by Harry. Both were perplexed and looked at her in wonderment when she said she had never been racing in her life. Talking to other people on the table, including a romantic novelist called Sandra, who owned a series of horses, each named after one of the titles of her best-selling books, and Max, the yard vet, they seemed to come from a variety of backgrounds, their only unifying factor being a passion for the sport. She also got the impression that winning was a little less important than the wonderful days out and the experiences provided by being part of the racing world. In the course of her various conversations, she managed to discover that nobody on her table had been with Westerby Racing ten years before. She wondered whether it was accidental or deliberate.

Harry's staff were working flat out, helping the caterers with the food and drink. She thought of Jane McNeil, ten years before and what Grace had told her. Had Jane met somebody at the party, maybe somebody she already knew, and then gone out with them later, once the party had finished? It would explain why she had cried off sick and left early, presumably to go and get ready.

Cheese and coffee were being served when she saw Harry threading his way through the throng towards her. He had been hosting another table at the other end of the marquee and she had barely seen him since they all sat down for lunch. He came up to her and kissed her warmly on the cheek and she thanked him for dinner.

'I hope you're enjoying yourself,' he said, smiling and apparently flushed with the success of the day. 'As you can see, racing's all about having fun.'

'It certainly seems to be.'

'You know, I really enjoyed our evening last night.'

The image of him standing under the porch-light as he tried to kiss her sprang to mind. She wondered if he really meant it. 'I'm glad you got home safely.'

'Sorry if I was a bit . . .' He struggled to find the word.

'The worse for wear?' She was still convinced that he hadn't been as drunk as he appeared, but if he wanted to use it as an excuse, that was fine by her.

He smiled. 'I had a bit of a headache this morning, but nothing that a few pills wouldn't fix. It would be nice to do it again sometime soon. How long are you here for?'

She was about to reply when Melissa tapped him on the shoulder. 'You need to come and talk to Bernie. He's interested in Slow Dancer.'

'Tell him I'll be over in a minute.' He turned to Eve. 'Before I forget, I promised to introduce you to Stuart Wade. Come with me.' He took hold of her arm and led her away to another table on the far side of the marquee, where a middle-aged man, with thick, greying hair, sat entertaining a group of giggling women with a story.

Harry tapped him on the shoulder and, as he looked around, Eve recognized him immediately as the man behind the wheel of the silver Range Rover with Harry, when she first went to Westerby Farm for dinner.

'Stuart, this is Eve,' Harry said. Stuart gave him a blank look. 'Eve's following up on a murder we had here ten years ago. You remember, Jane McNeil?'

'Yes, of course,' Stuart said flatly, with no visible reaction to the name. It was clear he had already been briefed by Harry. 'Excuse me, ladies,' he said, with a broad smile and a little, mock bow to the women surrounding him, and got to his feet, turning his back on the table as though it was something not for their ears.

He was very tall, maybe six feet four or five, broad-shouldered and heavy-boned, dressed in a well-cut tweed suit and tightly-knotted silk tie. Perspiration glowed on his deeply tanned face and the smile disappeared from his face as he looked at Eve.

'This is my son, Damon,' Stuart said, as a young man of similar height and build appeared at his side. He was equally tanned and wore a sharp, bright-blue suit, with a white shirt and no tie. Amongst the sea of pale, middle-aged faces and drab browns and greens, he stood out, looking as though he'd stepped out of the pages of *GQ* magazine.

Harry smiled. 'I'll leave you three to chat. And I'll catch up with you later, Eve.' He gave her a sideways glance, then turned away towards another guest.

'You want some bubbly?' Stuart asked, flashing a chunky gold Rolex at his wrist, as he topped up his glass from a bottle in a cooler on the table. 'It's not Cristal, of course, but Harry always serves OK stuff.'

She recognized the accent immediately as Manchester, although the look of him was pure Alderley Edge. Harry had described him as being 'in property', which could mean anything, from caravan parks to city centre skyscrapers. Whatever it was, it seemed to be lucrative enough.

'Elderflower, please.' She had drunk more than enough of the overly sweet mixture but she wanted to keep him company.

'Damon, get the lady a drink, will you?'

'Do you remember Jane McNeil?' Eve asked, as Damon disappeared into the throng.

'Damon was just a lad at the time, but I remember the case,' he said. 'It was in all the papers and it caused quite a stir at the yard. Why do you want to speak to me?'

'Because you called Jane on her mobile, the week before she died.'

He shrugged. 'Harry told me the girl used to work in Tim's

office. Maybe that's why I called her. Does that answer your question?'

'It was her personal phone you called. She didn't use it for work.'

'She must've given me her number, then.' He smiled, as though it was something that happened to him all the time.

Instead of Damon, a waiter appeared at her side with a small tray and handed her a tumbler of elderflower.

'So you don't remember what it was about?'

'Look, it was a very long time ago. I don't even remember what the girl looked like.'

'So, you have no recollection of her at all?' she asked, noticing how he didn't use Jane's name. 'You made five or six phone calls to her phone in the month before she died, as well as the two in the week immediately before.'

He spread his huge hands, as though it was par for the course. 'I'm a happily married man. Need I say more? I went through all of this with the cops at the time. They gave me a right going-over because of those calls, but I came out of it with a clean bill of health.'

'Did you see her at the party here ten years ago?'

He stared at her as if she were mad and gestured to the room with his glass. 'Look around you, luv. There are a couple of hundred people here. Do you really expect me to remember any of them ten years from now?'

'But you knew Jane. You had her mobile phone number and you used it several times.'

His face hardened. 'Harry said to help you, and I'm trying my best. But I told you, I'm a happily married man. End of.'

Again, he wasn't giving her a straight answer, but she had no authority and no leverage to force him to reply, as he well knew. It was futile pressing for more.

'I thought they caught the bloke,' he added.

'Yes. He's in jail. It's possible he didn't do it.'

'Really?' He let the word hang, looking at her with an amused expression. 'You saying the plods got it wrong?'

'It's possible.'

'Well, it wouldn't be the first time. Harry says you're a police-woman with the Met.'

'Yes. But I'm not here in an official capacity.'

He grinned, this time showing a wide arc of perfect, white crowns. 'Pleased to hear it. Pretty girl like you should be enjoying the party and not poking around in things that don't concern you. It's all dead and buried.'

'You mean like Jane McNeil?'

He was still smiling. 'Waste of your time. I'd give it a rest, if I was you, luv.'

In spite of the smile, she knew she was being warned off. It didn't bother her and, if anything, it intrigued her. Why should he care? If only she had access to the full police files, she could see how far he'd been questioned, although she assumed they had checked his alibi thoroughly.

'You're not me and I don't need your advice.'

'Sorry I can't help you, then,' he added, with mock politeness, then turned back to his group of ladies and sat down again.

She returned to her table and collected her handbag and coat, thinking that it was about time to go, when she saw Gavin coming towards her through the now thinning crowd. 'I'm glad I found you. I thought you'd already left. Do you have a minute?'

He pulled up a couple of chairs, removing a sleeping Jack Russell from one of them, and set them close together facing one another.

'Have you had fun?' he asked, as they sat down. From his expression, he didn't look as though he had been having fun at all.

'It was all very interesting. Very impressive. I never imagined anything on this scale. There must be a lot of money involved.'

'You can certainly say that,' he said, almost bitterly. 'Christ, it's so hot in here, I can't breathe.' He took off his jacket and tossed it over the back of his chair, then unknotted his tie and tugged it roughly out of his collar. 'Are you feeling any better?' he asked, leaning forwards towards her, as he ran his hand hurriedly through his hair.

'Better?'

'Yes.' He hesitated, as though he didn't know how to begin. 'I'm worried about you, Eve. I mean, I was worried when I saw you this morning. Are you really OK?'

There was something intense, almost emotional about the way he spoke. His face was flushed and it struck her that, like almost everybody else in the tent, apart from her, he had probably had

quite a lot to drink. One of the problems of being sober was how
people around you changed when they drank. They became
repetitive, told stories that weren't at all funny, lost their inhibi-
tions and said and did stupid, uncharacteristic things. Worries,
even simple ones, took on gargantuan proportions and even for
the most controlled of people, emotion overcame reason. It was
why she hated parties and large, prolonged gatherings. She
disliked seeing people embarrass themselves. Now she had the
feeling that Gavin – the most controlled and level-headed of men
– was about to say something he might regret. She had never
seen him so ill at ease before. Judging by the way he had been
that morning, he seemed to have enough worries of his own.
Whatever lay behind it, she decided not to add to them by voicing
her own concerns. No doubt he would probably think nothing of
it in the morning.

She met his gaze. 'Please don't worry about me. And I'm sure
you're right. It was just a poacher.'

He looked unconvinced. 'Even so . . . I've got to go back to
London. But I don't like leaving you here on your own.'

'I'll be fine.' He was right. The room was extremely hot and
she felt suddenly overcome by tiredness. She had barely had any
sleep and she needed to get back to the cottage and lie down.

'OK,' he said, nodding slowly, but she could tell he wasn't
happy. 'Look, I've got to leave in about half an hour. Someone's
giving me a lift. I really wanted to see you – on your own, I mean.
I want to talk to you.' There was a sharp explosion of female
laughter just behind them and he glanced briefly over his shoulder,
irritated, then turned and bent forwards towards her. She could
smell the whisky on his breath. 'God, I hate these stupid parties.
Every year the same bloody thing. I've done far more than my
fair share of glad-handing today. The only way to get through it
is to drink and I'm afraid I've probably had a few too many.'

Yet again, she pictured him as the outsider in the Westerby
world and saw how much it rankled – even more than she had
imagined, perhaps. Or maybe his disquiet was symptomatic of
deeper issues.

'I wouldn't worry. Everybody seems to be having a good time.'

'Not me, and not you either, I suspect. Can we meet up in
London, maybe for a drink or a coffee? Whatever suits you.

I'll be there all week. I need to talk to you. There are some things . . . Some things I need to understand.'

His tone was urgent, almost desperate. She gazed at him, wondering what he meant, and if she should say yes. Something was definitely bothering him. Surely, there was no harm in it, after all this time. Perhaps it would also do him good to get whatever was troubling him off his chest. Perhaps he needed to talk to somebody on the outside, who wasn't part of his world. Before she could answer, she heard Harry's voice just behind her.

'There you are, Eve. I've been looking for you everywhere. Was Stuart helpful?' He put his hand on her shoulder and gave it a little squeeze.

A flash of irritation crossed Gavin's face. She turned to look up at Harry, but felt suddenly dizzy. She blinked, looked back down again and tried to focus on Gavin, who was leaning back in his chair, like a grumpy child, arms tightly folded.

'Hope I haven't interrupted something,' Harry said, his hand still on her shoulder.

'You *are* interrupting us,' Gavin said sharply. 'I need to speak to Eve before I go.'

'What are you doing later, Eve?' Harry asked.

She tried to speak, tried to stand up, but found she couldn't. Nothing was working. Her body was like lead. She tried again and slumped forwards.

Gavin caught her and held her. 'Eve, what's the matter?' His voice was strangely echoey.

'Do you always have this effect on women, Gavin?' Harry said, from somewhere above her. There was a hoot of male laughter behind. Were they laughing at her?

She couldn't keep her eyes open. She felt strong arms around her, lifting her back into her seat, holding her up so she wouldn't fall. The din in the room reverberated around her head. She felt on fire. Everything was spinning. She was going to be sick.

'Poor thing. Is she ill?' A woman's voice asked in a motherly tone. 'It's SO hot.'

'She's had too much to drink, that's all,' someone else said. Another raucous laugh.

'She doesn't drink,' she heard Gavin say sharply, almost in her ear.

'If she's feeling faint, you need to lay her down flat,' the woman said. 'Let the blood get to the brain.'

'No, she just needs fresh air. It's very hot in here.' A man this time.

'You'd better take her home.' Another male voice. Was it Harry's?

'Is there a doctor here?' someone asked.

*Yes, a doctor. Get me a doctor.* Her lips wouldn't move.

'She probably just needs to sleep it off,' somebody else said.

The voices started to meld into one. She tried to speak. Even though she was struggling to stay conscious, her brain was still functioning, just about. She knew what had happened. All the classic signs. Rohypnol. GHB. Ketamine. So many options. Which one? When? Who? *I've been drugged. Someone's spiked my drink.* But the words wouldn't come. She had been anaesthetized, she wanted to scream.

# TWENTY-EIGHT

I t was almost midnight. Dan lay in the dark on the narrow camp bed in the back office, listening to music on his phone. He had finally been allowed to leave the police station a few hours earlier. From what he could gather, the police seemed to think Mickey's death must have been related to his personal life, which was reassuring. Although they hadn't explicitly said so, he got the impression that they thought it unlikely to be related to any of the cases Mickey had been working on, let alone the Sean Farrell investigation. Their assumption was that the man who had called Dan was some sort of sexual contact, who had tried to extort money from Mickey and, possibly helped by others, killed him, then tried to make it look like a robbery. They made much of the fact that Dan said the men both spoke with foreign accents. The police also still seemed to think that Dan might be tied up with it all too, and their new ludicrous theory was that maybe he, too, had had some sort of a sexual relationship with Mickey. At that point, Dan's solicitor had stepped in and halted proceedings. They had no proof of anything. They were trying to weave a story out of thin air.

Dan had no idea what had happened to Hassan, although the police still seemed certain that he did. However, the older man, Nasser, who he had met in Covent Garden, and whom the police had chased, was definitely dead. They had shown Dan a photo of him, eyes closed, presumably lying in a mortuary fridge somewhere. They said he had been hit by a car and killed outright. An unfortunate accident, apparently. They had no idea who he was but Dan identified him as the man who had approached him outside the Apple Store. He had to repeat several times, for the benefit of the recording, that he had never met the man before and had no idea who he was. Somehow, he still had the feeling that what had happened was all down to him, even though logically he knew it wasn't. He was so tired, so totally wrung out, he couldn't see straight. On top of everything, Kristen had called while he was still at the police station and had left a message saying that she had heard that the CCRC were going to decide on Farrell's case the following week. She had also heard from her source that, based on the evidence that they had so far reviewed, they were unlikely to refer the case back to the appeal court. He had tried many times to get hold of Eve, but she wasn't answering her phone and, after leaving several messages, he gave up.

The track on his phone changed to Bon Jovi's 'Always'. How ironic, he thought. Would his heart always bleed for Kristen? He listened for a few bars, then switched it off. It wasn't good to play that sort of sentimental stuff, particularly after the day he'd had. Kristen's message had been crisp and businesslike, as though she were talking to a work colleague rather than a former lover. Maybe to her, it was just another day-to-day failure for the charity, part of the nature of the beast. The odds were always poor when battling the monolith of the justice system, although 4Justice was as much her charity as his and he was surprised at her lack of emotion. She had once cared passionately about each case. It was one of the main things he had loved about her and it had cemented their relationship in the face of all sorts of differences. She had also felt passionately about him, or so she had once said. It suddenly struck him that she was trying to distance herself from him, not the charity, as though any tenderness or compassion might encourage him. He had never loved anybody with the intensity that he had loved Kristen, but he knew in his heart it was over.

He reached down for the bottle of vodka, but there was nothing much left in it. He stared at it for a moment, trying to work out how many nights it had lasted. He was drinking too much but, unlike the true alcoholics he had known, his father being one, it wasn't yet unthinking and automatic. He had a choice. He didn't need an eye opener in the morning and he could wait until the evening, most days, depending on how stressful things had been. He still took pleasure in each mouthful, as well as enjoying the dulling of the edges and the quick buzz and sense of lightness it brought. It was no different to taking painkillers or other forms of temporary medication, he kept telling himself. It was just for now and he was OK with that. He drained the last mouthful and was debating whether or not he could be bothered to go downstairs to the shop on the corner for another bottle, when he heard a sound outside in the main office. He listened more closely. At first he thought it was Zofia, having problems with her key, but she rarely came into the office at night and just an hour before, he'd bumped into her in the hall as he was coming in. She was on her way out in full Goth makeup, looking like she was going to make a night of it. He felt like quipping that Halloween had been and gone, but she was out the door too quickly. Apart from Kristen, the only other person who had a key was the cleaning lady, but she only came in on a Saturday morning. However, somebody was definitely fiddling with the lock.

He got out of bed, grabbed the bottle by the neck and tiptoed barefoot to the door of his room. He had left it ajar and he could see through the gap. The light from the street outside cast a yellow glow into the office and he watched as, after more rattling of the lock, the door slowly opened and a man entered. He was small and very skinny, dressed in a dark hoodie and jeans. He carried a torch in one of his gloved hands, which he shone quickly around the room and over the block of desks, then turned his attention to the bank of filing cabinets beside the window. Dan held his breath, wondering what to do. The image of Mickey's flat, and Mickey's dead body, flashed through his mind. Should he call the police? He dismissed the idea. By the time they arrived, the man would be long gone. He was a lot taller and bigger than the man, if it came to a fight, although he might not be a match for a knife, if the man knew how to use it, let alone a gun. Better to wait and see what the intruder wanted. The man took a scrap of paper from his jeans pocket, shone the torch on it, then scanned the filing cabinets. They were ranked alphabetically, everything clearly marked, thanks to a friend of Zofia's who had come in for a couple of days recently to sort everything out. Yet the man hesitated, as though he wasn't sure where to find what he wanted. He pulled one open, shone the torch along the row of tabs, then shut it again. He tried another, two above, and then another. This time it looked like he had found what he wanted, as he pulled out a thick manila folder from one of the hanging files.

Dan took a step forwards, trying to see which file it was and a floorboard creaked under his weight. The man started, turned and shone the torch at Dan.

'Hey,' Dan shouted, blinded by the light as he threw open the door. The man dropped the file and the torch, ran out the door and thudded down the stairs. Dan rushed out after him into the busy street, but he had disappeared.

Upstairs in the office, Dan switched on the lights and picked up the file. 'Sean Farrell Appeal' was written on the outside. The creased piece of paper the man had pulled out of his pocket was lying on the floor. *SEAN FARRELL* was written in capitals in ink on the inside. Also beneath it the name *MICKEY FRASER*. Using the edge of his sleeve, he picked up the slip of paper and put it in an envelope. The man had been wearing gloves in the office, but someone might have touched it with bare fingers at some point. Eve would know where to have it tested. Even if the CCRC had lost interest, the case was still very much alive for somebody.

# TWENTY-NINE

Eve heard the grinding sound of the rubbish truck as it came slowly down the lane and stopped outside the cottage. Heavy footsteps tramped up to the front door. A clatter of bin lids followed, then a man's voice shouted in a foreign language to somebody down below in the road. The footsteps retreated again, doors slammed and the truck moved on. She could tell from the

crack in the curtains that it was just starting to get light outside.
She raised her wrist to her face and checked her watch. Just after
eight. Monday morning, she assumed. The day after Harry's lunch.
She was lying on the floor of the bedroom, where she had fallen
earlier when trying to get out of bed. She was naked, the duvet
twisted around the middle of her body, leaving her arms and legs
very cold. She was still woozy, but it was a big improvement on
how she had felt a few hours before. Whatever she had been
given was finally wearing off. She pushed herself up into a sitting
position and pulled the duvet around her shoulders. Various items
of her clothing were dotted about the carpet like flotsam and jetsam.
Her handbag was sitting on a chair in the bedroom and she
wondered who had put it there. The last thing she could recall
from the party was talking to Gavin in the marquee, then feeling
suddenly sick and dizzy. That had been some seventeen or so hours
before, she slowly calculated.

The intervening period had been filled with a series of nightmares, familiar stuff dredged up from deep down, distorted,
terrifying images spiralling out of her subconscious. Voices,
screams, the whip-cracking rattle of gunfire, people running,
panic, breathlessness. She saw slaughtered animals come alive
on a butcher's slab, two little boys in pyjamas clawing their way
up through the dark, wet earth, then everything spontaneously
combusting and melting into ash. She felt an explosion, smelt
burning in the air. *Where's the girl? Find the girl.* Amongst a
swirling mist of images, she saw a woman's pale, oval face
morphing into an unknown man's, then a hooded, cloaked skeleton, the images rippling and swelling and changing like ink
splashed on oily water, then she saw the face of a different man,
with long hair and deep-set, mocking eyes, then Harry's face,
smiling, Gavin's face, worried, a man she had talked to at the
party. Was he the vet? Then Stuart Wade . . . Damon Wade . . .
The faces went around and around in her head. She felt a hand
clamped over her eyes, lips hard on hers, a tongue in her mouth
as a hand moved between her thighs. She felt the weight of
someone strong and muscular holding her wrists, pressing down
on her until she almost couldn't breathe. She couldn't move. She
couldn't cry out. He forced her arms and legs this way and that,
turning her over, turning her back, like a lifeless doll, something

over her face and mouth, all through it her skin dead to his touch. It was as though it wasn't her body at all and she was floating, detached, looking down, from somewhere else. Had she died? Was it some vision of hell?

She still felt the residue of paranoia that came with drugs, but she knew exactly what had happened. Breathing deeply many times, she tried again to shake off the images that still filled her mind. She had never been raped before, never even come close, but rage was pointless. It wouldn't get her anywhere. She needed to try and hold herself together and focus on what had to be done. If they thought she would give up and go home, they were wrong. When you had lost everything that had ever meant anything to you, there was little left to care about and nothing to fear. Wiping away tears, she tried to think back to the sequence of events the day before, re-imagining her every movement from the time she arrived at the party to when she started to feel unwell. Most so-called date-rape drugs were fast acting, usually twenty to thirty minutes and sometimes less. Whether in powder or liquid form, they were easy to add to somebody's food or drink and generally undetectable until it was too late. She had left her glass unattended on the lunch table on various occasions, the last being when Harry took her to meet Stuart Wade and his son. Wade had sent Damon off to get her another drink and a waiter had brought over a tray with a fresh glass. It had all happened very quickly, almost in front of her eyes, but that meant nothing. There was no point calling the police, she decided. What could they do? She had no idea who had raped her – there had been a good hundred or so men in the room – and they would laugh at her if she told them it had something to do with the Sean Farrell case. Nor did she want any word of what she was up to in Marlborough getting back to the Met. She knew exactly what must be done and she could do it herself, if only she could summon the energy. Hopefully the drug, whatever it was – some powerful fast-acting sedative, with psychotropic properties – would still be in her bloodstream, but she had to act quickly.

Holding onto the edge of the bed, waiting for each little wave of dizziness to pass, she slowly got to her feet and stumbled over to the window. The smell of him was all over her and the room reeked of what he had done. She wanted to vomit. She wrenched back the curtains, fumbled with the catch, then threw it open as wide as it would go. The curtains flapped and pulled against the little painted rail, as the freezing wind blew into the room. She stood for a moment looking out at the dark fields across the lane and the fading moon, which hung low on the horizon. She filled her lungs with gasp after gasp of fresh air, then yanked the window shut again, went into the bathroom and switched on the light. It dazzled her and she shielded her eyes as she peered into the shell-framed mirror that hung above the basin. Her pale, tired face stared back at her, remarkably untouched apart from the deep, dark circles under her eyes. For a moment, she saw her mother and two little brothers standing beside her, looking at her. It was a glimpse of the hidden world that was always there. She saw the ghost of herself, the girl she might have been if things had been different, the what-if that had haunted her whole adult life. Not for the first time, she wished she could step into the mirror and become that girl.

She remembered another time, some twenty years before, when she had looked at herself in a different mirror, wondering why she had survived. What was so special about her? Why had she been chosen to live? It was a curse, not a reward. She was standing on a chair in the safe house, dressed in purple velvet tracksuit bottoms and a matching top, with big, glitter stars on the front. It wasn't at all the sort of thing she would have picked, but she hadn't been given any choice. She always preferred boys' clothes to girls', but nobody listened. All her things were gone and it was the best they could do. The outfit had come from a local charity shop. She was very small for her age and it was difficult to find things to fit her. She was nearly thirteen, for God's sake, but she looked like a stupid child. She had stared at her pathetic reflection, with her round, baby-doll face, long mess of dark hair, scraped back in an Alice band, and scrawny, unformed little body, and felt like dying. What was there to live for? One of the police had come into the room behind her. They had helped her off the chair and comforted her as best they could until eventually she stopped crying. She remembered the exhaustion she felt afterwards and the sense of complete emptiness. Twenty years on, the image was still vivid and raw.

Eve fetched a chair from the cottage bedroom, climbed

unsteadily onto it and examined herself in detail in the mirror, checking every inch of her body. Apart from a little soreness around her wrists and the inside of her thighs, and a dark, angry red mark on one of her breasts, there were little outwards signs of what had happened. She wanted to rinse out her mouth, stand under the shower and scrub herself clean but she knew she mustn't. Samples must be taken. They needed to be profession-ally analysed and documented. It was the only way of catching whoever had done this.

She was about to get dressed when she heard a knock at the front door downstairs, then a moment later the sound of a key in the lock, followed by a woman's voice.

'Hello? Eve? It's Melissa. Are you awake?'

She heard the door close and Melissa's light footsteps in the hall.

'I'll be down in a minute,' she called out quickly. She didn't want Melissa coming upstairs.

She put on her dressing gown and went out onto the small landing. Melissa was staring up at her.

'Are you OK?' she asked.

'Yes.' Holding on tightly to the banister, she sank down onto the top step, as a wave of dizziness hit her. 'Who brought me home?'

'I did. With Gavin. You passed out.'

'You brought me home in the car?'

'Yes. Gavin carried you upstairs and we put you to bed.'

'In my clothes?'

'Yes.' She heard the note of surprise in Melissa's voice. 'Sorry, but I didn't want to undress you. In case you were cold, I mean. I just put the duvet over you.' She spoke quickly, sounding embarrassed, as though perhaps she thought she should have done more. Like everybody else, she no doubt assumed Eve had been drunk.

'Then what did you do? I need to know exactly what happened.' Her tone was a little abrupt and she saw a look of surprise cross Melissa's face. 'I don't remember anything,' Eve added. 'I just want to fill in the gaps.'

'Well, Gavin had to go back to London. Somebody was giving him a lift and the man couldn't wait. He was hanging around outside in the lane, which was a bit awkward. I stayed with you for about half an hour after they left, just to make sure you were alright.'

'This was what time?'

'Nearly six o'clock, I guess. You were, well . . . out for the count. I thought it best to let you sleep it off. Then I went back to the yard to help clear up. Most people had gone, or were going, and Harry and the staff had everything under control, so I took the boys home to give them their tea.'

Again it sounded as though she wanted to justify why she and Gavin had left so quickly, but there was no need. Drugs like the one Eve had been given lasted for hours, sometimes days. Whatever had been used to spike her drink, she was at least thankful she had had no alcohol with it. It would have made everything ten times worse and she might even have died. It was ironic that, after everything she'd survived in her life so far, she might have been killed by something as simple as a Mickey Finn.

'Thank you for doing that, for looking after me. I'm beginning to feel a lot better.' It wasn't true. Her head was in a fog and she still felt nauseous, but she wanted Melissa to go. There were things she needed to do. Somehow, she had to get herself to London, although she certainly wasn't fit to drive. She would use some of Duran's money to pay for a taxi.

Melissa was still hovering below looking concerned. 'Can I get you anything?'

Eve had the impression that Melissa felt responsible in some way.

'Honestly, I'll be fine. Apart from Gavin, was anybody else with you last night?'

'In the cottage?'

'Yes.'

'No. Just the two of us.'

'Did anybody else know I was ill? At the party, I mean.'

Melissa hesitated, again looking a little uncomfortable.

'Please. I just need to know.'

'Well, there were quite a few people around at the time. They were obviously concerned for you. But I don't think anybody will remember much about it. They were all quite drunk themselves.'

One of the last things Eve remembered was Gavin saying

loudly and forcefully to somebody 'Eve doesn't drink', but maybe nobody had been paying attention, or had believed him. Probably nobody cared. Part of her – her stupid pride – wanted to explain, but it was easier to leave Melissa with the impression that she had been drunk, than go into what had really happened.

'How did you get in?' Eve asked. 'I thought I took the key with me.' She had removed the key from above the front door after the incident the previous night with the so-called poacher.

'I found it in your handbag. I put it back where we keep it, above the front door, just in case I needed to let myself in again. In case *you* needed anything . . .'

So, somebody else had let themselves in. Somebody who knew, or who had been told, where the key was kept. She heard hurried footsteps outside, followed by a loud rap at the door. She hoped it wasn't Harry. Melissa went to open it, but instead of Harry, Dan stood outside under the porch. A gust of freezing air blew into the hall and Eve shivered, wrapping the dressing gown even more tightly around herself.

'Eve, I've been calling you,' he said, stepping inside and slamming the door shut behind him, his tone urgent and full of emotion. 'I kept getting your voicemail.' He stared up at her, his arms dangling at his sides.

'I got your message. I tried calling you back, but I've got no signal here. What's the matter?'

He glanced at Melissa, then back at her. 'Several things, in fact. We need to talk.'

'Dan's with 4Justice,' Eve said to Melissa. 'He's helping with Sean Farrell's appeal.'

'Well, if you're sure there's nothing I can do, Eve, I'll be off,' Melissa said briskly. 'I left my mother doing the school run, which she loathes, and I have to meet Harry now down at the yard for a run through on yesterday. The yearling sale went very well, apparently.'

'I'll be fine,' Eve replied firmly.

'Are *you* alright?' Dan asked, as soon as Melissa closed the front door behind her.

'No. I'm not. I need to go to London right away, but I'm not fit to drive a car. Can you take me?'

'Yes, of course. Where to?'

'A hospital. Central London. I'll give you the address on the way.' She saw the alarm on his face.

'What's happened?'

'I'll explain in the car. Really, I'll be OK, don't worry. Tell me first why you're here.'

He sighed heavily. 'We've had a tip-off that the CCRC are going to rule on Sean's case next week. They apparently want to get it out of the way before Christmas. Basically, we've run out of time and they're looking to throw the case out.'

'Oh, Dan. I'm very sorry.' Surely that couldn't be the end of it? There had to be another way. Holding onto the bannister, she slowly got to her feet. 'It was always going to be the most likely outcome. But you say we have a week? That may be enough. We mustn't give up just yet. If we can come up with something new, they'll be forced to change their minds.'

Her words had little effect. 'How the hell are we going to do that?'

What could she say? She didn't believe in God, or magic, or the Fates. You were on your own in life. You had to make things happen. Even so, it was wrong that a man like Farrell should waste his life away in jail because the system was flawed.

'Was that it? Or is there something else?'

He looked even more uncomfortable. 'There is something. But I'll tell you about it in the car.'

'You're not in any trouble, are you?' she asked, remembering Andy Fagan's message.

He sighed. 'No more than usual. And nothing I can't handle, I guess.' He looked down at his feet, avoiding her gaze.

The words 'I guess' said it all and she wondered what could have happened.

'You're sure about that?'

He nodded. 'It's a long story. But it can wait until later and it won't change anything much, at least not as far as poor Sean is concerned.'

'OK. Make yourself a cup of coffee while I get dressed. I've just got a few things I need to do before we go.'

# THIRTY

'Do you have any idea who did this to you, Eve?' Dr Margot Alexander asked, meeting her gaze with penetrating eyes, her pencilled brows arching a fraction over the rim of her glasses.

Eve shook her head. 'No. And, as I said, I don't want the police involved, at least not yet. But I do need the results back as soon as possible. I'm happy to pay whatever it costs myself.'

Margot pursed her plum-coloured lips and gave a precise, little nod. 'Understood.'

They were in her office in the basement of one of London's vast teaching hospitals, where she worked as a pathologist. She had examined Eve and taken all the necessary swabs and samples, including blood, all of which would be sent off to an independent lab for analysis. With her dark hair neatly pinned up in a bun, she looked bright and fresh in her white lab coat. Her rubber-soled shoes squeaked on the linoleum as she moved quickly around the small room, bagging up samples, filling out the necessary forms and tidying up. They had known each other professionally for the best part of ten years, since the first murder case they had worked on together, and occasionally met for a drink outside work. Margot could be trusted to be discreet, as well as very thorough. Although horrified at what had happened, and possibly even more shocked that Eve appeared to be so outwardly calm, she had finally accepted that Eve didn't want to go into any of the details or involve the police. But she kept darting Eve little concerned looks from time to time, as though she expected her to fall to pieces at any moment and must be ready in an instant to pick them up. Thankfully, whatever her views, she had the sensitivity to keep her mouth shut. Eve had no wish to discuss how she was feeling. She didn't even really understand it herself. She had worked for a while in one of the Met's Sapphire Units, dealing on a daily basis with crimes of a sexual nature, the victims both male and female. Each crime, each circumstance, each reaction was unique. It was impossible to generalize. Yet still she felt completely inadequate in her response. Maybe it had been easier for her to distance herself from what had happened, as she hadn't been fully awake. The vague memories were like fleeting dreams, melded with nightmares from the past and she wasn't sure what was real and what was not. She hadn't known terror, or desperation, or humiliation, or had feared for her life and there had been little physical violence other than the act itself. Moments of blind, senseless fury and a desire for revenge were the only emotions that punctuated the drifting fog of numbness that had set in. The distancing, the feeling of being an observer was her 'coping mechanism', according to one of her psychotherapists. 'It's how you survive, Eve. It's how you deal with the bad stuff.' How *bad* did it have to get, for her to rage and scream and cry like a normal person about what had been done to her? Maybe she was still in shock. Maybe at some point the full horror of what had happened would suddenly come crashing down over her. In the meantime, she had to keep going as best she could.

'When can I expect the results back?' she asked.

'I'll fast track them. The semen analysis will take a couple of days but, as you know, the tox results could be weeks. I'll also write an official report. As and when you need it for evidence, everything will be properly documented.'

'I've got a few more things that need testing, both for prints and DNA.'

She handed Margot a shopping bag, which contained, separately bagged, the mug and glass Harry had used the night he took her out for dinner, which she had retrieved, still unwashed, from the dishwasher, as well as his many cigarette butts from the kitchen bin.

'I can get the DNA profiles back in twenty-four hours.'

'Good. It may be a long shot – a precaution, really. But I need to know as soon as possible if there's a match with the samples you took from me.' She still couldn't quite believe that Harry was responsible, although there was often no rhyme or reason to rape and she barely knew him. But if her instincts were right and there was a link to the samples taken from Jane McNeil's body, Harry had an alibi, which had satisfied the police. If not

Harry, it could have been anybody at the party. It was a shame she couldn't get hold of Stuart Wade's glass too. He looked like a man with attitude and enough pent-up aggression to carry out a rape. 'This piece of paper also needs testing, both for prints and DNA.' She handed Margot the envelope that Dan had given her in the car, containing the slip of paper dropped by the intruder in his office the night before. 'It relates to a break-in. I've no idea if there's a connection to what happened to me, or if you'll find anything. The man who dropped it was wearing gloves. But whoever gave it to him may have been less careful. I just want to be on the safe side.'

'No problem,' Margot said. 'We'll process it as quickly as possible. We can sort out the finances later. But, as I said, the tox results will take a while. Any ideas what we should be looking for?'

'One of the dissociatives, like Ketamine. I was hallucinating and had a strange, out-of-body experience.'

Ketamine also seemed a likely candidate for so-called date rape on a racing yard, since its primary use was as a horse anaesthetic and it was easy to get hold of. She wondered if it had been used to knock out Jane McNeil too, although there had been no mention in the pathologist's report summary of any drugs being found in her system. Either the time elapsed was too long and the body was too badly decomposed, or they hadn't checked for it. It was equally likely that she had gone willingly with her killer.

Margot peered at her again questioningly over her glasses. 'You say you think this might be related to a cold case?'

'It's not just cold, it's dead and buried and someone's doing time for the murder.'

'But you think the real killer's still on the loose?'

'Maybe.'

'Can't you retest the exhibits?'

'The local police won't cooperate. There's a review of the case pending with the CCRC, but it's looking as though they may throw it out. The autopsy report was inconclusive, but sperm were found on the victim's thigh. Unfortunately, there wasn't enough biological material to develop a full DNA profile ten years ago. To give you the background, it had been raining heavily for many days at the time and the body had been partially set on fire, then half buried beside a brook, or a gulley, so probably exposed to more water. The man who's in jail had a vasectomy, so the prosecution case centred on the sperm having got there by secondary transfer, such as a towel at the gym, or some such ludicrous means. Unfortunately, the jury believed them. Much more likely, she had sex with somebody else, who then killed her.'

'Sometimes the science is too complicated for the man in the street . . .'

'Or the expert witnesses think they're talking to a load of academics and no normal person can understand them, particularly if the defence is not up to paraphrasing and giving a clear explanation.'

'Very true. You said that the sperm were deformed?'

'That's right.'

'Well, you can discount the rain or water as a factor. Spermatozoa resist, even submerged in water, very well; better than blood, in fact. One of my students recently presented an interesting paper on the subject. She had to use pigskin as a proxy for human skin, but the results are compelling. If the sperm were abnormal, it's likely to be for another reason. I know you're wondering if there's a link to what happened to you and the old murder.'

Eve nodded.

'Let's see what we have here.'

She took one of the slides she had prepared and added some liquid with a pipette. 'We call this Christmas Tree stain and you'll see why, in a minute. Very apt for this time of year, I think, and it's one of my favourites.' She placed the glass cover slip on the slide, slotted it into the tray of the microscope and peered down the eyepieces.

'Hmm. Very interesting,' she said, after a moment. 'You'd better come and look at this.'

She stepped aside and Eve put her eyes to the lenses, adjusting the focus until the image was clear. The background was a greenish colour and it was speckled with little red dots, which at first glance did look remarkably like Christmas tree baubles.

'The red bits are the spermatozoa,' Margot said. 'If you look closely, you'll see they are all irregular in size and shape. Some have deformed heads, or twin heads, some have twin tails, but the majority have no tails at all.'

Eve felt her stomach lurch and shuddered. It was exactly as the biologist giving evidence at Sean Farrell's trial had described. What were the odds? Blinking, she peered up at Margot. 'What causes sperm to be abnormal?'

'A variety of things. You'll find abnormal sperm in most samples, but it's the percentage that matters in terms of fertility. There's no way any of those are going to swim far enough to fertilize an egg.'

'How common is something like this?'

'I'm not an expert, but it's commoner than you'd think.'

Eve took a deep breath. What were the odds, she asked herself again. She didn't believe in coincidence. 'Going back to the man in jail, how would his sample differ?'

'With somebody who's had a vasectomy, you'll still have seminal fluid, and you might just possibly see a few red dots, depending on how well the operation was performed. But nothing like the number you'd expect in a healthy sample, or a sample like this one. Whoever he is, the man who attacked you certainly couldn't father any children.'

# THIRTY-ONE

'I don't see why somebody would go to the trouble of trying to steal this,' Eve said, closing Dan's file on the Sean Farrell case and handing it back to him.

She had leafed through it and, although it was full of interesting material relating to Jane McNeil's murder and Sean Farrell's trial, none of it was new to her, and none of it particularly sensitive. Bar the interviews with Farrell and various members of his family, most of it was in the public domain, if somebody had the will and the nous to look for it.

'There's got to be something else they're after,' she said firmly, studying Dan. But there was no visible reaction.

He stared at the cover blankly for a moment, then tossed it down on a pile of other papers beside him. They were in his office in Earl's Court, Eve sitting on the sofa under the window,

Dan perched on the edge of one of the desks facing her, chain smoking. Even though she'd opened the window a few inches, the air was thick with smoke and the smell was making her feel nauseous. Zofia was at her desk, behind where Dan was sitting, typing something at considerable speed into her computer. Occasionally she would glance down at a notebook, which lay open beside her on the desk, but most of the time she stared fixedly at the screen as though engrossed in what she was doing. However, it was clear from little sideways movements of her eyes that she was listening closely to their conversation.

Eve decided she didn't care. Zofia could listen in as much as she liked. It had been a long day and it was the least of her worries. Shocked by what had happened to her, as well as in a cloud of despondency about the imminent ruling by the CCRC on Sean Farrell's case, Dan had been happy to keep her company and act as her chauffeur for the day. He had waited patiently for her outside the hospital while Margot had examined her, then had driven her back to her flat, where he had again waited outside without complaint for three quarters of an hour while she showered and changed. He was even prepared to drive her back to Marlborough, if that was what she wanted, but she had decided to stay in London. She couldn't face returning to the cottage. Luckily, he had understood not to try and probe her about what had happened, although at one point she feared he was going to put his arms around her to hug her and she had turned quickly away. She felt too fragile. Even the smallest kindness, the warmth of human touch and sympathy might make her fall apart. However difficult, she had to try and block out, for the moment, what had happened.

A gust of wind rattled the window above her as a burst of icy rain peppered the glass like a handful of lead-shot. She shivered and wrapped her cardigan tightly around herself.

'OK, Dan. Answer me this. Did you take the Sean Farrell file from Mickey Fraser's flat?'

A look of genuine surprise crossed his face. 'No. I told you, the files were thrown on the floor. I had no idea what was there. Is it missing?'

'Apparently so.'

'How do you know? Did the police tell you?'

She nodded. 'Fagan said it's the only file unaccounted for in Mickey's flat, when they put everything back together. I'd say whoever took it – let's assume it's Mickey's murderer – came here, or sent somebody here, to get your file too. Which means there's something they want, that they think might be in your file perhaps, or in your possession. Once again, Dan, have you *any* idea what it could be?'

This time doubt and stubbornness clouded his face. She leant forwards towards him and met his gaze, lowering her voice, as though it were just the two of them in the room.

'We have to trust each other, Dan. We're all we've got. If it will help, short of your having actually murdered Mickey, which I'm sure you didn't, you have my word that I won't tell anybody, without your permission, whatever it is you've done. But I know you've done something, or got something you shouldn't have, so don't try and bullshit me.'

She stared at him for a moment, wondering what it would take to get through to him. In his eyes, she was a stranger and, worse still, a policewoman. Years of ingrained mistrust were hard to overcome.

'The stakes are already very high, and getting higher,' she continued. 'Think it through. Mickey was murdered, he was tortured, presumably to extract information. His flat is turned upside down and a file is missing. I start asking questions about Jane McNeil's murder and look what happens to me. Next thing we know, your office is broken into and somebody tries to steal your file. It all points to Mickey having found out something – some hard evidence, possibly – that relates to Jane's murder and Sean Farrell's innocence.'

'I'm not stupid,' he said morosely.

'Where it is now is anyone's guess, but they clearly want it badly and think you have it. They're likely to come back again.'

There was no reaction on Dan's face. He took out the pack of Camels from his pocket and, hand trembling slightly, lit up again, blowing a couple of perfect rings into the air.

'You smoke too much,' she said, waving away the smoke as it drifted towards her.

'Yeah, and I drink too much too. But who's counting? Don't you have any vices?'

He stared at her challengingly, his eyes watering and a little bloodshot, which made the blue of his irises even more intense.

'Of course. But we're getting off the point.' More pressing than anything was what Dan knew, what he was holding back.

He gave her a weary look. 'OK. What about the man in Covent Garden? I mean Nasser, the one who died, who wanted me to follow him. Where does he fit in? And what about the other one, the younger man, who called me on Mickey's phone and said he was Mickey's friend?'

'I don't know. I need to speak to Andy to see if he'll tell me exactly what happened, if he's found out who they are and what their connection to Mickey is.'

'You think *they* killed Mickey?'

'If they did, or worked for whoever did it, I don't see the point of getting in touch with you and luring you to Covent Garden.'

He nodded. 'That was what I thought.'

'Either they had some scam of their own going on the side, or it's just possible they had nothing to do with the murder. Which begs the question, *why*, apart from wanting money, get in touch with you? You say he knew Mickey was dead?'

'Yes. The younger one, Hassan, did, at least. He sounded genuinely upset.'

'Maybe he was Mickey's friend. But how come he has Mickey's phone, unless he stole it? You really have no idea who this man is?'

He looked affronted. 'No, I do *not*,' he said emphatically and, for once, she believed him. 'How the hell do we go about finding him?' he asked after a moment.

'We don't. We need to stick to what we're doing for Sean and forget about the rest. Leave it up to the police.' Fagan would be throwing all his resources at finding the man. 'Come on, Dan. There must be something. There *has* to be. It's me, Eve, you're talking to. Not the police.'

'You *are* the police,' Zofia muttered from behind her computer.

Eve looked over at her. 'No, Zofia. I'm not here as a policewoman.'

Zofia shook her head knowingly, still staring at the screen. 'Once police, always police.'

'You're wrong,' Eve said.

Zofia swivelled around in her chair to face Eve, her face red with emotion. 'I don't get why you here. Who sent you? Why you interested in Sean Farrell, may I ask?' She gesticulated with her hand for emphasis.

'No Zofia, you may not ask,' Dan said sharply, twisting around to look at her. 'I told you before why Eve's here.'

'I don't believe her,' Zofia said, her chin jutting out like a stubborn child's.

'Well I do,' Dan said. 'And that's all that matters. So, just shut the fuck up for once.'

Zofia shook her head angrily. 'OK. But you are fool, Dan. You see. She get us all in trouble.' Her ample chest heaving, she faced her computer again, muttering something to herself in Polish, the apparently universal words 'idiot' and 'cretin' discernible in the mix.

Eve stood up and stretched her arms and shoulders. 'I've had enough of this. I'm off home. You're on your own now, Dan.'

'You're chucking in the towel?'

'No. I'll carry on doing whatever I need to do. I'm just finished working with you, unless you come clean. It's your choice.'

Dan studied her for a moment. She saw a mixture of emotions cross his face. Perhaps he thought she didn't mean it, or perhaps he didn't care any longer. Zofia was staring at him, eyes stretched wide, willing him to keep quiet.

Eve picked up her bag and coat and turned to go. She was almost out of the door when Dan called out.

'Wait!'

She turned around. He stubbed out the remains of his cigarette and slowly and stiffly stood up.

'Don't trust her, Dan,' Zofia shouted, springing to her feet and taking a step towards him as though she physically intended to restrain him.

Dan shook his head. 'She's right, Zofia. We've got to trust her. We've got nothing to lose.'

'You being bloody stupid, Dan,' Zofia shouted.

'Maybe. It won't be the first time. But there's nowhere left to go. It's just one more week.' With a loud, throaty sigh he turned his back on Zofia and walked over to where Eve was standing. 'Let's go and get a drink.'

He grabbed his coat from the hook by the door, waited for

Eve to put on hers, then followed her down the stairs and into the street. They walked in silence for a couple of blocks until they came to a pub just after the Tube station. 'This will do,' Dan said abruptly, holding open the door for her.

Inside, the lighting was dim. The cavernous, high-ceilinged room was almost empty, apart from a middle-aged man sitting at the bar reading a copy of the *Evening Standard* and a pencil-thin young girl, who looked no more than sixteen, wearing an apron, who was busy lighting the myriad of candles scattered around the room.

'What will you drink?' Dan asked.

'Let me get these.'

He held up his hand. 'I can afford to buy you a drink,' he said sharply. 'It's the *least* I can do.'

'Diet Coke then, with ice and lemon,' she replied, wondering if he was usually so touchy about everything.

While he went up to get their drinks, she chose a table in a far corner of the room and sat down on a comfortable-looking velvet sofa. Van Morrison was blaring cheerily through the speakers, something about precious time slipping away, which was ironic, Eve thought. She hoped Dan wasn't listening. She watched as he had a brief interchange with the young girl, who was now behind the bar, making her laugh flirtatiously at something, as he placed his order. His face lit up in response, giving her a wide, confident smile. Momentarily he looked like a very different Dan to the version she was used to dealing with.

'Come and sit down here,' she said quietly, pointing to the seat beside her when he returned with their drinks. She shifted her bag and coat to a nearby chair and moved over to make room. 'I don't want anyone to hear what we're talking about.'

He sank down next to her, leaned back heavily against the cushions and put his feet up on the seat of a chair opposite. He took a large mouthful of his drink then, with a heavy sigh, turned to face her.

'I don't know why you still want to carry on, after what's happened to you.'

'Because I have to,' she said. 'I'll survive.' As she said it, she knew she would. It struck her that she didn't feel altered as a person, less of a woman, less able to confront the world, less anything, whatever somebody had done to her. She would not be defined or broken by what had happened, however fragile she felt inside. The will to keep going and move forward was still reassuringly there. 'There are worse things.' Seeing the shocked look on his face, she added: 'Think about what happened to Mickey.'

'I think of nothing else.' He took another swig then put the glass down on the coffee table. 'We've had difficult and disappointing cases in the past. But nothing ever like this. Four of us set up 4Justice, hence the "four". Myself, Kristen, and two other journalists. We raised money for the charity and co-opted a load of experts as advisors, who were prepared to give their time for free. We thought we had it made, that we'd set the world to rights. Maybe we were naïve, seeing ourselves as crusaders for justice and that sort of crap, thinking we could really change things. We've helped free a number of people who shouldn't have ever been put inside, so it hasn't all been wasted. We have made a difference . . .'

'Of course you have.'

'Thank God we don't have the death penalty in this country. Sure, we got it wrong sometimes. But the bottom line is we were just trying to do an honest, decent job for people who've been badly let down by the system. End of.' He met her gaze. 'I never signed up for anything like this. Finding Mickey . . . All the heavy stuff with the police . . . What happened in Covent Garden . . . Even though it was an accident, the man died almost in front of me. I can't stop thinking about it, particularly Mickey. The flat. The darkness. How I found him. The disgusting smell of it all.'

'It's normal to feel that way after what you've been through.'

'Is it?' He looked at her as though she was from an alien world.

She said nothing. She had no wish to explain why she was so familiar with the trauma he was describing. Maybe over time the memories would fade a little and lose their immediacy, but whoever said that time was a healer had lied. There was no peace. The images would always be there, like splinters dug deep into the skin, festering away. Worse still were the nightmares. She thought of her drugged visions the night before and with a shudder, tried to force them again from her mind. The horror, the terror of those memories, which sleep had brought alive again with a new and terrible freshness, would never leave her. Even though she had told herself over and over again that she looked completely different now, unrecognizable from her twelve-year-old self, and that there was no way anybody would be able to find her, the illogical fear was still there. She had no advice to offer him.

'You feel responsible for Mickey's death?' she asked after a moment.

He turned to face her, eyes burning. 'Of course I do.'

'You mustn't think like that, Dan. You can't blame yourself. Mickey was a pro. He knew the score.'

'And I'm some sort of stupid, dabbling amateur, well out of my depth.'

'That wasn't what I meant.'

'But it's how I see myself.' He spread his hands. 'What good am I doing? How is any of this helping Sean Farrell? It's hopeless.' His hands flopped to his sides and he tilted his head and looked up at the ceiling for a moment as though expecting some sort of divine intervention. 'I should probably just call it quits. The charity's on its last legs anyway, unless I can find a new source of funding.'

'Why do *you* keep going? Why does it matter so much to *you*?'

He sighed and looked down at his hands. 'Sometimes I wonder if I'm mad. But it's just something I have to do. Something I believe in.'

'There must be more to it than that, surely?'

He looked up and met her gaze. 'My brother's in jail for a murder he didn't commit. I don't want to go into the details and there's absolutely nothing I can do about it. I've had to accept that that's just the way it is. But at least I can help other people. At least I feel I'm doing *something*.'

'I'm sorry,' she said. 'I had no idea.' She now understood why his career had taken such a dramatic turn and why, in the face of everything, he still cared so much when most people would have given up.

'It's not something I talk about. It's really nobody's business. But I'm also not the only one who has had first-hand experience of the failings of the justice system. Zofia has an uncle and a cousin in jail in Poland, both imprisoned on trumped-up charges of political corruption. She comes from a little town near the Ukranian border. Her father used to be mayor there, until the scandal hit and, although he escaped jail, he was forced to resign and was financially ruined, even though she says he did nothing wrong. Maybe things are a little different in Poland, but when you've been through what we both have, justice is a very tainted word.'

She saw tears in his eyes, perhaps of bitterness or frustration or hopelessness, and she felt for him. 'You mustn't give up. Why don't you move to a cheaper office, or something? The rent and rates around here must add up to quite a bit.'

He shook his head. 'We get the office and flat upstairs for free for the time being, thanks to one of our benefactors.'

'There must be some other way to cut costs and keep going?'

'We haven't got the human resources. Kristen's sensibly fucked off elsewhere to do more important things, which just leaves me and Zofia, when she isn't working on her thesis, and a couple of very part-time helpers. We haven't paid ourselves in months and I'm broke. I should go and get a proper job.'

Eve sighed. 'Fine. If that's what you want to do, nobody would blame you. But I have no choice. I have to continue. I need to find out if Sean Farrell murdered Jane McNeil, whatever it takes. There's a lot riding on this for me. That's why I have to know what you know.'

He turned to look at her. Suspicion again filled his eyes. He downed his glass and slammed it on the table in front of him. 'You know, Eve, that's something I never understood. What exactly is "riding on this" for you?'

'I told you . . .'

He waved her away with his hand. 'Yes, I know you gave me some story about doing a favour for someone, this bloke who gave us some money. I knew at the time it was a crock of shit, but I let it pass. It didn't really matter then. But it does now. Honesty is a two-way street.' He leaned forwards towards her, his face only inches away from hers, and looked her straight in the eye. His breath was hot and thick with alcohol. 'If you want me to trust you, tell you everything I know, you need to trust me first. *You* need to come clean with *me*.'

She gazed at him for a moment, weighing it all in her mind, then she nodded. What was the harm in telling him, she decided. She should trust him.

'What are you drinking?' she asked.

'Stolichnaya.'

She went up to the bar and bought them both another drink, then she sat down again, facing Dan this time. She told him about Jason's murder, about her contact with Duran and about what a dangerous man he was. She described in some detail his brutal killing of Stanco Rupec and how she had helped to put him in jail. She then explained how Duran had told her that she had been deliberately tricked into going to the house in North London, looking for an informant who wasn't there, and how she and Jason had disrupted an ongoing, high-level, covert police investigation. She said how Duran had promised to give her the proof she needed, if only she would look into Sean Farrell's conviction. Dan listened in silence, his eyes fixed on a distant corner of the room as though he were being told an extraordinary story that he wasn't quite sure was true. Perhaps it did sound farfetched to someone who wasn't part of her world.

When she finished, he turned to her and said, 'Why does this man, Duran, care? What's Farrell to someone like him?'

'I don't know. I can't work it out.'

'So you've chosen to ignore it? To turn a blind eye?'

She nodded. 'He won't tell me the real reason, other than that he's dying and has developed an altruistic streak. I don't buy it, but in the end, I decided where's the harm? I know I was set up. If I can help Sean too . . .'

'You mean the end justifies the means?'

She met his gaze. 'In this case, yes.'

'Maybe you're right. Maybe the end is all that matters.' He reached into the depths of his jeans pocket and fished out a little red memory stick. 'This is what I found in Mickey's flat.'

# THIRTY-TWO

Eve turned away from the screen and looked at Dan. 'So this is it? This is the big secret you've been keeping from me?'

They were back at his office. Zofia had left for the evening and they had spent the last hour on Dan's laptop, examining the contents of the flash drive that he had taken from Mickey's flat. Eve scanned Dan's face but all she could see was disappointment and weariness. Perhaps he had thought she might pick up something he had missed. The flash drive contained a series of clips and interviews, mostly taken from an old Channel 4 documentary about corruption in the UK horse-racing industry. It must have been sensational stuff at the time, with a former Jockey Club head of security acting as whistle-blower and a number of trainers, owners and jockeys implicated in a series of dopings and race-fixing scams, all masterminded by a well-known, drug-dealing criminal. But eight years on, was any of it relevant? It seemed unlikely. Nor was there any mention of the Westerby yard, Tim or Harry Michaels, or anyone associated with them, as far as she knew. However, of more interest were a series of JPEGs. The location data said 'Ascot Racecourse' and they were dated only ten days before, the day Mickey had gone to the races. Several of the images were of Stacey Woodward looking quite cosy with Damon Wade in a car at the racecourse, others were of him handing her a thick brown envelope. By the shape of it, it could easily contain a big wad of cash, but proving it would be impossible. Further JPEGs taken that evening in Mayfair in London, showed Damon and Stacey going into a nightclub together and coming out again several hours later, arm in arm. The fact that they seemed to be close meant nothing. Even if he had been giving her some sort of a pay-off earlier, it was hardly the smoking gun that someone was searching for, something worth not only breaking into Dan's office, let alone torturing and killing Mickey. There had to be something else they were after.

'I didn't know what was on it, until Zofia brought it back last night,' Dan said defensively. 'I didn't want you running off to Fagan saying I'd taken anything from Mickey's flat. I'm in enough trouble as it is. I told you, he doesn't believe a fucking word I say.'

She held up her hand. 'I get it. You still need to hand it over to Fagan at some point. But it can probably wait a few days. My main question is, why did Mickey bother to hide it?'

He shrugged. 'He was the sort to squirrel all sorts of things away in little places.'

'But still . . . To put it in a bottle of headache pills. It seems a bit impromptu, but it must have meant something. Perhaps he hid it quickly, on the spur of the moment, from someone who came to the flat. You said it was in the bathroom?'

Dan nodded.

'Maybe the whole subject of corruption in horse racing is sensitive.'

He threw up his hands. 'Or he was just paranoid.'

'Given what happened to him, I'd say he had good reason to be.'

He exhaled sharply. 'OK. So what do we do now?'

'We need to go back to basics and focus on Jane's murder. Nothing else. We must tidy up the loose ends. There are three people Jane knew, who I still need to speak to. Holly, the girl who shared the cottage with her, who Melissa sacked. The woman who worked in the office with her . . .' She clicked her fingers, searching in vain for the name. Her brain was increasingly fogged and she was beginning to struggle.

'You mean Annie?'

She nodded. 'And the owner, Lorne Anderson, who called Jane several times the week before she died. He took his horses away from the Michaels shortly after, so maybe he'll be more open about what was going on at the time. I haven't managed to get hold of the other two yet, so he seems to be the best bet.'

'What about what's on the flash drive?'

'I think it's worth finding out what happened to all of the people mentioned in the documentary, see if there's any connection with the Michaels family.'

'I know one of the journalists listed in the credits. He's a mate of Kristen's. I'll try and get hold of him first thing tomorrow. What about you?'

She stood up, stretched her arms and shoulders and picked up her bag. 'I'm going to get some sleep. I think you should too. Let's talk first thing tomorrow.'

Outside in the street, while she waited for a taxi, she called Gavin. When he picked up, he sounded surprised to hear from her.

'Are you alright?' he asked. 'I've been very worried about you.'

'I'm fine. Feeling much better now.'

'Melissa said she went around to see you this morning and you seemed a bit wobbly. I was going to call you later.'

'Really, I'm OK now. It was just some sort of twenty-four-hour bug, that's all.'

'I'm so pleased to hear it. I didn't know what could be wrong. It seemed to come on so suddenly—'

'It's nothing a good night of sleep won't put right,' she interrupted. 'Anyway, I'm not calling you about that. I need your help.'

'Of course. What is it?'

'I'm back in London now. I need to speak to a man called Lorne Anderson. He used to keep his horses at the Westerby yard at the time Jane was murdered.'

'I know who you mean.'

'I asked Harry if he could put me in touch, but he wasn't very helpful.'

'No, he wouldn't be. There was a huge fuss when Lorne took his horses away. It was soon after my father-in-law committed suicide and it was a very tough time. He wasn't the only one to leave either, it's often the way, I'm afraid. But Harry saw it all as a personal betrayal, particularly with Lorne. It got very heated, I remember.'

'Do you know how I can find him?'

There was a pause at the other end. 'Is it important?'

'I don't know, until I speak to him. He called Jane's mobile a few times during the week before she died. I need to know why.'

Again another pause. Then he said, 'How urgent is this?'

'Very. We apparently have a week before the CCRC make their decision on Sean Farrell's case.'

He sighed. 'OK. You know I want to help you any way I can, Eve. Let me speak to Melissa first. If he's still in racing, she may know who's training his horses now. Failing that, I think he and I have a mutual friend at the Bar. I'll try and track him down somehow and get back to you soon as I can.'

She hung up and as she started to walk towards the Tube, a taxi came long and she flagged it down. She wanted to get home as quickly as possible. As she climbed in, it struck her how, in agreeing to help her, Gavin was going against the Michaels family and their tribal loyalties. He could have said no, she told herself, although she knew in her heart he wouldn't have. Again she saw him as an outsider in their midst, part of them but not one of them. He had never belonged to their world. Never would. He was well aware of it, from what she could see, and it rankled.

She called Fagan but his phone went straight to voicemail. She left a brief message asking him to call and was about to try another number for him when her phone buzzed with a voicemail alert. She didn't recognize the number. When she listened to the playback, she heard an unfamiliar, high-pitched female voice at the other end.

'. . . this Eve? Hope I've got the . . . number.' The signal was poor and the voice kept cutting out. It was also difficult to hear clearly over the rattle of the taxi's engine and the noise from the traffic outside. '. . . gave me a message . . . said you want to speak to me. Something to do . . . Jane Mc . . . . . . name's . . . Shepherd.'

Eve played it again several times, finally catching the words 'Blue Cross' and the Christian name 'Annie'. She sank back against the seat and exhaled. It was a piece of luck at a time when they needed all the luck in the world. She didn't believe in fate or telepathy or any of the unconventional ways that people tried to explain the happenstance of such things. But sometimes things just worked that way when you were least expecting them. She called Annie back and arranged to meet her the following morning at a gift shop in Avebury, near Marlborough, where she worked a couple of days a week. She would pick up her car and her things from the cottage at the same time. She had no wish to stay in the cottage again.

The nausea from the drugs she had been given the day before had finally eased off and she was starting to feel hungry. Realizing there was nothing to eat in the fridge, she asked the taxi to drop her at a Co-Op on the Uxbridge Road a few blocks from her flat. She bought milk for her morning coffee, a couple of croissants and a bag of salad, along with some eggs and cheese to make an omelette. Ten minutes later, she let herself into the house. Her neighbours on the ground floor were back from work, judging by the sound of their television. She switched on the lights in the hall and started up the stairs to the first floor. As she did so, she noticed a couple of small patches of what looked like mud on the buff-coloured stair carpet. There was another halfway up, and a further one on the landing, right outside her door. She was sure they hadn't been there earlier. Placing her bag and shopping to one side, she bent down and examined them, feeling the tiny blobs of sandy earth and fragments of leaf-mould between her fingers. They were still damp. Somebody had gone up the stairs very recently. As she raised her eyes to the door, she saw that the strip of magic tape at the bottom had come unstuck at one end. She stood up, heart beating fast, and took a series of deep breaths to steady herself as she examined the lock. The scratches on the cheap, brass-plated escutcheon and the white-painted door were familiar. There was no sign of a forced entry. Even so, somebody had definitely opened the door to her flat, which meant they knew how to pick a lock. Slowly and quietly, alert to any sound or movement, she unlocked the door and peered inside. The lights were switched off, as she had left them, but light flooded in both front and back from outside, which meant somebody had opened the curtains and blinds. At least, peering around, she could see quite clearly that there was nobody there now. She switched on the lamps and started to examine everything more closely.

At first glance, nothing appeared to be out of place. It wasn't as though she had many things to check, but if somebody had been through her drawers and wardrobe, they had been very careful. Her eye was drawn to the small desk in the sitting room, where she kept her personal files. One of the bottom drawers was open a few millimetres, the tab of one of the folders caught as it closed. She knew she hadn't left it like that. She stared at it for a moment, remembering how earlier that morning in her bedroom in the cottage, she had had the impression that the things in her small suitcase had been disturbed. She had assumed at the time it was either Melissa or Gavin, possibly looking for something to make her more comfortable, but had forgotten to ask Melissa. She wondered now if she had been drugged so that someone could go through her things more easily. Maybe the rape was an afterthought, rather than a warning. At least there was nothing sensitive for them to find. Her file on the Sean Farrell case was locked in the boot of her car and, even if they had taken her car key and found it, they would have learned nothing. Knowing that they had wasted their time was some comfort, but they had been in her flat, her private space, eyes restlessly seeking, their foul, questing hands touching her things. It felt like another violation. As soon as she had finished what she was doing for Duran, she would give notice on her lease and move out. If the disciplinary hearing went the wrong way and she was out of a job, maybe she would go abroad.

She heard the main entrance door of the house slam shut below. She went out onto the landing and looked over the banisters. Alison, her neighbour, was struggling with her key in the lock of her flat front door.

'Sorry to bother you,' Eve called out, starting quickly down the stairs towards her. 'I wondered if you'd let anybody into the house in the last few hours.'

Alison looked up and shook her head breathlessly. She was dressed in a dark grey tracksuit and mud-spattered trainers, her face bright pink and glistening with sweat. 'I've been out most of the day. Let me ask Kelly. She's been in bed with a cold.' Alison disappeared inside for a moment. When she came back she looked a little worried. 'She says someone called a couple of hours ago. He said he was an emergency plumber, from the landlord, that your boiler was on the blink. Is anything wrong?'

'He wasn't from the landlord.'

As Eve spoke, Kelly appeared in the hall, behind Alison, shorter and plumper, wrapped up tightly in a towel dressing gown, with a woollen scarf tied tightly around her neck. 'I wasn't dressed so I spoke to him over the intercom,' she said in a hoarse voice. 'I had a peek at him through the front window. He knew your name. He showed me some sort of photo ID. It looked pretty official.'

'You let him in?'

She shrugged sheepishly. 'He asked if he could wait for you inside, as it was raining. I'm *really, really* sorry if I've done anything wrong.'

'It's OK. Don't worry. What did he look like?'

'He was wearing overalls and heavy boots. I'm pretty sure he had a toolbox with him. I assumed he was kosher.'

'What sort of age and build?'

She frowned, as though trying to picture it all again. 'Small, wiry, in his twenties, short black hair, olive skin.'

The basics certainly fitted Dan's description of the man he

had disturbed in the 4Justice office the night before. 'Anything else you remember?'

'He spoke good English but he had an accent.'

'You mean foreign?'

She nodded. 'Eastern European, maybe, although I'm not very good at telling. He can't have been up there long, though. No more than ten minutes, I think. I heard the front door slam when he left. It always makes such a noise. I'm so sorry, Eve. I just wasn't thinking.'

'Really don't worry. Nothing's missing. But if either of you see him again, call me right away, will you?'

# THIRTY-THREE

E ve pulled up in the empty public car park at Avebury, opposite the gift shop where Annie Shepherd worked. She had arranged to meet Annie at ten o'clock, but she was early and the shop was still shut up and dark. She had caught a train from Paddington to Swindon first thing that morning, then taken a taxi to the cottage. Hoping to avoid seeing anybody, she had rushed inside, quickly cleared up the few things she had left behind, and put them all in the boot of her car. As she did so, she noticed that the Sean Farrell file had gone. Maybe now they would leave her alone.

The wind blew clouds of rain across the sodden fields and circle of ancient stones, which looked like shadowy giants in the mist. She sat with the engine running, listening to the rain drum on the roof. What was usually a soothing sound made her feel on edge. She turned on the radio to drown out the sound, letting the burble of voices wash over her, but her thoughts kept turning to Mickey's flash drive. What was so important about it? She had picked up a couple of voicemails earlier that morning, one from Alan Peters saying that Duran was asking for an update. It was bad enough being in any way answerable to a man like him; worse still, she had nothing to tell him. The other was from her solicitor, wanting to set up another meeting as soon as possible with her barrister to prepare for the disciplinary hearing. She had managed to put it all out of her mind temporarily but time was running out for her, as well as for Sean Farrell. She had a week, at best, to get what she needed from Duran. The old doubts resurfaced. Could she trust him? Did he really have evidence that she had been set up and, if so, would he give it to her, even if she were unable to fulfil her side of the bargain? Worse still, she was no further forwards in finding out who had raped her or why. The sick feeling in her heart, the rising swell of emotions, which she had tried so hard to keep at bay, was pressing in on her more than ever. She closed her eyes, tilted her head back and squeezed the bridge of her nose to stop the tears. She mustn't give into it. She had to keep going, just for a little longer.

She heard a car coming along the lane behind her. She opened her eyes and saw it pull up right outside the gate to the shop. Engine and headlamps off, a woman jumped out and, with her shoulders hunched and head ducked low against the rain, she ran up to the door and unlocked it. She disappeared inside and a moment later started raising blinds and switching on lights. Eve gave her a couple of minutes to sort things out, then turned off the engine, climbed out of her car and sprinted across the road. A series of little bells jingled loudly as she pushed open the door. It was cold inside, the air pungent with the stale odour of incense. For a moment, it took her right back to her series of childhood homes, where her mother was always burning joss sticks and scented candles, probably to mask the smell of dope which usually followed whichever boyfriend was in residence.

'We're not open yet,' a woman's voice called out shrilly from the back of the shop.

'Annie, it's me. It's Eve.'

There was a pause, then Annie shouted back, 'Right. I'll be with you in a mo.'

The low-ceilinged room was filled floor to ceiling with shelves of crystals, fossils and Celtic-style souvenirs, wrapping paper and cards, and books on Wiltshire chalk horses, crop circles, local guide books, astrology and tarot. Tall glass cabinets stood against one wall full of more crystals, ornamental daggers and letter openers, what appeared to be carved wizards' wands, as well as silver jewellery and knick-knacks. A moment later, Annie emerged from a room at the back of the shop, with a full mug of something hot. She was dressed in jeans and clumpy, brown, rubber-soled boots, and an oversized jade-green cardigan with a shawl collar and huge, chunky mother-of-pearl buttons.

'You want a coffee?' she asked, putting her drink down carefully on the counter beside the till.

'I'm fine,' Eve said, not fancying the look of it and not wanting to waste time.

Annie went over to the entrance door, where she flipped the sign from 'closed' to 'open', then came back to the counter, where she lit a large, pink candle. She looked to be in her early forties, a few years older than Jane McNeil would have been if she were still alive. Her dark brown hair was threaded with grey and knotted in a loose bun. But the white streak at the front was still very noticeable and some sort of tattoo peeped out from beneath the edge of her sleeve on the back of her hand, just as Steve Wilby had described.

They sat down in a couple of chairs behind the counter and Eve explained about Sean Farrell's application to the CCRC.

'I dunno know how I can help,' Annie said, when she had finished. 'I talked to the police when it happened and there's nothin' much I can add to that.' The West Country burr Eve had heard on the phone was even more pronounced in person.

'But you knew Jane,' Eve said, catching the slightly defensive tone and wanting to put her at ease. 'I'm just trying to get an idea of what she was like as a person.'

Annie shrugged. 'I just knew her from work.'

Eve decided to start with the basics. 'Who else was in the office, in those days?'

'Just me, Jane, Sally Michaels . . . that's Tim's wife. She used to do a lot of the client stuff before Tim's death.'

'Anyone else?'

'Melissa was there on and off, and Helen . . .'

'Who was she?'

'She used to help Tim with the entries, but she left a month or so before Jane went missing. Then there was Susan . . .'

'Is that Susan Wright?'

'Yeah. She came in once a week to do the books.'

'She apparently saw Sean Farrell outside Jane's cottage the night of the party.'

Annie took a sip of coffee. 'So she said.'

Eve looked at her curiously. 'She didn't see him?'

'I'm sure she saw *someone*, I just don't think she should've been so positive 'bout it being Sean.'

'Why do you say that?'

'Well, her eyesight wasn't that great, poor love.'

'If she wasn't sure, why did she tell the police that it was Sean?' Eve asked, wondering why Dan hadn't picked up on this detail.

'I suppose 'coz she thought it *was* 'im. If you ask me, she sort of talked herself into it. Once she'd *said* she saw Sean, they were all on her like a pack of hounds and it was difficult going back.'

'There was nothing malicious in it? She didn't have it in for Sean?'

'Nah. Anyways, they had other evidence against him, or so I was told. And maybe she did see him.' She opened her eyes wide and gave another shrug.

Susan Wright wouldn't be the first, or the last, unreliable witness, Eve thought, pressurized into giving the police what they thought they wanted to hear. But it was a shame Farrell's barrister hadn't cross-examined her more forcefully, or done his homework about her eyesight. It was yet another piece of circumstantial evidence against Sean Farrell that was questionable.

'Do you know where I can find Susan?'

''Fraid you're too late. She dropped dead of a heart attack a few years back.'

Eve tried to hide her disappointment. There was no way now of getting Susan to retract her statement, although it wouldn't have been enough on its own to persuade the CCRC to take up the case.

'I understand you drove past the cottage a bit before Susan,' Eve said.

'That's right. The lights were on so I thought Jane was in.'

'You didn't notice anybody hanging around?'

Annie shook her head.

'Did you ever see Jane outside work at all?'

'Once or twice, maybe, with some of the others from the yard, but we didn't really socialize much.'

'What was your impression of her?'

Annie hesitated, as though choosing her words carefully. 'She just got on with the job and she kept herself to herself most of the time.'

'Did you *like* her?'

'I'm sorry she's dead, if that's what you mean.'

'But you didn't actually like her?' Eve insisted.

Annie was silent for a moment, her lips forming into a tight pout. 'I didn't take to her, if I'm honest. She thought she was above us all, or at least that's the way it come across. I'm sorry 'bout what happened to her, but she was a sly little thing.'

'Sly?'

'Secretive.'

'What about?'

'Well, we had no idea she had a thing goin' on with Sean. Then he started hangin' around the office like a lost calf and someone said she'd dumped him. I was amazed. I didn't even know they'd been goin' out.'

Eve studied Annie's pale, pinched face for a moment, thinking that she couldn't blame Jane at all for wanting to keep her private life to herself, particularly in the claustrophobic atmosphere of such a small office. She also remembered what Grace had said about Jane disappearing off to see an unknown man. Maybe she had just wanted a bit of space from prying eyes, or maybe there was more to it than that.

'You knew both of them, at least superficially. Why do you think she went out with Farrell in the first place?'

'Sex, money, something to do to pass the time of day, I guess.'

She spoke as though it were normal. The idea that Jane might have been lonely didn't seem to have occurred to her. 'After she broke up with Sean, did she see anyone else, that you know of?'

'She certainly didn't confide in *me*.'

'But you introduced her to a man called Steve Wilby, who worked at the Honda garage.'

'We went out for a drink. That's all.' Her expression shut down.

Wilby had described Annie as being 'narked' that he had

preferred Jane over her, and Eve wondered if jealousy was still clouding her judgement even after so many years. She also wondered if Annie knew that Jane had seen Wilby a few times after that night, then decided it was probably another thing Jane would have sensibly kept to herself.

'But you told the police about him, didn't you?'

Annie met her gaze defiantly. 'I had to. Didn't I? But they checked him out and that was the end of it.'

'Were you surprised Sean was found guilty of her murder?'

'The police and the court did their job, I guess.'

'So you've never had any doubts about it?'

'At the time, no.' She put her head to one side thoughtfully. 'But now everybody's askin' questions, makes you wonder, doesn't it?'

'What about the two girls she shared the cottage with? Was Jane friends with them?'

'You mean Grace and Holly?' She shook her head. 'They didn't get on.'

'Any particular reason?'

'The usual female stuff. Always some stupid bloke, or other, hangin' around in the background causing trouble.'

'Anything else? It doesn't matter how trivial.'

Annie sighed and took another mouthful of coffee. 'Well, Jane never stopped goin' on about the mess the other two made. She was a bit OCD. Used to give us all a hard time about leaving dirty coffee mugs in the sink or hanging our coat on the wrong peg.'

'I've spoken to Grace, so tell me about Holly? I understand she was sacked a few days before Jane went missing.'

'She had it coming. She was always turning up late, or calling in sick whenever she had a hangover and couldn't be bothered gettin' out of bed. You know what young girls are like.' She gave Eve a knowing look. 'She thought she could charm her way out of anythin', that one, but she'd pushed it too far.'

'I thought there was more to it than that.'

'Well, some said she'd been up to no good with Harry, as well as one of the young lads. I was never much into all the yard gossip, and being sat in the office all day, it was always fourth- or fifth-hand, but there were certainly fireworks that morning.'

'Go on,' Eve said. 'It was ten years ago. Nobody's going to mind now.'

Annie drained her mug and plonked it down on the counter. She pulled the sleeves of her cardigan over her hands and folded her arms tightly across her chest. 'Well, I remember Holly stomping into the office, bold as brass, asking for Tim, saying she wouldn't take no orders from Melissa. She was effing and blinding, like we wasn't there. But Tim was out somewhere for the day, so in the end we had to call Harry. He paid her off and got rid of her . . .'

'I thought it was Melissa who paid her off,' she said, remembering the odd conversation between Harry and Melissa at the dinner table. She was curious that Annie's account differed in this small detail to what Melissa had told her.

'No. I remember very clearly it was Harry. Even if there was something goin' on between the two of them, he sent her packin' good and proper that day. That was the last we heard of her, 'til some poor sod of a trainer called in to ask for a reference. And blow me down if Harry didn't give her one.' She raised her thin eyebrows meaningfully.

'Do you know how I can get in touch with Holly?'

Annie shook her head. 'Haven't a clue. Sorry.'

'Do you remember the Christmas party?'

'Course I do. I had to go over it for the police many times.'

'Did you see Jane there?'

'I saw her at the beginning, when we were settin' up the tables. But I hadn't time to keep an eye out for her after that. We all just got on with what we had to do and I didn't notice she'd gone until someone said she was sick. I remember thinking it was very odd . . .' As she let the word hang, a sharp look came into her eyes.

'In what way?'

'Well, what I did see of her, she seemed to be spending a lot more time talkin' to the guests, than helpin' out. She didn't look like someone who was sick, to me, I can tell you.'

'Who was she talking to?'

'I don't remember. But she was popular with some of the owners – the *male* owners, if you get my drift.'

'A couple of the owners called her mobile the week before she died.'

'Doesn't surprise me. As I said, she was a sly one. I remember her going out of the office more than once to take a private call and she'd walk round outside with her phone in her lunch break, like she had something special goin' on.'

'You make it sound as though a racing yard's a hot bed of sex and intrigue.'

Annie's mouth cracked into a funny, lopsided smile. 'You wouldn't be far wrong there. It's the horse world really, too much testosterone and long hours and all those empty-headed young girls.'

And alcohol and drugs and money, Eve thought. It was a heady, possibly dangerous, mix.

The door blew open and banged against the bookcase behind, sending the bells into a frenzy of jingles. A couple of elderly women in hats and waterproofs stepped inside, one struggling to manoeuvre her dripping umbrella through the doorway. The umbrella jammed in the opening and, as she tried to free it, another gust of damp, freezing wind filled the room, extinguishing the candle by the till in a puff of sickly-sweet smoke.

Eve stood up. 'We're probably done for now. Thank you for your time.'

Annie shivered and got to her feet, tugging her cardigan even more tightly around her narrow shoulders. 'I should start charging. You know, you're the fourth person asking about Jane in less than twelve months. I'm beginning to feel like a celebrity with all the attention.'

Eve failed to hide her surprise. 'Four people? Who do you mean?'

Annie started to count on her fingers. 'Number one was this journalist . . . a young chap from the local newspaper. Number two was some private investigator—'

'Is this the PI?' Eve asked, taking out her phone from her pocket and showing Annie the photo of Mickey.

Annie peered short-sightedly at the screen. 'No. He's number three. I spoke to *him* only a few weeks ago. The second one was another investigator, or at least that's what it said on his card.'

'When was this?'

'About six months ago.'

'Do you still have the card?'

She shook her head.

'Do you remember his name? Or what he looked like?'

'Middle-aged, a bit fat round the middle, in a suit and tie. I thought he was a policeman when he come into the shop. But that's all I remember.'

'Do you know who he was working for? Could he have been sent by Sean's family, or by his solicitor?'

'No idea. He just said he was lookin' into Jane's murder, tryin' to trace everyone Jane knew. I heard from a friend of mine who still works for the Michaels that he'd been over at the yard askin' questions. He went into the office, bold as brass, then Harry came back from somewhere and saw 'im off. There was a real to-do, from what I hear and Harry gave him a bloody nose.'

Outside in the car, Eve called Dan. She told him about the other private investigator, but he had no idea who he could be and said he would contact Sean and ask him.

She was about to drive off, when her phone rang. It was Gavin.

'You'll be delighted to hear I've managed to track down Lorne Anderson,' he said a little hurriedly. He was outside in the street, judging by the noise of traffic and voices in the background and she had difficulty hearing him clearly. 'He'll be at Newbury Racecourse later today. He said he's happy to speak to you there. He's got some guests for lunch and a couple of horses running, but any time after around two will be fine.'

'How do I find him?'

'He'll be up in one of the hospitality suites in the Berkshire stand. Go up to the fourth floor and ask for him by name. I'll text you his phone number, in case you have any problems.'

'Gavin, I'm really grateful for this.'

'Don't mention it. I've got a load of meetings today, otherwise I'd come with you. But why don't we catch up this evening, if you're free, and you can tell me all about it? I'll be in need of a stiff drink after all the fuss I've had getting his number.'

# THIRTY-FOUR

The rain from the morning had moved eastwards and the sky above Newbury Racecourse was the colour of lead. It was a miserable day for any outdoor sport, Eve thought, passing the parade ring, where knots of racegoers were huddled under umbrellas in the centre and around the perimeter, watching as the horses from the last race were unsaddled. The announcer's voice blared cheerily over the loudspeakers, but anyone sensible was inside in one of the many bars, watching on a TV monitor. The entrance to the Berkshire Stand was just opposite and she took the lift up to the fourth floor, where the hospitality suites were located. Staff bustled in and out of the various rooms along the long corridor, carrying leftover food and empty plates, the buzz of voices and laughter floating out behind them through open doors. She asked for Lorne Anderson and was pointed towards a door about halfway along. The room was large and square, with a wall of sliding glass doors at the front leading out onto a wide balcony, with a clear view of the racecourse and finishing post below. Coffee and tea were being served at the back of the room, along with brandy and port. A few people were still seated around the dining table, chatting and watching a re-run of the previous race on a wall monitor. The rest of the party was gathered in front of the doors, glasses in their hands, staring out across the racecourse.

Eve asked an elderly man dressed in tweeds, who was seated in a wheelchair at one end of the table, where she could find Lorne Anderson.

'Out there, having a smoke,' he said, pointing towards the balcony.

She threaded her way through the other guests and pulled open one of the sliding doors, letting in a blast of freezing air. Two men stood outside, their backs to the room, talking animatedly.

'I'm looking for Lorne Anderson,' she said, peering out.

Both men turned around and the shorter of the two said, 'I'm Lorne. You must be Eve.' He stubbed out his cigarette and stepped back inside, giving her a very firm, cold handshake. 'Let's go and find a quiet corner. I understand you're an old friend of Gavin's.'

He was stocky, with a broad, puckish face, dressed in a well-cut, brown-coloured suit and a silk bow tie. Although he looked to be in his late forties, his shock of hair was prematurely white and he matched the description of the man Steve Wilby had seen with Jane in Berkeley Square, whom he had assumed was her father.

'We've finished lunch but would you like coffee or tea, or something stronger, maybe?' he asked.

'Nothing, thank you.'

He pulled out a couple of empty chairs and they sat down together at the table.

'Gavin tells me you're looking into Jane's murder,' he said. 'He's explained about the CCRC and that there's not much time. I'm very happy to help in any way I can. I knew Jane quite well, you see.'

She picked up a surprising softness of tone. 'By "knew" do you mean from the office, or something more?'

He peered at her for a moment. 'Both, I guess. There's no harm in telling you. I had to come clean with the police at the time, of course. They had logs of all my phone calls to her. Thank Christ I had a rock-solid alibi, otherwise I'm sure they'd have tried to pin the whole damn thing on me.'

'You were having an affair with her?'

He winced. 'I've been divorced and remarried since then, so nobody's going to mind now, but I wouldn't quite put it like that. We weren't exactly having a relationship, just more of a light-hearted flirtation, let's say.'

'Nothing more than that?' She looked at him enquiringly and he shrugged.

'Look, it was pretty dull for her working at the yard. She was also new to the area and didn't have many friends. I think the girls she shared with were quite bitchy. She also liked being taken out from time to time, and wined and dined. I occasionally bought her the odd little present, although nothing particularly expensive that would attract attention.'

'Someone saw you with her in Berkeley Square.'

'Did they indeed. Well, that's easily possible. My office is around the corner. We'd occasionally meet up for the odd lunch when she was in town. It was easier seeing her away from Marlborough. She was a nice girl, but she knew I was married and that I didn't want to take it any further.'

So far, he hadn't tried to deny anything, but she had the impression that he was glossing over what had happened. He made it all sound so simple and harmless, but things were rarely so light-hearted and balanced on both sides. Without knowing Jane, it was impossible to say if she had been dazzled, or even in love with him, or merely, as he said, happy with just a light-hearted flirtation, whatever that meant. The way he talked, he came across as the sort of man who was used to having 'flirtations', as he called them, and was probably good at handling them. She wondered why he bothered getting married. Maybe the mix of it all was part of the fun, or the thrill. But for the moment, it didn't matter. Unless the police had been completely incompetent, they would have checked his alibi very thoroughly, given all the calls to Jane's phone and his admission of their closeness. If Jane's relationship with Lorne Anderson was developing, or she had hopes that it might go further, it possibly explained why she had decided not to carry on seeing Steve Wilby.

'This went on for how long?' Eve asked.

'Oh, around three months or so, right up to the day she disappeared.'

She remembered Sean Farrell saying that Jane had been flush with cash. 'As well as the lunches and dinners and the little presents, you were also paying her, weren't you?'

He shifted his weight in his chair and stared at her, as though looking at her properly for the first time. 'Gavin said you're sharp. How on earth do you know about the money? That's something I never told the police.'

'Why was that?'

He continued to look at her for a moment, as though assessing her, then sighed. 'I suppose, if I'm honest, it all felt a bit grubby. It muddied the waters, so to speak.'

Curious that he had felt ashamed about the money, but about nothing else, she said, 'You gave her cash, am I right? Quite a bit, from what I hear.'

He nodded.

'Was this for sex, or something else?'

He grinned, revealing a gap between his top two front teeth, his small hazel-coloured eyes slanting upwards with merriment. 'I've never paid for sex in my entire life, or at least not directly. No, Jane was doing something for me. It was a business arrangement. It's really why I got friendly with her in the first place.' He hesitated, then leaned forwards towards Eve, resting his arm heavily on the table and using his shoulders to screen them from the other guests behind. He lowered his voice. 'I suspected something was up at the Westerby yard. I needed somebody on the inside who'd keep an eye open for me.'

'So you used her?'

He put his head to one side and studied her quizzically. 'As you're a good friend of Gavin's, I won't take offence. All I can say is, Jane didn't seem to mind. She was a nice girl, quite pretty, in fact, if a bit naïve and inexperienced. She was hard-up and lonely and I needed information. It was a happy bargain on both sides.'

Again Eve wondered if Jane really had been happy with the arrangement, although there was no way of knowing now. 'What sort of thing are you talking about?'

'Let's just say there were a few very odd results.'

'Race results?'

He nodded. 'A couple of my horses should have done a lot better than they did in certain races. I went to Tim Michaels about it and he got very angry, but I could tell I'd hit a nerve. He knew exactly what I was talking about. He tried to explain it away by blaming the jockey, or by saying that the horse must have had a virus, or an off day. Of course, it happens. Horses and jockeys aren't robots. But I wasn't the only one at the yard who was a little suspicious. To cut a long story, I kept a closer eye on things after that and for a while it was all hunky-dory. Then just when I thought I'd got it all wrong, it happened again. This time I went straight to the British Horseracing Authority, who had recently taken over as official regulator for the sport.'

'What do you think was going on? Race fixing?'

He nodded.

'Were the police involved?'

'I don't know if it got that far. I heard unofficially that the BHA had several enquiries going on that year, but although a trainer and an owner and two jockeys were eventually suspended, only the trainer and one of the jockeys received a ban. Interestingly, the jockey also used to ride for Tim Michaels.'

'Was Tim Michaels ever investigated?'

'I know from Jane that they were certainly talking to him. She said they came to the yard a couple of times, although Tim tried to pass it off as something routine. She also overheard an argument afterwards between Tim and his wife, Sally, about it. Everyone had gone home for the evening but Jane had gone back to the office to collect something she had forgotten. She said Sally and Tim were in Tim's office at the back, having a right old ding-dong. Even though the door was closed, she could hear Sally tearing a strip off Tim, telling him they'd be ruined if any of the owners got wind of the fact that they were being investigated. Apparently, Tim kept saying there was nothing to hide, but it sounded as though she didn't believe him. So much for trust between husband and wife. I don't know if you've ever met Sally, but she's a pretty strong type. She speaks her mind far too freely.'

'I've met her. I know what you mean. Were they aware that Jane had overheard what they were saying?'

'She said she managed to slip out again before they came out, so I don't think so.'

'When was this?'

'Several weeks before Jane disappeared. Then Tim committed suicide.'

'You told the police?'

'Of course. But they weren't that interested, particularly when I said I had no proof. Maybe they got as far as talking to the BHA, but I don't know. Not long after, the farrier was arrested and that was that, I guess.'

She wasn't surprised that the police had discounted it. Farrell, the jealous, stalking, ex-boyfriend was a much more likely suspect. Even so, if somebody had found out that Jane had been snooping around, and there was something criminal going on, which was worth hiding, it was a clear motive for murder. With the odd scene she had witnessed between Harry and Stacey Woodward in mind, she wanted to ask Lorne for his views about the Westerby Racing yard now, and if he thought it was clean. But she reminded herself that even if he knew anything about it and was prepared to comment, it had nothing to do with Jane's murder ten years before. That was all that was important.

'What was Tim Michaels like?'

He looked at her thoughtfully. 'Used to be very good, although not a patch on his father, I gather. I never had any problems with Tim on a personal level, until I started asking awkward questions. He was so vehement that I was wrong, it made me wonder if my suspicions might be correct. No smoke without fire, as they say.'

'What if Jane discovered something else and maybe he caught her? Is he the sort of man who'd kill her to keep her mouth shut?'

He folded his arms across his broad chest. 'I guess anything's possible. People do terrible things when their back's up against a wall.' He glanced down at the floor for a moment, studying the toes of his polished brown shoes. 'He'd certainly have been hopping mad if he caught her spying on him,' he said thoughtfully. 'But he'd have sacked her on the spot.'

'What if she was blackmailing him?'

He looked up and met Eve's eye. 'Jane wasn't like that. She liked the good things in life and having a bit of money, but I don't think morally she was that sort of person. Nor do I think she'd have had the nerve.'

'But if he knew he'd been found out, how would he have reacted?'

'Racing was his life-blood and reputation is everything at his level. He'd have fought tooth and nail to keep things quiet. But if he murdered Jane, why kill himself so soon afterwards?'

'Guilt?'

He shook his head. 'Not the type. Tim wasn't blessed with sufficient imagination or sensitivity to have much of a conscience. Also, even if I'm right about what was going on, it's not at all a given he'd be found guilty. These things are rarely cut and dried. BHA investigations can drag on for months, if not years and if the police get involved, they usually make a hash of things. There've been a number of cases recently where people who've been up to all sorts of dodgy stuff have managed to wriggle off the hook. But say things hadn't gone well for Tim and he's banned, I think he'd have found it very difficult to live with the shame. At that point,' he said, raising his index finger, 'he might very easily have felt life wasn't worth living. But why do it *after* getting rid of Jane, with everything still to play for?'

She nodded slowly. What he said made sense and as far as she could tell, he seemed a good judge of character. There didn't seem much point in killing somebody to shut them up, then committing suicide.

'Was Harry Michaels involved in the yard at the time?'

'Most definitely, although Tim was still very much in the driving seat. I never got on with Harry. He's an arrogant prick. After Tim's death, when I told him I was taking the horses away, we had a real bust up.'

'Do you think he could've been mixed up in any of this?'

He looked at her thoughtfully. 'I really don't know. He and Tim hadn't been getting along for a while and there'd been a bit of a schism. I heard on the grapevine that Harry had some idea about setting up his own yard, which would have been heresy in the Michaels family. Tim's suicide put paid to that, of course.'

'Do you know why they hadn't been getting along?'

'Father and son stuff, I guess. Tim was very old school, whereas Harry was very much the new blade, with all sorts of ideas Tim probably didn't approve of.'

She kept getting drawn back to Harry and the present which, while interesting in terms of background, meant they were getting off what really mattered: what had happened to Jane.

'Did you know one of the other owners, a man called Stuart Wade? He rang Jane's number a couple of times in the week before she disappeared, as well as before.'

'I know who he is, but I don't know anything about him, except that he and Harry were as thick as thieves.'

Eve thanked him for his time and made her way downstairs into the main foyer. She was about to walk outside, when she heard someone behind her call her name. She turned around and saw Harry coming towards her from the bar area. She froze.

'Eve, what a surprise. What are you doing here? I didn't think racing was your thing.' He was smiling, as though pleased to see her.

For a moment, the dark, dank bedroom in the cottage sprang to mind, the faceless man on top of her, moving her this way and that like a doll.

'Seeing Lorne Anderson,' she said.

The smile disappeared. 'I hope he wasn't spinning you some more of his ridiculous stories. The man has a really wild imagination. We should have had him for slander and taken him to court, but my father didn't want a fuss.'

She gave him a blank look. 'He called Jane the week before she disappeared. That's why I'm here.'

Harry's expression softened a touch. 'I remember your saying. Did he manage to explain it?'

'Oh yes. It was just something routine, that's all.'

'Good. Are you fully recovered now? You look great, but we were very worried about you.'

'Just a twenty-four-hour virus. I'm fine now.'

'Wonderful. Perhaps we can have dinner again. I—'

He was interrupted by a large hand on his shoulder. Stuart Wade's son, Damon, had come up behind him, towering over him.

'Are you coming, Harry? Dad's waiting outside.' It was the first time she had heard him speak. Unlike Stuart, he had no trace of a northern accent and she assumed from the short, clipped vowels that he had been sent to some expensive private school in the south. Even though they had met at the Christmas party, he made no eye contact with her, as though she weren't there. Was it a sign of guilt, she wondered?

'Sorry, Eve,' Harry said. 'I've got to go. Stuart's got a horse in the next race. I'll call you later.'

They marched off briskly together down the small flight of stairs and out of the doors, heading towards the parade ring, Damon's huge arm almost shepherding Harry away. As Eve watched them go, it struck her that it was almost as though Damon Wade, young as he was, was Harry's boss, rather than his client.

# THIRTY-FIVE

'Do you want a cup of tea?' Shona asked Dan. 'Or maybe a drink? I've got a bottle of red open, if you like.'

It was a few minutes past seven in the evening and they were standing in her small kitchen in Pimlico, Shona leaning heavily against one of the tatty old units, hair tied back in a bun, still in her work clothes, Dan hovering by the door. She looked tired, he thought, but nonetheless happy to see him. A large shoebox loosely wrapped in brown paper sat on the table, Mickey's handwriting recognizable on the front.

She had called him earlier that day to say she had picked up a parcel from the post office and, on opening it, discovered that it contained her husband Kevin's diaries, which she had given to Mickey. She was in a flutter about it and very apologetic. It seemed that Mickey had posted them back to her second class, but hadn't put enough stamps on the package. Not realizing it was anything urgent, she hadn't gone to collect it immediately and it had been waiting at the post office for nearly a week. According to the postage mark, Mickey had posted it the Friday before he was murdered, the day before he had gone to the races. Dan was itching to go back to his office to start going through the notebooks, but he had the impression that Shona wanted company, sensing a loneliness in her that had maybe been awakened by the sight of her husband's diaries and notebooks. He could also use a drink. It had been a frustrating day having to speak to Kristen, who had been unpleasantly brusque, and then trying to chase up the researcher from the Channel 4 programme, playing phone tag with him all day. A small, nagging voice in his head was also telling him that someone should call Fagan about the package. Maybe he could slip the little red memory stick in between some of the notebooks and get rid of it that way. It didn't appear that Shona had gone through everything in the box. He hated doing it. She had been so straight with him. But he couldn't think of any other way of getting it to the police without being hauled in for more questioning. He made a mental note to wipe off his prints first.

'Wine would be good,' he said. As he watched her pour out a generous glassful, and one for herself, he added reluctantly, 'Thinking about it, maybe you ought to hand these over to the police. They may have nothing to do with Mickey's murder, but better to be safe than sorry.'

She nodded. 'I was going to. I just wanted you to see them first. You could take copies, if you like. A few hours' delay won't hurt, I'm sure. I've got a scanner in my study.'

# THIRTY-SIX

E ve sat down at the back of the small bar just off Victoria Street, in Westminster, where Gavin had suggested meeting. The room was hot and almost full, with a lively after-work crowd, busy knocking back wine and cocktails and sharing plates of tapas, as they laughed and shouted over the loud music. Margot Alexander had called her half an hour before to say that Harry's DNA, recovered from the glass and cigarette butts from the cottage, did not match the samples she had taken from Eve. Nor did the samples match any of the DNA profiles stored on the national database. In a way, she wasn't surprised. Whoever had assaulted her must have known they couldn't be traced.

She hadn't been waiting long when Gavin appeared through the main door. She waved and as she caught his eye, he gave her a broad smile. Still dressed in his work suit and tie, his face flushed from the cold, he fought his way through a group of new arrivals waiting by the entrance to be seated, and crossed the room. He put down his briefcase and kissed her lightly on the cheek.

'Sorry I'm late. What can I get you?'

'A Diet Coke.'

He returned after a moment with their drinks, sat down opposite and took off his tie and undid the top few buttons of his shirt. 'That feels better already.' He raised his martini glass. 'To you, Eve. To your success with what you're doing for Sean Farrell. May justice be done.' He took a large mouthful of his drink. 'Mmm, that's good,' he said, putting the glass down on the table. 'How was Lorne?'

'Very helpful.' She didn't want to shout over the music and she moved her chair closer and leaned across towards him, elbows on the table. 'He and Jane were having some sort of relationship, although according to him that's too strong a word for it. Did you have any idea?'

The look of genuine surprise on his face answered the question. 'No. I was in London most of the time, but Melissa would've certainly told me, if she'd known. Do you think he . . .'

She shook her head. 'The police checked him out. But there's something else. The reason he approached Jane in the first place was that he suspected something was going on at the Westerby yard. Some sort of race-fixing scam, was what he said, although he had no proof. The BHA were apparently looking into it when your father-in-law committed suicide.'

'I can't believe Tim would've been involved in anything like that. He was always so straight down the line. But I do remember Melissa telling me that someone had gone to the BHA with a load of allegations, trying to stir up trouble. She said Tim suspected it was one of the owners, but I had no idea until now that it must have been Lorne.'

'I'd be grateful if you don't mention this to Melissa.' It was asking a lot, but instinct told her she could rely on him.

He frowned. 'OK. I remember her saying at the time that what was being suggested was a load of bullshit. Why would she lie to me?'

Wondering if Melissa might have indeed lied to him, she said, 'Maybe she didn't know what was going on, or maybe Lorne got it wrong.'

He still looked troubled and picked up his drink, draining it in one. He took the curl of lemon peel from the bottom of the glass and started to chew it. For a moment, he was silent. Then he said, 'What has any of this got to do with Jane?'

'It provides a motive for somebody other than Sean Farrell to have killed her.'

'I see. You mean because she was Lorne's little spy in our midst? She was feeding him information?'

Eve nodded.

'That's another thing I think I won't mention to Melissa,' he said bitterly. Holding her gaze, he leaned back heavily against his chair. 'My god, Eve, you're certainly stirring things up. No wonder they're all so antsy about your asking questions.'

'I shouldn't have told you.'

'I'm glad you did.' There was a pause before he said, 'It's hot in here.' He stood up, took off his jacket, which he hung over the back of his chair, and rolled up his shirtsleeves. 'OK,' he said, sitting down again and rubbing his hands together theatrically. 'What else have you got to tell me?'

He was half smiling now, putting a brave face on things, but she could sense the tension beneath. He was remarkable, she thought. She had forced her way into his life again and upset the balance, testing his loyalties and slowly turning everything he knew upside down. Yet he was pretending not to care. He had always been stoical, whatever was thrown at him. It was as though he were part of a brighter world, where things would always come right in the end. In so many areas he had succeeded against the odds. Whether it was blind self-belief or sheer optimism, she wasn't sure, but it seemed to work for him.

'Come on, Eve. Don't hold back. Spit it out.'

She leaned forwards. 'There's really nothing concrete.' She shared her observations about Harry and the Wades. As she spoke, it all sounded very tenuous and melodramatic. It was impossible to put gut feel into words.

'Harry has to keep them sweet,' he said thoughtfully when she had finished. 'Stuart's been very loyal to him, particularly after Tim died. He was one of the few people who stuck by him when it all looked like it was going pear-shaped, and he's worth a lot of money to the yard.'

She shrugged. She knew what she had observed. 'Harry's a fool to have a client like that.'

'Maybe. You and Harry seemed to be getting on so well. I was worried you were going to be my next sister-in-law. You'd be the third Mrs Harry Michaels, you know. He likes to collect them.'

She was pleased that he wanted to make light of things, although she didn't feel in the least like joking. 'No chance of that.'

'I'm glad. What changed your mind about him?'

Beneath the banter, she wondered if he had actually been a little jealous. 'Nothing, really.'

'Now you're being guarded. I thought we agreed you'd tell me everything.'

'I didn't agree to anything. But there is more. I'm sure now there's a connection between Jane's death and the racing world.'

She proceeded to tell him about Mickey, and about Dan's office being broken into. What had happened at her flat seemed to lead on naturally from that. He listened without comment, his expression growing darker and more distant as she went on, as though his thoughts were elsewhere. When she had finished, he reached over and took her hand, holding it tightly for a moment before letting go. The touch and the emotion in his eyes made her feel suddenly very awkward. She was sorry to have burdened him with it all.

'Thank you for trusting me with that,' he said. 'I don't want us to have any secrets. But I'm now very worried about you.'

'Don't be. I can look after myself.'

He shook his head slowly. 'Can't you leave this whole thing alone? Can't you let this journalist – Dan – get on with things?'

'No. I can't.'

She gazed at him for a moment. He looked hot and tired and drained and the light had gone out of his eyes. It was time to explain about Duran. As she started at the very beginning, with Jason's shooting, it struck her that it was the second time in only twenty-four hours that she was telling the story. It wasn't her inclination to confide in anyone. Usually, the thought of having to open up, and explain anything remotely important or sensitive, let alone personal, made her want to run in the opposite direction. But the events of the past few days had shaken her. She had to admit that she felt vulnerable and less certain about life than she had done for a very long time. She had been forced to tell Dan to get him to trust her, but with Gavin it was different. She had been closer to him than to any other man in her entire life. She wanted to explain, to be truthful as far as she could and, if nothing else, she felt she owed it to him.

He listened without interruption, his eyes on her all the time. When she had finally finished, he rubbed his face vigorously with his hands and sighed. 'I don't know what to say, Eve. You live in a very different world to me. But I'm here for you, if there's anything – whatever it is – you need. I understand now, there's no point telling you to stop this thing. You have to see it through.' He reached across the table again and took both her hands in his. 'I must sound like a complete arse, thinking I can tell you what to do. I'm sorry. I know you're not going to pay any attention to me. You think you know what you're doing. Just *please, please* be careful. I couldn't bear for anything to happen to you.'

Out of the corner of her eye, she caught the flashing light of her phone, which was sitting face up beside her drink on the table. She glanced down and saw Dan's name. The call cut off after a few more inaudible rings. Then it started to ring again almost immediately.

'I must take this,' she said, withdrawing her hands. 'It's Dan. He wouldn't ring at this hour unless it were important.'

She answered, but couldn't hear anything. Holding the phone tightly to her ear, she dashed outside into the street. She heard the burble of Dan's voice talking nineteen to the dozen, people shouting and sirens wailing somewhere close by. Even outside she could barely make out what he was saying, catching the words 'fire' and 'smoke' and 'Zofia', but that was about it.

She ducked into a doorway and turned her back on the road, blocking her other ear with her finger. 'Say that again, Dan. I didn't hear any of it.'

'They've set the fucking office on fire,' he yelled.

# THIRTY-SEVEN

Dan looked at his watch again. Eve had said she would be there in about fifteen minutes, which was over ten minutes ago. The firefighters had cordoned off the whole block on either side of his office, as well as the road in front. While they tried to put out the fire, police were still evacuating the last few remaining people from the neighbouring buildings. It was chaos, people shouting, others complaining about not being allowed through to get their things. He had given the police a brief statement and had also tried to get through to Andy Fagan, without success. Someone had given him an emergency foil blanket, which he had wrapped loosely around himself, but he didn't need it. He didn't feel at all cold. The sight of the cloud of black, billowing smoke that was pouring through the shattered windows of the first-floor office, along with the blazing light in the room behind, had lit a fire in his heart. He would find whoever had done this and he would kill them.

He had spent a couple of hours at Shona's, scanning the notebooks while they finished the bottle of wine and then half of another, and then shared a Chinese takeaway from across the street. She had talked a lot about her husband, Kevin, and the way he had worked. He had been meticulous, she said, with a real instinct for a story, if a little anarchic at times, which made him better suited to freelance work. The more she said, the more he couldn't wait to start delving into the scanned pages, which he had copied both onto his laptop and a spare flash drive. Just before he left, she had gone into the kitchen to make a cup of tea and call the police and he had taken the opportunity to slip Mickey's little red memory stick down the side of the box of notebooks, taking care to wipe his prints.

He had got back to the office just in the nick of time. Someone in the street had already dialled 999, but he had been able to push his way through the growing crowd on the pavement. His first thought was of Zofia. She had told him earlier that she was tired and was staying in that night. He had tried calling her from the street, but her phone was switched off. Maybe she had changed her mind about going out, but he had to check. The front door was open and he rushed upstairs to the top floor. He found her in her bedroom, dressed in pink flowery pyjamas, lying on her back in the middle of her bed in a star-shape, snoring loudly. He saw a packet of Nytols on the bedside table. He shouted at her, but she didn't respond. How many of the bloody things had she taken? He shook her and prodded her, but she just groaned and turned over. He shouted at her again and shook her even more violently and finally her eyes opened a crack and she gazed at him as though she hadn't a clue who he was. She was far too heavy to carry, but he managed to drag her out of the bed and help her unsteadily onto her feet. Just when he thought he'd got through to her, she pushed him away and started stumbling around the room trying to gather up some of her things, muttering all the time to herself in Polish. He could smell the smoke coming up the stairs. They needed to go. He shouted at her again but she seemed unable to grasp the situation. He grabbed hold of her and slapped her hard across the face. She opened her eyes wide and stared at him blinking and disorientated, as though she had just woken from a deep dream. He was able to yank her by the wrist, still clinging to some of her possessions, out of the flat, pulling her down the many flights of stairs and through the open front door, just as the first fire engine screeched to a halt

outside. Zofia had been taken off to an ambulance, where paramedics were examining her, but he had refused any medical
attention. Although his lungs were full of smoke, he didn't want
to go to hospital. He couldn't afford any delay in finding out
who had done this and he needed to see Eve.

Gazing across the road, he spotted her amongst the crowd,
her pale face looking here and there as she searched for him. He
was about to call out when he realized she was with someone.
He was tall and good-looking, with blonde hair. There was
something familiar about him and Dan suddenly realized he
was something to do with the Michaels family. He was married
to Melissa Michaels, that was it. The MP. Gavin something.
What was he doing there with Eve? Dan watched them make
their way through the crowd of onlookers towards the edge of
the cordon, then he lost sight of them. Why had Eve brought
him here? How could she have anything to do with any of the
Michaels clan after what had happened to her? He ducked into
a doorway, crouched down and pulled the foil blanket over his
head. He felt his phone vibrate in his jacket pocket, took it out,
saw her name on the screen and switched it off. A moment later
a text came through: *I'm here. Where are you? Eve.* Another
police car pulled up alongside and as the crowd parted momentarily to let it through, he caught sight of them again. They were
in the middle of the road, right at the front, by the cordon, no
doubt waiting for him to appear from somewhere. Gavin had
turned to face Eve. His hands were on her shoulders and he was
saying something to her, which looked important, as Eve looked
up at him intently. After a moment, she nodded and Gavin smiled
as though she had just given him some good news. Then Gavin
bent down, kissed her on the cheek, and turned and walked away.
Along with the shock that they clearly knew one another quite well,
there was something intimate in the way they had looked at each
other. From nowhere Dan felt an unexpected stab of jealousy.

He waited a moment, making sure that Gavin was not coming
back, then shed the blanket, leaving it behind in the doorway,
and crossed the road to where Eve was standing. He touched her
on the shoulder and she turned around.

'Oh, Dan. There you are. I've been looking everywhere for
you. Are you OK?' She reached up and wiped away a smear of

something from his cheek with her fingers. 'You're covered in soot.'

'I'm fine.'

'What the hell happened?'

'I wasn't here, so I don't know. But I found the front door open and when I went upstairs to look for Zofia I smelled petrol on the landing outside our office. It's definitely arson. Probably the same person who broke in the other evening.'

'Have you told the police?'

He nodded. 'I need to go to the local station later and give a proper statement.'

'You should also call Andy Fagan and tell him what's happened. This is all tied up with Mickey's murder.'

'I have tried calling him, but he's not picking up. That man I just saw you with . . . He's married to Melissa Michaels, isn't he?'

She nodded. 'His name's Gavin. I told you about him.' She looked at him questioningly.

Perhaps she had mentioned it in passing. If so, he'd forgotten the details or hadn't realized the significance at the time, that she and Gavin were so close.

'It's thanks to him I got to stay at the cottage,' she added. 'He's the person who arranged the meeting today with Lorne Anderson.' Her tone sounded a little defensive. She had called him after her meeting with Anderson but she had said nothing about Gavin. Perhaps he too had been at the racecourse. How much had she told Gavin, he wondered.

'Why's he being so bloody helpful, all of a sudden? None of the Michaels give a flying fuck about Sean Farrell and what happens to him.'

'He's not one of the Michaels. Anyway, he and I go back a very long way.'

'I see,' he said, although he didn't see at all. It was a loaded expression and no explanation of anything.

'Look, I trust him, Dan. Please don't worry.'

He shrugged. It was easy for her to say. She hadn't seen everything she'd worked for, for so long, go up in flames. A waft of fried onions drifted over him and he realized they were standing outside a Burger King, with people going in and out as though everything were normal. But it was the end of 4Justice, the final, lingering chapter in his relationship with Kristen. In the adrenalin of the last hour he had forgotten about the practicalities. He would have to find another job and, even more pressingly, somewhere to live. He still had a little money in the bank but it wouldn't last long. He would have to ring up his mum and try to borrow some money to tide him over. He was thirty-three, nearly thirty-four. By now, he ought to be able to stand on his own two feet. But it would be yet another mark of his failure, in her critical eyes.

'Dan?' He felt Eve's hand on his arm and looked up.

'Sorry. I was miles away.'

'I could see. What are you going to do?'

'I don't know.'

'My flat's tiny, otherwise you could stay there.'

'I'll check into a hotel for the night,' he said firmly. 'I'll sort out somewhere to go in the morning.'

'What about 4Justice?'

He shrugged again.

'Were your files backed up?'

He sighed. It didn't matter any longer.

She looked at him sternly. 'I know you're in shock, but you need to snap out of it. Do you have a backup?'

He sighed again, then nodded and patted the messenger bag slung over his shoulder. 'I've got my laptop. All my work's stored on it. Kristen also has a backup of the whole system at her flat. It's a bit out of date but we scanned most of the important documents and files.'

'Thank God for that.' She looked genuinely relieved and it struck him for the first time that she actually cared.

'We were worried about all the old wiring in the building. Of course, we never imagined something like this happening.'

Eve put her hand on his sleeve. 'I know everything looks black at the moment. But you mustn't give up. What you do is really important. Think of Sean, or your brother, and people like them, rotting in jail for years, their life slipping by, knowing that someone else is guilty and running around free as a bird. They *need* you. We will find whoever did this. I promise.'

It warmed his heart to hear her so firm and positive and strong and, for a moment, he found it difficult to speak. She reached into her bag and pulled out a thick brown envelope.

'Here, take this. There's the best part of ten grand inside. It's John Duran's money. He gave it to me for expenses for looking into the Sean Farrell case, so as chief investigator, it's yours by rights.'

He started to object, but she held up her hand. 'This whole thing is to do with Jane McNeil. If you and I hadn't been getting near the truth, this would never have happened. I will explain to Duran.'

He hated to have to take the money, particularly from her, he realized. He felt somehow ashamed. Eve was saying something about going to see Jane's mother in the morning and asking if he wanted to come, but he couldn't focus. He was staring down the road in front, past the fire engines, wondering what to do, when he caught sight of a face that looked vaguely familiar. The boy was some distance away but he was looking straight at him. It took a moment to place him. His heart missed a beat.

He turned to Eve. 'Gotta go. I'll call you.' He took off through the crowd.

# THIRTY-EIGHT

E ve turned off the car ignition and reached for the half-drunk cup of black coffee she had bought at a petrol station a few blocks away. It was below freezing, according to the dashboard display, and fat flakes of snow had started to drift down through the air like feathers, settling on the car window before slowly melting. The street-lamps were still lit, but the sky was gradually beginning to lighten and the small, suburban close on the outskirts of Grantham was coming to life, as people emerged here and there from their front doors to go to work, take their children to school or, huddled in thick coats and rubber-soled boots, walk their dogs gingerly along the frosty pavement. After seeing Dan the previous night, she had been so wired when she arrived home that she had stayed up until the early hours of the morning, mulling everything through. She had then left London just before five a.m., for the two and a half hours' drive north. She usually managed well on little sleep, but she felt exhausted as she gazed across the road towards the small, modern, detached house with the blue door where Jane McNeil's mother, Ruth, lived. The house was in a development of almost identical houses, each with a double garage to one side and a neat rectangle of lawn at the front. Ruth's house was screened from the road by a sparse, newly planted evergreen hedge. A shiny red Honda Civic was parked in the driveway and a ginger-and-white cat sat huddled on the roof, watching the comings and goings in the street. Bearing in mind what Dan had said about Ruth practically slamming the door in his face when he went to see her, Eve had not rung ahead. Surprise was often the best policy and hopefully she wouldn't have to wait long. Lights were on inside the house and she could see the shadow of somebody moving around on the first floor behind the drawn curtains. Jane's mother had moved several times since her daughter's death. According to Dan, she was now a widow and had reverted back to her maiden name, Weldon. Grantham was not that far from Lincoln, where Ruth and her husband had lived, and where Jane had grown up. Perhaps after everything that had happened, Ruth had wanted a fresh start, although many people in similar situations clung on as tightly as they could to the physical places and things that were filled with happier memories.

Eve's thoughts kept turning to her conversations with Gavin from the previous night, first in the bar and then later, standing in the Earl's Court Road, while they waited for Dan to appear. She could still picture the burning building, with the extraordinary, roaring, rushing, cracking noise of it, the fire engines, the crowds of stunned onlookers, the emergency staff running here and there, the air heavy with the acrid smell of smoke. She pictured Gavin, facing her, his back to the commotion in the road behind. 'Why don't you come with me. Stay with me tonight.' He spoke quietly, urgently, leaning in towards her, conscious of the people around them. His eyes said how much he wanted her and strangely it didn't scare her any longer. Part of her felt inclined to slip her hand in his and go with him then and there, wherever he wanted. It was as though reality was suspended and the last twenty years had never happened. She could forget about Jason's murder, forget about the rape, the pain and all the terrible things that had happened, and lose herself with him for a while. All she needed was to take his hand, close her eyes and jump.

She took a deep breath and shook her head. 'I'll be fine. They've been all over my flat and found nothing. They're not going to come back.'

'If that's what you want.' Although he masked it well, she sensed his disappointment. Perhaps he had realized how frighteningly close she had been to letting go.

'It is,' she replied firmly.

He took a deep breath and placed his hands lightly on the tops of her arms, holding her square in front of him, as though he demanded her full attention. 'Look, I need to get away for a couple of days and clear my head. My mother's had a fall. It's nothing too serious, but I'm going down to Lymington tomorrow night to check on her, then I'll spend the following day on the boat. Why don't you come? Whenever you like. However long you like.'

She gazed at him for a moment, her head full of doubt, still coupled with vague, bewildering feelings of longing.

'There's so much I want to talk to you about,' he said, with a sudden intensity. 'I mean properly, away from here and all of this.' He gestured towards the crowd. 'Will you come?'

What harm could it do? Maybe it was what she needed. 'Alright. I'll come.'

His face lit up and he smiled. 'That would make me very, very happy. I'll leave you to find Dan now, but text me as soon as you get home. Let me know you're OK.'

There was a moment's hesitation as though he wanted to say something else, then he kissed her lightly on the cheek, turned away into the crowd behind and was gone.

Eve drained the remains of the coffee. It was such a foolish, crazy idea. Would she go? *Should* she go? She was telling herself for the umpteenth time to stop over-analysing and put it out of her mind for now, when the blue front door opened. The ginger and white cat sprang from the car and took off into the bushes, as a stout, middle-aged woman with short, fluffy, blonde hair emerged on the doorstep. She wore an emerald green coat, with a black and white patterned scarf around her neck, and she was holding the hand of a little boy. He was dressed in school uniform and looked to be about five or six at most. The woman opened one of the rear doors of the Civic and waited as he climbed in. She fastened the seat belt around him, shut the door, then got into the front seat and drove off.

The car was barely around the corner when the front door opened again and a youngish, red-haired man emerged, dressed in jeans, trainers and an anorak. Hands in his pockets, ducked against the flurries of snow, he walked hurriedly down the street and turned the corner in the direction of the station. Wondering if Dan's information was out of date, Eve went up to the front door and rang the bell. The lights were still on inside but there was no answer. She tried the house next door and found a young woman, still in her dressing gown and slippers, who seemed quite happy to tell her, with the sound of breakfast TV blaring in the background, that the house with the blue door was occupied by the King family, Jimmy and Claire, plus their six-year-old son, Alfie, who was nearly the same age as her daughter. She thought the middle-aged woman was Jimmy's mother. The neighbour had only just moved in a few months before and had no idea who had lived there before the Kings. She had never heard of Ruth McNeil or Weldon. It looked as though Ruth McNeil had moved yet again.

Eve got back into the car and rang the phone number Dan had given her. A woman answered the phone.

'I'm looking for Ruth Weldon, or Ruth McNeil, as she used to be called,' Eve said.

'Who's that?'

'It's about her daughter, Jane.'

'You've got the wrong number.' The call was disconnected.

The woman on the phone hadn't sounded particularly old, but voices could be misleading and Eve wondered if she had just been speaking to Ruth McNeil. Whoever it was, there had been a second's hesitation before she said 'who's that'. From her intonation, Eve was sure the name Ruth McNeil or Weldon was familiar. It was the mention of Jane's name that had made her hang up. If she had moved somewhere locally, she would prob- ably have taken her phone number with her. Eve was on the point of calling Dan, to see if he could try and trace her new address, when the front door opened yet again and a young woman, who she assumed was Claire King, stepped out. She was carrying a briefcase and was smartly dressed in a black fitted coat with gold buttons, narrow-legged grey trousers and high-heeled boots. Eve got out of the car and crossed the road towards her.

'Excuse me,' Eve said. 'I'm looking for Ruth McNeil. She may be using the name Ruth Weldon. I was told she lives here.'

Claire stared at Eve for a moment as though she didn't understand the question. Snowflakes settled on her shiny, dark bob and as others touched her heavily made-up cheeks, she swotted them away like flies with her gloved hand.

'I can't help you, I'm afraid.' It was the same clear voice from the phone. Claire clamped her dark pink lips together and carefully skirted around Eve, walking in choppy little steps on the icy pavement.

'But she was living here a year ago,' Eve said, catching her up.

Claire shook her head. 'There must be some mistake.'

'No. A friend of mine visited her here. I need to try and find her. I think you know where she is.'

Claire stopped under a street-lamp and turned to face Eve, studying her in a strangely intense way. Her eyes were thickly outlined in black pencil, like a cat's, and there was something odd about her face, although Eve couldn't put her finger on what it was. Maybe it was the make-up, which gave her small, unremarkable features a frozen, doll-like look, particularly in the half-light.

'That must have been before we moved here,' Claire said crisply. 'Now, I really must go. I'm late for work.' She turned away and started to make her way carefully along the street.

Eve was used to people being evasive when put on the spot, but something definitely jarred. She replayed the conversation in her mind. She was convinced Claire knew who Ruth McNeil was, and possibly where she was, and was protecting her for some reason. Whether Ruth liked it or not, Eve needed to speak to her. She stood in the middle of the pavement and watched Claire totter out of sight around the corner. She shivered and felt for her gloves in her jacket pocket. She must have left them in the car. There was no point following Claire now and she would probably be gone for the whole day. She would have to speak to some of the other neighbours instead. There must surely be somebody living in the close who would remember Ruth and know where she had gone. She started back towards the car, but something still niggled, something she just couldn't quite place. Was it something someone had said? If only she wasn't quite so tired. What was it? Who had said it? Then it came to her. Out of the fog, a moment of sudden clarity. She heard Steve Wilby's voice talking about Jane, something about an actress . . . Eve froze. She had always thought of herself as a good detective, certainly better than many she had worked with, and it took her by surprise when occasionally she overlooked the obvious. But it was staring her right in the face. She took a series of deep breaths, filling her lungs with the freezing air, tasting the snowflakes on her tongue, as she allowed herself a moment or two to digest it all. She reached back in her mind, working through the full, startling implications. It was so shocking, it couldn't be true. Yet it was the only thing that made sense. She opened her mouth wide, took another gulp of air, then started to run as fast as she could without slipping down the street.

# THIRTY-NINE

'Stop right there, Jane,' Eve yelled, as she rounded the corner. 'I know who you are.'

The woman with dark hair froze mid-step, her back still to Eve, like someone paused in a video clip. As Eve reached her, she came alive again and turned around, the shock visible on her face.

'Don't try to pretend you're called something else,' Eve shouted. 'I know it's you. I can produce several people who will ID you, if necessary.'

Jane took a small step back, as though she thought Eve was about to hit her.

Eve stared hard at her for a moment, her heart still pounding with adrenalin. She could see what Steve Wilby had meant. Jane was still pretty, even ten years on. She had nice colouring, with her dark hair and pale, almost translucent, skin. But more than anything, Eve remembered what he had said about her eyes: one blue, the other brown, like some famous actress, whose name he couldn't remember. They were her most striking feature.

'I wasn't going to pretend,' Jane said quietly. 'How did you find me?'

'Not important.'

'But how did you recognize me?'

'Your eyes. They're very distinctive.'

Jane nodded thoughtfully. 'There was no mention in the papers, so I stopped wearing my specs to cover it up. I thought after all this time I was safe.'

'You were unlucky. Somebody I spoke to has a very good memory.'

Jane sighed. 'Sod's law, I suppose. Who are you? Why are you here?'

'I'm helping Sean Farrell. I'm a police detective, in my day job.'

'I told you I'm late for work.' Her voice rose plaintively.

'You won't be going to work today,' Eve said, holding her gaze, amazed that Jane thought any form of normality was either appropriate, or still possible. 'I need to ask you some questions. Then I'll drive you to the nearest police station where you're going to make a statement.'

'No. I can't do that.'

'You have no choice. If you don't, I'll call the police right away.'

Jane looked taken aback. 'Why do I have to go to a police station?'

'As I said, you'll need to give them a statement. I'll stay with you until it's done, to make sure you don't have second thoughts. If you try and run away, I *will* find you and you'll be arrested. Sean Farrell has spent the last ten years of his life in jail because of you. He needs to be released as soon as possible.'

Jane's expression hardened. 'He bloody well deserved it. And he can stay there and rot, for all I care.'

'How can you say that?' Eve asked, amazed at the ferocity of Jane's tone. 'He's innocent.'

'He's a disgusting pervert, that's what he is and I hate him.'

'Why?'

'Because he raped me.'

'Are you serious?'

''Course I bloody am. I know exactly what happened and I haven't forgotten it to this day.'

'You'd better tell me,' she said, holding Jane's angry, defiant stare.

Jane took a deep breath, drawing herself up tall. 'The first time I thought he'd just got carried away. He apologized and I tried to put it out of my mind. But the second time I knew that was what he was like, that was how he got his kicks. He didn't see it as rape at all. He said it was what I needed, what I wanted. Those were his words. He said I was asking for it. It was so frightening and he really hurt me. I dumped him straight after that.'

Her words shocked Eve and she felt for her. There was nothing about Jane's manner to suggest that she was either exaggerating or lying. For a moment, Eve saw herself again standing in front of the mirror in the cottage, the disorder of the bedroom behind her in the reflection, the clothes and twisted sheets lying around the floor, the reek of it all still hanging in the air. Was that what it had been like? Was that what had gone through somebody's mind? Had she 'needed it' in their twisted view? Had she 'asked for it'? Tears welled as she felt the fury rise again.

Jane shivered, brushing flakes of snow from her coat. 'Can we go inside? I'm freezing standing out here. I can't afford to get ill.'

'Let's go and sit in my car. It's parked outside your house.'

Jane shrugged as though it were all the same to her.

'Did you report it?' Eve asked, as they started to walk back up the road together.

'No. I didn't want any trouble. I didn't want people to talk. But then he started to stalk me. Wherever I went, he'd turn up. He'd hang around the cottage waiting for me, and at the office. I'd be in Swindon or Marlborough doing some shopping and he'd bloody well pop up. He made my life total hell.' Her voice rose shrilly on the air and a woman walking on the other side of the road looked around.

Eve remembered what Dan had said about the rape allegations that had dogged Farrell. They were the reason why the police had been convinced that he fitted the profile of Jane's killer so perfectly. However disgusting and depraved Farrell's behaviour had been, it still didn't make him a murderer.

'You should have gone to the police.'

'How would I prove it? *I* know what happened, but I also knew how *he'd* spin it. I don't want to go into the details, but I didn't think the police would believe me. I did tell them about it when he started stalking me, but they weren't that interested. I got the impression they thought I was exaggerating, like I had some sort of axe to grind.'

'They must have followed up on it, surely?'

'Oh yes,' she said bitterly, with a toss of her head. 'They went and had "a word" with him. Of course, he denied it all, made out that *he'd* broken up with *me*, like *I* was the one with the psycho problem. When they called on me afterwards to tell me they'd been to see him, it was pretty clear who they believed.'

'I'm sorry.'

Jane looked over at her angrily. 'What, as a policewoman?' She made the word sound almost dirty.

'No, as a woman, as a person. I *do* understand. But whatever happened between you, whatever he did, he still doesn't deserve to lose ten years of his life for a crime he *didn't* commit.' Even as she spoke, the words sounded hollow. 'So who was the girl they found in the woods?'

'Search me.' It was clear from Jane's tone that she didn't care.

When they got to Eve's car, Eve opened the passenger seat door for Jane.

'Get in.'

Shoulders back, head held high, eyes focussed on some distant point straight ahead, Jane did as she was told. Once inside, she plonked her briefcase down on the floor, tucked the skirt of her coat tightly around herself, then folded her hands neatly in her lap. There were tears in the corner of her eyes. Eve couldn't decide if it was nervousness, or self-pity, or the sheer relief at finally not having to pretend any longer. Thinking of the odd parallels between herself and Jane, she assumed it must be the latter. To live your life perpetually in fear of discovery, then finally to be free to be yourself, what must that feel like? It was something she longed for, that filled her dreams. She wondered for a moment if she would ever reach that place herself.

Eve climbed into the driver's seat, switched on the engine and turned the heater up high.

'So what do you want to know?' Jane asked quietly, after Eve had started the voice recorder on her phone. She was doing this for Duran's sake, more than anything. She wanted to give him the final proof that Sean Farrell was innocent.

'Let's start with why you disappeared.'

Still staring straight ahead out of the front window, Jane sighed. 'I was seeing somebody, one of the owners at the yard.'

'Lorne Anderson?'

Jane nodded. 'He thought something was going on, that someone was fixing his horses to stop them winning. I don't remember exactly how it worked, but they were making a ton of money out of the bookies, Lorne said.'

'Who do you mean by "they"?'

'Tim Michaels, or at least Lorne thought it was him.'

'So Lorne asked you to spy for him?'

Again she nodded. 'There was this party—'

'I know about the party. What happened?'

'Lorne wanted to see me. I'd texted him that morning to say I had some more information for him and that it was urgent we speak. But with everyone around in the tent, including his wife, it was tricky finding the right moment. She was like a demon. She wouldn't let him out of her sight.'

For good reason, Eve thought. 'You told everyone you were sick and had to go home.'

'I was hoping he'd make some excuse and slip away to the cottage for half an hour. But then he came and found me and I started to tell him what I'd learned.'

'Which was what?'

'I'd overheard Tim and Sally Michaels having an argument. They were talking about the BHA and the yard being investigated, something about one of the owners tipping them off and Sally also asked Tim if there could be somebody on the inside feeding them info. I assumed they must be on to Lorne, and possibly me too. Somebody then came over and interrupted us, so we arranged to meet at the back of one of the barns so we could talk properly. There's a sheltered place where they used to store all the bales of hay and shavings. I waited for him for quite a while, but he didn't come. It was already dark and I didn't want to hang around any longer on my own in the cold, so I started walking back to the marquee. When I passed Tim's office, the lights were on and I heard men's voices. It sounded like they were having a real argument, then there was a loud crash. I peeped in through the window and saw Tim with one of the owners.'

'Which one?'

'A man called Stuart Wade. He had two other men with him, neither of whom I recognized. They must've pushed over the big glass cabinet where Tim kept all his framed photos and cups and awards. There was broken glass all over the floor and I saw one of the men deliberately step on one of the photos. Then the other one pulled out a gun and pointed it at Tim.'

'You mean a shotgun?' Eve asked, thinking of Tim's suicide.

'No. A pistol. Tim looked terrified. I thought he was going to have a heart attack. They were calling him a grass and a snitch and threatening him, saying they needed to know what he'd said and what he was going to do about something or other.'

'Do you have any idea what they were talking about?'

She shook her head.

'Was this about the BHA investigation at the yard?'

'I don't remember. Then they told him what they'd do to him if he went to the police. I nearly wet myself, I was so scared. I didn't dare make a sound. Tim kept saying he had nothing to do with whatever it was. But they didn't believe him. Then one of them, I think it was Wade, said unless he did exactly as he was told, they'd kill him.'

'They didn't see you?'

'No. But Harry Michaels did. I'd decided I'd better get going, in case they came out, and I was trying to creep away without making any noise, when Harry appeared from nowhere, right in front of me. I must've jumped a mile and I nearly screamed. He just smiled and said "hello" as he passed, as though nothing was wrong. It was really dark out there, but I'm pretty sure he'd seen me looking in through the window.'

'What did Harry do next?'

'He just went into the office, cool as a cucumber, like nothing was wrong. Come to think of it, he was whistling.'

'Did you hear what happened when he went inside?'

She shook her head. 'I was so shit scared, I just legged it. I went back to the cottage and got my things. I'd been feeling pretty nervous ever since overhearing the row between Tim and Sally and my suitcase was more or less packed.'

'You called your mother?' Eve asked, thinking back to Jane's call log that night.

Jane nodded. 'I explained what had happened and she told me to get out.'

Eve was silent for a moment. Had Harry walked in and interrupted what was going on in his father's study, or was he a part of it? Was he in league with Wade? On balance, based on what she had seen and heard, it seemed likely. The thought made her shiver.

'Did you see anyone hanging around the cottage while you were there?'

'No. But I wasn't there long.'

She had probably got out in the nick of time, Eve thought, remembering Susan Wright's statement about a man in a suit whom she had seen hanging around outside when she drove past the cottage. It was likely to have been Wade, or one of his cohorts, and they must have been responsible also for the break-in.

'What did you do then?'

'I ditched my phone and got rid of the car. I had a lot of cash on me . . .'

'This is the money Lorne Anderson had given you?'

She nodded. 'I kept it hidden at the cottage. I didn't dare go home in case they tracked me there, so I checked into a hotel under a different name, bought a new phone and called my mum again. It took a couple of days, but she sorted another car for me. When I didn't show for work, they reported me missing. The following week Mum found out Tim Michaels had committed suicide. I was shitting bricks after that.'

'You think they murdered him?'

'Yes.'

'You didn't think to go to the police?'

She looked around at Eve for a moment, her eyes wide open. 'No way. Don't you understand, I'd never have been safe.'

'You could have gone into the witness protection scheme.'

Jane shook her head vehemently. 'I read up on what that involves. I couldn't just say goodbye forever to my mum and dad and they certainly didn't want to join me. Anyway, I was sure those men would still find me somehow. I cut my hair short and dyed it and did everything I could do to change my appearance. I was just going to lie low for a while, maybe go to Scotland, or Ireland, or somewhere far enough away, where I didn't need a passport. It would be easier just to disappear for a while until everything had calmed down and they had forgotten about me. I hoped that one day, maybe a few years on, I could come back to my old life again. Then everything went pear-shaped when they found that woman's body in the woods.'

'What made them think it was you?'

'Because the woods are so near the yard, I guess. Maybe I was the only girl missing from the area at the time.'

'They must have tried to match the body's mitochondrial DNA to your mother's.'

'No point. Mum can't have kids. I'm adopted, my mother untraceable and no idea who my father was.'

'The police had to have had something concrete for the ID. What about fingerprints or dental records?'

'I don't know what the police did, or how they decided it was me. But when they turned up on my parents' doorstep and said they were very sorry indeed to have to tell them that they'd found me and that I was dead, it was like a gift from heaven. Mum was brilliant at acting, or so Dad said. I kept worrying for ages they'd discover their mistake, but we heard nothing.'

'The woman's body would have been released to your parents. What happened to it?'

'It was cremated. My father thought it was better that way.'

'You mean so there was no chance of her being dug up again and found not to be you?'

Jane looked down, staring hard at her hands for a moment. 'I suppose so. She was dead. What does it matter?'

Eve shook her head despairingly. Somebody, somewhere, was missing a daughter, maybe a sister, or a lover, a family left in limbo for ten years, not knowing what had happened to their loved one and that she was dead. But it was clear it meant nothing to Jane. Revenge for what Sean Farrell had done to her, and her own safety, were all that had mattered.

'So when Sean Farrell was charged, and then found guilty, did it occur to you, or your parents, to come forward?' she asked.

'No. I told you, my life was still at stake. Anyway, as I said, Sean needed locking up.'

The windows had misted up inside so that it was almost impossible to see out and the lack of visibility felt claustrophobic. Even with Jane's testimony, it was unlikely Wade would be charged with anything after so much time. It would be Jane's word against his. He would dismiss it all as the wild imaginings of a girl, a proven liar, who'd gone into hiding for ten years and allowed an innocent man to go to jail. In spite of what Jane claimed to have seen and heard, there was no proof that Wade, or one of the other men, had actually followed through on their threats and killed Tim Michaels. She would call Andy Fagan and ask him if either Wade or Harry's names were listed amongst Mickey's recent phone log, but that's as far as she could go for now.

She turned to Jane. 'One last thing. Why was Stuart Wade calling your mobile in the weeks leading up to the party?'

'Why do *you* think?' Jane said sullenly. 'They're all the same. Just because they've got money they think they own everybody.'

'How did he get your number?'

'One of the girls in the office, probably. He's not easy to refuse.' She shifted in her seat and looked around at Eve. 'Will I be charged with anything?'

'I'm afraid so.'

Alarm flooded her face. 'Something serious?'

Eve nodded. There was no point lying. Perverting the course of justice was a serious offence and could carry a weighty custodial sentence.

'Oh my God.' With a gasp, she put her hands to her mouth, pressing her fingertips hard against her lips, her eyes wide with fright. 'You mean I'll go to jail? Oh, no. My poor little boy.' She turned away and started to sob.

'Jane, it will help you if you're seen to come forward of your own accord and own up to what you've done. It's very, very important you tell the truth.'

But Jane wasn't listening.

# FORTY

'You've done very well, Eve,' John Duran said. 'Although I expected nothing less from you.'

His face was expressionless and unreadable as always. Again, she wondered if Sean Farrell's innocence really mattered to him.

They were seated on either side of the table, facing each other through the glass again, in the interview room at Bellevue Prison. His scalp, with its black shadow of hair, and gaunt, sallow face glistened with a film of sweat. He had stumbled when he entered the room and needed support from the prison officer who accompanied him.

She had driven Jane McNeil to the huge glass and steel police station on the outskirts of Grantham, where Jane had given a signed statement, confirming everything she had told Eve. Jane had then been read her rights and formally arrested and taken away to await legal assistance. Outside, Eve had called Dan and told him the good news. He had immediately called Sean Farrell's solicitor, who was probably already at Bellevue by now, seeing Farrell and explaining what had happened as well as sorting out the necessary paperwork and putting into motion the lengthy procedure for his eventual release, which would start with a judicial review of the case. She imagined Sean's rejoicing, but after what Jane had told her, knowing what he had done to her and, possibly, to other women, it felt very hollow. She had also called Andy Fagan and left a voicemail asking him to call. Before leaving Grantham, she had texted Duran, using the phone he had given her, saying she urgently needed to see him. She had then emailed the recording of her interview with Jane McNeil to Alan Peters and he had played it somehow to Duran. All that was left now was for Duran to give her what he had promised her, the proof that she had been set up.

'I've proved that Sean Farrell is innocent, which is more than you asked me to do,' she said, studying his haggard face, wondering if he would try and wriggle out of it. 'He'll soon be a free man. It's time you honoured your side of the bargain.'

Duran looked at her thoughtfully, back ramrod straight as always, head ever so slightly to one side.

'Of course. As I said, you've done a very good job. You'll receive the proof you need shortly. I'm happy to give it to you. You've earned it.'

Although relieved that he was making no objections, she didn't let it show. She couldn't imagine his getting excited or joyous about anything, but she was still surprised that his reaction was so flat. Perhaps, after all, it really meant nothing to him; it was just some bizarre sort of a game. She still didn't have a clue about his motivation in helping Farrell, but it didn't matter any longer.

He yawned, stretching his mouth wide, not bothering to cover it with his hand, and she saw his perfect, Hollywood white teeth, which must have cost a fortune in dentist's bills.

'I'm just a little intrigued, Eve,' he said, with a sudden sharpness in his eyes. 'We had a murder victim and now you've discovered she isn't dead. The supposed murderer is innocent and the happy man will be released. Hurrah! As I said, well done. You should feel very proud of yourself. But aren't you forgetting something?'

'What do you mean?'

'There's still the woman in the woods. Don't you care about her? Someone needs to, surely. She needs a champion to stand up for her.'

'You're joking.'

He held up a large, bony hand. 'OK. Perhaps that's a little melodramatic. But aren't you interested to find out who she is, and how she got there?'

She had thought of nothing else since finding Jane, which he had clearly guessed. The loneliness of the dark woods and the unknown, unclaimed woman kept preying on her mind. It was as though she could hear her voice calling out, desperately wanting resolution. Somewhere, her family and friends were still missing her, thinking of her, wondering where she was and if she were still alive. They deserved to know what had really happened. Somebody also needed to pay for it. But she had kept telling herself that she couldn't solve every mystery. She must walk away and focus on the problems in her own life. It was Wiltshire Police's job to deal with it now, not hers.

She held his gaze. 'I've done what I set out to do and I'm quits.'

Duran sat up even taller in his chair and stretched his shoulders back, arching his neck for a moment like a swan, so that his chin almost touched his chest. He looked as though he was in pain.

'You surprise me,' he said, relaxing his body again with an audible groan. 'You keep everything buried so deep, you think you can con everyone. But I understand you. I've always thought of you as someone who cared, who'd always go the extra mile, who had to prise out every little detail, however painful and difficult, to get to the bottom of things. Like a grain of sand in an oyster, it drives you mad not to understand. It's why you're so good at what you do. It's why you're desperate to know why I killed Stanco.'

'I'm not desperate to know anything about you,' she said, although she could see from his expression he knew he had hit home.

He shook his head. 'The fact that you bother to deny it proves the lie. Maybe one day I'll tell you. Perhaps when you tell me who *you* really are.'

She stared at him for a moment. He would never know anything more about her, if she could help it. He would never know her real name or her history. But the fact that he had an inkling of what lay inside her, horrified her. The last ten days had been bruising, both physically and mentally. If she were honest, for the first time ever she felt overwhelmed. There were too many loose ends, but she had to let go. Let someone else deal with it all. She must focus on her disciplinary hearing. Yet try as she might to ignore them, all the unanswered questions kept nagging away at her; their tiny, persistent voices would not be silent.

'I heard about the fire at the 4Justice office,' Duran continued. 'Alan Peters tells me everything was destroyed. He said that somebody started it deliberately. He also says Dan Cooper was doing a good job too, so it seems very unfair. He just got mixed up, somehow, with the wrong sort of people.' He looked at her questioningly.

She almost laughed. The image of Duran's killing of Stanco Rupec flashed again through her mind. 'The wrong sort of people?

That's rich, coming from you. What Dan got mixed up in was trying to prove Sean Farrell's innocence. Whoever torched the office, also killed a PI who was working for Dan on the Farrell case. It's all linked.'

Duran's expression remained unchanged. 'Then it's even more important we should help him. Don't you think?' He was studying her, his impenetrable eyes fixing hers, and it was all she could do not to look away. She hadn't a clue what he was thinking. Then he said, 'Do you *like* Dan Cooper?'

'What sort of question is that?'

'I don't mean something cheap and smutty. Do you think he's a *good* person, who works hard and deserves good things to happen to him?'

'Yes.'

'And this charity, you think it's a worthwhile organization?'

'I certainly do.'

'OK, then. I'll make another bargain with you. Just solve this last little mystery, this woman's murder, like you've done so many times before. You can then put the ghosts in your head to rest for a while and I will make a very generous donation to 4Justice to get them back on their feet again.'

She couldn't hide her surprise. Did he really think he could buy everybody, that everything had a price? 'Dan won't take your money.'

'Then he's stupid. But at least let *him* decide.'

'Why are you doing this?'

'Because it entertains me. It's like watching a mystery on TV, only better. I've got nothing else to do and I've so much enjoyed watching you help Sean Farrell. These are the last few months, maybe weeks, of my life. I can't take my money with me when I'm gone. As I told you before, I want to help people, do some good.'

She still didn't believe him.

# FORTY-ONE

Room service was a great aid to productivity, Dan thought, putting his empty plate and cutlery back on top of the hotel trolley, next to the remains of his very late lunch. The bottle of iced Grey Goose sat unopened in the cooler, beside the salt and pepper and a tiny vase of pink carnations. For some unknown reason, two glasses had been provided, as though people didn't drink alone. Farrell would be a free man in a matter of days and he felt like celebrating, but there was still too much to be done and he needed to stay sober. It wasn't yet five in the afternoon but it was already dark. He drew the curtains and went back to the bed, where the copies of Kevin Steven's notebooks were spread out in date order.

After leaving Eve in the street the previous night, he had chased the boy he had spotted in the crowd. He had recognized him as the one in the navy anorak outside the Apple Store and later by the Christmas tree opposite the church in Covent Garden. He was Hassan, Mickey's friend. But by the time he had cut through the back streets behind the Earl's Court Road and worked his way around to the far side of the cordon, Hassan had disappeared. Had he been the one who had set the office on fire? Was that why he was hanging around? Why had he tried to lure him to Covent Garden? What was the point? He couldn't make sense of any of it. Afterwards, having made sure that Zofia was alright and had somewhere to stay, he had gone, as requested, to Kensington police station to give a formal statement about what had happened. He had then checked into a hotel not far from the office. It was a big, functional, charmless, modern building, which he had often passed on foot. The street outside was usually clogged with lines of coaches loading and unloading parties of tourists. It was not the sort of place he would have chosen if he had more time. But Duran was paying for it and, after everything that had happened, he was worn out. It would serve for a few days, while he worked out what to do. He had sent his filthy clothes for express cleaning and showered, enjoying the endless, power-stream of hot water, as he tried to get rid of the stench of smoke. He raided the mini-bar, then crashed out in the huge, crisp-sheeted double bed. He watched a trashy war film on a flat screen TV mounted on the opposite wall, luxuriating in the rare comfort of it all and eventually, for a change, drifted off into a deep, dreamless sleep. He woke just before nine that morning, feeling amazingly clear-headed and full of energy.

Several hours later, after the delivery of another room service trolley, with pints of tea and a full English breakfast, he went walking along the King's Road to look for replacement clothing and other essentials. He was in a clothes shop, trying on jeans, when Eve called to tell him what had happened with Jane McNeil earlier that morning. For a moment, he was stunned, struggling to take it all in. It was extraordinary; almost unthinkable that something like that could happen, and yet he had long since learned that the police were fallible. Eve was in a rush and sketchy about the details, but they had arranged to meet that evening at her flat. He had then gone back to his car and called Sean Farrell's solicitor, to tell him the good news. He had also asked him to check how the police had originally identified the body in the woods as being Jane's. Most worrying was Jane's account of overhearing Stuart Wade threatening to kill Tim Michaels. He had finally managed to speak to the journalist on the Channel 4 programme and had asked him about both Wade and the Westerby yard. The man said that, after such a length of time, he had no recollection and would have to dig out his old notes, if he still had them, and get back to him later.

The destruction of the office, with so many years' worth of work, filled him with an unrelenting gloom. Much of it had been backed up, and they could survive without what had been lost, but it was symbolic more than anything. It was the end of one important chapter in his life. Also, at odd, irritating moments, he kept thinking of Eve and Gavin Challis. He had Googled Challis but had found nothing particularly illuminating amongst the various entries, which recorded his academic prowess and his successful career first at the Bar and then latterly in Parliament. The many images of his ridiculously handsome, smug face were particularly irksome. He told himself it didn't matter what was going on between Challis and Eve. She could see whoever she damn well liked, but at the back of his mind, he knew he was deceiving himself. Part of the problem was that seeing them together had reminded him yet again how much he missed Kristen. It wasn't just the sex. He could easily go down to one of the many local bars in Earl's Court, or the Fulham Road, pick up a pretty girl and maybe, if he felt like it, bring her back to the hotel. But it wouldn't solve anything. He missed the closeness, the all-enveloping, unrelenting female presence that had filled his life for several years. Losing it had left a deep, dark hole.

Finally, that afternoon, he had felt sufficiently strong and clear-headed to read through Kevin Stevens' notebooks. He had pored over the copies, page by page, until he was dizzy, still with the smell and sound of the fire in his head. As he analysed the endless detailed entries, people interviewed both on and off the record, including a former head of security at the BHA, lists of suspect racing results and accounts of odd betting patterns, all documented in the meticulous, but difficult to decipher notes, his heart grew dark and heavy. Taken together, they documented a wide-reaching conspiracy of corruption. Stuart Wade's name, and that of Westerby Racing, appeared over and over again, along with others, which he didn't recognize. Had Stevens lived to see his scoop published, it would no doubt have had as dramatic an impact as the Channel 4 programme. Dan was sure the information contained in it had cost Kevin his life. The catalyst for it all coming alive again had been Mickey. There were a few more pieces he needed to quickly piece together, then he would call Andy Fagan.

He was about to make himself a quick coffee from the Nespresso machine in the room when he heard the ping of his phone on the bed next to him. Checking it, he saw a text from an unknown number. *Come outside hotel*

His heart missed a beat. Who knew he was in a hotel? He thought of the fire, of what had happened to Mickey. It felt like a trap. He gathered up the papers and stuffed them hurriedly into his bag, ready to run if he had to.

He texted back: *Who are you? What do you want?*

*I am Hassan. I wait outside for you*

Hassan must have followed him last night from the Earl's Court Road. He had probably been watching Dan after he had given up the chase. There had been so many people around, plus he was so distracted by everything, he hadn't bothered to check behind him when he went to the hotel.

*Why did you run off last night?*

*Too much police*

It was just like Covent Garden, all over again. Once bitten, twice shy.

*Why should I trust you?*

*Because you Mickeys friend too*

*What do you want?*

*I want to talk with you*

A few minutes later, having, on reflection, left his bag and laptop with the hotel reception for safekeeping, Dan stood outside on the steps, scanning the dark street. But there was no sign of Hassan. It was a joke, after all. He was about to go back inside, vowing to turn off his phone so he wouldn't be disturbed again, when he caught sight of a figure standing in the shadows by the railings on the far side of the square, behind a line of parked cars. Dan took a deep breath and went down the steps, walking slowly and deliberately towards him. No point in hurrying this time. If Hassan wanted to run off again, he didn't care. He had had enough of the games. But Hassan – if it was him – didn't move. As Dan got closer, he saw that it was definitely the boy he had seen the night before.

'Hello,' Dan said, approaching him warily, keeping one car between them, in case he tried to do something aggressive.

Hassan stepped out of the shadows. Shoulders hunched, hands in his pockets, he was wearing jeans, the same navy-blue anorak, with white trainers. The haze of orange light from the street-lamp cast shadows on his face, but he looked to be in his late teens or very early twenties, with short, curly, black hair and olive skin. His body language was uncertain and hesitant. It struck Dan that maybe he was equally fearful, although it still had the feel of a trap.

'I am Hassan. I am Mickey's friend.'

It was definitely the younger voice from the phone.

'You mean you *were* Mickey's friend. As you and I both know, Mickey's dead.'

'That's why I come see you.'

'I'm not giving you any money.'

'It's OK. I don't want money.'

'Your friend certainly did,' he said, sharply.

'The money, it is not my idea.'

'You mean Nasser, or whatever his name was, talked you into it, right? The man I met in Covent Garden?'

Hassan nodded. 'He want money. He say he make you pay.'

'And he's dead too.'

'I am there. I see you. I see what happen. Police chase him. He is hit by car. I want to talk to you but police are there.'

'They were following me and tracking Mickey's phone. What do you want now?'

'To talk. I give you Mickey's phone.'

'You have it with you?'

'Yes.'

'Jesus! It's not switched on, I hope?'

'No.'

'Thank God for that.' Dan moved around to the other side of the car so he was face to face with Hassan. He was small and slight, and seemed to present no physical threat. Dan wondered if he had been Mickey's lover. 'Why do you have his phone?'

'He give it to me. I was in garden having cigarette and making call for him . . .' He searched for the word, with a gesture of his hand. 'When men come.'

'What men?'

'Bad men. Who kill Mickey.' There was a slight tremor in his voice.

'Where was this?'

'In his flat.'

Slowly it dawned on Dan what he was saying. 'You were *there* when Mickey was killed? You *saw* what happened?'

'Yes. I hide in garden. But I see what they do, before they close curtains.'

Dan saw the tears in Hassan's eyes and felt suddenly sick. What Hassan must have seen didn't bear thinking about. There was only one thing that was important.

'You really cared about Mickey, didn't you?'

Hassan nodded, wiping his face with the back of his sleeve.

Dan wondered if maybe, deep down in Mickey's cynical old heart, there was a core of softness, which had met Hassan halfway. He hoped so.

'Then you must trust me, OK?' He held out his hand.

There was a beat before Hassan nodded again, then took it.

# FORTY-TWO

E ve sat in the armchair by the window in her sitting room, with her laptop on her knees. She had downloaded the file that had been emailed anonymously to her. She assumed that it had come from Alan Peters, but the address was from a Hotmail account, with no recognizable name. It was easier that way, as the police would want to know where it had come from and she could truthfully say that it had been sent to her anonymously. The file consisted of a voice recording dated over four weeks before, just a couple of days before Jason's murder. The sound quality was not particularly good, with a lot of background noise. From the buzz of conversation and clink of glasses, it seemed as though it had been recorded in a bar or a pub. However, she recognized one of the voices immediately. It belonged to DS Paul Dent, Jason's close friend and best man. What was also clear, from the conversation that followed with another, unknown man, was that they were discussing the police surveillance operation at the house in Wood Green, where Jason had been killed. The address of the house was specifically mentioned twice, along with details of the basement flat.

'Thanks for the information,' Paul Dent said, after a moment.

'You're very welcome, Mr Dent.' It was a rich bass voice and sounded Eastern European.

'It's Paul.'

'OK, Paul. It's what you wanted, yes?'

'It's exactly what I wanted. How much do I owe you?'

'Nothing this time. It's on the house.'

'Really? That's very generous.' There was a pause. The recording picked up a female voice, asking if she could clear their glasses. A minute or so later, Paul said, 'You're absolutely sure the operation's still ongoing?'

'No doubt of it. My sources tell me it's costing an arm and a leg and the big boss is complaining as always, but they're nearly done. Probably only another couple of weeks now, then they'll have what they want and they'll pull out. You better get on with whatever it is you want to do.'

'Thanks. I really owe you. How'd you find this out?'

'It was no trouble,' the other man said, with a gutsy laugh. 'You think this woman friend of yours – this policewoman . . .'

'Eve.'

'Yes. You told me her name but I forget. You think she'll fall for your little prank?'

This time it was Paul who laughed. 'Hook, line and fucking sinker. Miss Perfect's got a blind spot.'

'She trusts you?'

'Not exactly. But I'll feed it to a friend of mine. She's screwing him and he'll do absolutely anything to please her. She'll swallow it without question, if it comes from him.'

'OK. But tell your friend not to go there after dark.'

'Why?'

'You just want to get her in a bit of hot water, right?'

'That's right.'

'OK. Let's just say it's not advisable to go there at night.'

'Copy that.'

Rage filled her as she played the recording again several more times, making sure she hadn't missed any detail and that it was all written down. Don't go there after dark. Not advisable. Had Jason delayed in telling her, or had Paul wanted to up the stakes? Whichever, Paul would hang for this, at least in terms of his career. He would be finished in the Met and finished, most likely, with his friends. His petty jealousy had cost Jason his life. She wondered who the mystery man was, with the Eastern European voice. It was also not clear who had made the recording. The mic seemed too far away for it to have been him, unless it was sitting in a bag under the table. If so, it was surprising Paul had showed no sign of suspicion. Clearly he trusted the informant. The other, burning question was how Duran had got hold of it, but for the moment, it didn't matter. The recording was enough for the disciplinary hearing and she would forward it to her solicitor in the morning.

She put down her laptop and sat for a moment, looking out at the night sky. She had been cooped up for almost the entire day, either in her car, driving, or at the police station in Grantham. She had about half an hour before Dan was due over. Before that, she needed to get out, fill her lungs with fresh air and clear her mind. She went into her bedroom and changed into her running gear. As she let herself out of the flat and went downstairs to the hall, the front door opened and her neighbour, Alison, came in, carrying a large bag of shopping and a bunch of bright pink tulips.

'Going for a run?' Alison asked cheerily, as the door banged shut behind her.

'Just a very quick one. Need to clear my head.'

'I wish I could join you, but I've friends coming over for supper. Did you find out who broke into your flat?'

'No. But they didn't take anything and they haven't come back, so far.'

'Well, Kelly and I will keep an eye out, don't worry. If we see anything suspicious, we'll call you.'

Outside, apart from the odd person on their way home from work, the street was dark and quiet, the drone of traffic on the Uxbridge Road the only distant disturbance. She stopped at a neighbouring gate and was stretching out her legs, holding onto the iron post, when she heard a car come up fast behind her. It screeched to a halt, doors opened and heavy feet thudded on the tarmac.

'There she is,' a man shouted.

As she turned, someone grabbed her from behind. She felt a huge hand press something over her mouth, as another hand covered her eyes, pulling her backwards off her feet. She smelt the sweet, chemical odour of chloroform. She tried to scream, fighting against a wet rag that was stuffed in her mouth, kicking and ducking, trying to shake herself free. Her foot landed a blow against something hard and she heard a yelp and a gasp.

'Can't you fucking hang onto her? She's like a bloody cat.' She recognized Damon Wade's voice.

'Hit her, grab her legs, or something,' a second voice said. 'I can't get near her.'

'Man up and get on with it,' another, gruffer voice replied, right in her ear. 'Someone's coming.'

'Fucking hold her arm, will you?'

Somebody grabbed her by the wrist and wrenched her arm

straight. It was being pulled out of its socket and she felt a sharp sting through her sleeve.

'Got her. That'll do for the bitch.'

'Quick. Get her in the car.'

'Hey! What are you doing?' a woman yelled, somewhere further down the street. The voice sounded familiar.

Eve tried to call out, tried to pull away from whatever held her, but her legs collapsed beneath her and everything went black.

# FORTY-THREE

'How long before this stuff wears off?' a man's voice asked.

It echoed, as though under water. As he spoke, Eve was aware of somebody prodding her shoulders with the toe of their boot. Her eyes were tightly closed and she knew to keep still, not show any sign she was awake.

'Looking at her, I'd say half an hour at least,' a second voice replied gruffly.

'Well, that's fucking useless, isn't it?' the first voice said. Was it Damon Wade who spoke? It sounded like him. 'We're wasting precious time. I tell you, we need to find out what the bitch knows. Can't you give her something to make her talk?'

'No. It's not like in the movies.'

She had been drifting in and out of consciousness for a while when she heard them come into the room. They had stood over her talking, although at first she was too groggy to focus on what they were saying. Someone pulled her up off the floor, her feet dragging on the ground, as other strong hands held her under her armpits. Somebody slapped her hard across the face several times, shouting 'wake up'. Then they poured freezing cold water over her. Still she didn't react. They must not know that she was conscious. Through the blindfold, she was aware of a bright light being shone at her face. Somebody grabbed her by the hair and yanked her head back and they ripped off the blindfold, peeling back each of her eyelids momentarily. For a second, she was totally dazzled. They let go of her hair and her head flopped forwards on her chest. She groaned incoherently as though she was still drugged. They hit her again and she tasted blood, but she let her body flop heavy in their arms, then they threw her back down again. Her head was spinning and she felt nauseous, the voices reverberating around and around, becoming increasingly distant.

*For a moment, she was twelve again, high up in the arms of the old apple tree at the bottom of the garden. She loved the shape of it, the feel of its rough, knotted bark. The apples made the best purée and crumble and it was where she went whenever she wanted to be alone. She had seen Daz come home with the long-haired man in motorbike leathers, who called himself Dr Death, and his tall, scrawny friend. They had gone into the small sitting room at the front and started to argue almost immediately. She ran down the passageway and hid in her bedroom, but there was no lock on the door. Then she heard shouts, followed by footsteps outside in the hall. They mustn't find her. She climbed out of her bedroom window and ran into the garden, shinning up the tree and hiding behind the curtain of soft, green foliage. It was almost dark and lights were on inside the house. She could see right through the small, open window into the kitchen. A moment later, the man with long hair came into the room, pushing Daz in front of him. Then another man, much older, dressed in a suit and tie, appeared in the room. She had never seen him before but he seemed to be in charge, pointing and gesticulating and making Daz sit down in a chair in front of him. Daz had his back to the window, so she couldn't see his face, but the older one looked very angry. He was asking Daz something, but Daz kept shaking his head. Then the long-haired man started shouting at him and hitting him. Then the older man pointed something in his face. She strained to see and realized it was a gun. She felt sick, her heart beating so fast, the blood pumping deafeningly in her head, she could barely breathe. Daz was yelling something, then her mother rushed into the room and screamed, followed by two quick pops. It sounded like a firecracker. Daz fell forwards and Eve closed her eyes. Another scream. Another couple of pops. When she opened her eyes, all she could see were the two men in the kitchen. Where had her mother gone? 'No witnesses,' the older man shouted, his voice carrying through the open window. 'You find the little boys. I want the girl,' the long-haired man shouted. 'I'll deal with her.' Eve clamped her hands over her mouth, holding them as tight as she could so no noise would escape.*

Somebody kicked her hard in the buttocks and she was back in the room.

'You gave her too much,' Damon Wade was saying. 'She's not going to answer anything now.'

'I tell you, it will wear off. Trust me.'

'Well, I haven't got all night and she's no bloody good to us like this.' It was Stuart Wade this time.

'Whatever you intend to do, she's got to be out of here by three a.m. at the very latest. Understood?' It was Harry Michaels, his tone flat and measured as though he was talking about something routine.

The sound of his voice jolted her, but even in her woolly state, it made sense. Why wouldn't he be there? He had been part of everything right from the beginning.

'No problem,' voice number two said. 'It's only ten. We've got bags of time. Once she's properly awake, it won't take long. We'll try again in half an hour.'

'Come on,' Stuart Wade said, with a clap of his hands. 'Let's go. I want her wide awake. In the meantime, I need a drink. Where's Damon gone?'

The footsteps receded, a heavy metal door clanged shut, followed by what sounded like a key being turned in the lock. Gradually, she became aware again of her surroundings and opened her eyes. She was lying on her side, her left cheek pressed against a cold, gritty floor. The darkness that surrounded her was absolute, not even a chink of light. The ache in her shoulder beneath her was excruciating, stabs of pain reaching up through the numbness. As she tried to move, she realized that her hands were tied together tightly behind her back and her ankles were also secured, the ties cutting deep into her flesh. There was no gag over her mouth. She must be somewhere where it didn't matter if she made any noise. She tried to focus and think back to what had happened. For a moment, she was in the dark street outside her flat. Of the three male voices that she had heard, one definitely belonged to Damon Wade, with his clipped, private school voice. He was the person she had kicked and the thought gave some meagre satisfaction. Neither of the other voices were familiar; the deeper one had a London accent, the other, who sounded quite a bit older, had a similar northern accent to Wade. Lancashire or Yorkshire. She couldn't tell the difference. She wondered if either of the men had been with Stuart Wade in Tim Michaels' study ten years before, if one of them was the man who had pointed the gun at him. Did they intend to kill her too, once they had found out what she knew? Given what they had done to Mickey, it seemed likely.

Somebody had just mentioned that it was ten o'clock. She assumed they meant night, as Harry had said they must be gone by the early morning. So it was less than four hours after she had been abducted. The air in the room was damp and smelt strongly of leather and something waxy and chemical. It occurred to her that she might be in one of the tack rooms at Westerby. The one in Old Yard, which Harry had pointed out when he gave her the grand tour the week before, had a large metal door with rivets. She also remembered that the room had no window. Security was important, he had said. There would be no means of escape, except through the door. Even if she had a lock-pick or a blowtorch, it would do no good. She couldn't do anything with her hands and feet tied up so tightly. But at least she had left some sort of a trail behind her. A woman in the street had definitely seen her being bundled into the car. Was it someone she knew? The voice had sounded familiar. Hopefully whoever it was had called the police. Even if she hadn't, Dan was coming over around seven. He would have seen her car in the street, parked almost outside. When she didn't answer either her phone or the doorbell, he would have rung Alison's bell and Alison would have told him that Eve had gone out for a run. After everything that had happened to them both, surely it wouldn't take him long to realize something was wrong and to call Fagan? But how would they know where to look for her? She must play for time. She closed her eyes again and felt herself drift away.

*Dr Death was in the garden somewhere behind her, yelling something unintelligible to his friend. Even in the branches of the tree, she smelled petrol and heard the clatter of bins in the side passageway as he must have stumbled. 'Get the fuck on with it,' the other voice said. 'We need to get out of here.' Silence. More footsteps running. Then an explosion ripped through the air. For a moment, she was flying through a cloud of coloured lights. Then she hit the grass below very hard. Her ears were ringing and she couldn't breathe. Distant voices, more shouting. Her heart was about to burst. 'Her window's open. Check the garden,' Dr Death called out somewhere behind her. 'Look, she's there. Get her. I want her. She mustn't get away.' She shot back up the tree as fast as she could, more bangs rang out from the house. Something pierced her side, and her arm. The searing pain made her cry out, but she kept going, pulling herself higher and higher into the tree, then scrambling along the thick, gnarled branch and dropping down into a pile of long grass in the next-door garden. She picked herself up and ran.*

Somebody was shaking her. 'Eve? Are you awake?' a man's voice whispered right above her.

She didn't move.

He shook her again. 'Eve. Please wake up. It's Harry. We haven't got long.'

Through her eyelids, she was aware of a weak light shining on her face. Maybe he had a torch, or was using his phone.

'Please, Eve, if you can hear this, you've got to trust me. We haven't got much time.'

The use of the word 'we' and the softness of his tone reached out to her. Even if it were a trick, if he was trying to trap her into showing that she was conscious, she didn't have much to lose. She couldn't keep it up forever. They would soon be back. She opened her eyes a crack, trying to make out the dark shape behind the light. As far as she could tell, he was on his own. As her eyes gradually focussed, she saw he had a small knife in his hand. Her heart missed a beat.

'Thank God you're awake.' He knelt down beside her and started to cut through the ties holding her feet together, then he did the same for the ones binding her wrists. He picked up the pieces of plastic and put them in his pocket. 'Come on. You've got to get out of here.' He lifted her up onto her feet, but her legs wouldn't support her and he caught her.

'I'll carry you. I've got to get you out of here.'

'I can walk,' she mumbled, pulling away from him and flexing her feet and legs until the blood started to flow. She felt suddenly dizzy again and bent forwards.

'Here, take my arm. Stop being stubborn and let's go.'

'You need to call the police,' she said groggily.

'I can't. The office is locked. So is my flat, and the keys and my phone are in the study, with Stuart.'

Holding tightly onto him, she stumbled out of the room. The cold night air hit her with force and she took several deep breaths until gradually her head began to clear. The sky was cloudless and full of stars, with a bright, almost full moon, bathing the quadrangle and stables in an eerie, bluish light. A clock tower loomed above them. They were, as she had thought, in Old Yard.

'This way,' he said, guiding her towards the arch on the far side.

'Where are they?'

'Back in my study, enjoying some very expensive brandy. They won't be coming out for a bit.'

'They'll know it was you who let me out.'

'It doesn't matter. They won't hurt me. I've spent the last ten years gathering all sorts of information together. It's my little insurance policy. If anything happens to me, a bomb will go off for them. Stuart and his boys will be finished.'

She hoped he was right, but Stuart Wade didn't seem to be the rational, logical type, the sort of man you could blackmail, who would then happily leave you alone to enjoy the rest of your life without retribution.

'Was it you who drugged me at the party, or was it one of them?'

'It was me. I just wanted to stop you asking questions, to keep you out of their way. You just couldn't leave it alone, could you? Even though it had nothing to do with Jane.'

Whatever else he had done, at least he hadn't raped her, she reminded herself. The DNA sample had confirmed it. Her legs still wouldn't work properly and she needed his help again as they crossed the cobbles. They went through the arch under the tower and, sticking to the deep shadows made by the moon, slowly made their way around the back of one of the new barns. Neither Harry's shoes nor her trainers made any sound on the concrete, but a horse whinnied in the barn as though aware of

their presence, setting off another as they passed. She hoped
Stuart and his cohorts couldn't hear. They were halfway along
one of the outer sides of the indoor school when she was suddenly
hit by another wave of nausea.

'Wait,' she said, heart beating fast. She bent over, palms on
her thighs, gasping. She was going to be sick. She was never
going to make it to the road at this rate. Maybe it would be better
to hide. Everything was spinning. Harry's hand was on her arm,
steadying her. The sickness passed after a few moments and she
slowly stood up and looked at him. 'Why are you doing this?
Why are you helping me?'

'They're going to kill you.'

'Why?' It still didn't make sense.

'You know too much, or at least they think so. Stuart doesn't
like leaving loose ends. I have to say, I didn't bargain on that. I
thought they just meant to scare you. Whatever you think of me,
I'm not a murderer.' She picked up the urgency in his voice,
surprised that after everything he had some sort of a conscience.

'What about Mickey Fraser?' she asked, as they started moving
again, half walking, half jogging. It was the best she could do.
'Were you involved in what happened to him?'

'The PI, you mean? No. He came to Newbury and asked for
me. I tried to make him go away, but he started shooting his mouth
off about all sorts of wild stuff. He then confronted Stuart, which
was a very stupid thing to do. He said he had proof of something.
He said something about a dead journalist called Kevin, who used
to work for the *Racing Post* and some notebooks. I had no idea
who he was, but it certainly meant something to Stuart. It was like
somebody had lit a fire under him. I still didn't realize they intended
to kill Mickey, then I read about his murder in the papers. I recognized his photo. He'd come to the yard only a few days before.
Then you mentioned him and showed me his photo.'

'Someone overheard Wade threatening to kill your father ten
years ago. They saw one of Wade's men pointing a gun at his face.'

'You mean Jane? How the hell do you know that?'

She glanced up at him. Even in the half-light she could see
the shock on his face, but there was no time to explain.

'It doesn't matter.'

'They didn't kill her, if that's what you think. I never told them I saw her there at the window. I knew what they'd do to her. I went around to the cottage later, to talk to her, but she'd gone. I swear I didn't kill her.'

'So it was you who broke in?'

'Yes. I couldn't find the key. I was worried. I wanted to make sure she was OK.'

'What about your father? Did they kill him?'

'He took his own life. He discovered what I was mixed up in. It would have ruined him if anyone had found out. They'd never have believed he wasn't involved. He did it to save me.'

'How can you be so sure?'

'I found him, in his study. There were two notes, one for my mother, which I gave to the police, and one addressed to me, which I never showed anyone. I still have it. It's the most godawful, shaming thing I've ever read. He was trying to protect me, put all the blame on himself. After that, Wade wouldn't leave me alone. The BHA dropped the investigation, but he had me in his pocket.'

'Why didn't you call the police?'

'I'm in too deep. I don't fancy a spell in jail, so I'm going to disappear abroad for a while. I'll call it a sabbatical. It's all planned. I'll leave things in Melissa's capable hands.'

'Wade's not going to let you go.'

'I told you, I know too much. Once I'm gone, once he realizes I'm not going to do any damage to him. He'll soon forget about me. He's got fingers in lots of pies. I'm not his only stooge.'

As he spoke, they heard somebody calling Harry's name from the direction of the yard.

'I told them I went to check on a horse that's got colic,' he whispered. 'They can't get into the tack room without the key, so you've still got a bit of time before they realize you've gone. If you go up that bank there, then over the top, you'll see the house at the bottom. Melissa should be home by now. Call the police from there.'

'What about you? You should come with me.' She could barely see his face but he seemed surprisingly calm.

'I can't. He might do something stupid, like set fire to the stables. Let me handle this. As I said, when they find out you're not there, they're not going to hurt me. I know too much. I'll go back now and try and hold them off. I'll pretend I've lost the key.'

He was being stupid, but there was no time to argue. Also, even if his conscience had made him stop short of murder, he had been mixed up in it all for years. It was his lookout. She scrambled up the steep, muddy bank as best she could and crossed the soggy grass to one of the gallops. She climbed through the railings and followed the soft track for a good hundred metres, hoping to hide her footprints. Then she ducked under the railings on the other side, crouched down low and ran as fast as she was able along the ridge at the top. More shouts came from the direction of the yard. She hoped when they found out she had escaped they would assume she was making her way to one of the main roads, either at the back or the front of the estate. She cut off left, heading over the brow of the hill, as Harry had suggested. The farmhouse was just visible down below in the valley, half-hidden behind some trees. Lights sparkled at the windows and she could just make out Melissa's car parked on the drive, in front. She heard more shouts in the distance. Then she heard the sound of gunshots. Two in quick succession, then a third. It sounded like a pistol. She kept going, slipping, almost falling, down the bank, then tripping and smashing her way through the bracken at the bottom and into the small copse. She was making a lot of noise. Anyone on top of the hill would know exactly where she was, but she didn't care. Gasping for breath, she climbed over the fence that separated the wood from the garden and sprinted the final stretch up the drive to the front door.

She rang the bell and banged the knocker as hard as she could several times, but nobody came. A light was on in the kitchen window, at the side of the house. The curtains were only partly drawn. A sleepy-looking young girl sat on the sofa, in front of the television, the brindled whippet curled up on the cushion next to her. She must be the babysitter, Eve thought. She hadn't seen her before. She hammered on the glass, but the girl didn't appear to hear. Eve picked up a stone from the path and hurled it as hard as she could at the centre pane of the window. The glass smashed and the stone fell at the girl's feet. She looked up.

'Open the door. *Now*,' Eve shouted.

Still staring at Eve, mouth open, the girl didn't move.

'Let me in. We need to call the police.'

The girl stood up, pulled off a set of ear-buds and said something Eve couldn't hear.

'Let me in,' Eve shouted again. 'Help me. I need to call the police.'

The voices were getting closer, somewhere high up on the ridge above, maybe on the road leading to the main gate. If they looked down, they would have a clear view of the house below, and possibly a clear shot at her too, although hopefully she was out of range. She was about to try and smash open the window with a garden chair when Melissa walked into the room. She still had her coat on and looked as though she had just returned from an evening out.

Eve hammered again on the window and Melissa looked around alarmed.

'It's me, Eve,' Eve shouted. 'Open the door.'

Melissa ran across the room and unlocked one of the French windows. Eve pushed past her into the kitchen.

'Where's the phone?'

'My God, Eve. What are you doing here? Was that you making all that noise just now?'

'Call the police.'

'There's blood all over your face. What on earth's happened? Has someone attacked you?'

'Harry's in danger, and so am I. I think they just shot him.'

'What? Who?'

'Just call the police,' she shouted.

# FORTY-FOUR

Just after two thirty in the afternoon, the following day, Eve drove through the barrier and down the hill through the woods to the little marina on the Beaulieu River. She had tried to call Gavin several times but his phone kept diverting straight to voicemail. She wondered if Melissa had been able to get hold of him to tell him what had happened the previous night. Melissa's voice still filled her ears in a disjointed loop.

*'I can't get hold of Gavin. He's on that stupid boat of his. You think he'd come back here, to be with me? He doesn't care about any of us. This is all your fault. Now Harry's been shot because of you. Why did you have to come here, stirring up trouble? None of this would have happened without you.'*

Eve had spent part of the previous night being interviewed in the little police station in Marlborough, after which she had been driven by a member of Fagan's team back to London for further interviews earlier that morning. Dan had taken Hassan to see Fagan and he had given a statement about what he had seen at Mickey's flat. Harry had been shot twice and badly wounded. He had been taken by ambulance to Swindon hospital, with Sally Michaels at his side. One of the bullets had nicked his lung and he had been rushed into surgery, but he had since regained consciousness and was expected to pull through. Stuart and Damon Wade had been caught, trying to escape, and had been arrested and charged with a variety of offences, along with two of their men. Hopefully, Hassan would be able to identify one, or both of them and that forensic evidence would place them at the scene of Mickey's murder. The third man had run off some-where on foot, but was finally captured later, trying to hitch a lift on the road to Swindon.

At the bottom of the steep hill, the dark trees gave way to a wide, open area of brown, brackish marshland, feathered with little inlets of muddy water. She parked her car next to the yacht-broker's cabin, which appeared to have already closed for the day, and walked through the boatyard. It was packed with about fifty boats of varying shapes and sizes, the hulls lifted high off the ground on sturdy wooden props. A radio blared from one of the boats, accompanied by the sound of drilling and hammering, but other than that there was little sign of life. The harbour master's hut looked over the water. She stopped and asked for directions and the man behind the desk pointed through the window towards the neat lines of boats beyond, giving her precise instructions. Outside, the air was heavy with the smell of brine. The river curled into the distance, milky and still under the huge grey sky. Physically, it looked little different to how she remem-bered it from twenty years before, except that the sun had been shining, the air hot and dry and the landscape bright with colour.

She crossed the bridge and walked down the narrow gangplank onto the main pontoon, which ran parallel with the marshland. A flock of gulls were feeding on the muddy banks, exposed by the low tide, and their intermittent cries pierced the silence. Five narrow pontoons stretched out at right angles from the main walkway, like the branches of a tree, each festooned with neat lines of white yachts, with hardly an empty berth. Most of the boats were dark, locked up and in hibernation for the winter.

Even without the harbour master's directions, she couldn't miss Gavin's boat. Again she heard Melissa's shrill, bitter voice:

'*You know what it's called don't you? It's* The Eve. *I should have guessed the minute I first saw you. You've ruined all our lives.*'

The yacht sat low in the water, about thirty-feet long, gleaming white, with navy trim. Her name was written in large black italics on the stern. It must have been a rebuke to Melissa every time she saw it. No wonder she didn't enjoy sailing. Music drifted from inside, Mozart, she thought, and could just make out Gavin through the window, leaning against a pile of cushions, reading some sort of document. He must have heard her as he looked up and came out on deck.

'Oh, Eve,' he said, helping her aboard. 'I wasn't expecting you. Are you OK?'

She nodded.

He studied her face anxiously. 'Melissa called me. I was going to come, but she said you'd gone back to London with the police. I didn't realize those men had hurt you, as well as Harry.'

'It's nothing. Just bruising, that's all.'

A gust of wind blew her hair into her eyes and for a moment she was blinded. He brushed it gently away with his fingers, still gazing at her.

'I'm so sorry you ever got drawn into all of this.' It was as though he felt he and the Michaels family were to blame for everything.

She followed him inside through the small door, stepping carefully down the ladder into the warmth of the small cabin. It was fitted out in glossy cherry-coloured wood and cream leather upholstery, with a slatted, wooden floor. He took her coat and hung it up in a small cupboard at the back.

'You know, I never thought you'd come,' he said, turning off the music and hastily clearing away the remains of his lunch. 'Would you like a cup of tea, or coffee, or something?' he asked, quickly washing them up in the galley. 'I've got nothing else, apart from some wine, I'm afraid. As I said, I didn't think you'd come.'

'I'm fine. I've had enough caffeine in the last twelve hours to last me a week. How's your mother?'

'Luckily, just a bit of bruising, that's all.'

She sat down on one of the long, cream benches and he joined her after a minute.

'Will you tell me what happened? I'd like to hear it from you.'

She felt suddenly awkward and looked away, folding her arms tightly across her chest as she gazed out of the window towards the woods in the distance. She had told Andy Fagan everything. Why was it so difficult to talk to Gavin?

'Look, if you don't want to, it's fine.'

'No. I'd like to.' Taking a deep breath, she started with what had happened in the street outside her flat, then in the tack room at Westerby, Harry, the gunshot, Melissa . . . As she listened to herself talk, it suddenly seemed a terrible, confusing blur. She didn't know if she was making sense or not, but it struck her suddenly how close she had again come to dying. When she finished, there was silence for a moment, then he put his arms around her and pulled her to him. From nowhere, tears filled her eyes.

'I'm sorry,' she said, pulling away and wiping her face hurriedly with her fingers. 'I shouldn't have come. I'm very tired. I'm in no fit state . . .'

'Eve, it's me. It doesn't matter. I'm just so happy you're here. You can rest. I'll look after you.'

She shook her head. The weight of his emotions and expectations were too much. She felt suddenly claustrophobic and stood up again. 'I've got to go, I'm sorry.'

'But you've only just got here. What's the matter? You feel unwell? I can call a doctor.'

'No. I just can't stay.'

'Please, Eve. Will you just sit down for a minute and tell me what's wrong.'

She stared out of the window again, trying to make sense of how she felt, then turned back to face him. She didn't know what to say or where to start. None of it would make any difference, nor would it make him happy.

'Eve, please. I'll do anything I can . . . Anything for you . . .' He was looking at her, as though not sure what to do, then reached for her hand and pulled her down next to him again on the bench. 'You don't get it, do you?' he said, trying to catch her eye. 'And I sense you don't want to hear this. But I have to tell you. I love you. I always have. I've never stopped. Not for one single minute. I felt that way from the moment I first saw you.' He took a series of deep breaths. 'You know, I used to go outside into the back garden on the pretext of having a cigarette, even though I didn't really smoke, and I'd stand gazing up at your window, just wishing I'd catch a glimpse of you or that you'd open the curtains and look out at me. I just wanted to see you, to feel close to you, to be with you. I don't feel any different now.'

She saw the sadness in his eyes and pressed her fingers to his lips. There was nothing that she could say that would make it any better.

He took her hand again, holding it tightly. 'You don't understand the effect you have on people, on me, I mean.'

'Please don't say any more.'

'I have to. You know, I've always believed in myself, ever since I was really small. I've always set myself goals. I knew if only I put my mind to it and worked incredibly hard, I'd do well at school, get into a good university, then the Bar, and then, later on, win a seat in Parliament. I've never felt inferior to anybody and I've always thought that everything was possible, if I wanted it enough. I've never doubted anything, ever, until you appeared in my life. I mean both twenty years ago and now. I feel suddenly lost all over again. Why did you come today?'

She pulled away, took a deep breath. 'Because I owe you an explanation.'

'You mean about why you ran off and left me before? It doesn't matter. You're here now. That's all that's important.'

She shook her head. 'Nothing's changed. I couldn't marry you when you asked me and I can't be with you now.'

'I don't understand. To be honest, I've never understood.'

She held his gaze, struggling to form the words. She had never spoken them before and it felt suddenly frightening. Once out, there would be no return. She stood up and moved away from him, looking out at the water, wanting to put some distance between them.

'Eve? What's wrong?'

She turned back to face him. 'My name's not Eve.'

'What do you mean?'

'My real name's Pagan.'

'Pagan?'

'It's the name of a character in a stupid bestseller my mother was reading when she was pregnant with me. She lived in a world of fantasy most of the time. It's one of the many ways she tried to escape everything.'

'You never talked about your mother.'

'She's dead. I've been Eve for over twenty years, now. Pagan . . . she seems like another person.'

'You didn't like your name?'

'It's not that, although I hated my name. I used to get teased about it at school.' She took a deep breath. It was almost painful to speak. 'I was twelve. Something happened to me. I was put in the witness protection scheme and given a new identity, a new life. I've never told anybody before.'

'My God. What happened?'

She bit her lip, wishing she didn't have to explain. But she had to go on. 'I was living with my mother and my two little half-brothers. There were two men. They used to come to our house to see my mother's boyfriend, Daz, whenever he was around. He was mixed up in a whole load of bad stuff, I discovered later. On the night when it happened, they brought a third man, Ray McAllen, with them. He was a really bad man. I found out later he was their boss.'

'Where was your father?'

'No idea. He left long before I was born. My mother wouldn't talk about him and I've never known who he was. She had one hopeless relationship after another when I was growing up, so I assume he was another bad lot. We moved around a great deal. I've never really felt at home anywhere.'

'Tell me about the men.'

'One was a paedophile. I don't know his name, but the other man called him Doc and he had a tattoo on his arm of a skeleton. I called him Dr Death. The other man was called Clive Ripley. It was McAllen who killed Daz and I saw it happen. Then they murdered my mother and my brothers. I was shot as I ran away. That's why I have those scars. When they'd finished, they set our house on fire. Everything was destroyed. Everything.'

From nowhere, she heard the screams, the gunfire, then the explosion, followed by the roar of the flames. She could smell the smoke. She pressed her hands tightly over her ears but she could hear their voices. She shivered and shook her head vigorously, trying to get rid of the images, and looked up at Gavin. She needed him to understand.

'I was the only witness. I was taken to a safe house until after the trials. McAllen was a very dangerous man, a member of a well-known crime family. I'm sure he did absolutely everything he could to find me and he would have killed me if he had. But he failed. Once the trials were over, I left immediately to start my new life with Robin and Clem. Even though it was all done and dusted, as far as the police and CPS were concerned, it wasn't for me. It will never be over. It's why I had that meltdown when you asked me to marry you, why I had to leave. It was just too much and I couldn't handle it. I realized I – we – had been living a lie.'

He exhaled loudly and looked down at his feet for a moment, then back up at her. His face was red and there were tears in his eyes. 'What happened to the men who killed your family?'

'Both Ripley and McAllen were caught and sent to prison. I identified them and my testimony helped put them both away. McAllen died of a heart attack a few years ago, but Ripley's still in jail on a full life term, although he still claims he wasn't there, that he was innocent. The other man, the so-called doctor, got away. He's German, I found out later, a doctor of philosophy, not a medical doctor. I used to think he'd come after me, that he'd want to finish the job. He's long gone now, probably on the other side of the world if he's not dead. I keep telling myself, there's no logical reason for him to come and look for me after all this time. Anyway, why would he make the connection to the person I am now? I look completely different, with a new identity.

But the nightmares don't stop. What happened still haunts me. When I close my eyes, I see . . . I hear . . . I still feel the fear.'

'You're safe here with me.'

She shook her head. 'The fear's in my bones, in my blood, in every beat of my heart. I will never feel safe until I know he's dead.'

'Do you have any idea what happened to him?'

'No. I've done everything I can over the years to trace him, but so far nothing. One day, though, I'll find him, wherever he is, if he's still alive. And I'll kill him.'

He sighed. 'You mean that, don't you?'

She nodded.

The ringing of her phone broke the silence. As she took her phone out of her pocket, she saw Dan's name on the screen and answered.

'Yes?'

'I've found out how the police ID'd the body of the woman in the woods,' Dan said. His voice sounded very loud in the quiet of the cabin. 'They used fingerprints and DNA taken from personal items belonging to Jane. The solicitor gave me a list of the things they used, but if Jane's not dead, how's that possible?'

# FORTY-FIVE

E ve hung up and stared at the dead screen for a moment, trying to think through the implications of what Dan had just said. Whilst the sensitivity of DNA extraction and analysis had moved on leaps and bounds in the past ten years, the processes used for identifying a body remained the same. The coroner required primary identifiers, such as DNA and finger-prints to confirm an identification. Odontology would also be used where the body showed signs of unique dental work, which could be compared to records. But there had been no mention of this in Jane McNeil's post-mortem report. Tattoos, scars, old fractures, breast implants and other signs of medical intervention were only secondary identifiers and, where possible, X-rays and serial numbers would be needed. Again, there had been no mention of any of these in the autopsy report. The first basic step would have been to compare the body's DNA and fingerprints with the national databases. If there was no match, the police would go to a possible victim or missing person's home, or office, and take away personal items for ante-mortem matching. A hairbrush, a comb, a razor, a toothbrush, a book, a mobile phone, all might hold a person's DNA and, or, fingerprints. These would then be compared with the DNA and prints taken from the body. Dan had just said that this was what had been done. But somewhere along the line, a mistake had been made.

She texted Dan. *Where did the items come from? Does it say in the list? If not, can you find out? I need to know exactly. ASAP!*

Wondering how it could possibly have happened, she gazed out through the window across the slick of brown water towards the muddy bank opposite, where another flock of noisy gulls had just descended.

'What's the matter?' Gavin asked, behind her.

She had forgotten he was there. She tucked away her phone and turned to face him. Taking a deep breath, she explained about Jane McNeil being alive. He sat down on the bench and rubbed his face vigorously with his hands, staring at her. It was a lot for anybody to take in in such a short space of time.

'So whose body was it?' he asked after a moment.

'I don't know.'

'How can the police have made the wrong identification?'

'I don't know the facts. Everything's always easier with the benefit of hindsight. Jane was missing. A body of a woman of similar age and build turns up only a couple of miles away. She's in no state to be identified visually, but the DNA and fingerprints recovered from Jane's things, if that's what the police used, matched the samples taken from the body . . .' She shrugged. She didn't need to make excuses for what was usually a straightforward process. It just didn't make sense. She felt suddenly hot in the cramped, airless space.

'Do you mind if we go outside for a bit? I need some fresh air and I'd like to stretch my legs.'

'Of course. Whatever you want.'

Gavin fetched her coat from the cupboard, put on a waterproof jacket and boots, then locked up the boat. They walked back together in silence along the series of pontoons to the boatyard where a man was sweeping the front porch of the harbour master's office, whistling. The radio was still playing cheerily from one of the boats and it was as though nothing at all was wrong with the world.

She heard the ping of a text and took out her phone. *All items were taken from the cottage according to Sean's solicitor.*

Attached was an image of the typed list. She studied it for a moment, then put her phone away again. None of the items used to identify the body had come from the office. She remembered Harry saying that people often shared desks, so the police would have looked elsewhere. As far as Jane's family home was concerned, Jane hadn't lived there for a while and she imagined that Jane's parents would have come up with all sorts of excuses and stories so as not to give the police any of Jane's personal items, if they still had any. The cottage, where Jane had lived for six months, had been the obvious source.

They followed the path along the edge of the river to the woods. Her muscles ached from the previous night and her throat was dry and scratchy, but it felt good to be outside. The wind had dropped and a fine mist tinged the air, softening the browns and muddy greens of the landscape and gathering in thicker drifts by the water. Once under the canopy of tall pine trees, it was much darker and several degrees colder, the atmosphere heavy with damp. Three girls living at the cottage: Grace, Jane and Holly. Grace had left the previous month and Eve had also spoken to her. Jane had said she had taken all her things, so the items that the police recovered from the cottage for DNA and fingerprint matching could only have belonged to Holly. She had been sacked on the spot a few days before the party and told to clear out. She wouldn't have had time to pack up everything, which was why she had texted Jane, asking to come and collect her stuff. That had been on the Friday before the party. But Harry had told Eve that Holly had been employed by two other racing yards after leaving Westerby and that he had been asked by both for a reference. This had also been confirmed independently by Annie, although perhaps she was only repeating what Harry had said. Eve thought back to the peculiar conversation with him and

Melissa over dinner on her first night at Westerby. They had definitely been hiding something. Had Harry been having some sort of relationship with Holly and had he killed her? It seemed very likely. Why Holly had never been reported as missing was another matter, but maybe she had fallen out with her family; maybe she had no family. Or maybe they, too, had been told that she had been sacked and had moved on.

The only person who really seemed to care about the mystery of what had happened was Duran and she would tell him as soon as she could. She had more than fulfilled her side of the bargain and hopefully it would be enough for him to agree to give Dan the money. As far as Holly's family were concerned, Jane had said that the body had been cremated. However, the items taken to identify the body, which must hold Holly's DNA, if following the theory that the body was in fact Holly, would still be in the Wiltshire Police exhibit store somewhere, along with the rest of the crime scene exhibits. She would call the police later and explain what she had learnt. At least, stuck in his hospital bed, with a tangle of tubes attached to him, Harry wasn't going anywhere. They could also trace Holly's next of kin and confirm the ID.

Gavin's phone was ringing. He took it out of his pocket, checked the screen, then switched it off and quickly put it away again.

'Was that Melissa?' Eve asked.

He nodded.

'Shouldn't you speak to her?'

He sighed. 'At some point, yes. I've told her I'm leaving her.'

'What's happened between you?'

'It's been a long time coming. We've been falling apart for years.'

'Why?'

He stared at her. 'How can you ask that? It was never right from the start. She wanted me. She pursued me. If I'm honest, I was flattered and eventually I just fell in with it. It seemed the best, the easiest thing to do. We've been through a lot together and Melissa was determined to make it work, whatever happened. But seeing you again . . . Well, it's reminded me of what's been wrong all along. I just can't go on.'

'What about your little boys?' Her heart felt suddenly heavy at the thought of them and of so much unhappiness.

He exhaled loudly, his breath pluming out on the air. 'Sadly, they're not *my* boys, which I'm sure she'll make a huge deal of now. Although, obviously, they mean just as much to me as if they were mine.'

She glanced over at him. 'They're adopted? They look just like you.'

'They're Melissa's. I can't have children.'

She stopped and turned to face him, grabbing hold of his sleeve. 'What do you mean?'

'I have a condition. A medical condition. I can't father children. We used a sperm donor.'

Her heart missed a beat. She felt the darkness roll towards her again like a huge, unstoppable wave. There was no air. She put her hands to her mouth and stared at him. All she could hear was the blood humming in her ears. Could it be? Was it possible? The man she thought she knew so well dissolved before her and she was looking at a stranger. Everything she had ever thought about him, everything that had happened between them took on a new light. *I'd stand gazing up at your window, just wishing I'd catch a glimpse of you or that you'd open the curtains and look out at me. I just wanted to see you, to feel close to you, to be with you.* How the hell had she missed it? It had been staring her right in the face. With all her strength, she swung her arm and punched him.

He stumbled backwards, rubbing his chin. 'Christ. What's that for?'

'You raped me,' she shouted. 'It was *you*, all along.'

He caught her hands as she swung at him again. 'Wait, Eve. It wasn't like that.'

She shoved him away. 'Wasn't like what? I was drugged. Out cold. Unable to give any form of consent. What the fuck do you call it?'

'I didn't drug you.'

'That's irrelevant. You took advantage of me. You of all people. How could you?'

'I—'

'Shut up. Let me get this straight. You put me to bed . . .

Melissa was there. You had someone waiting for you, to give you a lift . . . So you must have come back later?'

'Yes. I wanted to make sure you were OK, that's all. But I didn't *rape* you! I wasn't violent. I love you, Eve. I told you, I always have. I always will. It was a moment of madness. Forgive me.'

He stepped towards her, but she held up her hand. 'Don't come anywhere near me. You disgust me.' She took a deep breath, almost unable to speak. '*Why* did you do it? What made you? I need to understand.'

He shook his head slowly, as though he didn't know where to start.

'Come on. Tell me. I have to know.'

'I saw you the night before, with Harry. You went out to dinner together. I watched you come back. You both went into the cottage. He was there for a long while. I imagined the two of you together . . . I know what he's like. I thought I'd lost you again. Please forgive me.'

'So it was *your* footprints I saw on the grass, you were the person I heard in the woods?'

'I didn't mean to scare you.'

She stared at him, still struggling to take it all in. Whatever the reason, whatever pathetic thing he said, it made no difference. Then something else clicked into place. In the heat of the moment she had forgotten all about it. It felt as though everything had turned upside down all over again.

'You were screwing Holly Crowther too, weren't you?'

He looked surprised. 'Yes, now you ask. I don't deny it. But what's that got to do with anything?'

She took a deep breath, trying to think through what must have happened. 'Melissa found out, didn't she? That's why she sacked Holly and Harry paid her off, to get rid of her. He knew about this, didn't he?'

He nodded. 'Melissa tells him everything. She didn't want Tim to find out. I didn't blame her. I was stupid and it was all my fault. My only excuse, for what it's worth, is that Holly looked very much like you.'

'Are you serious?'

'It's true. Melissa noticed it when she met you. It gave her quite a shock. I guess it's what attracted me to Holly in the first place. Sometimes, I'd pretend to myself that she *was* you. But she was a poor substitute. She meant nothing to me, I swear.'

'So what happened? Was Holly blackmailing you?'

'No. There was nothing like that.'

'When was the last time you saw her?'

'The night she left Westerby. I agreed to meet her, in a car park . . .'

'In the woods?'

'Yes.'

'You had sex with her?'

'We had sex. Then we had another row. It had become a pattern. She had some crazy fantasy that I was going to set her up in a flat and carry on seeing her, and that maybe I'd run off with her eventually. It was ludicrous. Why do you want to hear all of this? She meant nothing to me.'

He was talking normally, as though describing something trivial. She stared at him for a moment, wondering how it was that he didn't understand. 'Because it was Holly Crowther's body in the woods,' she shouted.

He took a step back as though she had hit him again and stared at her dumbstruck. Even in the dim light, she could read his expression clearly. He was either an incredibly good liar, or he really didn't know.

'My God. Holly? Are you absolutely sure?'

'A hundred per cent. So you had sex with her, had a row and then you killed her, because she wouldn't leave you alone? Was that it?'

He looked at her aghast. 'What? *No!* When I left her, she was very much alive.'

'*You killed Holly Crowther,*' she shouted, wanting to get more of a reaction. 'Why don't you just tell the—'

A shot rang out, then another, hitting a branch just above Gavin's head and whining off at an angle. She looked up the hill into the woods, but saw nothing. It was impossible to tell where the shots had come from.

'Get down,' she screamed.

'What do you—'

'They're shooting at *us*. Get down.' As she spoke, there was another shot. Gavin cried out and fell to the ground. She dropped down on hands and knees, fumbling for her phone in her jacket pocket. One of the bullets had hit him in the arm and he was bleeding.

'Jesus,' he said. 'What the fuck's going on?'

He struggled to his feet and started to examine the wound.

'Get down,' she shouted again, as another shot rang out. It hit him and he spun around, falling back again into the bracken. She crawled over to where he lay, propped up on one elbow, his hand clasped to his stomach where he had been hit. Blood was seeping through his fingers. Shielding him with her body, she pushed him down into a large mass of dead ferns, then lay down beside him on her stomach and dialled 999. The dispatcher answered quickly and, in a low, urgent voice, she explained where she was and what had happened.

'I didn't kill her,' Gavin whispered, when she had finished. 'Please . . . You've got to believe me. I didn't even know she was dead . . . until just now. When I left her . . . she was angry . . . but still alive.' The words came in short, staccato bursts. 'I heard nothing . . . after that . . . from her. I thought it was extraordinary . . . I just hoped she'd seen sense . . . given up on me . . . and gone away somewhere. I *swear* I didn't kill her.'

He was dying, his life ebbing away right in front of her, but all she felt was numbness.

'Melissa knew about the two of you?'

'Yes. Hold me. Please.'

She shook her head. 'I do believe you,' she murmured. 'But it doesn't excuse what you did to me.'

With a sigh, he sank slowly down into the long grass. His eyes were still open and he was mumbling something. She put her face close to his, trying to hear what he was saying. She made out a few more words, felt the warmth of his breath on her cheek, then his body relaxed.

She heard the distant sound of a siren and stood up. She didn't care if somebody shot her.

'Eve?'

It was a woman's voice. She turned and saw Melissa on the path below, looking up at her.

'Where's Gavin?'

From where Melissa was standing, Gavin was hidden from view in the undergrowth.

'*You* killed Holly Crowther,' Eve shouted. 'I know you did, Melissa.'

Melissa stared at her for a moment. 'What are you talking about?'

'Jane's alive, Holly's dead. You've known all along, haven't you?'

Melissa was silent for a moment, then said in a cold, flat voice, 'You've gone mad.'

'Gavin told me everything.' It wasn't true. The only words he had said to her before he died were 'I love you', but she now understood what had happened.

'He said what? Where is he?'

The siren was very close now. Turning, she saw flashing blue lights flickering in the distance coming down the long drive to the marina. She started to scramble down the hill towards Melissa.

'Why don't you just admit it?' she shouted. 'It's just the two of us here. Nobody's listening.' Although she knew she was right, she wanted to hear Melissa say it.

'You've got blood all over you again. What's happened? Where's Gavin?'

'It doesn't matter. Just admit it, Melissa. *You* killed Holly Crowther. I know you did.'

There was a moment's hesitation, then Melissa shrugged. 'I don't know what you're talking about. It's Jane who's dead.'

'No. I've met Jane and she's very much alive. It was Holly's body in the woods and you had a strong motive to kill her.'

'You're talking total crap.'

'The crime scene exhibits are still held by the police and can be retested. Forensic science has come on leaps and bounds in the last ten years and it's amazing what they can do now with the tiniest speck of DNA.'

'So what?'

'You'll have touched Holly at some point, either when you killed her, or afterwards. Maybe you left a hair, or a drop of sweat or blood behind, something that in the heat of the moment you didn't think of. Even though you tried to burn the body, it will still be there.'

'I tell you, I had nothing to do with it.'

'We will be able to prove you killed Holly . . .'

As she spoke, a shot rang out, the bullet glancing off one of the trees right in front of Melissa, sending splinters of wood and bark into the air.

'Shit. What was that?' Melissa looked around towards the marina below.

'Get down,' Eve shouted, taking cover behind a tree. Melissa was lying. She knew in her own mind what had happened and she believed Gavin.

'What the hell's going on?'

'For Christ's sake, get down.'

'Tell me where Gavin is, *now*. He's clearly been telling you a pack of lies.'

Craning her neck, Melissa took a few steps forwards off the track, moving out into the open.

'I know you killed Holly,' Eve shouted. 'You couldn't have disposed of the body on your own, so Harry—'

Two more shots echoed in quick succession through the woods. Melissa was thrown sideways. Crouching low, Eve ran to where Melissa's body lay face down in the undergrowth. In the gloom, she could just make out the dark, wet hole at the back of her head. There was nothing she could do for her.

The last few shots had come from way above, to the right. Zigzagging through the trees as fast as she could, Eve ran back up the hill. She heard the whip-crack of breaking branches some-where above and saw someone dressed in dark clothing streaking away up the hill towards the road. Moments later, she heard the roar of an engine and the screech of tyres as a car drove off at speed.

# FORTY-SIX

Eve stared across the table through the glass at Duran. 'Why? That's all I want to know.'

He returned the stare. 'Why what?'

'You know exactly what I mean.'

It was two days later and she was back at Bellevue Prison.

Duran sat upright, hands folded on the table in front of him, chin slightly lowered so his black eyes were almost lost under his dark brows. For a moment, she was back in the woods, in the dying light, listening to the car drive off. As its engine faded into nothing, it had struck her how none of the shots had been fired at her. Not even close. The shots had only been aimed at Gavin, and then at Melissa. Also, Gavin and Melissa had been shot almost immediately after she had accused each of them of killing Holly. But the sniper had been far away, somewhere up the hill, close to the main road. How could he possibly have heard what was being said?

She had gone back to the marina and spent the next few hours being interviewed by the local police, not that she could tell them much. She had no idea what the sniper looked like, let alone who he was. After that, she had checked into a Travelodge nearby and, before showering, had stripped herself, examining all of her clothing and the contents of her pockets and her bag. She had then checked her car. Eventually she found what she was looking for. The first device, a tiny black chip, had been hidden in the Nokia Duran had given her, which had been tucked away in her coat pocket all that day. The second, a small rectangular black box, about the size of a cigarette packet, had been attached magnetically underneath her car. She had taken them both that morning to someone she knew in London, who used to be with the Met and who knew a lot about such things. He confirmed that the first was a wireless voice transmitter containing a SIM card. Someone had been listening in on her conversations whenever the phone was close to her. The second was a waterproof GPS tracking device. Both had been programmed by, and linked to a mobile phone – the sniper's, she was sure. They were both the latest technology, although relatively inexpensive and easy to come by either from a specialist shop or via the Internet. They had to have been planted by the same person and that person had to be somebody acting for Duran. She felt such a fool. She had assumed that the phone he had given her was safe because it was old technology and couldn't be tracked. She had also been so keen not to use her own phone for anything that might link her to him, it hadn't occurred to her to take the Nokia apart and check inside. No doubt this was something he had anticipated. It had been in the pocket of her outdoor coat at the marina. Luckily, when she went on board Gavin's boat, he had hung her coat up in a cupboard well away from where they were sitting. The buzz of the nearby generator would have drowned out any sound from outside in the cabin. She reassured herself that Duran, or whoever it was, would have heard nothing of her confession. What was suddenly clear was that right from the start Duran's interest had been in Holly, not Jane.

'Come on,' she said. 'You owe it to me, to tell me. That's all I want.'

'Dear Eve. Always so curious.'

'Just tell me. Then I'll go, and leave you alone for good.'

'But I don't want you to leave me alone. I like you coming to see me.'

She pushed back her chair violently, the legs screeching on the floor, and stood up.

'This is not a social visit. If you won't tell me, I'm off. I'm not wasting my time here any longer.'

He held up his huge, yellow hands, palms towards her. 'OK. Calm down. Please sit down. You want to know why Holly Crowther is so important to me?'

'Yes.'

There was a long pause as he stared at her before he said, 'She's my daughter.'

'I don't remember your having any children.'

'There's a great deal you don't know about me. With regard to Holly, I was seventeen when I fathered her, out of a stupid whore of a girl. But she's still my blood. I've been looking for her for the last five years, ever since I discovered the mother had died. It's become even more pressing now that I don't have much time left. The trail ended at Westerby. I had a really good PI looking into it. He tracked down Jane's mother, trying to get more information on Holly, and something she let slip made him wonder if Jane wasn't dead after all. Two girls go missing more or less at the same time, from the same area, what are the odds?'

'Why the hell didn't you tell me?'

'Because I didn't know for sure. It was just a possibility. I needed you to look at everything with a totally fresh, unbiased pair of eyes. Also, if my Holly was dead, whoever had murdered her was likely to be associated with Westerby Racing. But the PI couldn't get much further than the front gate.'

'Was this about six months ago?' she asked, remembering the second investigator that Annie had mentioned, the man whom Harry had punched.

He nodded.

'So I was your Trojan horse?'

He gave the slightest of shrugs. 'What's wrong with that? I gave you what you wanted in return, so it was a fair deal.'

'You don't know the meaning of the word fair.'

He frowned. 'Look, you're annoyed because I didn't give you the full picture, but it's just your ego talking. You didn't need to know everything. As I said, I didn't want it to colour your judgement or line of questioning. I wanted a thorough job, from soup to nuts, and I was more than happy to pay your price.'

There was no point arguing. She folded her arms and stared at him. 'Why choose me? There must have been any number of people who could have done what I did.'

'You're wrong, there. You're the best, Eve. I told you, I know everything about you and your career with the Met from the research we did on you when you first interviewed me in that foul police station. I'm very thorough. I like to know exactly who I'm dealing with. I also knew about your connection with Gavin Challis. I found out about your relationship and how very close you once were. He wanted to marry you, I understand. You walked out on him. First love, first break-up, can be very scarring. You were both so young, but it's often difficult to get over that sort of thing. From everything I heard, he hadn't.'

'You were taking quite a risk. Gavin might have hated me after what happened. He might easily not have wanted to see me, let alone help me.'

'What was there to lose? I heard his marriage was on the rocks. Even if *you're* not the sentimental type, I thought, twenty years on, he might be happy to see you again. I took a gamble and it paid off.'

A glimmer of light pierced the fog. She felt suddenly sick at the realization. In the confusion of everything that had happened, she hadn't had a moment to see things clearly before. But looking at him now, seeing how vital it was to him to find out who had killed Holly, she realized what it all meant.

'You've been behind everything from the very beginning, haven't you?'

'What do you mean?'

'Right from the moment I went chasing after Liam Betts at the house in Park Grove. You couldn't give a stuff about redemption. That was just a load of bollocks.'

He stared at her unblinking, eyebrows slightly raised, but said nothing. Maybe he hadn't expected for her to work it out.

'The man talking to Paul Dent in that recording you sent me, his informant, was *your* man, wasn't he? *You* planted the information on him . . .'

'Now you're going too far. The informant – his name is Dmytro – is someone known to us, I admit. When the policeman – this Paul person – went to Dmytro and told him what he was after, that he wanted to cause trouble for you, Dmytro came to us. He's one of my contacts. He was close to me at the time I was charged with murder, and he knows I'm interested in you. He thought I'd like to hear what Paul had planned for you.'

She shook her head. It didn't ring true. '*Why* are you so interested in me?'

'All sorts of people interest me.'

'*You* set me up, not Paul. You could have got me killed. How would that have helped your search for you precious daughter?'

'You've heard the recording. Paul was specifically told you weren't to go there after dark.'

She had been the key to it all, she realized. Duran's 'research' on her hadn't stopped after his being sent to jail. He knew about Jason, he knew about Paul Dent and his jealousy and he had used it to get what he wanted. Rather than Paul Dent seeking out Dmytro, she wondered if it had been the other way around. Maybe Dmytro – Duran's man – had initiated things, planting the information that Liam Betts was going to be at the house in Wood Green, knowing that Paul Dent couldn't help but take it and would run with it. Knowing Paul, he had probably delighted in the idea of sending her blundering right into the middle of a highly expensive and important undercover investigation, the cock-up that would cost her her career. From Duran's point of view, even without Jason being killed, she would have been suspended, making her open to his offer of help to clear her name.

'You're lying again. You're incapable of telling the truth.'

'And you don't lie to me? I know your name's not Eve.'

'Who I am – what my name is – doesn't matter.'

'It matters to me. Very much. Now, are you going to tell me who killed my daughter?'

'Your sniper . . .'

'Not my sniper . . .'

'That's another lie. You and I know the truth.'

'Truth, as you call it, is a matter of subjectivity. It's open to interpretation.'

'Are you saying you didn't give me a phone? That you weren't tracking me, listening to all of my conversations?'

'The phone, yes. But what's this about a tracker and a bug?' He spread his hands on the table and shook his head. 'Why would I bother? What would I gain from it? I knew what you were doing. I knew roughly where you were and that was enough. Someone else was keeping an eye on you.'

'No. The phone was with me all the time.'

'Really? Are you absolutely sure? It's kids' play to plant these things, if that's what you say they did. Maybe they didn't realize the phone wasn't yours.'

A niggle of doubt slithered into her mind, but the idea was ludicrous. He was teasing her. The whole point of tracking her and listening in on her conversations was to find out who had killed Holly and to enact revenge. Nothing else made sense. Perhaps Duran was denying it for the benefit of the prison guard standing behind him, or maybe he thought the walls had ears and didn't want to be had up for two more murders. But however much he denied it, she knew the truth.

'I don't believe you.'

'What happened in those woods to my daughter was a bad, bad thing,' he continued in a low, insistent tone, as though he hadn't heard. 'The *only* point of your coming here is to tell me who killed her and why. That's all I ask.'

It struck her how very much it meant to him. 'I'll let you work that one out.'

'I had a bargain with you.' His tone was suddenly harsh.

'You broke that by killing two people.'

'My daughter, she was young, beautiful,' he said emphatically. 'She had her whole life ahead of her, so very much like you in many ways. She didn't deserve to die. Just tell me, was it your former lover? Or was it his wife? Which one? Or were they in it together? What about Harry Michaels? How was he a part of this? *I must know.*'

She almost smiled. The urgency in his tone and the mention of Harry's name had given him away. The news of Gavin and Melissa's murders had been all over the media, but only the person listening in – Duran's man – would have heard her mention Harry's name just before he took a shot at Melissa. It also struck her that in spite of the listening device, Duran had no clear idea who had actually murdered Holly, or why. She thought back to the woods and the interchanges with Gavin, and then Melissa. The phone had been buried deep in the left-hand pocket of her padded jacket. The listener had heard her accuse Gavin of killing Holly. But after Gavin had been shot the second time, they had both been on the ground and she had been lying on top of the phone. The exchange of words between them had been in a whisper. It was unlikely that anything much could have been heard. What she had shouted at Melissa would have been a lot clearer, but probably still accompanied by the type of shuffling, deadened sound of a pocket call. Whether anybody listening could hear all of Melissa's responses was anyone's guess. Whether they had, or not, they would have still struggled to follow the full thread of what was going on. No wonder Duran was confused and he was the sort of person who wouldn't rest until he had the full facts. Only she knew what had really happened and why, although it gave her no satisfaction. It occurred to her how Gavin's adultery – a small, inconsequential thing in itself compared to the following chain of events – had been the real beginning, the trigger, for the downward spiral. It had led in a direct line to Holly's murder, to Sean Farrell's imprisonment, to her being set-up by Duran, to Jason's murder, to Mickey's murder, her rape, the burning of the office, and finally the shooting of Gavin and Melissa. The tally of destruction was horrific. If Holly hadn't looked so very much like her, if Gavin hadn't been so obsessed, would he have been so easily tempted? It was a chilling thought. Even though Harry hadn't murdered Holly, she was sure he had helped Melissa get rid of the body. He had then lied to protect his sister, telling Eve and Annie that he had been asked to give Holly a reference. But whatever exactly had happened, Eve owed Duran nothing.

He was staring at her, unblinking, waiting for her response.

'Neither of them killed her,' she said, meeting his gaze. 'Your man shot the wrong people.'

His face hardened. 'That can't be. Now I know *you're* lying.'

'I tell you, he got it wrong.'

'That's not what I—'

'Two more innocent people have died because of you. I hope you rot in hell.' She got up again and turned to the guard behind her. 'I'm done here. I'd like to go now.'

'But I'm not finished,' Duran shouted. 'You can't go. I *must* know.'

With her back to him, she waited for the door to be opened, then left the room. Not knowing who had killed his daughter or why would be his punishment for everything he had done. He would go to his grave without that certainty and the thought gave her some small but meaningful satisfaction.

'*Tell me. That's all I ask.*' His voice boomed after her. '*I'll find out who you really are.*'

Out in the corridor, she heard more bellowing, the words full of rage and more or less unintelligible. It sounded as though he had gone berserk. There was a crash. He must have thrown something hard and heavy, like a chair or the fire extinguisher hanging on the wall behind him, at the plate glass partition. The miracle was how he had the strength to do it. A siren cut through the air and the guard who had been accompanying her, turned and rushed back towards the room.

# FORTY-SEVEN

Just after five thirty in the afternoon, Eve finally emerged through the huge revolving glass doors of the Met Police building in central London, her male barrister following closely behind her. Dan watched as they walked down the steps together and stopped on the busy, windy pavement outside. She was smartly dressed, in a dark, fitted coat and trousers and was carrying a small, black briefcase. It was impossible to tell from her expression, or her body language, how the hearing had gone.

She had been there since first thing that morning and had texted Dan at lunchtime saying that they would be finished by the end of the day. He had been waiting for her for the past hour in the little café opposite, on tenterhooks, wondering if it was a good thing, or a bad thing, for the hearing to be taking so long. Watching her, as she stood talking to the barrister, the wind whipping her hair in her face, he felt increasingly apprehensive. He was also very worried about her. A dark cloud seemed to have enveloped her after what had happened in the woods ten days before. It had brought out a whole range of other emotions that she struggled to keep at bay. She wouldn't tell him much beyond the barest of facts about what had happened to her at Westerby, and at the marina, but from the little he gleaned it all sounded horrific. How she was feeling about Gavin Challis's death, he couldn't begin to imagine. But he let her be. It was clear she didn't want to talk about it, or about anything much that had happened in the past few weeks. Not for the first time, he sensed her fragility. She was barely holding herself together for the hearing and he felt that if he just scratched beneath the surface, she might fall apart.

He quickly left a handful of change on the table to cover his several coffees and, once the lawyer took his leave, went outside to join her. Eve was scanning the pavement, looking for him, and he called out and waved as he sprinted across the street.

'How did it go?' he asked, as he joined her.

'Better than I expected.' Her expression still gave nothing away. 'At the last minute, somebody came forward saying they had overheard me trying to get clearance to speak to Liam Betts and that, just as I clearly remember, Superintendent Johnson had given his approval, even though he's still denying it.'

'Why didn't they come forward before?'

She shrugged. 'Nobody likes to be a whistle-blower, particularly when it's going against the word of somebody much more senior and it's all so politically sensitive. What happened caused

Jason's death, as well as wrecking a top-level surveillance operation. Heads will roll. The recording of Paul Dent in the pub,
showing that I had been set up, was also very helpful. Of course,
they were very curious to know where it had come from. Luckily,
I'm sure they won't be able to trace it.'

Dan knew what had really happened. Not for the first time,
he was amazed how she could be so economical with the truth
when it suited, yet so black and white at other times. Maybe,
after everything she had been through, she was becoming a little
more pragmatic.

'So what happens now?' he asked nervously.

'There's an investigation going on into the information leak,
in particular how Duran's man, Dmytro, knew about the surveillance operation on the house in Park Grove and also his links to
Paul Dent. Dmytro's not on the registered list of informants,
so Paul should not have been talking to him either officially, or
unofficially. But Dmytro is no doubt long gone by now, so I'm
not sure how far they'll get. As for that shit, Paul Dent, he's for
the high-jump and he deserves everything that's coming. It's clear
from the recording that he knew that the operation was top secret
and that he didn't care about jeopardizing it to get at me.'

She was ignoring the main question, the one that really mattered
to him. 'What about you?' he asked.

'Oh, they've offered to reinstate me . . .'

His heart missed a beat, but he forced a smile, trying to look
as though he was pleased for her. 'That's wonderful. You must
be so relieved.' The words sounded hollow.

She was studying him and he caught a mischievous glint in
her eyes. Was he so totally transparent? Had she guessed how
much he wanted her not to return, that behind it all, he hoped
she would come and work with him? Perhaps there were other
things too she had guessed. The thought made the colour rise to
his cheeks, but there was nothing he could do about it. There
were worse things in life than a woman knowing he fancied her,
he decided.

'You accepted?'

She hesitated, still holding his gaze, then shook her head.
'Don't worry. I told them where to stick it.'

'Seriously?'

'Yes.' She shivered and pulled on a pair of leather gloves. 'Come on. Let's go. It's too cold to stand around out here.'

They started to walk together, following the crowd of people making their way towards the Tube. The silence felt like a chasm between them.

They stopped at a crossing and, while they waited for the lights to change, he turned to her. 'What will you do now?' It was the million-dollar question and he dreaded her response.

'I don't know. I haven't decided.' She looked up at him. 'More to the point, what are *you* going to do? Will you take Duran's money and start over again?'

He sighed. What could he say? Duran's solicitor, Alan Peters, had offered him a sizeable donation to keep the charity afloat. 'Mr Duran takes a great personal interest in your charity', Peters had said. 'He wants to make sure that it will keep going long after he's dead.' Blood money, was what Eve had called it. He didn't blame her, after everything Duran had put her through. She was also surprised that even after she had left Bellevue prison without telling Duran who had killed his daughter, he was still prepared to offer Dan the money. Maybe Duran hoped she would relent in the end. If so, he was wrong. But however terrible he was as a man, however dreadful the things he had done, the money was clean, as far as Dan could tell, or at least no dirtier than a lot of money from far more so-called legitimate sources. Was it right to be so principled and refuse the money, when it might make the vital difference between surviving or going under? What charity in its right mind could afford to be so scrupulous? Perhaps the money could also be cleansed through the good work it would do. He had tried that argument with Eve over and over again, but she refused to accept it.

She was looking at him, her eyes dark and stern. 'You are going to take it, aren't you?'

He sensed her disappointment. 'Maybe. Are you angry?'

'No. Not angry. You must do what *you* feel is right. On balance, you probably should take it. Forgive the pun, but it would be a crime for 4Justice to disappear. The justice system needs you.'

'You said Duran's very ill, that he's dying?'

She nodded. 'It's about the only thing he's said that I actually believe. I guess if *you* don't take it, maybe he'll leave it to a cats' home or something. *They* probably won't care at all where the money came from.'

Were it not for her expression, he would have laughed. The idea of a man like Duran leaving a legacy to a load of homeless moggies was wonderfully ludicrous. He decided to take the plunge.

'If we do carry on, maybe . . . Perhaps . . . If you've got nothing else planned . . . you'd come and work with me for a while. Until you find something else, that is.'

'You are funny,' she said, suddenly laughing as she reached out and touched his sleeve.

He had never seen her laugh before and he felt sudden relief. It was as though the dark clouds above them had parted and the sun had come out.

'I knew that's what you wanted to ask me the other night,' she added teasingly. 'Why didn't you?'

'I thought you wanted to go back to the police.' It was a lie. He hadn't dared ask, that was the truth. He hadn't wanted to be shot down in flames.

'Well, I'm done with that life. I want to move on and I'm looking for a challenge.'

'Working with me would be a challenge?'

'No. That part would be easy.'

'It's just an idea. Temporarily, if you like.'

'That sounds good, at least for now. But I've got some savings tucked away for a rainy day. We can use that for the moment.'

He shook his head. 'I'd rather take Duran's money than yours. Anyway, we may not need it. All the publicity and stuff in the press has sent the phones ringing. Channel 4 want to commission a documentary about what we did for Sean and, apart from a whole new wave of people trying to get us to take on their cases, I've had several pledges of financial support. We've also been offered the use of an office free of charge for the time being, while the owner applies for planning.'

'OK. Let's start with that and see how we get along. But first I need a holiday. I haven't had one for God knows how long. I fancy somewhere really hot and far away. I want to pack a small bag, go to the airport and just pick a destination from the departures board. But I promise I won't be gone long, maybe just a few weeks, or a month at most, that's all. I get easily bored with nothing to do. Then I'll come and join you, if that's what you really want.'

He could hardly believe what he was hearing and was speechless for a moment, emotion and excitement welling inside. He took a deep breath, trying not to let it show. 'Yes. You sure that's what *you* want to do?'

She nodded. 'It is. Let's shake on it, then.' She held out her small hand and, as he took it, she looked deep into his eyes and smiled. 'Here's to a new beginning. And to 4Justice. Long may it continue and thrive.'